On the Night

SCEPTRE

Also by Peggy Woodford

Cupid's Tears

On the Night

PEGGY WOODFORD

Peggy Woodford

SCEPTRE

First published in 1997 by Hodder and Stoughton
A division of Hodder Headline PLC
A Sceptre Book

10 9 8 7 6 5 4 3 2 1

British Library Cataloguing in Publication Data

Woodford, Peggy
On the Night
I. Title
823.914 [F]

ISBN 0-340-63959-8

Typeset by Hewer Text Composition Services, Edinburgh
Printed and bound in Great Britain by
Mackays of Chatham PLC, Chatham, Kent

Hodder and Stoughton
A division of Hodder Headline PLC
338 Euston Road
London NW1 3BH

For Walter

George holds up the birthday card: above an unreal autumn woodland scene are the gilded words *FOR MY SON*. There's a quatrain inside beginning *May your years be filled with joy* which Lena has crossed out. He re-reads the shakily written message.

Darling George, Happy birthday and many happy returns of it! You're fifty-five – I can hardly believe it. Where do the years go? Come and see me soon. Your loving mother Lena. PS. Forgive the card – Mrs Harris bought it for me in Chichester because I haven't felt well enough to go out for the last few days. It was very sweet of her though I wouldn't exactly have chosen it myself.

He must go down to see her – he could go tonight, to celebrate his birthday of yesterday. If he leaves within the hour he can be there by dinner-time. He rings her to say he will be coming for the evening with food and drink, and buys what is needed on the way out of London. As he sits in heavy traffic, his thoughts go round and round: My life has reached a crossroads. My life has reached a crossroads. The lid has been screwed down on so many things, crucial matters that I have stifled or ignored. I put up so many defences to prevent myself getting hurt that I disappeared inside them. My thick skin has helped me be blind to anything that might pierce through it; and in the last few years I've been so busy, that same thick skin has been an advantage. George Warne QC: clever, trenchant, tough. Known to be a hard man, a formidable opponent. And now I am faced with a dilemma I did not expect, a request that could change my life permanently.

Two days have passed since he received the critical phone call, and George finds he is still no clearer in his own mind: should he leave a life he relishes to become a High Court Judge, an honour but a prospect he doesn't relish in the least? He wishes he could ask his mother's advice, but the Lord Chancellor's Department insist on secrecy until the formal announcement of the appointment is made. He knows anyway that Lena would advise him to take up the offer and then tell everyone in the village; he also knows that the prospect of her son being given the usual knighthood when appointed would heavily colour any advice she gave him.

Besides, he wants her to save her energy for a completely different conversation, a conversation neither of them is likely to enjoy.

'It's too late to drive back now. Stay the night for once. You never stay these days. I can't remember the last time you stayed here—'

'Is everything still in my room?'

'Who would touch it?'

'All right, I'll stay. But on one condition.'

'Oh Jebs, don't keep on about it. It would make no difference if you knew. And don't criticize me for calling you Jebs again – if you will keep dragging me back to the past then you can't complain if I use your old nickname.' Lena pulls her wrap higher over her shoulders; the soft fold of blue wool under her chin flatters her dark brown eyes and white hair.

'You can't assume it would make no difference, Lena. I want to know who my real father is, and I – I find I need to know.'

'Why? You've lived all this time without knowing. What difference would it make to your existence to know his name? And he's probably dead by now.'

'He might not be.'

'He was older than me, I'm nearly eight-one, so I'm sure he's dead. I told you, Jebs, I haven't been in touch with him since before you were born. Please don't ask me any more questions tonight. My head is buzzing, it's late, I'm tired. Those early years were very painful, very difficult. I hate remembering them.'

'I'm sorry, Lena, but you must see my side of things

too. Don't let me go back tomorrow without knowing his name.'

'Goodness, you're hard on me, Jebs. Hard on everyone. I wish you'd married Marcia, she'd have softened you.' Lena pulls herself out of her chair and walks painfully over to the doorway. When she is sitting her eyes and skin and expression look no different from the ageless image of Lena George holds in his mind's eye. But when his mother walks he can see the stiff hip, the tilted body, the agony of grinding joints. Not long ago she moved like a sixty-year-old, but since breaking her hip she has aged at an alarming rate.

'Let me give you a hand—'

'I'm all right.' She leans against the doorjamb, her wrap hung now over one shoulder. 'I liked Marcia, you know. She may have been a lot younger than you but she had your measure. More than those two stupid women you did marry. I really thought it was going to be third time lucky for you with Marcia.'

'Lena, you promised never to go over that subject again.'

'I only want you to be happy, Jebs. It seems to me you're not a happy man.'

'Telling me about my father would be more use.'

'Darling Geoffrey was your father all your life! He did everything a father should, he was so good to you!'

George stares at her, hears her harsh, distressed breaths that don't come easily, sees the tears start to gather in her eyes. He knows he's on the point of giving up hope she will ever tell him. He takes a deep breath.

'I realize that.' There is a silence which he is too dispirited to break. Then his mother says with effort: 'It'll make no difference to you to know, but if you like I'll write it all down, his name as well, when I wake in the morning. I always wake early these days, and feel at my best in the morning. You can take the letter back to London and read it later.'

'That's a very good idea. Thank you.'

'It will change nothing.'

'Can't you understand, Lena, that I need to find that out for myself?' He takes her hand, surprised she has given in so suddenly, and wonders whether after all she has felt, like him, an unacknowledged need to end the secret.

'Help yourself to some of the whisky you brought.'

'Why don't you have some with me?'

'It's time for me to go to bed. I'm always awake at five every morning, whatever time I go to sleep. It's very trying.'

'Some whisky might relax you, help you forget the aches and pains.'

'Alcohol quarrels with the drugs I have to take.' She moves towards the staircase, and George follows her.

'At least let me give you a hand up the stairs.'

'It's easier to go at my own pace. Don't watch me, I hate it. How I hate old age.'

'Goodnight, Lena.' George kisses her cheek.

'I'm so glad you came – such a lovely surprise. I couldn't believe you were coming straight away like that and bringing such a delicious dinner for us. You must do it more often.'

'I will.'

They give each other a stiff, unpractised hug while she kisses him, and then she starts her painful progress up the stairs, propping herself between wall and creaking bannister rail.

'Are you sure you don't need help—'

'Go and have your whisky. I can manage.' She freezes, her back stiff with awareness of his gaze. 'Please shut the sitting-room door.'

'Sleep well then.'

'And you, Jebs. Do let the cat in if he asks.' She is waiting until he shuts her out of sight. Through the closed door he can hear her puffing and grunting as she proceeds to bed.

George pours himself a large whisky and lies on the sofa sipping it. The fire crackles softly as it dies, and an insistent gentle tapping starts at the window behind him. He sees his mother's black and white cat Raj batting on the pane and lets him in. Raj immediately settles himself as near the fire as possible after a couple of perfunctory purrs.

Jebs. His old childhood name, now used by no one save his mother. Jebs.

The luggage, the docks, his mother and his Aunt Cynthia, the screaming of the cranes as they winched cargo on to the liner, the screaming of the gulls. His first memory, coloured by later descriptions but still the apex of all his other recollections. He remembers how he swung his own little case full of his toys, how the crowds poured past them on to the ship, and their own moment of embarkation came nearer when he and she would sail back to India. Then it happened.

'Jebs, my little one, my darling baby, when I next see you you'll be such a big boy!' She hugged him, tears starting suddenly, her tweed coat rough on his skin.

'Go on, Lena, not too big! The war isn't going to last that long.' Aunt Cynthia's voice was hearty. 'Two years, no more, that's what they say.'

'But Jebs will change so fast even in two years! My little darling.'

Ears ringing, terror-struck, Jebs struggled free, grabbed his precious suitcase and tried to run towards the gangway. His mother pulled him into her arms again and sat on a crate, cupping his face with her hands.

'Listen, precious Jebs. I don't want to leave you behind, I hate doing it, but this voyage is going to be dangerous. It's better you stay with Cyn on the farm – think how you'll love living on a farm. And you've got all your things in your own new suitcase—'

'I want to be with you.'

'Think of all those lovely animals.'

Jebs started to scream, his noise blending with that of the docks around them.

'I told you not to leave it until now to tell him. Poor little scrap.' Aunt Cynthia patted his tense little body as he continued to scream.

So his luggage – one large new case and his little one – was divided from hers, hers was loaded on board, time passed – numb, empty time – and then his mother walked up the wooden gangway, high heels twisting on the wooden struts, and after more numb time the liner pulled away from Tilbury docks and he howled in concert with its mournful hooter.

When his aunt tried to pick up the large case, Jebs lay on it and would not let her move it. His mother would change her mind, the ship would turn back, he would join her . . . What hurt most of all was the sight of all those other happy waving children sailing away with their mothers down the Thames.

George has still got that case, stored with other childhood things in the loft of his mother's house. It was bought at the Army and Navy stores on the day his mother had successfully battled to get on to the last liner out to India just after the outbreak of World War Two. The case had always been the embodiment of betrayal.

He used to run his fingers over the raised metal letters bearing the name of its make. Only much later could he read them: REVELATION.

George finishes his whisky, decides against having another, and lies watching the fading embers of the fire. He cannot remember anything after that scene at the docks – nothing of the journey to Somerset, the settling in at the farm, the new life he'd been dropped into. Misery wiped it from his conscious memory. He supposes his cousins Sophie and Laura and his Uncle Julian were kind to him, he knows his aunt loved him. He also knows, because she told him, that he gave them little help. He went silent, became an elective mute. If he spoke at all it was only in Hindi, pretending he was talking to his beloved ayah. He even sung himself to sleep, imagining it was her.

> *Nini, baba, nini*
> *Roti, maccan, chini,*
> *Roti maccan hogia*
> *Nini, baba, sogia.*

Every English child brought up in India was sung this monotonous but effective ditty, with the powerful soporific of its nursery words – sleep baby sleep, bread, butter and sugar finished, sleep baby sleep. Every night Jebs would sing it, on and on, in his hoarse, flat little voice, until sleep stopped him. Often his aunt would listen outside his door, despairing.

'You drove us mad, you know. You did well at school without saying a word, you knew exactly what was going on, but for three years not a word did we hear you speak except that wretched Hindustani.'

'I'm very sorry.'

Aunt Cynthia occasionally came and stayed with his parents in their house in Harrow during his teens. She would make sure she and George had time together away from Lena and Geoffrey, because he always went quiet in their presence.

'You didn't speak from the moment she left for three whole years. She should never have left you behind but nothing would make her change her mind. I suppose she was right – the voyage was dangerous. The Germans might have bombed the ship. But it was full of mothers and children and I used to look at you, poor little scrap, and know you'd have been better off on it.' Aunt Cynthia was a squat, plain version of Lena; her shy, brusque manner hid great warmth. Her sister Lena's seeming warmth and friendliness hid a more chilly soul. 'You used to stand silent and miserable in a corner of the kitchen clutching that toy you loved.'

'Chota, my mongoose.'

'I can't tell you what a relief it was when that wonderful teacher unlocked your tongue. I've forgotten her name now—'

'Miss Tompkins.'

'So it was.' They both heard the voices of Geoffrey and Lena coming out into the garden to join them. Aunt Cynthia leaned forward and took his hand. 'I just wanted to tell you, Jebs, that though we had such a difficult start it was lovely having you in the house. I felt you were like a son. You weren't a burden, despite what your mother thinks. Not at all.'

Six months after this conversation his aunt died of cancer. She was forty-five. He was sixteen.

George wanders round his mother's sitting-room looking for a photograph that used to stand at the back of a row of family images in frames propped by little stiff flaps. It showed Lena and Cynthia as girls sitting together against a photographer's backdrop of the 1930s. He longs to see a picture of his aunt's face, but he can't find the photo he remembers. He suspects it's been retired to make space for one of himself wearing the full ceremonial dress of a Queen's Counsel, looking rather ridiculous in silk stockings and breeches that do nothing for his legs.

If Cynthia had lived he could have asked her whether she knew anything about his mother's early years in India. All he has ever been told was that Lena had gone out very young to marry an Indian Civil Service officer called Eric Leith who died in a shooting accident only six months after the wedding. Five years later the young widow married Geoffrey Warne and Jebs was born in the same year. What Lena had done to keep body and soul together in the five intervening years had never been clarified. She remained vague and uncooperative on the subject.

George picks up a photograph of his mother taken in the forties in India and sent to her family back at home. She is smart, pretty, deliciously dressed in bias-cut silk, with black open-toed shoes on her neat little feet. George remembers how a copy of this photo was propped on the kitchen mantelpiece in the farmhouse, looking incongruous amongst the faded sepia postcards and bills. He would stare at it, unable to make sense of it.

'Quick, Jebs, it's your mother! Hurry, she's ringing from London!'

Jebs, aged nearly nine, had never used the phone in his life. He gazed in horror at his aunt and nearly ran off through the back door.

'Come on, silly billy!'

The telephone was screwed on to the wall of the lobby outside the kitchen, and since its fairly recent arrival at the farm had mainly been used by Julian Roper to order lists of fertilizers and farming aids. Sophie and Laura, twelve and ten, had not yet woken up to its potential.

Jebs held the receiver high on the wall above him to his ear and stood on a box to speak into it. An unfamiliar crackly voice was saying, 'Cynthia, don't bother him if he doesn't want to, I can talk to him another time—'

'Hullo, Mummy.'

'Heavens, it's my little boy! How are you, darling?'

'Very well, thank you.' He stared at the black bakelite receiver. It didn't sound like his mother, but then how would he know anyway after so long what she sounded like?

'I'm sorry we haven't been down yet to see you but we both thought it best to get a house for us here first. Then we'll come down and fetch you and the three of us will be a family again. Won't that be lovely, Jebs darling! I'm so longing to see you! Are you longing to see me?'

'Yes.'

'You sound very grown-up, I must say. Not the little chap I left behind.'

O cruel betrayal.

'But it had to be, and I'm sure now you're bigger you understand that. All the little English boys in India knew they must be parted from their mummies and daddies one day, to go to school. Parting is part of life. Are you still there?'

'Yes.'

'How are you enjoying school?'

'It's all right.'

'That's one of the many many things we will talk about together.'

'When are you coming?'

'As soon as we've found the right house. We're going to look at one tomorrow that sounds very promising. In Harrow. Geoffrey doesn't want to commute too far.'

'Is Harrow far from Somerset?'

'Harrow's just outside London, Jebs. I must say, they haven't taught you much at the village school, have they? Just as well we'll be looking for a nice new school.'

He stood in the lobby for some time after his mother had stopped crackling into his ear and he'd hung the receiver back on its hook. Then he heard his aunt's footsteps and ran away, up to the top of the house, up to his room in the eaves with its dormer window. He loved his room. He sat on the windowsill and stared out at the gentle valley below him, at the group of horses on the opposite hill, their coats shining in the sun. One started to gallop and they all followed, round the field and out of sight.

He loved Bellwether Farm. It was home. The Ropers had become his family; he was part of their web. He liked his school in Taunton, and when he thought of having to leave it, his heart froze. They may not have taught him where Harrow was but he didn't want to know, he didn't want to go there.

He left the window and lay on his bed, numb with misery. His aunt had to fetch him to eat that evening; usually he was waiting by the kitchen table, his hunger so sharp he could think of nothing but food.

'Are you feeling ill, Jebs?'

'Not really.'

'It's difficult when you've got big changes ahead, isn't it? Did you have a good talk to your mother?'

'Yes.'

'And your father?'

'No.'

'Well, he's very busy, making a new career for himself here. And finding somewhere to live. Come and eat, Jebs. Your food will be getting cold. Shepherd's pie, your favourite.'

His father. He hadn't thought of him. His mother hadn't mentioned him except as 'we'. It had never crossed their minds that his father ought to speak to his son, or would want to.

George picks up the photo of Geoffrey Warne taken on his sixtieth birthday when he had just become chairman of the small merchant bank he'd joined on his return from India. Long nose, large, curiously fleshy ears, thick black eyebrows recalling the departed black hair, pursed determined mouth. Tough dark eyes whose main message was pride and self-love. George remembers those eyes. They made him quake. The smile on the lips only reached them when he was talking to Lena, never to George.

George's inner conviction that Geoffrey was not his father went through many stages: at first, it was a nebulous desire to rationalize the fact there was no bond between them and not an iota in common physically or psychologically. He could do nothing to interest, attract or impress the man his mother called his father. Geoffrey was strict, he gave measured praise where necessary, he grew irritated sometimes, but never showed any deep emotion to his son.

*   *   *

'Jebs! Come down! They're here at last!' His aunt's voice was hoarse with excitement as she shouted up the stairs; Jebs watched from the lavatory window as she rushed out of the house and fell on her sister as she climbed out of a car. Both of them were weeping as they hugged each other.

Jebs's diarrhoea threatened to attack him again as it had on and off all morning, but he stayed watching the driver's door as it opened and a black-haired, black-browed man got out. He shook hands formally with Cynthia, whom he'd only briefly met in 1939 before his abrupt recall to India as war broke out. Jebs gazed at him, disappointment flooding him. He saw Lena take Geoffrey's arm as they followed Cynthia into the house, and incontinence overcame him again.

'Jebs! Where are you, darling?' His mother's voice came up the staircase.

'Just coming.' He wiped his sore arse with more sheets of shiny hard Jeyes paper, and pulled up his good school shorts, too long and so big round the waist they were held in and up by a new elastic belt with a snake's head clasp which he loved. His white aertex shirt was clean, his hair newly shorn. As he washed his hands he looked into the mirror to see the boy his parents would see: a thin, pale face, a high forehead, a few small tufts of curly fair hair left by the barber, greenish eyes, heavy freckles, a beak of a nose. He looked like a frightened animal; he tried to practise a smile.

'Jebs!'

So at last he ran downstairs and was hugged by his mother, kissed and examined and exclaimed over.

'Hasn't he grown tall, Geoff!'

'Hullo, my boy.' Jebs found his hand being shaken in a large cool grip, looked for a second at his father's dark eyes and saw his own disappointment reflected in them. 'Up to your mother's shoulder. Well done.'

'Oh, it's so lovely to be a mother again! I hope I haven't forgotten how.' Lena hugged him once more and gushed and laughed all through the otherwise sticky lunch they had to endure before Jebs and his luggage would leave the farm for good. Sophie and Laura were as silent as Jebs, Julian tried to find common ground with Geoffrey by asking about farming methods in India, Lena and Cynthia spent a lot of time chatting in the kitchen.

Jebs sneaked looks at his father. His smart tweed jacket, his pale, beautifully kept hands, his immaculate cuffs, made him seem a different animal from Uncle Julian, who was all roughness and redness and untidy sprouting hair. Jebs could sense his uncle did not like Geoffrey Warne.

When Jebs saw how near was the moment when his Revelation case would be loaded into the car, and he would be taken away from the family he loved, the farm which was home, to live with strangers, a new spasm gripped his gut, his heart, his whole being: a spasm of purest anguish.

'You were a complete bastard to me. An utter bastard.' George controls a desire to dash the portrait of Geoffrey Warne at his late-life apogee to the floor. 'Cold, mean-hearted bastard. You made sure I could never call your house my home, from the first moment I arrived in it.'

'I think George should have the room at the side.'

'But I've put him in the back room next to ours—'

'We must keep that one for guests. We can't really put them in the other, it's not big enough. Put the boy in it.'

'Come with me, Jebs darling. I'm sure we can make it very cosy.'

When Jebs saw the room that was his, he stood blankly in the middle of it. Square, with just enough room for a single bed, a table and an ugly coffin-shaped wardrobe, it had a view of the next-door house's wall, an expanse of red brick with no break in it. It was going to be difficult to make his dismal room feel like anything but a prison.

Later he saw the spacious room looking out over the back garden that Lena had allotted him originally, and feared that whatever his father had in mind for him in the future, it wasn't going to be enjoyable.

And it wasn't. A minor boarding school in Sussex where, along with most of the boys, he was deeply unhappy, a minimum of exeats, poor food all the time and not enough of it, too little pocket money – every aspect of his schooldays was unpleasant except for the work. George was clever and found the work easy.

'They're actually managing to teach you something.' This remark of his father's after the first successful year when he came top of his class in most subjects had a faint undertone of disappointment in it, covered at once by 'Well done, my boy, well done.' Nothing could eradicate George's conviction that Roddick Manor had been chosen because it was third-rate and unlikely to give him more than a basic education. It was also much cheaper than Marlborough or Radley, Lena's preferences.

Lena always let him down. That first betrayal was a pattern for them all. Husband came first, husband was deferred to on all decisions, not because she was a weak woman but because she found subjection obscurely exciting. George only realized this when he was an adult; as a child he simply knew he could never count on his mother. But he could count on his Aunt Cynthia, and since Geoffrey and Lena liked to pack him off to the farm for his long summer holidays, he survived the year in between more or less. He learned to show no enthusiasm about going to Bellwether Farm; his face never showed the leap of his heart when he arrived there. And the same canniness made him hold his tongue about the misery of his home life when he talked to his aunt. He knew if a whisper about it reached his parents he would never be sent to the farm again.

Sophie and Laura treated him like a brother; in other words Sophie ignored him most of the time and Laura teased him and taught him games. They would spend hours locked in canasta, bezique, cribbage, draughts. Sophie didn't mind occasionally playing Monopoly, and these games could last days.

In the summer of 1951 Laura taught him to dance. Sophie owned a gramophone, an enviable object with grey casing and red grilles, and when she was out Laura would put a Glenn Miller record on and push him round the bedroom floor. Laura at fifteen was fat and spotty and unappealing to the local boys, so Jebs was useful as a partner, and dancing fascinated him. When Laura took his hand and put his arm round her fat waist he was in heaven. He was hardly ever touched at home; his mother would peck his cheek now and again, but his father never touched him at all. Since his babyhood when his ayah cuddled him and held him and hardly ever put him down, he had suffered a dearth of physical contact. Aunt Cynthia hugged him when she greeted him and again when she said goodbye. Two hugs a year had been his ration and here was Laura in his arms, prodding at him impatiently as she tried to teach him to waltz and to quickstep.

'Look, it's one-two-three forwards but not on to my feet, and hold me here, I won't bite.'

'I feel as if I've got three legs.'

'I feel as if you've got six feet.'

His feelings for Laura were a milder version of his devotion for his aunt; she was family, she accepted him for what he was. Without a hint of anything beyond this, their dancing sessions progressed until Laura said, 'You're better than Neil Roundhouse.'

Since Neil Roundhouse was her designated partner at the weekly ballroom dancing sessions held in the village hall, Jebs glowed. He never had any further dancing lessons later in his life, but remained an excellent dancer.

That was his last summer at Bellweather Farm. He has never been back since. His aunt developed cancer that winter, and died the following summer.

George finds the photograph of the two sisters in his mother's roll-top desk. He carries it back to his chair, refilling his glass with whisky on the way.

It was taken in 1932 when Lena was about to leave for India to marry Eric Leith, aged twenty. Cynthia, two years older, has soft long hair loosely caught into a chignon; Lena's is cut into a sharp bob. The sisters have identical smiles, but where Lena's eyes are bright and guarded, Cynthia's are full of humour, as if the photographer's antics have amused her. In this photograph, it is Cynthia who holds the viewer's gaze.

'Did you ever know how vital you were to me, beloved Auntie Cynthia? Probably not, for I never told you. Let's hope you sensed it. When I heard you were dead my life changed for ever. I still don't know how they could have done it to me.'

Lena was a fierce and nerve-racking driver and had her own Austin A40 because Geoffrey wouldn't let her drive his company Bentley. Her car was almost too small to hold Jebs's school trunk at the end of the summer term of 1952, but somehow they got it in with the unexpected help of various boys who'd noticed the slim, smart woman in black, with nails and lips and high-heeled shoes an eye-catching red.

'We'll stop for lunch at the Three Pigeons.'

'Oh good.'

'You're looking very tired, darling.'

'It's been a tiring term. I had exams, remember.'

'Oh my goodness, how did they go? What with everything I'd forgotten to ask you.'

'OK.'

'That tells me nothing.'

'I didn't like the maths much.'

They talked about the School Certificate exams but Jebs could see his mother wasn't really listening. He had the feeling she was brewing up to tell him something, and he knew, given his home life, that the something wouldn't be pleasant. So he stopped talking and thought about the excellent steak and kidney pudding with a slightly gooey suet crust that he always had at the Three Pigeons, followed by apple crumble and clotted cream.

'What's happening to me this summer, Mum? The farm as usual?'

'Ah. No, Jebs, not the farm. No. Haven't you noticed I'm wearing black?' Lena's voice was strained. Jebs began to feel cold despite the hot day.

'Black?'

'I'm in mourning for my sister.' Her hands were gripping the steering-wheel, her eyes were staring glassily ahead. Tears began to pour, to choke her voice. 'She's dead, Jebs, she's dead. My Cynthia—' His mother started to sob. She pulled the car over to the entrance of a field and stopped so suddenly that the car behind screeched its brakes, honking furiously. Jebs saw Blakeney Minor's father make despairing gestures as he passed.

Lena sobbed and Jebs sat there, unable to take in what he had been told. Aunt Cynthia couldn't be dead, she couldn't be. She had stayed with them in the Christmas holidays, she was fine then—

'It was cancer, Jebs. Six months was all they gave her when they found out. Oh God. Look at my makeup.'

'I saw her at Christmas—'

'We didn't know then.'

'When did you know?'

'Soon after. She was losing weight – you remember how thin she was? Then the lumps started.'

'Mum.'

'I know it's a shock for you.'

'Mum, why didn't you tell me she was ill?'

'We thought it best not to. You had exams to concentrate on.'

'You mean my father thought it best.'

'Well, Geoffrey did tell me to tear up a letter I'd written to you, but I'm sure he was right.'

'He wasn't. Now I've got no one.'

'What do you mean? You've got me. Think of poor Sophie and Laura, without a mother.'

'You should have told me. You should have told me.' Jebs's voice was nearly a shout as he struggled to open the car door. His mother clutched at his arm.

'Jebs my darling—'

'I needed to know. Now I've got nothing!'

'I don't understand all this shouting—'

'And the funeral, why couldn't I come to the funeral?'

'You had your exams—'

'But *when was it*?'

'The day before yesterday.'

Jebs stared out at the green hedge, the green field beyond, the clear blue sky, the flatness, the emptiness.

'I'd finished my exams by then, I could have come, you should have told me. Now I've got nothing.'

'Well, it seemed better not.' She tried to start the car and stalled it. 'I'd no idea you'd take it like this.'

You've no idea what I am, you've no idea what I feel, you've no idea what you've done to me. And you'll never know, never.

George lies on the sofa, the photograph of the sisters beside him. He watches the cat re-organize himself on the hearthrug, turning his body anti-clockwise in an effort to crush invisible undergrowth and settling just as and where he had been. George hears the creaks of his mother getting out of bed above him, going to the lavatory, going back to bed. He replays in his mind's eye the scene he so often imagined, of his father picking up the letter ready to post to him at Roddick Manor, of him asking, 'You didn't tell the boy about Cynthia's cancer by any chance?', of Lena's flustery 'Yes, of course I did, he's very fond of his aunt', of his father tearing the letter in half unopened. 'It's not appropriate, Lena. He will learn soon enough. It's for the best he doesn't know.'

The death of his aunt had devastated him, but it also freed him from any lingering hope that his home life would improve. Jebs perfected the first of the many tough layers he grew to protect his inner being; up till now he had responded to events like a boat at anchor, but now he grew wily and proactive. Even by the time he and Lena got home after that journey from Roddick Manor he'd decided not to let his father see his grief. He sobbed when he was alone in his bedroom, but appeared for meals stonily indifferent.

'We're sorry you can't go down to the farm as usual.'

'It doesn't matter. It was boring down there.'

'I'm afraid it's going to be even more boring for you here all summer.'

'I'll find something to do.'

He could feel his father's unease at his stoicism. He stared at the cruet in the middle of the polished table made in the form of a pair of scales with salt and pepper shakers balancing each other, inwardly vowing he would get a holiday job and start saving for the day when he could leave home for ever.

His strategy against his father arrived fully formed out of his hurt. He took the lack of resemblance, the lack of bond between them a stage further and decided that Geoffrey Warne was not, could not be his real father. He started calling his parents by their first names from that moment, and though Lena objected, he took no notice. He insisted they stopped calling him Jebs and eventually the name atrophied, though Lena found it difficult to stop at first.

George also decided that if he stayed near Geoffrey he would never thrive. Geoffrey nudged him towards the second-rate, wanted him to shine but dully. But George had other ideas. He got a job that summer as a hand in a local factory making paper goods, and saved twenty pounds seven shillings and sixpence, a considerable sum in 1952. He returned to Roddick Manor in the autumn with excellent exam results, and started the sixth form with a secret goal in his head – Oxbridge. Roddick Manor sent few boys on to university, and rarely any to Oxford or Cambridge.

'You're getting so secretive, Jebs.'
  'George.'
  'Why can't I call you Jebs? I like it and it suits you.'
  'It's a baby name and I'm not a child any more.'
  'You come home for the Christmas holidays and we never see you. What are you doing all day?'
  'Earning money.'
  'Not at that dreadful factory again—'
  'No.' This time he was working as a temporary postman, but he didn't tell her. She'd find out soon enough.
  'Anyway, darling, you don't need to do these holiday jobs – it's not as if we're badly off.'
  'I like earning my own money.'
  'Geoffrey's afraid it's going to affect your school work.'
  'I don't care what he thinks.'
  'Jebs – George – please don't talk like that. Oh, hullo, darling. We were just chatting—'
  'Since for once you're actually in the house with us, George, I thought we might have a discussion about your future.'
  George was lying on the sofa and his father came and stood behind it. George resisted his natural inclination to sit up and stayed floppy in front of the stiff figure of Geoffrey.
  'Does this passion for holiday work imply that you'll be keen to go into a job straight after your schooling ends?'
  'Possibly.'
  'Then I must insist you choose something that offers an integral training.'
  'It's a long way off. What's the point of talking about it now—'

'Eighteen months or so is not so long. I think you should get your hair cut, by the way.'

'People are wearing hair longer.'

'Not in my experience. You'll find when you enter the world of real work, things like long hair and careless manners count heavily against you.'

There was an edge of violence in the way he said 'heavily'; George knew he itched to pull his lounging son off the sofa by his long curly hair.

'Please don't put your feet on the sofa, Jebs, there's a good boy—'

George swung himself out of the sofa and went to the french windows as Lena plumped the cushions. The garden was iced with a thin layer of snow, and Harpo, their lugubrious cocker spaniel, was sitting in the middle of the white lawn. George tapped the window but Harpo, slightly deaf now, took no notice.

'George doesn't seem to be interested in his future.' Geoffrey sat firmly on the sofa.

'I didn't say I wasn't interested. I just said it was too soon to think about it.'

'Nineteen fifty-four starts tomorrow. I would have thought it was an ideal time to talk about the future.' Lena talked brightly to cover the tension. 'What about university, Jebs? Surely the school are encouraging you to think of going to one after those good exam results? What do your masters say?'

'I haven't been to the careers beak yet.'

'What about Oxford and Cambridge? Think of all those lovely old colleges—'

'Lena, don't encourage him to aim too high – disappointment is worth avoiding, it seems to me.'

'But there are lots of other good universities too—'

'George may not be the university type. He seems to be attracted to the world of commerce.'

George tapped noisily on the windowpane and this time Harpo heard him and came bounding over to jump at the glass.

'Make sure that dog has his paws dried when he comes in.' Geoffrey opened *the Daily Telegraph* at the business pages. 'How much did you earn for being a postman?'

'I'm not sure, I haven't been paid it all yet.'

'You'll get exploited if you don't know where you stand. Always read the small-print.'

'I do love the thought of Oxford for Jebs.'

Spurred by the desire to stop his mother talking, Jebs suddenly undid the french windows and let the dog in. Harpo rushed across the room in manic delight and leapt on the sofa beside Geoffrey, wetly pawing the newspaper. In the fury and confusion that followed Oxford was forgotten, and George slipped off upstairs. The need to keep his plans secret was almost painful.

George gets up to fetch a glass of water from the kitchen. The sink is full of dirty dishes; there is a smell of decaying food from the dustbin. He checks the fridge and sees only a saucer containing two cooked sausages, another with a portion of something white and gooey, milk in a familiar blue earthenware jug, a small piece of Edam cheese and two eggs. He is sure Lena is not eating properly – her diet since Geoffrey died has been mainly packet soup, toast, sausages, and tinned Ambrosia creamed rice. She has plenty of money but has lost interest in food.

He makes himself some tea, knowing he is putting off the moment when he has to climb the stairs and settle himself between musty sheets within earshot of his mother's snores. There is no Geoffrey beside her, but his spirit endures.

Peter Dawlish arrived at Roddick Manor in January 1954, temporarily taking the place of the old history master who'd died of a heart attack on Christmas Day. Dawlish, fresh from Oxford, was half the age of the next youngest master, and his face amongst the other members of staff at the first assembly gave George a shock. Whispers announced he was the new history beak. To George he was a miracle: young, approachable, enthusiastic and friendly. Like George, he was tall and blond, but there the likeness ended: George's flat secretive face gave nothing away, whereas Dawlish's expression was open, eager and usually smiling.

'Warne, this essay has real promise. I wish you'd gone more into the reasons for Mussolini's rise to power but otherwise it's a good survey of Italy's position at the outbreak of the war. You obviously know the country well.'

'Never been there, sir. I just like atlases and maps.'

'As all good historians should. Have a mint.'

George often hung about at the end of the modern history session just before recreation, and Dawlish never used to rush away to the staff-room, probably because he had more in common with the sixth-formers than with the staff.

'I didn't go to Italy until last year, but it knocked me out. You should go, you'd love it. By the way, there's an exhibition of Italian surrealist painting on at the moment in London, and I'm planning to take a group to see it. Mackie and Stubbs have shown interest – what about you?'

No teacher had ever suggested anything so alluring; school outings were sparse and deadly.

'Yes please, sir.'

Dawlish talked the maths master into lending his car, and one freezing February afternoon George found himself in the front seat beside his hero, going too fast on the A22, his heart singing. Mackie and Stubbs played cards in the back while Dawlish filled the car with smoke from his cigarettes. He offered the boys one, in flagrant breach of school rules.

'I can't believe none of you smoke. Have one, I won't tell.'

But none of them did. George was tempted to try, and would have had he been on his own. He'd always felt sick before when he'd tried his parents' cigarettes, but he was impressed by how deeply Dawlish inhaled and with what gusto.

'Unless anybody has a better suggestion I'm going to park off Piccadilly and then we can walk up Bond Street to the exhibition, do a few other galleries, and then I'll take you to a new coffee bar, Il Paradiso. A bit of grub – it's very cheap, you get a good big plat of spag for one and sixpence. Then back to Alcatraz.'

They laughed dutifully, not daring to admit they didn't know what Alcatraz was. George was relieved he'd brought a precious half-crown with him; Stubbs and Mackie always had plenty of money but he'd have starved rather than borrowed from them.

Peter Dawlish started to sing, and for the rest of the journey he taught the boys risqué songs. As George bawled them out he knew his life had turned a corner and ahead lay heaven. He also knew that Dawlish wouldn't last long at Roddick, but prayed he'd be there long enough to help him get into Oxford.

The exhibition was the only disappointment in a perfect outing; George stared at the jumbled metaphysical world of de Chirico and Carrà in uncomprehending unease. Dawlish inspected the pictures in rapt silence while the boys wandered blankly round the gallery like travellers in a foreign railway station where even the script is unfamiliar.

'Very well painted banana, sir.' Dawlish ignored Stubbs, who then went outside with Mackie to look at the shops in the street.

'Don't worry about their meaning, Warne. Don't expect to understand anything at this stage, just try and feel their power.'

'It's difficult, sir.'

'You will, one day. And I wish you'd stop saying sir when we're not in school.' With an impatient sigh he led George out to find the others.

'Stubbs. What do you think of your namesake's paintings?'

'Sir?'

'Look.' Dawlish pointed at the picture in pride of place in another smart gallery. It was of a large dappled grey horse being led by a groom. 'Stubbs painted that.'

The boys stared in relief at the picture in the window. Everything was as it should be – legs, hooves, mane, groom.

'Stubbs, the greatest English painter of livestock. Is he related to you?'

'Don't know, sir. How much is this painting?'

'Get your father to buy it, Stubbs.' Mackie nudged him.

Dawlish laughed and disappeared into the gallery for a moment, and was still laughing as he came out. 'A snip at five hundred guineas.'

Stubbs and Mackie hooted in disbelief as they followed Dawlish up Bond Street. George lingered, aware that this was a day of revelation. Five hundred guineas for a picture. The little water-colours in the high-street gallery at home were one guinea each, too expensive even for a Christmas present for Lena.

A woman wearing a dark green jacket and skirt, the jacket

nipped in to show a tiny waist, the skirt long and full, brushed past him. A fur hat and collar framed her face; he smelt her scent, her powder, he saw her pretty ankles in pale nylons, seam-lines in perfect parallel, as she waited beside him, poised to cross the street. Her profile was beautiful. He could not take his eyes off her. His mother was smart but this woman was different. Five hundred guineas and one guinea, that was how different—

'Warne! We thought we'd lost you! Get moving!'

George watched the woman start to cross the street, and then ran to join the others.

'Il Paradiso here we come!'

Dawlish lasted at Roddick Manor just long enough to help George achieve a place to read history at Oxford. On New Year's Eve, 1954, he was arrested in Trafalgar Square for drunk and disorderly behaviour, and his teaching career came to an abrupt end. But George had got where he wanted, as much thanks to Dawlish's maverick vision as his own brain. He longed to keep in touch with him but had no address.

'Ask the bursar,' said Stubbs. 'He'll probably have left a forwarding address. Wormwood Scrubs, I should think.'

'Alcatraz.'

'So what is Alcatraz?'

'An American prison.'

'Oh, I get it.'

But the bursar could not help either.

Goerge lies on the sofa in Lena's dusty sitting-room, his tea gone cold, unable to move. He is George Warne QC, he has just been asked by the Lord Chancellor to be a High Court Judge, he is successful, he is not happy, and at the moment he longs for one thing: to know who his real father was. Having invented the idea that Geoffrey wasn't his father and lived through his teens with this comforting prop, he remembers the night when he returned very drunk from a twenty-first party to find his mother in the kitchen with a mug of Horlicks, sitting at the table reading an article in *Tatler* about famous fathers with famous sons. He banged the kitchen door and staggered to the sink to pour some water.

'Shh, do be quiet, you'll wake Geoffrey.'

'Why are you up so late?'

'I couldn't sleep. Would you like some Horlicks?'

'God forbid – you know I hate milky drinks.'

'So soothing.' She sipped at her drink, her eyes returning to the article. He peered over her shoulder.

'What a bunch of creeps. Slimy fathers and equally slimy sons, all dead pleased with themselves.'

'They have a lot to be pleased about.'

'I can't believe Simon Taplow junior is an MP already – he's only a few years older than me.'

'Like father like son – perhaps forceful genes do run in families.'

'Lena. Right. Now for a bit of truth—'

'Please don't raise your voice, you know how lightly Geoffrey sleeps.'

'Geoffrey is not my father, is he? Not my real father.' George watched Lena as closely as the swaying room allowed him. 'His forceful genes did not beget me. We have nothing in common, nothing.'

'Jebs.' She had not used this name in years.

'Tell me the truth. I'm over twenty-one. I should know.'

'Please don't ask me.'

'Yes.' George knocked a chair over as he moved round the table to face her. '*I am asking you!*'

'Oh, don't shout. I couldn't bear it if we woke Geoffrey—'

'Bugger Geoffrey. I am right, I can see I'm right. He's not my father.'

'No,' She whispered, eyes down.

'Does he know?'

'Of course.' Her self-control began to return. 'Of course.'

'Why didn't you tell me this before?'

'We both thought it was wisest not to. Family life is better without secrets like that coming out.'

'Family life is *better!* Lena, can you honestly say we've had a good family life?'

'You're drunk.'

'Yes, I'm drunk. *In vino veritas.* Who was my father then? TELL ME.'

'No. Never.'

'You must. You bloody must!'

'Please respect me over this, George. I have just half-broken a promise I planned never to break, and I refuse to go any further.' She stood up, her eyes steely. George stared at her in surprise. His mother was usually so conciliatory to her menfolk, as she always called them, he could hardly accept she meant what she said.

'But I need to know his name.'

'No you don't. Your life would have been no different if you'd always known, and will be no different if you don't. Geoffrey has been marvellous to us always, and I promised him right at the start of our marriage I would never tell you. I've half-broken that promise tonight and I feel dreadful.' For once she looked dreadful too: white-faced, bags under her eyes, hair untidy, hands shaking. But her eyes remained obdurate.

'Lena—'

'Promise me you will never, never tell Geoffrey you know what you now do. And don't ask me for that name again.'

George wished he wasn't so drunk. The water had made him feel worse if anything.

'Promise me, George.'

'I don't mind promising not to let Geoffrey know I know, but damn it, Lena, why shouldn't I ask you the name of my father!'

'Please stop shouting. It won't achieve anything. Just promise.'

They stared at each other until finally George shut his eyes, mainly because he felt so queasy.

'All right. I promise.'

'It would be best if you forgot this conversation ever happened.'

It was as if she was hypnotizing him into accepting half of the truth and burying it. By the time he'd woken up with a massive hangover, the conversation with his mother was like an ill-remembered dream. He let it sink out of sight, but did not lose it. It was there, inert but ready to resurface, like a brick on the end of a rope.

*   *   *

George pours himself another very small whisky and paces about the sitting-room recalling that night encounter with his mother with difficulty – he'd been so drunk that the nuances were blurred, lost. Thirty years have passed and only now has he raised the subject again with his mother. Perhaps one reason he has let it lie for so long was that he was shocked by what he'd learnt, profoundly shocked to find his boyish ploy – deal with a father you dislike by imagining he's not your father – was true. But he also realizes now that there was something in his mother's reaction that made him fear to probe: a darkness, a hidden shame perhaps, a desperation that she might spoil the life she had and loved with Geoffrey.

George looks again at the pompous English face of Geoffrey Warne: immaculate suit, hair and tie, watchful eyes, solemn mouth with the slight indication he might smile if you were lucky. So this face always hid the knowledge that his son was not his son; and that son, once possessed of the same knowledge, could not use it.

Poor Geoffrey – soon after he had this portrait taken epitomizing the successful businessman, chairman of companies, honourable member of societies and clubs, propped and buffered by personal secretaries and a supportive wife, he developed little signifiers of a terrible fate to come: his wine-glass clicking against his teeth, his keys proving difficult to guide into locks. The maddening certitude of his expression slipped into fear and puzzlement as Parkinson's disease took its hold. Deference turned to pity and distaste, power melted into dependency. Poor Geoffrey.

George puts the photograph back in its place and yawns. It's late, one o'clock. He ought to go to bed, but needs five minutes of fresh air first.

Lena's house is on the edge of a nondescript little Sussex village. The pub flourishes, the church is open one Sunday in four, the post office no longer exists, the general store closed at the end of the summer. Lena's supplies are brought once a week by her neighbour from the superstore ten miles away. George walks quickly past the store's empty windows looking for a track he remembers which led up between fields to the Downs. But the track now has a gate across marked Private, and a dog starts to bark furiously at him. Giving up on the track, he heads back towards Lena's house, setting off more dogs.

He lets himself into the overgrown garden and sits on a bench. The old man who had gardened for Lena died the very day the store closed, and she hasn't found anyone to replace him. The sight of the ragged grass, overgrown shrubs, a climbing rose hanging off the house, gives George a fierce pang. He's a most remiss son; he could have come and tidied up her garden for the winter. The whole place looks sere and utterly decrepit. Many panes in the little greenhouse are broken, clearly deliberately, and the inside has been desecrated. George switches off the torch he'd picked up off the shelf by the front door. The garden depresses and rebukes him; better not to see it. He must come down soon and tidy it up for her. But he has been so busy recently, and if he becomes a judge, he will be as busy and much more restricted in the time he can take off. A judge – the prospect chills him, and he pulls his scarf more closely round his neck.

George loves the life of the advocate, he loves the unpredictability, the constant change, the variety of cases, the daily challenge of court procedure. He has refused to specialize in any particular branch of the law, and enjoys the switch from a civil case to a fraud to a murder. He has a good rapport with juries and judges alike: he can sway a jury, yet also, when needed, impress the judiciary with his incisive grasp of complex legal issues. He knows that as a judge he will still have the variety of cases, the court procedure, the constant change, but the unpredictability will go and, most importantly, the advocacy, the thinking on his feet as a witness blows up and he has somehow to save a situation, the sheer risk of it all. A judge is salaried, operates within a structure, has the heavy weight of adjudication always with him. He has to accept the prescribed system and abide by its rules. It is not a life of freedom.

Yet George also knows he is delighted and flattered to have been invited and that if he asks for a postponement he will not be asked again. George Warne is a surprising choice for the High Court Bench, and the announcement will cause some consternation at the Bar. For that alone, he is tempted to accept. He is also aware of an obscure sense of duty towards the Lord Chancellor; judges are needed and he has been asked.

But. But. Does he really want, could he bear, the life that goes with the appointment? Six-week periods on circuit all over England, based in Judges' Lodgings with other judges, some of whom he knows only too well from appearing before them, and in a few cases dislikes intensely? Sharing the breakfast table with the likes of Mr Justice Pellet-Hicks, for instance, is a prospect he can do without. Only yesterday, while discussing the downside of High Court life, he'd described him to Freddie Mentieth (who, as his Head of Chambers, could be told of the Lord Chancellor's approach) as a rude, port-stained Fascist. Freddie had laughed, but George could still see the regret in his eyes that it was the unlikely George Warne QC and not the more expected Frederick Mentieth QC who had been put forward for the Bench.

A fox moves across the corner of the garden, orange pelt grey in the moonlight. Stars are faintly visible in the permanently polluted English night sky above him; he longs for the bright stars of his childhood; the sky here is murky, reddened at the edges by the urban complexes along the south coast. He can hear the murmur of a distant dual carriageway; it has drowned out the sound of the sea which used to be audible on still nights like this one. The fox stares boldly at him as it saunters past.

He'd earn less as a judge, much less. But he'd get a pension at the end of it all, a good pension, way beyond the provisions he has made as a self-employed person. Yet why worry about a pension when he is currently well-off, owns a handsome house in Kensington, and has no dependants save his mother? Financial security would be a poor reason for giving up the life he loved; if he took up the appointment it should be for a better one.

There is a squeak from the hedge: the fox has caught a small animal. After frenzied rustlings, the fox runs past him with a limp form in its mouth.

I live alone. I like it. I'm not much good at sharing my house with anyone, even the women I've loved. How could I endure weeks in Lodgings at close quarters with judges like Pellet-Hicks or Jane Niven? How could they endure me?

The dogs in the village start barking again, this time in chorus. Night cold is biting into him despite his thick coat. George goes back into the house through the front door and eases off Geoffrey's wellingtons in the porch; it is five years since he died but his gardening shoes and clothes still lurk in the untidy cupboard. George throws the boots into the confusion and makes his way through the inner door into the hall. When Geoffrey was alive, those shoes stood in neat rows and thick socks for his wellingtons hung pegged to the top of each boot.

'If ever thou gavest hosen and shoon
  Every nighte and alle
Sit thee down and put them on
  And Christe receive thy saule.

But if hosen and shoon thou gave'st none
  Every nighte and alle
The whinnes shall prick thee to the bare bone
  And Christe receive thy saule.

As these words come unbidden into his mind, George remembers the night Geoffrey died. Summoned at four in the morning by Lena, George had immediately driven down to the house, The Lyke Wake Dirge drumming through his brain as he sped through empty dark roads. He'd chosen to learn the ballad at school because it was short, and once committed to his memory it had thrown a long shadow, had chimed in his head often over the years, refusing to be forgotten. He began to chant it to keep himself alert.

This ane nighte, this ane nighte
  Every nighte and alle
Fire and fleet and candlelight
  And Christe receive thy saule.

When thou from hence away art past
  Every nighte and alle
To whinny-moor thou comest at last
  And Christe receive thy saule.

If ever thou gavest meat or drink
  Every nighte and alle

> *The fire shall never make thee shrink*
> And Christ receive thy saule.

> *If meat or drink thou ne'er gav'st none*
> Every nighte and alle
> *The fire will burn thee to the bare bone*
> And Christe receive thy saule.

It was an ancient Norse dirge for the dead soul, where the gorse-moor – the whinny-moor – was an image for the pricking torment a soul received in Purgatory as it waited for judgment. *This ane nighte, this ane nighte.* Geoffrey had given him hosen and shoon, Geoffrey had given him meat and drink. Geoffrey had done the right thing; cold, without obvious beliefs, he had kept faith with his basic commitment and brought up his wife's son. Perhaps it is not the motive that matters, but the act.

The poem filled George's brain in that darkness before dawn until he became aware that light was creeping into the eastern sky behind him, and as the light grew the words dimmed. It was just daylight when he stopped outside the house containing Geoffrey's cooling body, the house that Geoffrey and Lena had chosen with such care for their retirement. He followed Lena upstairs into the bedroom – the early sun streamed straight on to the bed from a side window.

Geoffrey lay tidily on his back, hands hidden under the covers, his feet at ten to two poking up under the smooth bedding. His head was tipped sideways, his mouth was open, his eyes shut. There was a strong smell of fresh faeces in the room.

Lena stood frozen in the doorway, eyes staring. 'He's messed himself. Oh God, he's alive—'

'He's dead, Lena.' He put his arm round his mother's tense shoulders. 'Sometimes bodies do that after death.'

'I didn't know,' she whispered. 'I didn't know anything about death.'

'He looks very calm. He didn't die in pain.' George couldn't quite take in the body. He knew a lot about the technicalities of death, had looked at many photographs of corpses in course of his work, but never at a real dead body before. He touched the nearly cold forehead, then pulled back the covers slightly to see Geoffrey's right hand. It was a clutching claw, spread as if to grip desperately. He quickly re-covered it.

'Come downstairs, Jebs.' Lena stumbled out, leaning heavily on her son. 'I can't bear the smell. I had to clean him up so often at the end.'

'It's over now.'

'You'll never know how hard it's been.'

He held her tight but said nothing. The doorbell rang as they reached the hall.

That'll be Dr Knights. He's been very good to us but Geoffrey didn't like him very much.'

'I'll take him upstairs. You go and sit down, darling.'

'No, no, I must come too. This is George, Doctor, our son.'

'My condolences to you both. I know my way, you can leave me to it.' Dr Knights was squat and red-faced; he puffed a little as he climbed the stairs, showing the shiny seat of his trousers and his worn-down heels.

'We'll have some coffee ready for you in the kitchen—'

'Righty-oh.' He shut the bedroom door.

'Not exactly overflowing with charm, your doctor.'

'He's old and tired too. Jebs, what shall I do about the announcement? It's got to go into *the Daily Telegraph*. Geoffrey's favourite reading was the Deaths column. He always read it first. Oh, Jebs.' As she started to cry, the doorbell rang again and George let in the undertakers. The day passed in a blur of arrangements, phone-calls, drafts of the death announcement. George stayed the night and left at dawn to return to London and his case, promising to be back that evening.

This ane nighte, this ane nighte – George turned his radio on very loudly to silence the ballad hovering in his brain.

George, still cold from sitting in the garden, hesitates at the foot of the stairs, wholly unwilling to go to his unaired, clammy bed. He goes into the kitchen and puts a kettle to boil while he searches for a hot-water bottle. There used to be several on the back of the larder door, but that hook is bare. He briefly thinks of a hot bath until he remembers that the hot water only comes on in the mornings. He is reduced to pouring the kettle into the washing-up bowl and warming up his feet and hands that way. He then takes off as few of his clothes as possible and slides between the cold sheets. He longs with all his being for his bed in London.

But he sleeps remarkably well and wakes four hours later at six o'clock more refreshed than he expects. Good hot water and a shave with an old but just serviceable razor restore him further, and he goes down to breakfast feeling spruce. His mother is sitting in the kitchen with her hands round a mug of tea, looking worn and tired. As he kisses her he notices a sealed blank envelope lying near his plate. Neither of them refers to it.

'The kettle's just boiled. Tea or Nescafé? And put some toast on for yourself. You have to hold the lever down or it won't work.'

'You must get a new toaster. I'll buy you one.'

'I'm fond of that one. I don't mind humouring it. The sliced bread's over there.' She rubs her forehead, shutting her eyes tightly.

'Did you have a bad night, Lena?'

'I always have a bad night. My hip keeps me awake.'

'What does Dr Knights suggest?'

'Dr Knights? He retired years ago. Someone told me he'd died of a heart attack. No, I go to the clinic. I never know which doctor I'm going to get. They just give me painkillers. Could you let Raj in? I can hear him miaowing.'

The cat jumps up on to the top of the fridge and settles himself over the warm grille at the back. George goes back to holding the toaster down.

'This is taking a long time.'

'Sorry, but of course time doesn't matter to me any more.'

'I'm at an age when every second is precious.' He can see the envelope through the corner of his eye and cannot stop his next remark. 'Have you really no idea whether my father is alive?'

There is a silence broken only by Raj's purrs and the fridge's blending whirrs.

'I've put all I know in the letter. Please don't ask me any more questions. Don't spoil your last half-hour here with me. I see so little of you.'

'I'll come down again soon.'

'You always say that and weeks go by.'

'I promise I will. I can't come next weekend but I will the following one. Just for the day, on Sunday. I'll take you out to lunch.'

'Jebs, I would love that. Bring Marcia down with you. We had such a marvellous time when the three of us went to Brighton.'

'Lena, I don't see Marcia any more.'

'It breaks my heart. You were very happy together.'

'I'll take you to Brighton again if that's what you'd like. There, two perfect slices of toast.'

'I told you I didn't need a new toaster.'

2

What makes a girl believe she has been raped by a god? *Apollo raped me. In a cave on the north side of the Acropolis in a place called the Long Rocks, Apollo raped me.* Did the girl wander round the borders of the sanctuary brooding on the beauty and power of the god's statue until, half-crazed by the physical representation of the spiritual, rape by a handsome young temple attendant might be seen in retrospect to be the visitation of Apollo himself? Or did she simply use the story to cover up an ordinary affair or a lapse into lust? Or did the god indeed impregnate her as she claimed?

Marcia lies back on her sofa, the marked copy of her part lying open on her thighs. In order to play Creusa in Euripides's *Ion*, does she need to believe in the truth of that statement, *Apollo raped me*? And that when the teenaged Creusa left her newborn baby in the same cave in which she claims she was raped, did she believe the god would take care of his son? Or was it done in blind panic? She had kept her pregnancy secret; she was the King of Athens's daughter – she had too much to lose if her secret got out. And the secret did not get out, because here is Creusa about eighteen years later, privately agonising over the fate of that lost baby as she stands with her tough, tricksy husband Xuthus before the oracle of Apollo at Delphi, whence they have come to beg the god to end their childless state.

Marcia's never been to Greece, has never acted in a classical play before. She picks up a postcard of the Acropolis and stares at it. It is extraordinary, perched above the ugly modern city against a cobalt blue sky in seeming weightlessness on its rock. The Long Rocks. She wonders if the cave is still there.

You came to me, with the gleam of gold in your hair,
As I was picking an armful of yellow flowers . . .
You gripped me by my bloodless wrists,
Dragged me, shrieking for help, into the cave,
Bore me to the ground – a god without shame or remorse—
And had your will – for the honour of Aphrodite!

Spring. Crushed yellow flowers. Screams, panting, grunts, virginal blood, semen. A god? A godlike man playing on a young girl's naivety? A lover who wooed but deserted her once he'd had his will? Whatever the truth, Creusa claims she bore Apollo's son. And the play seems to bear it out.

Marcia puts her script aside and goes into her untidy kitchen to make a drink. Light-headed from three days' incarceration she is dithering between Earl Grey and peppermint tea, when the phone rings. It's Suzanne Baker, whom she's known since drama school.

'Marcia! I've got it! I'm the Priestess.'

'Brilliant. Brilliant.'

'Thank you for ever for suggesting me. I still can't really believe John Alsopp has chosen me.'

'I'm pleased it's worked out, Suzanne. You deserved a break.'

'So did you. Let's hope this play will finally make our names!'

'I've been around too long to have hopes like that.'

'Are you all right?'

'Suzanne, I'm still in the middle of a long haul of part-learning. I don't really want to get out of the mood. Let's talk later.'

Marcia decides to have a coffee instead, then remembers she's run out. She pours herself a glass of water and goes back to the sofa. She thinks of the young Creusa's horror when she crept back to the cave and found it empty and her conviction that wild animals had killed the baby. Then no further children came to help heal the guilt and pain.

Marcia shuts her eyes and stares at the bars of light on the insides of her lids to distract herself from the pit that is opening within her. It is all too near the bone. She is thirty-eight, about Creusa's age; she is childless. She longed for a child once – but no, no, she doesn't want children, her life is good, she has Edward, what would she do if she had a child, how could she cope . . . The pit closes. The phone rings.

'Marcia.'

'I was just thinking about you.'

'Good. I'm round the corner at Rosie's. If I come round now you can see me as well as think about me.'

'Edward, please don't. I *must* get this bloody part learnt.'

'Take a break, Marcia. I haven't seen you at all this week.'

'I haven't been out all week.'

'I could test you.'

'You'll just distract me. I test myself against my tape recorder – much more effective.'

'It's the first time someone has said I'm less effective than a tape deck.'

'Oh, Edward, don't be silly, you know what I mean. This part is such a milestone—'

'So you won't be coming to *Waiting for Godot* tonight? There's a ticket for you. Last night of the best production there's been in years. And Timothy Tugwell has asked us for a quick drink afterwards.'

Marcia stares at a crack in the wall which seems to have grown tributaries since she last paid any attention to it. She can hear the heavy grinding of Todd Reid's rowing machine directly above her. Could it be causing the cracks perhaps—

'Marcia?'

'I'm still here.'

'Don't you think you should make an effort for the producer of *Ion*?'

'Of course I should. I'd forgotten *Godot* was another one of his. All right, I'll come. Thanks, Edward. I'll see you at the theatre ten minutes before the show goes up.'

'Why can't we make an evening of it? If I come round now we can go out later for a quick bite before the show—'

'*Please* don't undermine me any more – I have to go on with what I'm doing until the last possible moment!'

'You're such an obsessive, Marcia—'

'See you later.'

She pulls the phone out of the wall and attacks her part

with a sustained burst of concentration. She gets on so well she leaves for the theatre at the last minute, having thrown on black silk trousers and grabbed her best coat – red – before rushing out to her car. It hasn't been used for several days, and the weather has been cold and damp, so naturally it refuses to start. The battery sounds as tired as Marcia feels.

'Now come on, car. Just behave.' The engine almost catches and Marcia waits another precious minute, deep breathing the while and trying not to think about the fact she can't afford to run any car let alone this dying old Fiat whose MOT is about due followed by its annual insurance, ridiculously high because actors are assessed as bad risks.

'Come *on*, car.' It starts and Marcia promptly stalls the engine as she starts to manoeuvre out of a tight gap. She finds an equally tight gap to park in twenty stressful minutes later, runs to the theatre, grabs her ticket from the box office and slides into the seat beside Edward just as the curtain rises.

'Sorry.'

Edward rolls his eyes reproachfully. Marcia sinks backwards, letting her tension pour out of her as she watches the tramplike figure of Estragon struggling in vain to pull off his boot. Vladimir enters.

'*Nothing to be done.*'

'*I'm beginning to come round to that opinion.*'

The opaque dialogue progresses, Godot is hinted at, expected, invoked, and Marcia thinks of Xuthus and Creusa waiting for illumination from the Oracle of Apollo at Delphi and wishes she hadn't come. She is densely in another imaginary world.

Edward takes her hand, squeezes it, and puts it on his thigh.

'Darlings. Sorry to keep you. Let's all have a glass of champagne.'

Timothy Tugwell is a large sweaty man; his expensive clothing is always rumpled and creased, his handmade shoes look as if he spends his time kicking stones down a dusty street. Edward, as tall but thin and always in complete control of his clothing, seems dwarfed by him.

Despite queues at the bar, three glasses of champagne appear at once.

'To the success of *Ion*. You have started rehearsing, I believe.'

'Not yet. On Monday.'

'John Alsopp is so brilliant – in many ways the finest director working in London. I can't think why he isn't better known.' Tugwell drinks half his glass in one swallow.

'He is within the theatre world.'

'But not in the wide world, Edward. Not a name the backers know. He talked me into doing *Ion*, sheer bloody persuasion. He'd get me to back an OAP production of *The Red Barn* in a village hall if he put his mind to it.' Tugwell chuckles at himself.

'I hope you don't regard *Ion* as being of that ilk.' Marcia tries to keep the edge out of her voice.

'Of course not. Of course not. Mind you, I do admit it's the first Greek play I've ever produced, and out of the West End, too. My wife thinks I'm mad! But I trust John Alsopp, and let's hope the crowds flock to *Ion* at the New Fortune. Well, good luck Marcia, and good to see you, Edward.' His champagne has disappeared. 'Now, if you'll forgive me, I ought to go backstage. Nice to talk. Bless you both.'

They watch him sweep through the bar, acknowledging greetings but not stopping.

'He clearly doesn't expect it to do well.'

'Bastard. He could afford to back a hundred *Ions*. But I agree, the subtext of all that was that he expects to lose money.'

Marcia yawns before she can stop herself. 'He probably will. There aren't any big names except Alsopp's.'

'Cheer up, Marcia. You've been working too hard. Let's have another drink.'

'I really must go. I've still got the last scene to memorise, and I'm still very shaky in the long scenes—'

'No you mustn't go.' Edward puts his hands on her shoulders and moves his hips against hers. 'I didn't know you were such an obsessive, my darling. John isn't going to expect you to know the whole bloody play on Monday. Come back with me, have a complete break – it's Saturday night after all.' He puts his mouth against her ear and touches the lobe lightly with his tongue. 'I need you. I've missed you.'

'Edward, I can't. I am obsessive, I'm hopeless, but I always do it this way. It's like a sort of ritual preparation, and I've already broken the ritual by coming here to see Godot with you.'

'Then there's every reason to go on breaking it. Haven't you missed me?' His mouth is still against her ear. Marcia pulls herself away from him, smiling.

'No, I haven't.'

'Thanks a bunch.'

'You're the same when you're about to start a big project. You don't give me a thought for days and I wouldn't expect you to. You're just not used to me doing the same. This is the best part I've had in years, with a good director and a powerful producer, and I'd be a cretin if I didn't give it my all. Once rehearsals have started and I know where I am I'll give you a ring. But right now I'm going straight back to my car and home if it will start. Alone!'

'All right, all right! I had a weekend of lovely things planned for us to do together and there's a party tonight you'd enjoy, but I can see the flint in your eye. I give in.'

They walk out of the pub next door to the theatre together and stand holding hands on the pavement, their eyes joined.

'Where's this party?'

'At Geoff's – round the corner from me.'

'So I can't give you a lift.'

'Not unless you're feeling very kind.'

'But it's in the opposite direction—'

'And besides it's only three stops on the tube.' Edward and Marcia chorus this together, laughing.

'And my car is not behaving well.'

'Does it ever.'

They hug each other.

'I'll give you a ring on Monday night when I've got my schedule. Thanks for dragging me out. That was a good production.'

'Mike! Wait!' Edward has seen a friend, and with a wave disappears into Soho.

Marcia stops at a late-night grocery and buys what she needs absentmindedly, her mind on Edward. She could easily have

gone home with him, she could have left early in the morning
and returned to her flat to work. But Edward is not the sort of
person who lets those whose company he wants leave easily. He
is never content with the hours she has given him; he always
wants more. He is not a respecter of other people's time and
space. Whereas George – George never encroached. He never
pushed and hassled her. George – she hasn't thought of him
for months. She stands blankly staring at her change, seeing his
greenish eyes, his freckles, his thin sardonic mouth which could
curl into the best of smiles. That his smiles were rare made them
arresting.

'The change isn't right?'

'Oh, yes. Thanks. I'm just dreaming.' She gathers up her
shopping and drives the last two streets home, her exhaustion
suddenly surfacing and pushing other thoughts out. She eats a
simple meal – the remains of some carrot soup and a boiled egg
– and runs a hot bath. While she soaks in it she plays the tape
of her cues and is pleased with her progress. Then she comes
to an area of the play where she has had problems with the
word order, and finds they haven't gone so she stops the tape
and wallows, aware that close behind her search for words is
the thought of George, like a hidden card, and behind him two
more: Miriam and Martin, her parents.

She feels guilty about George. She hurt him. She allowed her
inchoate feelings about her Jewish roots to surface in the messiest
possible way. And she can't even blame her parents – they did
their best to make her rootless. She's typical of many Jews of her
generation who are the children of prewar refugees; no longer
believing or observant, they will eat an *insalata di mare* full of
prawns and *maiale al latte* to follow without a thought beyond
the recognition of good Italian food. Fridays are the end of the
week, Jewish New Year passes unmarked. Mixed marriages are
common. The only observant Jews of her age she knows well
are the Kleins; she was at college with Rachel who at the time
wasn't observant but after her marriage to Jonathan has become
increasingly so.

Marcia climbs out of the bath, dries herself, puts on her thick
towelling bathrobe and returns with the tape recorder to the

sitting room intending to clear up the area in the play where her memory is faulty. But the past grips her. She goes over to the mantelpiece and picks up a photograph of a young couple sitting together on an elaborate scroll-armed sofa, hands lightly linked, smiling insouciantly out: Miriam and Martin Fleckner at the beginning of their married life, very much the fashionable Berliners, liberal Jewish intellectuals who never expected life to take the turn it did.

Miriam has a thirties' bob, sharp and shiny, and wears a smooth crepe dress with intricate tabs, buttons and seaming. Her eyes greet the future, expect success after hard work, are almost arrogant in their sparky confidence; yet her hand is touching Martin's as if she has had to reassure herself that the good-looking man with his smile almost masked by his black beard is really her husband. At this point in their lives Miriam is showing promise as an editor in a big publishing house; Martin is teaching at the university, a book already published, another on the way. He's respected, he's arrived, his students love him.

The photograph holds the gaze. Humour, intelligence, promise: Marcia knows that if she saw a couple of strangers looking like this she'd cross the room to get to know them.

Miriam. The mother Marcia remembers is a worn, prematurely grey-haired, humped woman who rarely smiled and whose store of resilience had run out. When she fled to England in 1938 she could not speak the language; Martin could at least make himself understood, and later became fluent. Miriam eventually learned English but was never at home in the language or the country. She lost her sense of style and confidence; every vestige of the buoyant young woman in the photograph was obliterated by menial jobs, three miscarriages, and tragic family news from Germany.

Tucked away insided the frame out of sight is another photograph. Marcia can hardly bear to look at it. Miriam is breastfeeding her; the lined face and thin grey hair above the baby head could be that of her grandmother, *die alte Bobbe*, the grandmother who died in Treblinka. Miriam's mouth is smiling and tender as she reacts to the pulling and sucking on her breast, but her eyes are full of tears. She is clearly unaware of the camera.

'Your mother only really began grieving for her mother after you were born. The birth seemed to unlock everything. For ten years after the war she bottled her feelings up, then you arrived and she was always crying. Perhaps it was because she was old to give birth – forty-five after all is very old to have your first child. She would breastfeed you with tears splashing down onto your head. I took this photo through the open door without her knowing – I never showed it to her.' Martin only showed Marcia the photo long after his wife was dead.

'I don't remember her crying all the time.'

'It only happened when you were a baby. Her stock of tears ran out.'

Marcia pushes the photo out of sight and puts the frame back on the mantelpiece. The Shoah killed all the close relatives on both sides. Her parents always referred to the Holocaust by its Yiddish name, Shoah; Marcia found it a strange soft word for such a stark horror.

Marcia, born in 1955, was Miriam's one success story in England; she called her her *Wunderkind*, born when she'd given up all hope of ever having children. Miriam made sure of three things: that her daughter was baptised a Christian, educated in a Church of England school, and told nothing of her Jewish background. All Marcia knew as a young girl was that her family was German, that they had left their country because they loathed Hitler. They lived in the seedy end of Notting Hill, well away from the popular Jewish areas of north London. If there were any Jews at her primary school, they seemed as integrated as she was.

'If your family came from Germany you must be Jewish.' The boy was older than her, a powerful force in the playground.

'My parents are *German*. From Berlin.' Marcia, aged then about nine, remembers how puzzled she was by the boy's sudden approach.

'Then you must be Jewish like me. My family ran away because Hitler was killing the Jews.' The boy, whose name Marcia can't remember, fiddled with a Dinky toy, running the little rubber wheels up and down his arm. 'Germans didn't have to run away. Only Jews. You ask your Mum and Dad. They ran away because they were Jews.

Brrm, brrm.' He raced his car off along the playground wall.

But Marcia couldn't bring herself to ask any questions until after her mother was dead, and when her father poured out their story she realised the sacrifice he had made to abide by his wife's rule of silence.

John Alsopp sits with his cast round him in a big uneasy circle. 'Don't forget that *Ion* is a myth. All the main characters are one stage on from fantastic mythical beginnings. Creusa's father was born of the earth, as she herself tells us, as if it's a normal way of beginning life. Her husband Xuthus is the son of Aeolus, god of the winds, himself descended from Zeus. They accept these lineages, they ask no questions. Ion's name is also clearly mythical: it is later given to a large area of Greece, Ionia. So the story is a fable, but it is presented in an intensely human way and we're going to play it straight. Let the audience work out the implications, the equivocations. We mustn't do it for them.'

'But surely Euripides and his contemporaries didn't believe all this nonsense of being born of the earth and the winds?'

'How do you know, Damian? How can you be sure?'

'He seems to leave it open—'

'Perhaps. But we play it straight. When Creusa tells you her father was born by being pulled out of the earth, then believe her.'

'But Euripides is subtle—'

'Of course he is. His words will do their own work in spite of us.'

'Ion	– *Damian Frapp*
Creusa	– *Marcia Fleckner*
Xuthus	– *Andrew Lockwood*
Priestess	– *Suzanne Baker*
Messenger	– *Peter Newman*
Hermes & Athena	– *Roy Obula*
Chorus	– *Penelope Hill, Ros Trigg—'*

Marcia looks up from the cast list at the top of her schedule, suddenly aware there is silence. (She finds these lengthy discussions a trial and wishes Alsopp would get on and block the moves.) Everyone is staring at her. Alsopp repeats his question.

'What do you think, Marcia?'

'Sorry – I missed your question.'

'How literally should we take Euripides?'

'I spent days beating my head against that particular problem and gave up. Does Creusa really believe she was raped by Apollo? What's your view?'

Alsopp picks up the Penguin edition from the floor beside him. 'Let me read one opinion that caught my eye. "*Creusa never looks beyond the moment. Each successive scene has made more evident the credulity, or rather suggestibility, which has been her character and her curse since the first fatal weakness eighteen years ago. Once she has made up her mind to believe, she pursues belief like a duty.*" What do you think of that analysis?'

'I don't find it at all helpful. And on any view it's wrong to call her experience "her first fatal weakness". She was *raped*. It was frightening. Why should she lie about the rape? I have no doubt she was raped. She had a child to prove it. The hard bit is believing Apollo did it.'

'Suzanne, what do you think of the theory that you, the Priestess, who brought him up, is Ion's real mother?'

'I think it's bollocks.' There is so much laughter that the discussion loses impetus and to Marcia's relief Alsopp calls a break before he starts to block the play. Marcia always enjoys the plain physicality of blocking – enter right, exit left, try it further upstage, no you're masked, move to stage left. Masking tape on the floor indicates the size and position of Apollo's sanctuary, circles indicate the columns. Chairs mark the low walls of the precinct. The company are rehearsing in the large upper room of a pub which has been converted into a simple theatre space. Alsopp has brought a model of the final set and Marcia drinks her tea while she examines it. She sees the problem imposed by the central sanctuary: all exits and entrances except those of the temple attendants and Hermes and Athena have to be from the wings. Alsopp comes up beside her and she mentions this.

'Ah. Well, I wanted that limitation. The ancient Greeks didn't approach a temple direct, you know, but by deliberately winding paths. A sort of stalking of the numinous. So I want you and Xuthus and the chorus to make your first entrances through the auditorium to give this winding effect. Don't look worried, Andrew. You'll have time to rehearse it in the theatre – we get in on the Monday of the week we open. Mind you, if your approach is nervous, it would be in character. Approaching the oracle sent shivers through people. I want it to be difficult.'

Marcia knows exactly how hard it will be to manage moving through the auditorium of a theatre she hasn't acted in before in full heavy costume, but the challenge does not worry her. She winks at Suzanne, who mouths the word 'typical'.

'Well, let's start blocking the first scene. But just bear in mind, everyone, that though I see *Ion* as a play working on many levels, from the simple uniting of a mother with a longlost son to the heights of equivocation, ambivalence, sophism and casuistry, we're going to let those levels take care of themselves.'

The actors gaze at Alsopp, busy with their thoughts.

3

The outside of George's house is so conforming – a white-painted Victorian terraced house almost identical to its neighbours – that the interior comes as a shock to most visitors. Huge modern pictures cover every wall, some from corner to corner. George has rebelled against the pastel walls of his childhood bearing the odd small, instantly forgettable print by buying works from the degree shows of young artists newly graduating from the Royal College, or Goldsmiths, or the Slade. He chooses very big oil paintings in colours he likes mainly for the purpose of filling up his walls. He never buys from established artists, nor follows the careers of the painters he has bought if they happen to become famous. His acquisitions are cheap, and often good as well as big. He tries not to buy anything too gimmicky which he knows would annoy him before long. Sometimes he's made mistakes and been forced to get rid of a painting, which he does very simply. He puts it out on the pavement leaning against his railings, and attaches a note saying: 'Please help yourself to this painting if you fancy it.' All three paintings given this treatment disappeared as soon as darkness fell.

Starring Marcia Fleckner. The unexpected sight of her name on a leaflet in his post makes George catch his breath. He stands motionless in his hall, just back from his visit to Lena in Sussex, and gazes at the leaflet *Ion* by Euripides, directed by John Alsopp, at the New Fortune Theatre. Cast includes Marcia Fleckner, Damian Frapp . . . John Alsopp is well known as a meticulous and challenging director; George smiles as he sticks the leaflet into the edge of a picture frame, delighted that Marcia is in what will clearly be an interesting production. Memories flood back as he climbs the stairs to his bedroom to shower and change.

'Is the whole house full of these mammoth pictures?'

'Come and see. Let's start at the top.'

Marcia's clothes – long skirt, textured layers above it – rustled against the bannisters as she followed.

'When I bought this place I had it all painted white for simplicity's sake. But it felt very cold and clinical, so I hit on the idea of filling the walls in this way. Now they're covered with pictures they will never need redecorating, which is very convenient.' Their feet echoed on the uncarpeted boards of the top floor.

'What are you going to do with all this space? Two big empty rooms full of pictures and nothing else. And two more floors below us – why did you buy such a big house to live alone in? I've lived all my life in small crowded rooms – I think this space would get me down.'

'I don't mind empty rooms. And I like space because of having lived in small rooms. Are you thinking it's rather immoral to have all this house to myself?'

'It never crossed my mind it was immoral, just not very snug.' She laughed. 'But then, you don't strike me as a snug person.'

George was staring at a large picture of sketchy figures enacting some strange rite in a field. 'I'm beginning to think that one is a mistake. Magic realism isn't my thing. But the colours are so beautiful I think I'll give it longer. No, perhaps I'm not snug, but my kitchen is, so why don't we hurry down and have a drink while I finish cooking the dinner?'

Marcia's skirt made even more noise descending as it trailed behind her on the stair-treads. She stopped in front of a long picture halfway down. 'This is the one I like. All those reflections in the mirror are like inner worlds – it's very clever. Who is it by?'

'I forget, but Freddie Mentieth – that's my Head of Chambers – got very excited when he heard I had a big one and told me her stuff now fetches daunting sums of money. He knew exactly how much because he'd bought a small painting by her. I only paid four hundred pounds for that.'

'And of course you told him.'

'Of course. Freddie would have thought it out of character if I hadn't.'

Marcia: dark-haired with almost black eyes, big nose and white, white skin, the skin of someone whose ancestors have always lived packed together in the middle of a landmass far from the sea. Marcia Fleckner, whose Jewish forebears had come from Poland and Hungary and settled in Germany during the early nineteenth century. Her parents were dead and she was alone now, her tough self-sufficiency masking her vulnerability with considerable success. George recognized a fellow-traveller, and was unsurprised that when they first made love it did not go very well; they were both so chary of giving themselves it took a while before sex improved. By then she was staying a couple of nights a week with him; he once stayed with her but the bed, inherited from her parents, collapsed, and though she propped it up with judiciously placed bricks until she could afford to replace it, they decided against putting it to a further test. If Marcia was in work she wouldn't stay at all, and her independence pleased him. He felt their arrangement could last for life. And then it all ended.

'George.'

She came into the bedroom wrapped in a yellow towel, her hair in a wild frizz from getting damp in the bath, her eyes ringed with smudged mascara and tiredness He watched her move to a narrow upright chair he used for current clothes. She had never sat on that chair before.

'This is very difficult to say, but I think we ought to part.'

His silence only partly hid his shock.

'We're getting nowhere, you and I. I can't help it, I suddenly want a child before it's too late.'

'Then let's have one. I'm not against having children, I'm not even against marriage despite my bad showing. But I didn't think you wanted marriage and all that goes with it—'

'I don't. Suddenly I just want a child.' She jerked the towel round her body and clenched and unclenched her bare toes.

'It's perfectly natural you should—'

'You don't understand. Oh God, life's so stupid! I want a child, and there you are, so what am I waiting for?' She stared at him pinch-faced. 'Then, only then did I realize I didn't want your child. Oh George, this sounds awful but it's not meant to. We've been happy together, and you've been so good to me. But I don't want to have your child. It's like a toad in the heart of me; it's got nothing to do with reason.' Unshed tears collected in her eyes. George got out of bed and walked blindly to the window.

'I can see why you think we ought to part.' He felt he had borrowed a voice because his own was too wounded to function.

'George, George. I always believed my Jewish side was good and buried, but now I find it isn't. Why should a ridiculous atavistic desire to have a baby by somebody Jewish, Jewish like me, suddenly spoil everything? I can't understand myself. And I can't change what I am. I wish I could.'

'I've kept all your Dinky toys. I put them in a box in the loft. You might have a son one day, and he'd love those Dinky toys. Some of them are in mint condition – you were such a careful little boy.'

'I didn't have siblings to fight with over them.' George can hear his mother's voice, see her bright meaningful smile as she mentions a grandson. His son. No son. Marcia destroyed any hope he might have kept in a hidden part of himself that he might one day have children with her. Lena had never mentioned grandchildren before Marcia's advent in his life: she too had had hopes. To be told what he had been told left him profoundly bruised. No child, because she could not contemplate bearing his Anglo-Saxon flesh and blood.

Marcia left that Sunday morning, tears running down her cheeks, hands flapping helplessly at all she had broken. She threw her things into two Safeway carrier bags – he kept staring at the printed name, beyond thought and feeling. He hasn't seen her since, though her name has occasionally jolted him in television previews or theatre reviews. She has been busy in the last two years, seemingly too busy to have taken off time to have the baby she wanted. But he doesn't know and there is no one he can ask. He did not meet her friends, nor she his; their lives in the law and the theatre remained distinct, without overlap. Each was a secret kept from their other friends. For George, that wasn't difficult. He never let his guard down except to Marcia; for him that was part of the attraction between them, or at least so he felt. Perhaps for her it was simply caution.

George has searched papers for reviews with her name in, and has wondered often if she ever looks for his in law reports. He doubts it. He has never been to see her act, or watched anything she has been in on television, but he can feel the day is coming when he will. He looks at the leaflet again and sees that *Ion* is opening in mid-November. Did she mail him this flyer herself? He is not on the New Fortune's mailing list, and cannot think of any other source. The company is called Classic Renaissance and that too means nothing. He has occasionally been an 'angel' and put money behind a production but he hasn't done it since Marcia left him. In fact it was at a backers' party that he first met Marcia.

He can't help but be cheered by the leaflet: he is sure Marcia must have sent it. This is clearly a step upwards in her career. She's a good actress who has lacked good opportunities to show her full range; her voice is exceptional in its range, though not instantly recognizable. She has none of the very individual delivery of many actors which makes their voices instantly known.

'I've chosen a profession that ensures poverty except for a tiny proportion of people.'

'You'll get your break one day.'

'I've had lots of breaks. In the eyes of some of my friends I'm successful. Marcia Fleckner has arrived, but the money never does. And no, I don't want you to give me any, my darling. You've given me enough as it is.'

'Nobody can live on so little—'

'Look, I'm alive!'

'Please let me tide you over until the next job – I hate the thought of you on the dole—'

'There's a telly serial next month. I'll be fine. You're too generous to me, you know. It's not good for me!'

Money. *Where your treasure is there will your heart be.* George's reputation at the Bar is of a hard man, whose first question to his clerk about a case is the size of the fee, and who, unlike many others, talks openly about his earnings. This has encouraged the view that he is money-driven and tight-fisted – generosity is certainly not a quality his fellow-barristers see in him. Most of them aren't generous either: in George's opinion the intrinsic insecurity of a barrister's life seems to erode the impulse to be open-handed. They live in fear that each case may be the last, that their solicitors may desert them, that other barristers may displace them in the eyes of solicitors, clients and clerks.

'We're both in paranoid worlds, but mine is ridiculously better paid than yours. I can earn in a few weeks what you live on for the whole year. It's rather chastening.'

'Comparing incomes is a mug's game, George. Anyway, what do you do with all your money? Apart from buying a big house and a swish car?'

'Hoard it. I have to live up to my reputation as a mean bastard.'

'Well, you're not mean to me and that's for sure.'

George finds he cannot tell Marcia, or indeed anyone, that he gives away a sizable proportion of his income in the form of covenants to favourite charities, particularly those helping the sufferers of injustice, torture, lack of freedom. Keeping it hidden from others is crucial; he fears if people knew about his giving he would stop doing it, though why he feels this so strongly he does not know nor wants to know. Thus, when a fellow barrister airs the view he's a mean bastard, it's a comfort to him.

George changes into a fresh suit and collects his briefcase. He still has not read Lena's letter, nor did he keep his side of the bargain and tell her his news. He knows it was wiser not to tell her, but he feels guilty all the same. He puts the letter into his briefcase to read later in the day. The emotional ambush might be less if it occurs in working surroundings. He's beginning to wonder if he wants to read it at all; it is bound to be a Pandora's box.

George parks in the Temple and hurries up the staircase into his Chambers; his own room is small and of no apparent charm, being tucked away down a corridor past the clerks' room. The rent is low, and there is no view from the window; it's not really regarded as a suitable room for a QC, and the fact George doesn't want to move is generally perceived as a part of his tight-fistedness. But George, who's been in it for years, knows its main advantages: it's away from the body of Chambers, and close to the clerks. He passes their door to reach his – this keeps him in their minds. Paul, one of the junior clerks, sees him pass today and promptly follows him with the diary.

'Sir, I've had to fix a consultation for five-thirty today on the Donaldson case – I hope you don't mind having it so late but the solicitor can't get here earlier, and there's the strike tomorrow.'

'What strike?'

'Train, sir.'

'I'd forgotten. Oh well, five-thirty it has to be. Does that suit the client?'

'Everyone's happy. And Douglas said to tell you it looks like the Feathers fraud is coming your way, sir. He's with Bray, Sitch and Campbell now.'

'Good solicitors, good news. Tell you what though, Paul, I'd like to do less crime and more civil in a perfect world.'

'Never noticed the world could be perfect, sir.'

'You have a point.'

Paul goes off whistling in his peculiarly musical way, as if his lips are a mellow-noted reed instrument. Feet pass him and Francis Bates puts his head round the door.

'Paul is a demon whistler. Good morning, Francis.'

'Your room being where it is, you'd know.'

There is enough edge in Francis's voice to make George realize that his choice of room is generally understood as being for tactical as much as financial reasons.

'And what can I do for you?'

'I heard that your long case settled. Annoying for you – you looked as if you'd be there until Christmas.'

'Not annoying at all – it was quite the best thing, and we achieved a good settlement.'

'Since you're free, would you be interested in leading me in the Clarkson custody case? A bunch of unprincipled millionaires fighting over twin boys? It's starting next week, assessed at four days, which I'd say was about right.'

'Francis, can I think about it? I've only just got in, and I need to talk to Douglas first. But thanks for thinking of me.'

'The client is a full-blown shit – I'm sure you could handle him. Not many could.'

'I'm not sure that's a compliment.'

'Oh, come on, George, since when did you become a sensitive flower? You and I are known as the biggest shits in Chambers – my client is getting counsel he understands. Ring me later, I hope with the answer yes. Ciao.'

George wants to punch Francis's foxy face but smiles instead as the younger man leaves him. He has never liked Francis, but the Clarkson case is a good earner.

He slumps into his chair. He has been in Chambers for twenty minutes and already the life of a busy advocate has swallowed him. This is what he will give up if he decides to accept the Judgeship. He thrives on the uncertainty, the variety. He loves the moment a case shifts from desk to court, and a large amorphous group of people is linked for a while by its progress. Never again will he get to his feet and feel that tightening of intense anticipation as he begins to put his case. Of all legal processes, it is cross-examination that he enjoys most. George leads the witness gently along in a pleasant and accommodating manner, and then – ah, the snare is set and the witness is trapped, puzzled and confused. And the jury – George always tries to make eye-contact with as many of them as possible when he addresses them, and can feel the chemistry working as he outlines his case. And how he loves to fence politely with the judge, particularly when he makes a point that is unusual, perhaps without precedent. Such a pleasure it is to feel he might be making law, that this case or that one will be reported and contested all the way to the House of Lords.

Instead he could, perhaps should, exchange it all to sit on the Bench, making and mulling over lengthy case notes, trying to decide how good a certain point really is and what place to give it in his judgment. Complex judgments can take weeks to assess and write. George knows that he is the type who likes to raise the issues, make the points; will he ever get the same satisfaction from weighing their worth? He loves the licence advocacy gives him to put to a case forward on behalf of another human being with whom he feels intellectual but no emotional involvement. It is like a game but it is not a game: it has a serious purpose with serious consequences. But it is as exhilarating as a game to him, and a good win leaves him with the same wave of satisfaction. It is also almost a drug—

His direct line rings and he picks the receiver up. 'Warne.'

'Freddie here, George.'

'I know what you're going to ask me, and the answer is no, I haven't finally made up my mind yet.'

'I wanted to tell you I was working at home today, reading through a mountain of paper. So if you need to talk it over, ring me here.'

'No one else can help me with this decision, alas. But as soon as I have decided, I'll let you know, Freddie. Even before I ring the Lord Chancellor's Department.'

'No need to give me quite that precedence!'

'It should be you deciding, not me.'

There is a silence, one of those brief pauses that says everything.

'I am sure you would find the decision easy, Freddie, and accept wholeheartedly and do the job wonderfully. Can't think why the blighters asked me instead of you. I haven't done nearly so much judging as you, either. But life's not fair, as we all know.'

'I'll look forward to your call, George.' The line clicks dead.

George fetches himself a cup of coffee from the dispenser in the little kitchen between his room and the clerks', and firmly shuts his door. He looks contentedly round his book-lined room, and tidies a row of Law Reports. Like Freddie, he has a complete set, and allows younger members of Chambers to borrow them. Those who accuse him of being tight-fisted conveniently forget the thousands of pounds the set has cost him.

He picks up Lena's letter and again hesitates. But for some reason the letter is becoming a part of his decision-making process – I will find it easier to make up my mind when I know my father's name – and so at last he pulls out the single sheet. Lena has written half a page in black ink, her writing surprisingly firm.

Dear Jebs,
Your father's name is Philip Symes. When my first husband died,
he was very good to me. We fell in love. We couldn't marry because
he already had a wife, and he was Roman Catholic. He never
knew that I became pregnant, because I decided to move away from
Jodhpur. I met Geoffrey on the train to Delhi – it was the luckiest
train I ever took. He took care of me from that moment on, and
we married as soon as I'd had you. We left you with your ayah
for a few months, and then moved with you to a new posting.
No one in India ever knew you were Philip Symes's son and not
Geoffrey Warne's, but I think it's just possible that Philip might
have guessed who you were.

I have never contacted Philip since I left India, and I have no
idea even if he's alive.
                    Your ever loving mother Lena.

At the bottom of the page she has written *Helena Warne, her*
statement. Written on 4 November 1992.

George opens and shuts his eyes several times, a slow, dazed
blink. Philip Symes. A neat, colourless name. He stares at the
far from colourless words in front of him and reaches for the
telephone. He dials his mother's number but there is no reply.
He lets it ring for some time, knowing she often does not hear it
. . . She refuses to wear a deaf aid because she says she can hear
perfectly well, and turned down his offer of a portable phone
on the grounds she would surely leave it somewhere and lose
it. George usually rings when the cleaning lady, Mrs Harris, is
there but knows that today is not one of her days.

He longs to find out more about Philip Symes. What did he
do? How can he trace him? Lena's letter is so short he longs
for her to fill it out; now that she's taken this step, surely she'll
talk more.

'George?' Patricia Saban has knocked and walked in and he
hasn't heard a thing. He covers Lena's letter with another.

'Patricia.'

'Have you a minute? I would love to pick your brains if
you have the time. I need a second opinion on this medical
negligence case—'

'Colin's the man to ask—'

'I know, but he's down in Winchester all this week. I'll come back later if now is a bad moment.'

'Sit down, sit down.'

Patricia is not one of his favourite women in Chambers, but he has to admit that behind her fluttery manner she's got a good brain. He has heard Paul doing a wicked imitation of her voice to the delight of the clerks' room, and knows they judge her more by her mannerisms than by her abilities.

'I don't know what Colin would say, but in my view ten thousand pounds is about right.'

'Thank you, George. You've been a great help.'

'I haven't done much. You'd already got there on your own. You must learn to trust your own opinions, Patricia.'

'I know.'

'Simon Hardy or Francis Bates would have steamed ahead and sent their paperwork off full of confidence in themselves.'

'I'd rather not be like them, thanks.' She starts to collect the brief together.

'I don't blame you, but take on board some of their arrogance, and in you it will come out as justified confidence.'

'I could tell you to stop being a patronizing silk, but I won't, because I know you have a point.' She gives him a quick smile. 'Nat keeps telling me the same thing.'

As she leaves, Douglas Dean the senior clerk comes in. George wilts, knowing that he has to talk about future cases in a normal manner and keep his possible move to the Bench wholly concealed. It is harder than he thinks.

'Are you all right, sir?' Douglas does not meet his eye while watching him closely.

'I'm tired, Douglas. Went down to Sussex last night to see my mother, didn't get much sleep.'

'Parents are a worry. My old mother decided to go to Boulogne for the day last week – first time she's been to France – and she fell down the steps getting on the ferry at Dover. Sprained her ankle, can't walk, had to move in with us because she can't manage on her own.'

'I'm sorry. How's your son doing in Gray's Inn by the way?'

'He's not keen on the law, sir. Not a chip off the old block at all. Three generations of barrister's clerks and he wants to give up a good position and go off travelling round the world. Says he's earned enough to take two years off. I don't approve of his attitude, I don't approve at all.'

George looks at Douglas's gloomy face above his immaculate suit, shirt and tie and imagines he might be a fearsome parent.

'Fathers and sons. Ah well, nothing new. So will you be doing the Clarkson case, sir? Mr Bates needs to find a leader today if possible.'

'If you could keep people away from my door and not put any calls through, I can finish something I'm doing and think about the Clarkson case. Just till lunchtime.'

'No problem, sir.' He glides out.

George immediately uncovers Lena's letter and redials her number while his eyes run down her writing and rest on the phrase 'it's just possible that Philip might have guessed who you were.' Again there is no answer, and he tries Lena's next-door neighbour Dora. She too is out. Annoyed rather than worried, he decides to try again after lunch. He knows Lena could be out having coffee or lunch with a neighbour. There are so many questions he wants to ask his mother, the frustration is intense.

The morning passes as George deals with a heap of overdue matters and rings his mother every hour or so. He usually enjoys the sense of freedom a collapse of a case can bring, but today he is too tense about too much to relax. After lunch in Hall and a visit to his tailor, it's after three when he gets back to Chambers, where he finds a note in Paul's handwriting on his desk asking him to ring Mrs Cunningham urgently. He goes along to the clerks' room.

'Who is Mrs Cunningham, Paul? You took no number.'

'She said you knew it. I tried to get her to leave a message in your voice mailbox, but that really flustered her.'

'I don't know anyone called Cunningham.'

'Something to do with your mother, she said—'

'*Cunningham* – of course, it's her neighbour.' Dora Cunningham has never rung him before.

Paul's light blue-grey eyes meet his without expression. As a coldness creeps into his being, George finds their extreme paleness odd, ominous, as if leached of life. He drags his gaze away and hurries to ring Dora.

'I can't get an answer from Lena, George. Her cat is sitting outside the house miaowing its head off. That's what alerted me. I heard the miaowing. I don't have a key any more. I had one but she took it back the other day when she lost hers.'

'Have you contacted Mrs Harris? She'll have a key.'

'She isn't on the phone, George, and she doesn't live in the village. I rang you first because I don't know what best to do next.'

'We must get the police at once, and the doctor. Do you happen to have the surgery number? I have it at home but not in Chambers.'

'One moment.' The rustling goes on for interminable minutes, until George is about to give up. 'So sorry. Here we are. It's one of those health centres now.'

All the getting of names and numbers, of trying to control his impatience with the police, the doctor (a locum) and Dora herself becomes part of avoiding what by four o'clock he knows he can no longer avoid: the fact that Lena might be lying dead or dying and that he must go straight down to Sussex again as soon as the police ring him back having broken in. He sits with his head in his hands. His direct line rings and he snatches at it.

'Warne speaking.'

'Ah, good afternoon. This is the Lord Chancellor's Department. The Permanent Secretary has asked me to ring to see if you are any nearer a decision and would like to make an appointment to come in?'

'A decision . . . not yet.'

'Unfortunately, pressure is mounting because of a number of factors outside the Department's control. The Lord Chancellor had been hoping you would come in by the end of this week . . .'

George listens to the precise, careful voice and waits for it to stop.

'You catch me at a most difficult moment, I'm afraid. My mother has collapsed behind locked doors and I am waiting at this moment for a call from the local Sussex police. They may find – they may find she is dead.'

'I am so sorry—'

'So please tell the Lord Chancellor I am very sorry but I am in no state to make a decision for a few days . . .'

'Naturally. Quite understandable.'

'I promise not to keep him waiting much longer. You'll have my decision without fail next week.'

Douglas comes in the moment George has finished this call. 'Mr Bates needs to know about the Clarkson case, sir.'

'Douglas, there's a family crisis looming. I think I must turn it down.' As he starts to explain, the police ring to say they have found Lena at the foot of the stairs, very near to death.

His house has never felt so desolate and empty. He changes his clothes, hurries round checking windows and doors. His answerphone winks at him, its four messages asking for release. He leaves them, unable to think about his social life. The huge pictures everywhere press on him. His sits down on a chair in the hall, preparing himself Russian-style for his journey by quietening himself for a few moments.

Chekhov. *The Cherry Orchard*. Marcia as Masha.

He longs with his full being to talk to Marcia, to take her with him tonight to see his mother, to have her with him as he sits in hospital waiting-rooms and wards, to discuss his mother with her. He rings her number, which he still knows by heart.

'This is Marcia Fleckner's phone. Please leave a message giving time and day and your number and I'll get back to you as soon as I can.'

Perhaps she's away on tour. No, she must be rehearsing this new play . . . He leaves no message, suddenly unable to trust his voice.

Lena must have collapsed as he drove away that very morning. She obviously turned to climb the stairs and had a heart attack then and there, her world spinning and dissolving with the sound of his car still turning in her drive. The breakfast things are exactly as they were when he left; a half-eaten piece of toast still on her plate, the butter and milk still on the table.

False teeth grin at him from the hall table, neatly placed there beside the telephone by someone involved in taking Lena to hospital. The cat screeches frantically from the kitchen and George feeds him, noticing that apart from the tin in the fridge there appears to be no more cat food. There is a stink of rotting food from the kitchen bin, and the sweetish smell of old woman throughout the house.

George goes upstairs to put together a bag of night-things for Lena. Raj follows him, needing company more than food.

Lena's bedroom is in complete confusion, almost as if a burglar has been at work. Cupboard doors and drawers gape. In closed drawers George finds a quantity of old but good silk and satin underwear and lingerie, clearly unused for years, perhaps since Geoffrey died. Lena seems to have been existing on baggy cotton underwear and flannelette nightdresses, yet hanging visibly in her wardrobe is a row of lace-trimmed negligées with matching nighties which he remembers her wearing round the house; floating, flattering, very feminine garments which she wore to please Geoffrey. They too look as if they have not been touched for years. Faded lavender bags are still tied to the hangers, dangling in the neck of each negligée. Negligee. Is the word ever used now? Marcia wore nightshirts and towelling bathrobes.

The faint scent of lavender is quickly banished by other smells in the bedroom. George quickly takes one of the more substantial negligee sets, palest green trimmed with daisies round the yoke, and puts it in a carrier bag. Instead of her worn felt slippers he drops in a pair of satin mules he finds under the negligees. He keeps to her current choice of white cotton underwear, and goes to find a sponge-bag. She doesn't appear to have one, so he puts soap, a stiff dry flannel, a bottle of Oil of Ulay, her denture cleanser and two towels into another carrier bag. While he has been busy, Raj has settled himself on Lena's pillow, curled up with his back to the door. George groans; the animal is going to present a problem whatever happens. Before leaving for the hospital, he knocks on Dora Cunningham's door and entrusts the care of the cat and a set of keys to her. She doesn't look very happy about this arrangement, particularly when George gives her a £20 note to buy more cat food.

'I'm not very fond of cats—'

'Nor am I, Dora. I would come and feed him but I live fifty miles away.'

'I'll see it's done.'

'You're a very good neighbour to have. Many, many thanks.'

> If ever thou gavest meat and drink
> Every nighte and alle
> *The fire shall never make thee shrink*
> And Christe receive thy sawle

He drives to the hospital in Chichester with *The Lyke Wake Dirge* running through his brain again and begins to wish he could wipe his mind clean of it. But since he cannot think about Lena and the future, cannot rise above the mechanics of the route, his empty stomach and his tiredness, the poem drums on.

He needs to eat. He ought to eat something before arriving at the hospital. He goes into a garage to fill the car, and notices sandwiches in a large upright refrigerator. He stands in front of it for long minutes, unable to take a decision between cheese and pickle and ham and mustard. When he eats the sandwiches sitting in the hospital car park, rain beginning to stream down the car windows, his sense of dislocation is intense. He has never eaten food alone in a car park before. The visitors' cars around him are beginning to fill up and leave; a distraught young woman dragging two small crying children gets into the car next to his. He watches her spend long minutes strapping them into their seats, wiping a nose, rescuing a wet toy from the tarmac. When she finally pulls herself from the back of the car and straightens up, she stands for a moment facing George, her eyes pressed shut and her mouth pulled open in a silent scream. When she opens her eyes George has already turned away, no longer an observer.

George is in a small stuffy office off the ward, drinking a welcome cup of tea as he waits to see the houseman.

'Have a biscuit. Someone's just given us this boxful – a grateful patient who wants us all to get fat!' The bright-eyed Geordie nurse is already rounded, with arms and legs like a stonemason's. 'I just love these wafers with white chocolate, so do me a favour and eat some before I finish the lot.'

'A biscuit would be good. Thanks.'

'Not just one. Take plenty. Here.'

George finds his saucer heaped willy-nilly with biscuits.

'Who are you waiting to see then?'

'Dr Bradshaw. Apparently he admitted my mother.'

'What's happened to her?'

'That's what I hope he's going to tell me. She was found semi-conscious at the foot of her stairs.'

'If you give me her name I'll go and see what I can find out.'

'Helena Warne.'

'That's a beautiful name, Helena.'

'She always called herself Lena, I don't why.'

'You eat those biscuits, they'll give you energy.'

She hurries off and George obediently eats his biscuits, surprised by how much he is enjoying them. Time passes.

Dr Bradshaw, stringy and fair-haired, looks about fifteen. He has cut his chin shaving his vestigial growth of beard; past acne makes a clean shave difficult. He looks, as every houseman does, exhausted, and probably is. George is finding it difficult listening to him. People walk in and out of the office constantly.

'Your mother is now unconscious, though when she was admitted she still retained some consciousness. She has had a severe heart attack. I suspect she has suffered from coronary insufficiency for some time, but ignored the signs, and that her pericardium is diseased but no one has picked up on the infarction. One blood clot and you have coronary occlusion. For your mother it was not if, but when, I am afraid, as I am sure you realize.'

'What are her prospects now?' Dr Bradshaw stares at the notes he is holding. 'Please be frank, Doctor.'

'To be honest, not good. I would be surprised if she lasts very long, but you never can tell.' A bell starts ringing in the distance and two nurses run past. 'If you'll excuse me.'

George picks up his two carrier bags and finds his mother's bed. The sight of her toothless, breath rasping, skin grey, upsets him considerably. He sits beside her and takes her hand, but she makes no sign she's aware of him. He calls her name softly but her hand remains flaccid and cold. He continues to hold her hand, an hour passes, then there is a commotion in the next bed as an old woman starts to wail and is curtained off by two nurses. George leaves the ward, suddenly near tears. The nurse who showered him with biscuits sees him leaning against the corridor wall and takes his arm.

'Now you come and sit down for a moment, Mr Warne.'

'I've brought all her things—' A carrier tips over and the negligee spills out.

'Leave them with me, pet. I'll put them in her locker for you. What a beautiful nightie!'

'Do you come from Newcastle?'

'I do.'

'I'm very fond of Newcastle.'

'I can't stand the place which is why I've come south.'

'Most Geordies won't have a word said against the North.' George knows he is clinging to the company of this robust young woman, whose name he sees from her lapel is Vicki Robertson.

'They all think I'm mad. If I didn't have a boyfriend down here I suppose I might feel different. I'll take those things now.'

'You will let me know if my mother's condition changes?'

'Make sure you leave a number, and I personally will ring you. I'm on until six.'

'If I haven't heard, I'll ring the ward direct in the morning.'

'Will you look at these lovely daisies. All hand-embroidered.'

> This ane nighte, this ane nighte,
> Every nighte and alle
> Fire and fleet and candlelight . . .

George sits in his car not knowing what to do next. He can't believe he can be of any use sitting beside his comatose mother.

It's now half-past nine and the hospital car park is almost deserted. He could drive back to London, or he could sleep in his mother's house. Or he could find a hotel nearby. He drives out of the gate in total indecision, longing for a whisky.

Quickly he decides he cannot sleep at Lena's. He turns the car brusquely towards London and then sees a large sign advertising a nearby castle that has been transformed into a hotel. He pulls off the road and rings the number from his carphone; they sound surprised at such a late booking but agree to let him have a room. Twenty minutes later he walks into an improbable Victorian gothic castle, with rich panelling, plaid carpets, a real though dying log fire, and even a suit of armour in the great hall. His spirits lift, though his sense of dislocation remains. He orders whisky and hot soup to be brought to his room and follows the plaid-skirted receptionist upstairs.

'No luggage?'

'Nothing. I have someone in hospital down here after a crisis, and I decided not to drive back to London.'

'You will find a spare toiletry kit in the bathroom. And there's a bathrobe of course—'

He is shown into a room papered in dark green with massive polished wood doors and a marble fireplace. Someone has lit the gas log fire and today's papers are on the low table beside it along with a bowl of fruit.

'Your whisky will be up in a minute. Your soup might take a little longer. What about some nice cheese as well?'

'Wonderful.' His voice is husky.

As she leaves George turns away because he suddenly wants to cry. The contrast with the hospital, the unrolling of luxury and comfort, the sensual euphoria, overwhelm him. He stands still and breathes deeply. Whatever this costs it will be worth it. *Fire and fleet and candlelight* . . . goodness knows what fleet means, nor does it matter. He sits down and stares at the dancing fire, at the regularly irregular flames that give off no scent. He watches them mesmerized until there is a knock on the door and a waiter comes in with a decanter of whisky, a soda syphon, a jug of water, a bowl of ice and a large tumbler.

'Your soup will be five minutes.'

'Many thanks.' George pours himself a drink but before he

tastes it he rings the ward and leaves his hotel number with Nurse Robertson. Lena's condition is unchanged. He then takes a sip and lies back in his chair while the whisky creeps under his tongue and the fumes go up his nasal passages. From the colour and flavour he is sure he is drinking Justerini and Brooks, one of his favourite blends. Freddie Mentieth prefers it too, he seems to remember—

Freddie. He never rang him. George reaches at once for the phone and a voice replies instantly, though not an immediately recognizable one.

'Natalie Mentieth speaking.'

'It's George Warne. How are you, Nat? You sound a bit under the weather.'

'I'm getting over the worst bout of flu I've ever had so I'm not surprised. I'm in bed reading cosily so don't feel sorry for me – I feel sorrier for Freddie, who had no desire whatever to go out to yet another boring dinner. When he gets back I'll get him to ring you – he said he wouldn't be too late. I take it you want to speak to him?'

'Let me give you the number. I'm not at home – I'm at a hotel in Sussex because my mother has had a heart attack and the hospital she's in is nearby.'

'I am sorry, George. When did it happen? Freddie didn't mention anything.'

'He didn't know. She collapsed early this morning and I had to rush down.'

'What a shock for you. And you're in the middle of that long case—'

'It settled earlier this week, luckily.'

'How is your mother now?'

'Not good. The doctor wasn't hopeful.'

'I am sorry.' She has a coughing fit and has to end the conversation. 'Freddie will ring you.'

'I'd really appreciate that.'

So she knows nothing, Freddie has told her nothing; there was no undertone whatsoever of hidden agenda. As he puts the receiver down the soup arrives, along with hot rolls, celery and a piece of mature Cheshire. George eats slowly and with pleasure, has a hot bath, tries to read a newspaper for a while, but Freddie doesn't ring. Perhaps he still has not returned; Nat will be asleep by now. George lies on the sofa watching the fire make patterns on the green walls.

Peter Dawlish took him to a bonfire party in Roddick village to distract him from the looming Oxford entrance examinations. (Roddick can't be so very far from this hotel. He must look it up on the map.) The village had an age-long tradition of burning three effigies after a march round the village boundaries. The effigies were tied on to a wooden frame made to an ancient pattern and this was carried by four men dressed in green with wild wigs of raffia.

'It's not to be missed. Definitely a pagan rite. Those green men remind me of the Green Knight. They're definitely woodwoses.'

'What's a woodwose, sir?'

'For God's sake stop calling me sir, George! You are all brainwashed, you boys. Anyway, a woodwose is a wild man of the woods, a satyr, a faun. The word "wood" as used here is linked to the same ancient word that became "voodoo". Fascinating.'

They watched the group of men prancing through the crowds holding the effigies high. The bonfire was ready to be lit, and as soon as the frame was put on top of it, with the three figures facing outwards, the flames leaped.

'Watch, the woodwoses are going to dance. Then they will throw their tunics and wigs on the fire, as if they are done with magic and are returning to the community. Watch.'

The green figures were tall and faintly menacing as they stamped and jigged round the fire, silhouetted against it. When the effigies started to burn, they drew off their all-enveloping hooded tunics and wigs, and flung them on the flames.

'One of them's our school groundsman, look. It's Ben Meades.'

'So it is. How surprising. Come on.' Dawlish pushed up to the man who was still facing the fire. 'Hullo, Ben. That was quite a performance.'

Ben Meades ignored them as if he didn't hear. His eyes were glittering, fixed on the burning clothing. There was a nasty acrid smell as the cheap fibres shrivelled. The fireworks started and Dawlish and George moved away to watch them.

As George turns off the fire and stumbles to bed in the darkness he wonders again what happened to Peter Dawlish, who opened so many doors for him and broke down so many assumptions. Dawlish would be about sixty by now. Perhaps it would be worth another try to contact him through his Oxford college; often people got back in touch as they grew older and began themselves to be curious about other contemporaries. George himself had recently been to his first college gaudy out of the same curiosity.

Teachers and fathers. In his case, a teacher had in a brief period done more for him than his adoptive father in a lifetime, but perhaps it was always so. And would the same have happened had he been brought up by his real father?

George's next conscious thought is at seven-thirty when a wake-up call rouses him. He lies in the unfamiliar green room, temporarily disoriented. His mother, the hospital, the heart attack. He lies there, unable to move after his heavy sleep. He has not been contacted so Lena must have held on to life. Will he sit with her all day? How can he plan anything while she lies so close to death? And if she recovers she won't be able to live alone. And his work, his own future. He must ring Freddie. He must ring Douglas. He must ring his accountant to discuss the effect on his financial situation if he should accept the Judgeship, he should have rung him already . . . Lena, what must he do about Lena . . .?

Tension grips him. He needs advice, he needs . . . he needs Marcia.

He needs to talk to a friend who knew and liked Lena; keeping his private life so private has left him bereft of sympathetic ears. He has no close family to talk to. He has not spoken to the Ropers for years. Aunt Cynthia. She was such a good listener, so warm. Even though she's been dead for over thirty years he can still evoke her face and voice in his mind as if he'd seen her last week.

Her hens. 'Would you like to come and help me collect the

eggs?' Those curved indentations of pressed straw, the smell of feathers, of hen, the warm egg next to the false china one, so ugly it surely couldn't fool the hen. The search for the nests hidden in strange corners by two birds who always chose odd, unorthodox places.

'Why do they do that, Aunt Cynthia? The nesting boxes are much more comfortable than this broken old shed.'

'They're so naughty but I love them for it. It's my challenge from them: find the nest. Mrs Batty and Mrs Scatty, you're bad.' Mrs Batty and Scatty looked just like the other hens to George, but he liked the indignant noises they made when he felt underneath them to count the number of eggs they'd manage to lay secretly.

'It pleases me when animals don't do what you want them to do.' He remembers his aunt's smile as she carried the bucket of eggs back to the kitchen, her messy hair, her patched pre-war wellingtons, her ancient working clothes. When he saw her dressed up for a wedding or a special party he hardly recognized her, so dramatic was the difference. From scarecrow clothes to an elegant outfit, also all pre-war: black dress with diamanté dress-clips in the corners of the square neckline, black suede shoes with buckles, hair carefully done. Suddenly she looked like Lena, but softer, prettier. The scarecrow would be back next day, swinging the empty bucket as she went to see to her beloved hens. Julian didn't like hens and got rid of them all after her death.

'You're a quick-change artist like my Aunt Cynthia.'

'Oh yes? Is that a compliment?'

'Absolutely. She either looked a complete mess or wonderful.'

'Thanks.'

'No, no, I don't mean you look a mess, you just look completely different in different clothes, but always wonderful.'

'Butter, butter, bullshit.'

'Marcia, if you only knew how important that aunt was to be you'd see what a compliment I was paying you.'

'Who was she?'

'Cynthia, my mother's sister. She was a farmer's wife and looked after me during the war. I adored her. She died a long time ago.' And as he kissed Marcia, he wanted to add, I've never talked about her to anyone since she died, never. She was too precious to be shared. But the moment passed.

A long time ago. George sits up with a start when he realizes he's been lying thinking about the past for so long it's now getting on for nine o'clock. He shaves in a hurry and dresses, and before going down to breakfast rings the hospital.

'Could I speak to Dr Bradshaw?'

'He's not available at the moment.'

'Nurse Robertson?'

'Not on this shift. Can I help?'

'I'm ringing up to find out how my mother Helena Warne is. I take it she's come through the night because I haven't been contacted.'

'Just one moment, Mr Warne.'

The minutes go by and at last the voice returns.

'Very sorry, but I've been trying to contact Dr Bradshaw. Are you coming in now, Mr Warne?'

'As soon as I've had breakfast.'

'Dr Bradshaw will see you then.'

It is only on the way down to the dining-room that George realizes the rather cool-voiced nurse hasn't told him anything about Lena. Halfway through a delicious breakfast of croissants, rolls and damson jam, all homemade, it occurs to him that maybe the nurse didn't mention Lena because she had died in the night and she didn't feel it was appropriate she should tell him. Surely not? He'd given Nurse Robertson his hotel number, she'd promised to ring. No, surely the cool nurse was just being cool . . .?

But he can't finish his breakfast. Another coffee while he settles his bill, and he is on his way to the hospital again, knowing without a shred of doubt that his mother is dead.

'We phoned all the numbers we had. Obviously not your work number, but your house in London and Mrs Warne's house.'

'But I rang and left my hotel number with Nurse Robertson herself.'

'It's not on the notes, unfortunately. Look.'

George finds he is quite extraordinarily distressed that the nurse let him down and he has therefore come too late. He starts to shake.

'I really am very sorry, Mr Warne. We did our best to find you when we saw she was sinking.'

'I was so close by. I could have been here in time.'

'I know. It's a great pity Nurse Robertson did not follow usual procedures.'

'Did my mother ask for me?'

'She didn't speak, but her eyes were searching for you when we mentioned your name and said we were trying to find you.'

'It's so bitter I missed her.'

'She was barely conscious at the end – the moment of lucidity was brief.'

'But she knew you were trying to find me?'

'Absolutely.'

'I've let her down.'

'We let her down. It wasn't your fault.'

'She would only have known that as usual I wasn't there when she needed me. Can I see her?'

'Of course. She's in a side ward. I thought you'd prefer to see her here than in the morgue so I delayed her transfer.'

'Thank you.'

'She died calmly and with dignity.'

George follows Bradshaw's slight figure, comforted by his straightforward yet sensitive way of dealing with death. A mixture of panic and apprehension fills him when Bradshaw opens a door and stands aside to let George pass. He then pulls back the cheerful curtains closing off the bed and leaves George alone after saying he'll be around on the ward.

Lena is in her own nightdress and negligée; the embroidered daisies pick up the yellow in the curtains. Soft folds of lace surround her neck. Her teeth are in, her face is peaceful, even beautiful. Bradshaw is right: she's dignified. Her lids lie over her eyeballs so lightly George half-expects them to flip back and reveal alert eyes.

'Lena. Helena.' He touches her forehead and his fingers recoil. She looks so natural and warm-blooded the cold flesh is a shock.

He stares at her face, at the lines and stains of age on her skin, at the neatness of her nose and nostrils, at the strong growth of white hair from her hairline. He has the same robust hairline, even though his hair is so different in colour and texture. He looks at her small, odd-shaped ears, at the lobes with their holes stretched from wearing heavy drop-earrings. (They are bare; he wonders what has happened to the gold and amethyst earings she has worn day in day out since Geoffrey died.) His ears are large, flatter, different. His nose is like hers, but his line of jaw and firm, prominent chin are not at all.

He sits down beside his mother's body, unable to stop looking at her features. The aura of her personality appears stronger in death, as if it has refused to leave. Confident yet also hesitant, tough yet submissive, dignified yet self-indulgent, reserved yet sentimental, good social company yet insensitive. Lena. A bad mother to her son but a seemingly excellent wife to the man she loved. The daisies on her nightdress dance as his tears well and flow.

4 ∫

Marcia has started dreaming about George, even though they haven't seen each other for nearly two years. It is as if the guilt she has to simulate while playing Creusa is seeping through into her dreams, fed by the memory of that weekend when she decided she would have to leave George.

'Is your friend Rosie Jewish?'
   'With a name like Amsterdam?'
   'Well, she looked Jewish to me when I saw her on telly the other night, and you know as well as I do that names don't tell you everything.'
   'Someone did ask her once, now I think of it, and she ignored them.'
   'Probably is then.'
   'I never think about Jewishness except when I'm with you. How's Jonathan?'
   'Very, very Jewish!' Both women laughed, and Marcia noticed how soft and plump Rachel was looking. For a while after her divorce she grew very thin, but in the last year since her remarriage she slowly changed back to the rounded shape she had as a student.
   'Everything is going well?'
   'I'm so lucky, Marcia. He's such a sweetie, and he's wonderful with the twins. He's firm, he loves them, they treat him as if he's always been there. And they like the fact he's more observant about our religion than David was. Kids love ritual, they really do.'
   Marcia and Rachel meet about once a month, sometimes to

go to an exhibition, sometimes just to have coffee before one or other has some appointment that brings them to a convenient central point. Their friendship picked up as a direct result of Rachel's divorce, after years when they hardly saw one another. On this occasion they were waiting for the twins to join them after a children's matinée.

'I'll never again let my own life slide away like I did with David. I only met his friends, I thought about him and the kids all the time and forgot how much my girlfriends meant to me. I tell you, Marcia, when I was picking up the pieces on my own, being able to talk to you was what kept me going.'

'I don't really understand how you could have let David swallow you whole like that.'

'Wait till you meet a swallower. Mind you, kids are great swallowers too. Talking of kids . . .' Rachel hesitated, fiddled with the end of her piece of chocolate cake. 'I shouldn't have eaten all that, it's too rich. But I was always a sucker for chocolate cake. Oh well.'

'What about kids?'

'I've just heard I'm pregnant again. The test came through yesterday. Jonathan's over the moon. So am I.' Her eyes were full of light.

'How wonderful, Rachel.' But Marcia was flooded with purest envy; her whole being was dipped in it and emerged as if gilded with envy. Rachel couldn't help seeing, and her eyes lowered as she took Marcia's cold hand.

'I wanted you to be the first of our friends to know. Even the twins don't know yet.'

'Congratulations. I really am pleased for you. I'm jealous too, you lucky cow!'

'A cow is what I will feel like if it's twins again.'

'Is there a chance?'

'There have always been lots of twins in my family. Here come Judith and Simon. Don't say anything to them. I want Jonathan to tell them.'

'As if I would.'

Marcia walked back to her flat that Saturday haunted by children. Christmas was approaching and the streets were full of people shopping: families with dazed, glazed looks, focused couples, lone mothers with monster-sized carrier bags full of boxed toys. With no close family she had no one save friends to buy for; usually this was a relief but today she ached to have someone to spoil, someone young for whom the giving and receiving of presents was still a magic ritual. A child, her child, not someone else's.

For George she had bought two Victorian linen handkerchiefs embroidered by sheer chance with GW. That purchase took five minutes in Camden Market. He would be embarrassed by any more presents. She planned to give him his handkerchiefs that evening, as he'd mentioned he went away for Christmas to his mother's.

She let herself into the flat and seemed to see it for the first time. Untidy hall, with a bulging coat-stand crammed into one corner, as hung about with paraphernalia as any of the laden shoppers she'd just seen. Bare sanded floors, worn rugs. A large box full of empty bottles on their way (for weeks) to the bottle bank. A broken lamp, on its way to an electrician. Untidy rooms off the hall, no Christmas decorations anywhere. A pile of cards waiting to be put out on the mantelpiece. A rather flyblown mirror above the hall table with a dozen or so old photographs and postcards stuck into its frame. A dismal flat, not a place for a child. Why be jealous of Rachel, why imagine she could cope with a child? But she could change the flat, she could adapt her life. And George – what would George think about having a child?

She stared at herself in the mirror, seeing her mother's eyes, her father's nose, all those lineaments of generations of Central European Jews, survivors of the unimaginable. The women always, without exception, taking Jewish seed into their bodies, giving birth to wholly Jewish babies. Marcia looked into her dark eyes as into bottomless wells of Jewish blood, and closed her lids over them. She stood for some time remembering how her parents would chatter in Yiddish or in German when they thought they were alone, and how she felt like a changeling because she couldn't understand them. She was a baptized little English girl. It was as if she'd been given a change of blood.

But she hadn't. Marcia opened her eyes again, her Jewish eyes, and was overcome with a desperate longing not to break the tradition, not to bear the child of an Anglo-Saxon with light hair, greenish eyes, tall long bones. Ginger body hair. The fact that George was circumcised, like so many English boys of his class and age, made no difference. She could not have his child. She didn't know where it left them both, but she couldn't have his child. It was a gut reaction she could neither control nor articulate.

She put off seeing George that evening and got very drunk and miserable alone. The following weekend she broke off their relationship, and for months after wondered bitterly why she felt so strongly about her blood. As time went by, she began to see that by confronting her Jewishness and giving in to it she had exorcized it, but the price she had paid was high.

Miriam and Martin lived in an ugly flat in any ugly house on a noisy road, but having accepted it as home they stuck to it. Their real home was gone, the home full of the family furniture, the inherited objects snug in their appointed places, the silver cutlery, the china, the thick white damask tablecloths and napkins, the remnants of countless Middle European dowries over the years – embroidered mats, delicate nightwear kept for those special visits that never happened, jewellery that rarely saw a neck or ear or finger.

Martin told Marcia once that he and Miriam felt like icebergs just showing above water: they would never lose the weight of the past. 'We all thought we would see our families again, even if we lost our possessions. Some people couldn't bring themselves to leave all their precious family things behind, and died because of furniture and silver. At least we broke free of that. But never underestimate the wrench it was to leave everything behind that we'd all been brought up to cherish. Just to walk out on those voiceless things hurt more than we expected.

'I often think about a tea-set we both loved, Marcia. So stupid to think about a tea-set, but I do. It was delicate, of the thinnest, lightest porcelain, covered with pale blue convolvulus flowers with trailing leaves and stems, exquisitely hand-painted. The shape of the cups, the deep, rounded saucers, the pretty plates, gave so much pleasure. Miriam had inherited the tea-set from her mother who hadn't broken anything despite being known for her clumsy touch. We used it occasionally for coffee and cakes. So I wonder what happened to it when we had to leave it behind – who stole it or smashed it, whether somewhere in Europe there is an odd piece of it still whole and in use. I suppose it's the epitome of all the things Miriam and I no longer had when we set up home in England.'

Instead they used thick cups and plates, white with a blue line at slightly the wrong place, all seconds; they had a tin tea-pot, cheap stainless-steel cutlery, and ate at a lino-covered kitchen table (the same lino as lay on the floors). But Miriam had some silver teaspoons which she had brought with her because they were light and easy to carry: ten teaspoons with well-balanced handles and long elegant bowls, as elegant as any English Georgian silver, she used to say. Not long before she died, a burglar relieved them of their television, electric kettle, and those spoons.

Marcia was incandescent with rage that the only things that linked her to her great-grandmother had gone.

'You must report it to the police, Mutti.'

'What's the point? They won't find anything.'

'But it's horrible we've lost our spoons!'

'Martin's gone to look in the secondhand shops. That's better than asking the police.'

'I'm upset.'

'Things aren't important, Maüslein. Only people.'

Maüslein. Little mouse.

'Rachel, I'm sorry I didn't ring back earlier—'

'Talk about incommunicado. Half the time your phone's switched off.'

'I've been working hard on my part.'

'So rehearsals have started, I take it?'

'They have.'

'You're purring.'

'It's so wonderful to be working with a good director and a good cast on a good play. Yes, I'm purring. How are you?'

'No, Judith, not that sugar. Use the brown. I'm all right. We're making biscuits.'

'I'm making biscuits!'

'Judith is making biscuits. I'm just her culinary adviser. I was wondering if we could go to the exhibition at the Royal Academy later this week, Marcia?' There is a clattering of tin baking trays in the background, causing Rachel to shout down the phone.

'I'm sorry, no exhibitions until the play opens. We're rehearsing every day.'

'Judith, do you have to make such a terrible noise? Look, I'll ring you later, Marcia. The early evening is never a good time to talk.'

'Sorry, I always forget.'

Marcia does an hour's yoga exercises and follows them with a bath; she thinks of Rachel's evening routine of children and cooking, and rejoices in her absence of duties. Edward is in Newcastle for a couple of days. There is no one to make any demands on her. She turns on the television, and masked by the noise, declaims Creusa's speeches into the mirror.

5

'Marcia, it's George. Please ring me. Lena died last week and I'd value it if you could come to her funeral. It's next Saturday, November fourteenth, down in Sussex. Please come if you can.'

He actually composes the message on the back of an envelope before recording it, and finds when he replaces the receiver that his hands are shaking slightly. The first communication for nearly two years has taken a disproportionate amount of energy. He looks at his list and then rings Julian Roper, who takes some time to grasp who is speaking.

'Jebs! Why didn't you say so to start with? Sorry to hear about Lena. Of course I will come if Laura will drive me. I'll get her to ring you when she comes in from the horses.'

Julian bangs down the phone as he always did. Within ten minutes Laura has rung, her warm voice totally familiar though long unheard.

'So sorry to hear Aunt Helena's died. Of course we'll all come to the funeral, Jebs.'

'You must stay for lunch afterwards. It will be lovely catching up. I'll send you a map and all the details. How are you all?'

'Chugging along. Oddly enough, Jebs, Sophie and I were talking about you only yesterday and wondering how you were. It's years since we saw you last. Sophie says it was at her wedding.'

'And you're not married?'

'I run the farm for Father.'

'We can catch up on Saturday. I'm so glad you can come. Give me Sophie's number and I'll ask her too.'

Throughout the evening George telephones everyone who had any connection with Lena. He goes through what numbers he can find in her address book, and mostly draws a blank. Her friends have died, have moved to residential homes, have not lived there for years. But he reaches some, and finds it surprisingly therapeutic to talk about his mother's life and death with these sympathetic strangers. Only one old woman, clearly a little demented, shouts 'Who? Who? Never heard of her,' before cutting him off.

He finally exhausts the list and goes to the kitchen with a sore wrist and ringing ears. By now it's after half-ten and too late to make any more calls. He beats up two eggs and puts butter on to heat, but as soon as it browns and smells nutty the phone rings. Cursing, he turns off the gas.

'George? I've been trying to get through for hours.'

'Marcia!'

'I couldn't believe you'd left the phone off the hook so I kept trying.'

'Marcia—'

'I am sorry to hear about Lena. I liked her a lot.'

'She liked you. She was talking about you the day before she died.'

'Really? What on earth was she saying?'

'Oh well, nothing much.'

'Tell me.'

'I can't.'

'Let me guess then. Why didn't you marry that lovely Marcia Fleckner, instead of letting her slip through your fingers!' Marcia laughs.

'Not quite but nearly.'

'She rang me a couple of times, you know.'

'But she didn't know your number—'

'Yes she did. She asked for it once when you were out of the room. She rang me to talk about you, and she wanted me to stay with you. I had to tell her we'd already parted. We talked for ages. I admired her spirit.'

'Please come to her funeral. Will you?'

'What time is it on Saturday?'

'Eleven, followed by lunch at a hotel nearby.'

'I'm rehearsing in the afternoon, but I could come just for the funeral.'

'Stay for lunch. I can't tell you how nice it is to talk to you again. So few of my friends knew Lena, or saw her in the last few years. You did. I find I need to talk about her.'

'Tell me how she died.' Marcia listens without interrupting. 'Poor, poor Lena. But how lucky she'd just seen you.'

'I'm afraid it was the strain of seeing me that brought the attack on.'

'She loved you – why should your visit have strained her?'

'I arrived unexpectedly. Maybe surprises are more like shocks to the old.'

'Don't be silly, George. She longed to see more of you. A surprise visit would have been lovely for her.'

'It's nice to talk, Marcia. How are you?'

'Fine. Very busy rehearsing *Ion*. Did you get the flyer I sent?'

'I thought it was you.'

'It seemed far too long since we'd been in touch. How's your life, George?'

'Busy.'

'Not become a judge yet?'

'What makes you say that?'

'Just the feeling you'd be good at it. Do you remember I came and watched you when you were judging some case at the Old Bailey?'

'So you did. I'd forgotten.' It is on the tip of his tongue to ask her advice; for days he has relegated his dilemma to the back of his mind, knowing that after the funeral it will have to be resolved.

'I must ring off, George – I haven't eaten anything yet and I'm ravenous.'

'I haven't either, so why don't you come round and we'll eat something together?'

There is a brief pause before Marcia says, 'No, George. Thanks, but it's not a very good idea.'

'You're probably right. But you'll come to the funeral?'

'Yes. Send me all the details plus an idiot-proof map. Thanks for letting me know about Lena. I'm sorry her end was painful.'

As the phone goes dead George finds his pulse is racing. Elated, he returns to the making of his omelette. Marcia's voice is striking. He has heard her shrink it to an adenoidal toneless mutter, he has heard her expand and deepen it to fill a large theatre with a cascade of natural tonal subtlety. Her ordinary speaking voice has this tonal richness, remaining always natural. George has had fantasies about her voice; he has dreamed her low tones, her particular way of saying hullo and goodbye, her varied sighs and grunts of pleasure in food or sex, her creamy chuckle and her strange laugh. Her laugh is a sort of harsh bark, at complete odds with that chuckle.

'It's not a very good idea.' The weight of meaning she put into the last two words remains in his mind. Has she got someone else? Why shouldn't she have got someone else? He isn't the only man to have found her deeply attractive. His elation fades as he considers this, and he overcooks his omelette.

Marcia is also a realist. She would remember only too well what went wrong between them, how she blighted the relationship by rejecting him as a father of her children while still apparently accepting him as a lover. It's not the sort of attitude that changes, reflected George, arising as it does from an unexpected and possibly subconscious atavism.

He props a book up beside his plate and eats surrounded by his brash canvases, his pulse now quiet, his habits – table just so, whisky just so, Bach partitas playing quietly in the background – bringing necessary calm.

The fateful letter from his mother remains hidden in his desk. He feels no frustration now because there is nothing to be done. Philip Symes remains a name without resonance, belonging to a man most likely to be dead. George's grief for his mother has no space in it for the paternal side of his creation.

The village church is very small, no more than the original chapel of a now vanished big house. The twenty or so mourners look like a crowd packed into the short pews; the empty trestles wait for the coffin, almost blocking the aisle. It is after eleven but George is waiting for Marcia to arrive before telling the undertakers to move. Julian Roper stands beside him, leaning on a stick. Laura and Sophie have gone to sit down. George cannot quite accept that his cousins are now fat and grey-haired. Julian has worn better, looking much as he always did but more desiccated. His right hand, all bones and veins, is clamped on his stick; he's clearly very lame. Laura comes out of the church.

'Come and sit down, Father, you shouldn't be standing there in the cold.' Laura's weather-roughened face is not flattered by the dark green trilby hat she is wearing.

'I'd like to walk in with George behind the coffin.'

'We'll be starting in a minute, Laura.'

Laura stomps heavily off. Slow, quick quick, slow – her agile dancing days are over. George feels intense sadness at the change in her: her tight mouth, her unquiet eyes. The unmarried daughter trapped into caring for her father, dressed in a best suit that is out of fashion and too tight. Sophie is fatter but her eyes shine, her clothes suit her, her skin glows.

Julian is fumbling with his fob-watch. 'Ten past, old boy. Perhaps we ought to start.'

'Yes, I agree.' George nods at the vicar, and the undertakers lift the bare coffin from the hearse.

We brought nothing into the world and we take nothing away . . .

Lena brought an oblique character, a seeming fragility that attracted certain kinds of men, and a liking for male dominance; George follows the coffin up the church knowing she has taken away a lifetime of secrets. He sits in his pew beside the coffin and feels possessed by the past of the body inside it, particularly that past in India which he will now never learn any more about. He wants to beat on the coffin and weep.

George slowly becomes aware that everyone, Reverend Sefton included, is staring expectantly at him. He is amazed that the service, which he has barely followed, has already reached the point when he said he wanted to say a few words about his mother. Nervous and unprepared, though giving no sign of either, he stands beyond the coffin at the start of the chancel and waits for a moment. His audience perceives him as he wishes them to: the well-known Queen's Counsel, immaculately dressed, with thick silvery-yellow hair, cool, intelligent green eyes, and a highly developed ability to build long, complex, satisfying sentences ex tempore.

• Peggy Woodford

Why my mother Helena shortened her name is one of the many secrets she has taken with her. One would have thought the name that launched a thousand ships would have been appropriate: my mother was a beautiful woman, and always aware of this beauty. A Helen, a Helena. But no, she was Lena.

I have been sitting here thinking about the enormous span of Lena's life and the paucity of my knowledge of it. I chose Psalm Ninety because it considers the human span, and uses the image of grass, green and flourishing in the morning, withered and dry by evening.

"The days of our life are three score years and ten, or if we have strength, four score."

Lena had strength, she died aged eighty, but the years I long to know more of are the green ones, the early years in India. She went out there at twenty to be married, lost her husband not so long after, and a few years later married again. Geoffrey Warne rescued her from what I imagine must have been difficult years as a young widow. I long to know more about this period of her life, and now I never will.

George suddenly sees, tucked away at the back behind a large local farmer, a woman wearing a rich red coat and a black hat. Marcia is here, she has slipped in unnoticed. He swallows, thrown for a moment; he drops his gaze to the coffin, knowing that his audience will put hesitations down to his genuine sense of grief.

She spent the war years in India with Geoffrey, while I was left in the capable hands of her sister Cynthia. Cynthia died of cancer many years ago, but her husband Julian is here beside me, as are my cousins Sophie and Laura. All during the war they were my family, they looked after me and loved me as if I was one of the Ropers . . . They were more important to me than my own family. It seems disloyal to say that, but I hope Lena would understand.

Laura is weeping into her hands; Sophie hands her a tissue. Julian coughs, looking at his two hands crossed on top of his stick.

Lena made a choice in her life, of total loyalty and support to her husband at the expense of everything else. Including me, including me. She was a whole-hearted wife, but not a wife and mother. She adored Geoffrey, lived only for him, and when he died a great deal of her died too. I am sure she embraced her own death; and I'm glad for her sake she didn't linger in pain and disfigurement.

I miss her acutely and will continue to do so in ways I can't foresee. She had an unerring sense of style. I remember how proud – and relieved – I was as a schoolboy to have a mother that other boys considered a dish. She was my only claim to fame at school, but a big one! My mother would drive up, smart as paint, and a hundred hidden eyes would be on the lookout. I remember also the one occasion she came to hear me in court; I can see her now, sitting in the public gallery looking stunning, catching every eye. That was her gift to life: when she arrived, the view improved dramatically. Many people who have claimed more have given less. She was well named Helen.

A storm of wind buffets the windows of the little church as he sits down. The vicar follows him with a short homily about Lena's devout attendance at this church in her ten years in the village, and her Christian view of death. As George listens, the *Lyke Wake* Dirge floats through his brain again, its message bleak and unsettling.

> *If meat or drink thou ne'er gav'st none*
> Every nighte and alle.
> *The fire will burn thee to the bare bone*
> And Christe receive thy saule.

He is pleased and relieved he has invited everyone to lunch at the Castle Hotel where he spent the night of Lena's death; it is as if he has placated an uncompromising spirit who has been pestering him.

As he stands outside the church gate giving people directions for the crematorium before following himself with the vicar, a black hat dances past him in the wind. The vicar stops it with his foot, and George sees Marcia standing some way off; she has clearly come out first and moved away from the other mourners. She smiles and makes a gesture towards her hat but does not move.

'Excuse me a moment, would you? Here are the keys to the car, do let yourself in and get out of this dreadful wind.'

'There's no great hurry, the hearse will crawl. Thanks. I will get of the wind.'

Holding the hat like a shield, George hurries towards Marcia. Her hair is looking messy and flattened, and her face white and tired against the strong colour of her coat. She immediately puts the hat on again.

'It disguises the dreadful state of my hair.'

'Marcia, I'm so glad you've come.' He kisses her cold cheek and notices traces of dried tears. He hugs her.

'Your speech choked me. It was so sad.'

'It's good to see you.'

'I've never heard a funeral speech – is that what you call them? – quite like it before. I'd love a copy of it.'

'I just said what came into my head. I didn't prepare it.'

'No one would have guessed.'

'Are you coming to the crematorium? Then we all go on to lunch.'

'Forgive me, George, but I really have to rush back to London. We're in intensive rehearsal.'

'You look tired.'

'I am. It's very hard work.' Her eyes glimmer. 'But exhilarating too.'

'I wish you could stay. If you go now the party will feel incomplete.'

'Don't be silly, George. You've got all those members of your family and the friends and neighbours to look after – and some of them will look after you if you give them half the chance. You'd better go – all the other cars have disappeared.'

'So you won't even come to the next part?'

'I can't abide crematoria. And I haven't got the time anyway. What a pity Lena couldn't be buried in this pretty churchyard.'

'No chance. I tried.'

A flock of crows settles in a tree above them, cawing lustily. The vicar's face can be seen peering at them from the car.

'I must go, Marcia.'

'Come and see the play.'

'I will.' George runs to his car as she stands there watching him.

The days of our life are three score and ten or if we have strength four score.

'Wicked Helena,' whispers Marcia to the crows. 'How you hurt him.'

6 ∫

When Marcia arrives at the village pub to collect Edward she tells him to hurry.

'What do you mean, hurry? Marcia, you agreed to go for a walk on the Downs!'

'I never did – I told you I wouldn't have much time. My rehearsal's at two, and it's now well after twelve, so I really must get going.'

'Well, at least come into the pub and have a quick sandwich. Five minutes isn't the end of the world.'

'Only five then and no more. I'd love a tomato juice and a round of cheese and pickle.' She quickly pays the barman and walks over to the open fire with her plate and glass.

'You're being so obsessive about these rehearsals, Marcia. It's Saturday, damn it. A good walk on the Downs would set us both up. We need some fresh air.'

'I could leave you behind if you like and you could find a bus or train back.'

'I really thought we were going to make a day of it. I wouldn't have come with you otherwise. Come on, Marcia, we're here now. Let's make the best of it.'

Marcia doesn't answer. Edward hears what he wants to hear, and bends events to suit himself. He is obviously expecting to win, expecting her to ring in with a feeble excuse and cut the rehearsal.

'This is a lovely old pub. I wonder why it's called The Prisoner's Solace – is there a prison round here?' She warms her hands at the fire.

'French prisoners during the Napoleonic War were held

somewhere near here, so the landlord told me. They used to build beautiful flintstone walls like the one outside and then presumably were allowed a jar at the end of the day before going back to their prison. The landlord also told me there's a sculpture park nearby we could go to as well as having a walk—'

'Edward, please get it into your head that as soon as I've finished this sandwich I am leaving. Stay if you want to but I can't. I'm not going to miss a rehearsal for anybody.'

'Goodness me, we are tetchy today. You managed to get time off for the funeral.'

'I wasn't needed this morning luckily. Right. I'm off.' Marcia hurries out to the car, pursued by Edward, who is enjoying her bad temper.

'Marcia – I've just lit a cigarette.'

'Well, smoke it in the car. Edward – look, I'm sorry if you misunderstood me about going for a walk while we were down here.'

'I was pretty sure I'd get you to change your mind.' He winds down the car window and holds his cigarette out of it.

'Devil. This time I'm not going to.'

'Ah well. It was worth a try. You look marvellous in that hat. I think hats are very sexy things.'

'They hide a multitude of sins.'

'Perhaps that's why they're sexy. Whose funeral was it, by the way? You never got round to telling me.'

'An old woman called Helena Warne. I didn't know her well, but I liked her.'

'A long way to come for someone you didn't know well.'

'I wanted to be there, to be counted as a friend.'

'She wasn't there to count you.'

'Maybe she was. Her son George certainly counted me.'

'You've never mentioned him before.'

'Why should I?'

'What does this George Warne do?'

'He's a lawyer.'

'Not your usual field of play.'

'How do you know?'

'*Misteriosa Marcia*.' Edward has often called her that, and starts to sing it to a vaguely Verdian melody as they drive for some miles without talking.

'This car's not going well. It's not pulling – oh no. I've got the handbrake on.'

'No wonder then, poor old car.' He throws his cigarette butt into the road and winds up the window.

'I'm getting rid of it soon. I can't afford to run it, and it will never pass its MOT without serious amounts of money being spent on it.'

'I keep telling you it's cheaper to take taxis everywhere than have a car in London.'

'So you don't want to buy it off me even at a bargain price?'

'Like hell.'

Marcia laughs. 'Do you know anyone who might?'

'Never sell your old car to friends. Look, a sign saying Footpath to the Downs. Your last chance to change your mind.'

'You are incorrigible.'

Edward puts a jazz tape on and leans back, eyes half-shut. His dark hair is collar-length, as is his beard, and both are infiltrated with grey. Someone once told him he looked like Simon Magus and he hasn't forgotten. Marcia flicks a glance at his hawked profile, at the long fingers with grubby nails drumming out the beat on his thighs. Edward Wintlesham is a director/designer beginning to make a big name with his innovative interpretation of operas; he started life as a graphic designer, migrated into theatre design, and oozed across into direction when a project he was involved in suddenly lost its director through a car accident.

Edward's women friends have been more submissive than Marcia; he finds the domestic side of life a chore and has always up till now managed to live with willing women, who though they professed independence and sexual equality, found that their partner, while agreeing wholeheartedly with their sentiments, still managed to turn them into drudges. Each relationship had come to an end for much the same reason: each woman would tell him they were tired of being the slave of a selfish, self-confessed genius, and leave. Marcia knew all this about Edward and kept her distance. He wore her resistance down by pursuing her as he'd never pursued anyone else. What began as a game for him turned serious, because he fell in love with Marcia, and she (to her surprise) with him. But she still refused to move in with him however often he suggested it. Domesticity played no part in their relationship.

'I think I might try and get into the matinee of *Death of a Salesman.*'

'Good idea – with luck you'll be there in good time.'

'And then we could meet up again at Rosie's party.'

'Rosie's party?'

'Don't tell me you've forgotten about it!'

'I had. Today's been quite a strain. Funerals take it out of one.'

'Tell me more about this George Warne.'

'Why?'

'I'm curious.'

'There's nothing to tell.'

'Marcia, when you say there's nothing to tell in that tone of voice I simply don't believe you. You may be a good actor but you don't fool me. Look, I don't care one way or another—'

'Good.'

'But I like to dig into the reasons why you lie to me, because you don't lie very often.'

'How can you be so sure I'm lying?'

'I'm a human lie detector. Why, Marcia, unless you had an affair with this George person, would you be so cagey?'

'I'm cagey by nature. I'm the sort of person who would rather keep a secret than spill it. Most people seem to be the opposite, so they view me with suspicion. Blame it on generations of my family surviving pogroms by keeping mum.'

'I wish Jews wouldn't see themselves as special cases. Every Jew I've ever known does it. It seems to be inherent.'

'I think it probably is. But come on, Edward, you see yourself as a special case too – as an artistic type. So it's not exclusive to us.'

'Actually, I suppose an artist of any sort has to be like that in order to survive life in the philistine world. What I meant though was the old cliché, that Jews see themselves as victims.

You mentioned the word pogrom when there was no need to – the victim attitude is so ingrained.'

'Maybe. Being from a victimized race is a foreign concept to an English person, unless their family was caught up in some horror outside England.'

Marcia remembers George talking about old Raj families whose forebears were killed during the Mutiny, of an anguished letter home from a woman confined in Cawnpore who later met her death in the infamous well, along with all her children. Marcia realizes how much she has missed George's wide knowledge of history, knowledge worn and given lightly, unlike Edward's which was the result of research done for a particular project with a slant in mind, information passionately held until it faded permanently. But Edward, unlike George, had not been to university; he said, and repeated often within invisible inverted commas, that he'd been educated by the university of life.

'Drop me by the underground station, Marcia. Thanks for the ride, no thanks for no walk.'

'What time is Rosie's party starting?'

'Seven. Drinks and finger-food. It'll probably go on late, though – Rosie's parties tend to.'

'If I don't make it, don't worry. I've no idea how long we are going to rehearse, and I'll be shattered anyway afterwards.'

'You *must* turn up, Marcia. Rosie's invited Sedley Mortimer and you've got to meet him. No excuses, you're coming. See you at seven or soon after. No chickening out.'

Marcia watches Edward lope across the street while she waits at a light. A woman swings her gaze to watch him as he passes. He's a striking, attractive figure, and success has given him allure. Marcia knows all about the allure of success; most of her working life she has had to try to invent the allure without the success. A good part, good reviews, regular income from a West End show, and the difference in any actor is remarkable. Marcia's version of the cliché is that success breeds allure plus success.

She pulls away from the light as Edward disappears into the station. Sedley Mortimer. London's current top theatrical agent, but not hers. Edward dislikes her agent, Christina Platt, and keeps urging her to change, but Marcia's been through so much with Christina she can't imagine life without her.

'I can't kick her in the teeth just when I've got my best part in years.'

'The right moment to do so. You can only change agents from a position of strength. You know that, Marcia. Sedley isn't going to be interested in you until he sees you in *Ion*. Then he might take you on.'

'Christina got me the part.'

'*You* got it through an audition. She just alerted you to it. And it's the only good part she's sent your way for years according to you.'

'Not for want of trying.'

'So what are you saying, Marcia? That she tried and failed because you are no good? Or she's no good? If it's the former, forget Sedley Mortimer. If it's the latter, then you're a fool not to approach him.'

Of course she has done nothing, and now Edward is determined to introduce her. She's not sure of his motives, either; some people might do this out of pure kindness, but not Edward. His kindnesses were complex, and gratitude was often hard to feel.

'So, Creusa, your plot has gone awry, you are condemned to death by the court at Delphi, you flee to the altar in the sanctuary of Apollo for safety. Ion follows you intent on killing you, but is checked by the Priestess who at last tells him her secret – that she knows he is Apollo's son by a mortal woman, whose identity he will discover through his cradle and coverings which she has kept hidden all his life. Naturally enough, Creusa recognizes them, convinces Ion he is indeed her son by Apollo, and mother and son are reunited. Xuthus is going to be kept in the dark about this latest twist: he will continue to view Ion as his son. Nice little twist.

'Yes, you all know the story, but don't forget, so does the audience. They were told at the beginning by Hermes, messenger of the gods, exactly what was going to happen. And yet there's still a tension in the unfolding of the drama, it's more than a dance in which the steps are known.

'As I said, I want the audience to sense the layers of meaning under the story without our stressing them at all. Play it straight, but strange – I want the otherworld feeling of an ancient religion to be powerful. Any story of lost sons being found is a winner, and if we bring tears to the audience's eye, well and good. And if all the questions you have been asking occur to them too, excellent; if on the other hand they accept the play straight, again excellent. Right. On with the business. Chorus, Creusa, Ion, and the Priestess for the altar scene.'

'He wants to have his cake and eat it,' mutters Suzanne to Marcia. 'Two-cake directors are usually hot on theory and not so hot on the nitty-gritty, but Alsopp is good on everything, I have to admit.'

'Don't you like him?'

'He makes me nervous.'

'Not a bad thing.'

'Marcia, I've decided to change your entry. I think you should rush through the theatre taking the same route as with your first entry, and Ion and his crowd of would-be killers will do the same. Damian, did you hear?'

'Good idea. It will help raise the adrenalin. Come on, Marcia, let's run up the pub stairs before we enter to get the feel of it.'

Alsopp smiles at Damian. He likes bumptious young men.

'Marcia, think winding paths, altars and sanctuaries, cicadas and heat. You've been to Sicily, remember those temples at Agrigento and run through them in your mind. But you're frantic. All the running round impediments just means your pursuers are catching up. You can hear them baying. OK then. From your entry.'

'*Women, they are after me to kill me! Apollo's court demanded my life – I am in their hands . . .*'

Because Rosie Amsterdam's flat is very near hers, Marcia knows as she arrives home at seven-thirty that however tired she is, she will have to put in an appearance at the party. She has a hot bath, rings Rosie to say she's on her way, and dresses herself in black trousers and a loose red silk shirt. It's well after eight by the time she arrives and she can see at a glance that most people are fairly drunk and Edward more than most. He's sitting on a sofa with a blond actor called Moonie whom Marcia doesn't like, so after waving in their direction she ploughs on through the noisy crowd towards the kitchen and Rosie. She can hear her loud, inimitable voice.

'Darlings, he then took the shoe and threw it at me with all his might. If it had hit me I could have lost an eye but it sailed past and went straight through the window. Shoe-shaped hole in the glass. And where is my shoe? Sailing off down the street on top of a removal lorry that happened to be passing. I know, it's unbelievable, and they were good shoes, Manolo Blahnik's, I got them for half-price in a sale, but even so. Marcia darling, you've made it! Darling, you look as wonderful as ever. Have a great big drink to catch up with us all. Now, come with me and meet Sedley Mortimer. Edward was afraid he'd leave before you arrived.'

Rosie has Marcia by the hand and is dragging her through the crowd to the front room. Their progress is slow.

'Marcia darling, how lovely you're here! Edward said you weren't coming.'

'Lies. Hullo, Mervyn. Is Roger here?'

'Gone to New York.'

'Work?'

'Work. Play. We're not an item any more, by the way.'

'Oh Mervyn, I'm sorry. Look, Rosie wants me to meet someone but I'll come back afterwards and you can tell me about it.' She kisses Mervyn's cheek; she's known him a long time. He has dyed his hair a rather fierce dark brown.

'Same old story. He met someone else.'

'I'll come back soon.'

Rosie pulls her towards Sedley Mortimer's impressively tall back view. He has a sycophantic group around him.

'Sedley, you've been monopolized by this lot for far too long. Come and meet some new faces. Start with Marcia Fleckner. Marcia, this is Sedley Mortimer.'

'Hullo, Marcia. We haven't met before, but your face is familiar. I know *Spotlight* off by heart, so that is probably why.'

'Meet the rest of her, then.' Rosie gives a raucous screech as she catches sight of another new arrival, and disappears.

Marcia can see the lack of enthusiasm behind his polite smile and his cool handshake. He's a man who knows his own power and influence, and she's not going to add to either. She breaks the brief but growing silence.

'What do you do and how do you feel when your clients are disloyal?'

'I beg your pardon?'

'Say one of your rising actors goes off to another agent?'

'They don't. It's not a problem in my agency.'

Marcia meets his eye, aware his attention is still only partly on her.

'So you poach rather than suffer poachers?'

'Are you deliberately trying to annoy me?'

'I'm trying to get through to you.'

'Go on.'

'I've seen agents rise and wane, just as actors do. All except you, you just rise. So it occurred to me that either you had a very tough contract with punitive clauses that stopped people leaving, or that people never wanted to leave you, or that if someone did leave (actors can be disloyal) there were dozens to fill the gap.'

'There's a bit of truth in all three of your suppositions. Who's your agent?'

'Christina Platt. Has been ever since I started.'

Marcia is watching his face closely, but he gives nothing away. Not for him the smallest movement of the eyes or head to imply deprecation.

'Why did you say I poach?'

'I've heard it said.'

'I'm accused of poaching because actors come to me dissatisfied with the service they are getting from their agents. I take on a very small percentage of those who approach me and inevitably I'm accused of poaching.'

'I suppose other agents find it galling when they've been nursing someone's career and you benefit just when that career takes off?'

'Tough. Why shouldn't the actor move to someone who'll do better for them?'

'But isn't it true that most actors join you just when their career's about to take off anyway?'

'Marcia, I have the feeling you are trying to tell me something. It's not the first time I've heard an actor express your views.'

He smiles at Marcia, a warm, attractive smile that more or less reaches the eyes, and though those eyes don't move, Marcia gets the impression they have taken in someone behind her.

'She's trying to tell you, Sedley, that she's about to play a big part in a new production, and she wants you to go and see her act.'

'Hullo, Edward. Didn't know you also knew Rosie Amsterdam.'

'Everyone knows Rosie.' Edward puts an arm round Marcia. 'Marcia is a near neighbour of hers.'

'So what's the play, Marcia?'

Marcia boils inwardly but is good at hiding her feelings, particularly when she feels she is being patronized.

'*Ion*, by Euripides. John Alsopp's directing. It opens at the New Fortune in about ten days.'

'I've heard about it actually. Alsopp's a stringent director.'

'Indeed.'

'Who's in it with you?' As Marcia reels off the cast she knows that none can be from his stable or he would not ask.

'I've heard Damian Frapp is good.'

'You should watch him then, Sedley. Get him at the start of his career.'

'Edward, you're so full of good advice you ought to be an agent yourself.' Sedley Mortimer grins at him without malice.

'I've thought of it, actually. I'm good at picking talent. If directing doesn't work out, there's another career I could try.'

'I shall have to watch my back.'

'No one will overtake you, Sedley, and you know it. All the best people are on your books.'

'I love all this praise, but I've just seen the time. I really have to leave now. I must go and find Rosie. Nice to meet you, Marcia. See you around, Edward.'

Marcia pushes Edward into a corner as Sedley Mortimer disappears rapidly. She is hissing with rage.

'That was unpardonable, Edward. You should never interfere like that.'

'I thought you needed a good word.'

'I was doing perfectly well on my own, thank you.'

'No one does well with Sedley Mortimer – he makes the running if he's interested.'

'Even less reason for you to butt in. He certainly won't come and see *Ion* now.'

'Don't be ridiculous, why shouldn't he come?'

'Not that I bloody care anyway. I'm staying with Christina whatever happens.'

'You are so pig-headed, Marcia.'

'I know, and right now I don't care about that either. I'm going home, Edward. I'm on my knees. I only came to meet Sedley Mortimer and I've met bloody Sedley Mortimer and I'm off.'

'Marcia – wait a minute—'

'Goodbye.'

Marcia is so tired and angry she feels manic, and knows that more alcohol would be very unwise. After resisting Rosie and Mervyn's protestations she runs back to her flat and collapses on the sofa. She can see the light winking on her answerphone but switches it off without listening to her messages. Tomorrow will do.

She puts some Mozart on, makes herself an omelette and a salad, and sits eating in the kitchen until she is calm enough to read a book. It's months since she spent a Saturday night on her own; Edward insists on something happening at a weekend even if it's just a visit to the cinema followed by a pizza. He is incapable of spending a Friday or Saturday night at home, he likes busy weekends whatever the previous week has been like. Marcia knows she can only function properly if she has fallow time, and fallow time has been in very short supply. She feels profoundly drained.

George didn't drain her. They tended only to meet at weekends, and often spent them in George's house doing very little – reading, eating and drinking, making love sometimes. She remembers how she even thought, when the weekend followed a quiet week (she was between work), that it verged on the boring. But as she sits in her kitchen, her rage now gone, her exhaustion taking over, she sees how tired she is of Edward's incessant activity. Exhibitions, plays, films, operas – he misses nothing he considers important. He sees everything and is seen everywhere, and that is how he likes it.

*   *   *

'Rachel. It's me.'

'Marcia! So you did get my message this evening.'

'Sorry, I haven't listened to them.'

'Oh well, great minds.'

'What does it say?'

'I wanted you to come over this evening and take pot luck – we hadn't seen you for so long. It was Jonathan who said get Marcia over.'

'Oh Rachel, what a pity. I'd love to have seen you both instead of doing what I did.'

'I'd say come over now but it's a bit late and we've eaten anyway.'

'So have I. I just wasted an hour going to a party I didn't want to go to, and I'm sitting here on my own and the only person I wanted to talk to was you.'

'So talk. That's what friends are for. I'll take the phone into the bedroom and leave Jonathan to watch his programme in peace.'

There are rustles of movement and a door shuts.

'I feel I've been a lousy friend since your miscarriage. How are you now, Rachel? You sound lots better.'

'I am. I am. I really am. I've got two lovely children and there's nothing to stop me trying again. But I tell you, Marcia, losing that second baby was the worst thing that's happened to me. I lost the other so early it didn't hit me in the same way. This baby looked so perfect. I asked to hold him and they left him with me. His little nose, his hands, his toes – all just like Jonathan's. I cracked up completely when they took him away. I honestly went mad for a bit. Poor Jonathan was quite terrified.'

'You never told me you'd held him. Oh, Rachel.'

'I couldn't talk about it before.'

'I've been a useless friend. I haven't given you any support at all.'

'I didn't ask you for any support because I didn't need any – I've got Jonathan. You've got troubles of your own. And you haven't got kids, so you wouldn't know what it was like.'

'I understand better than you think.'

'I'm not criticizing you, Marcia, please don't misunderstand me. It's just a fact of life – having kids, not having kids – one of those things. When you have children you can't help seeing things differently, and when you haven't got them, you don't understand that there's a difference.'

'Well, I'm one of those blind ones and yet I'm playing a woman who has a baby and abandons it.'

'Not *blind*, I never said that. Don't put words in my mouth, naughty Marcia. As for abandoning a baby, that's something I can't understand and never will.'

'I'm finding it quite hard myself, even if I'm only eighteen or so and believe I've been raped by the god Apollo, and therefore leave the baby boy at birth at the scene of the crime for the god to take care of.'

'In other words, leave him to die.'

'Not clear. This is ancient Greece. You can't assume anything.'

'I can't understand how any woman can just leave their child and walk away. How can you make a character like that sympathetic?'

'Rachel, I told you, this is ancient Greece. You have to accept she thought the god would do something.'

'So tell me the story.'

'Creusa – my part – is a king's daughter, mid-thirties or so when the play starts, married to a foreigner called Xuthus, and they're childless. They have arrived at the oracle of Apollo at Delphi to ask the god to give them a son.' Marcia walks about the flat as she talks, occasionally looking at the photo of Apollo.

'Does the foreign husband know about the first baby?'

'Nobody knows. Anyway, the keeper of the sanctuary is this lovely teenager who has no parents and since childhood has been in the service of the god. Yes, he's the lost baby, but Creusa only learns it after Apollo has played her a dirty trick.'

'Dirty tricks seem to be in his line.'

'He tells Xuthus the next person he sees will be his son. He sees Ion, accepts him at once as possibly the result of some fun and games at a bacchanalia, and immediately adopts him. Creusa is furious that this bastard by-blow is to join the royal family, and decides to poison him.'

'Her own son?'

'She doesn't know it yet.'

'Don't tell me she tries to kill him a second time and succeeds!'

'No, this is a Greek play with a happy ending.'

'So somehow she finds out in time—'

'Her plot doesn't work luckily, and it all sorts itself out in the end.'

'I'll come then. I couldn't take it if she did kill her child. It's more like a fairy story by the sound of it.'

'More subtle – lots of layers. The superficial story is not the only explanation.'

'It never is, but often it's the only one I follow. That's another effect kids have on you, Marcia, your powers of attention seem to fragment. I feel as if I've got a melon instead of a brain sometimes. But you sound really excited, Marcia – it's a good part.'

'And a good cast and director. It's the best thing I've been in for ages.'

'It's time you had a big success. You're so good, much better than many who seem to get the big parts.'

'Edward says I should change my agent.'

'And what do you say?'

'I hate to hurt Christina after all she's done for me.' Marcia goes into the kitchen and switches on the kettle.

'And Edward says be ruthless and leave her?'

'Of course. And you?'

'Marcia, I'm not in your world. I just come and watch you and know that you're as good as anyone but not as successful as some. If it's because of your agent, then change from her. You've only got one life to live—'

'And it's not a dress rehearsal.' They say this in chorus and laugh.

'Who was it always said that at college?'

'Vicky Calman. Voluptuous Vicky.'

'I wonder what's happened to her. But to get back to Christina Platt. She's always struck me – and I hardly know her, so don't lay too much importance on what I say – she's always struck me as a woman who likes control.'

'So?' Marcia mashes the herb teabag roughly in a mug of boiling water.

'Well, real success is out of people's control, isn't it? Once it's happened, vroom. Your life changes in unforeseen ways and you change too.'

'She was over the moon when Jolyan Welsford hit Hollywood with such a bang.'

'He's a man. She'd have had less control over him from the start. It's a sort of nanny syndrome she's got – men are better at shaking it off.'

'I think you're talking rubbish, Rachel. I'm sorry, but I do.'

'Quite likely. I told you I didn't know her very well.'

'I don't think you'd have liked the agent I was introduced to at the party tonight. Edward thinks I ought to join him if he'd take me.'

'Who?'

'Sedley Mortimer.'

'I don't believe this.'

'Do you know him?'

'He's a cousin on my mother's side – distant but definitely there. Known to be seriously arrogant—'

'And seriously successful.' Marcia stretches out in the sitting-room, her mug of tea resting on her stomach.

'Well, our Sedley wouldn't suffer from nanny syndrome and that's for sure.'

'How well do you know him?'

'Hardly at all. We've met at the occasional bar mitzvah, he always looks as if he'd rather be elsewhere. He married out of the faith, but he's now divorced as far as I know.'

'He's London's hottest agent, which is why Edward is pushing me at him, but he's not going to want to take me on, so why am I worrying?'

'His father was English. I remember Mum saying that the Mortimers were very grand, so goodness knows what they made of him marrying Sadie Nussbaum!' Rachel giggles. 'And her father was a rabbi. But cousin Sadie was beautiful – a real stunner. Sedley's not bad-looking either.'

'Not my type.'

'Well, you've got Edward. One great hunk is enough at a time.'

'That's another problem. I feel – I feel very unsettled about Edward, Rachel. Up and down. Drained.'

'Is it his fault?'

'I think so. He's always on the go, always looking for the latest thing. Relentlessly avant-garde.'

'Sounds exciting. You should try my life.'

'But I'm drained by it all.'

'I'm drained too, most days, and all I've done is look after a family. So I can't be sympathetic about your life, Marcia. When you start moaning I just want to say you don't know how lucky you are.'

'You're right. I'll stop. Perhaps the funeral I went to this morning has put me in a dismal mood.'

'Whose was that?'

'Nobody you know. The mother of an old friend.'

'I hate funerals.'

7

'Who was that interesting-looking woman who came in late and then disappeared?'

'An actress called Marcia Fleckner. A friend of mine who knew Helena.'

'Heleena, Heleena – why did she shorten it?'

'I've no idea, Laura, as I said in my little speech.'

'Such a beautiful name, Helena. Your friend reminded me slightly of Aunt Lena as she was when she used to bring you down to the farm. I remember the first time she came, our famous aunt from India. I expected her to be wearing a sari! Instead she looked so smart and chic and pretty I couldn't believe she was Mum's *sister*!'

'She always dressed well.'

'Why didn't your friend come here to this lovely hotel?'

'She had to go back to London for a rehearsal.'

Laura has taken her green hat off and is looking much better without it. Her clothes smell of mothballs, and have the dim look of fabrics which don't get much use so never get cleaned because they're not dirty, just fusty.

'You live such a glossy life, Jebs. London, the Bar, the theatre. I moulder away at Bellwether Farm and have nothing to show for my life.' She takes another swig of champagne despite the fact she is driving.

'Your father would never have coped without you.'

'Oh, that's true, that's absolutely true. Laura the packhorse, that's what I've been. And now I look like one – what we used to call as children a ten-ton-tessy.' Her nose is red from cold and champagne, her grey hair is thick and inexpertly cut, her ankles bulge above her tight court shoes. George tries to think of something to say but luckily she continues.

'I had a good cry when you said we mattered more to you than your family.'

'I loved the farm, and coming every summer was what kept me going.'

'I loved the farm too when we were young. I loved it because I was going to get away one day, go to college, get a job. Get married. Instead Mum got ill and died, and bang went my future. Sophie was the lucky one, she was already away at college, with a steady boyfriend – I'm sure she married Monty so young to make sure she wasn't sucked back into Bellwether. The wedding was the last time we saw you.'

'It's ridiculous I've left it so long.'

'Well, I could see that without Mum there wasn't much draw for you. She adored you too, but you know that – it used to make me quite jealous how well the two of you got on.'

George stares wordlessly at Laura.

'Only joking. So anyway, what could I do? Mum died just as I was thinking about the next stage after school – instead I had to become Dad's partner on the farm.'

'You could have refused – he could surely have employed someone else?'

'There was no money to pay someone else. Dad needed me – I'd taken Mum's jobs on while she was ill and he could see I'd cope.' Laura looks at her father's frail figure sitting by himself by the fire. 'He needs me even more now, poor old thing.' The sudden bitterness in her voice fades again, and she and George go over to Julian Roper. They fetch him more drink (whisky) and a plate of food, and bring a small table close to him. He starts to eat with focused concentration, his hands unsteady. George decides to talk to him later, but before he moves on to talk to other guests he takes Laura's hand.

'Don't feel you've lost out. What you've done is admirable and I do admire you for it. I always admired you – remember how you taught me to dance?'

'How I loved dancing! Well, those days are over, good and proper.'

Sophie comes up to them at this moment, a streak of mayonnaise on her cheek. 'My goodness, the food's good, Jebs. How did you find this place?'

'By accident. I'm glad you're enjoying it.'

'You look so distinguished these days, Jebs. But no one calls you Jebs any more, do they?

'Don't stop – I don't mind.'

'Are you going to become a judge soon? Monty says QCs usually do.'

'Not true, actually. A lot don't.'

'Are you?' Sophie's gaze and manner are as direct as they used to be, and George mumbles in reply as he always did.

'Unlikely.'

'You haven't gone to seed like us, Jebs. Monty says country bumpkins go to seed, ha ha, but I think it's in the genes. Your father was so tall and thin and kept his figure too, just like you.'

'Your father's hardly a big man—'

'He used to be quite burly, don't you remember? He's shrunk. Mum had heavy bones too, and we girls both inherited that. Aunt Lena kept her shape though.' Sophie rubbed her hands on her plump thighs. 'None of this.'

'She worked at her figure all her life. She called it Banting for Beauty.'

'Never speak ill of the dead, but Aunt Lena was always a bit too smart to be real, if you know what I mean.'

'I must go and talk to Julian now he's finished eating.' George walks away, feeling a certain comfort in the fact that he likes Sophie no more than he used to. She heads back to the buffet table for another plate of food.

George fully intended to drive back to London when the wake was over, but as the last guests – Julian, Sophie and Laura – disappeared down the drive of the Castle Hotel, he knows it is beyond him. He walks back into the hotel as if he is carrying a load of lead.

'Are you all right, sir?' The bright receptionist looks concerned.

'I'm exhausted. That was a very good lunch party, very well done by you all. Many thanks.'

'It's our pleasure.'

'I think I might stay for the night, if you have a room.'

'We do have a group of business delegates here for a weekend conference, but let me look and see if we can squeeze you in. Ah. We only have the Tower Suite – the bridal suite – available, sir. I could ask the manager if he'd let you have it at the ordinary rate.'

'See what you can do. Where do I go?'

'The bridal suite's on the third floor, sir.'

'A fitting place to sleep after a funeral.'

'Sorry?'

'It doesn't matter.'

The Tower Suite is on the top two floors of the central tower; an internal wooden staircase leads from the sitting-room to the bedroom. The views over the valley are exceptional, and George stands for some time in the bedroom staring at the curves of hillside, the bare trees, the patch of red-brown bracken growing deeper-coloured in the fading light. He hears a tray of tea being left in the room below, calls down an acknowledgement but does not move.

He has more than enough to do in London, he has brought none of his work with him, and yet here he is again in the anonymity of a luxury hotel. Rites of passage. He needs to immerse himself in today's rite of passage, to feel its full weight, to give his mother's departed spirit proper space. He could have gone back to her house, been close to her there, but the recent past is too strong in that house, and Geoffrey himself still too resonant.

He will have to go back to that house soon though, and sort through all Lena's dusty possessions; he will have to brave the sweetish stale smell of her clothes. He couldn't leave the job to strangers, but help from someone like Laura or Marcia would ease the work. Impossible, alas.

Marcia. The sight of her, tired but dashing, moved him unexpectedly this morning. If only she could have stayed, been with him now. This last thought creeps in, ignoring boundaries.

He recalls what Laura said, that Marcia resembled Lena. Dark hair and eyes, a stylish look, that's as far as it went in his view. Marcia looks Jewish, Lena looked Celtic. He can't put his finger on the difference, but wonders if it lies more in things like the cheekbones and shape of the mouth than in the area usually chosen, the nose. Lena gave herself cheekbones by means of makeup; Marcia's tilt in a natural bony slant.

He goes down the short staircase to the sitting-room and pours himself some tea. There is a newspaper, there are magazines, but he has no desire to read. He eats a muffin without hunger, stares at the tidy flames of the gas-coal fire. Dusk is now falling, rooks are cawing, someone whistles repeatedly for a dog. The valley is filling with mist; the bracken is black against a charcoal hillside. As dark falls the mist thickens, and his tower is isolated in silence.

He lets the weight he has been controlling all day drop inside his body, fill him, flood him. His mother is dead. He does not know his father. He is alone.

When George wakes next morning the silence and the light – there are windows on three sides of the bedroom and he hasn't drawn the curtains – are almost tangible. The glow of a crisp bright autumn morning fills the room, and he shuts his eyes again as he registers he is in the Castle Hotel, on the Sunday after his mother's funeral. He has slept for ten solid hours; the weight has gone. He is floating in light. Church bells ring in the distance. His aunt adored him. He will accept the Judgeship; having been at the very back of his mind for days, the dilemma is solved, the solution is sitting at the front of his brain waiting for him to pick it up. Yes, he will accept. He will ring the Lord Chancellor's Department tomorrow. All decided.

He leaps out of bed, shaves, bathes, breakfasts, and suffused with his new clarity and energy goes to his mother's house to begin the sorting process. She was a hoarder of boxes, and he puts as many as he can find in the hall and on the landing. He decides to leave the first floor for another day, and goes into the sitting-room. Lena's desk sits there, one of those with a flap that closes up. He pulls it down and a crush of papers, letters and bills falls forward. He quickly heaps them into a box to deal with later, and pulls open the drawers. These are tidier but crammed full, one with letters.

The letters are tied in bundles; he recognizes Geoffrey's writing on one bundle, his own on another. There's a bundle from Cynthia, another from some friend with neat writing on dark blue Basildon Bond. His own bundle is meagre – mostly letters written from school, a few from his years at Oxford, the odd postcard from abroad. Lena has kept everything. He leafs through the group from Roddick Manor and finds another letter tucked in with them, in a faintly familiar hand. The postmark on the envelope is also Roddick. Curious to see whose hand it is, he opens it.

Peter Dawlish. It's a letter to Lena from Peter Dawlish. His curiosity intensified, he begins to read it.

Dear Mrs Warne,

Please forgive me for writing to you out of the blue. Let me introduce myself. I am George's new history master at Roddick Manor. I came to help out in the Spring Term after Mr Hunt's unfortunate sudden death.

I find your son a delight to teach, and am pleased about his excellent progress. He is extremely intelligent and I like his sense of humour. But I'm not writing simply to tell you that, but to make a suggestion which I hope you will consider. Let me give you the background first. My parents have bought a small farm in Italy, in a bad state of repair, and have asked me to get a team together to tidy the place up this summer. Everyone helping will get free board and lodging and living expenses, plus plenty of time off to pop off to Florence, Arezzo, Assisi – the rich culture of Italy is on our doorstep. I wondered if you would allow George to come and join the team – I know he would enjoy it, see Italy, and no doubt learn a lot if not about art, then about painting and decorating! The plan is for a small group of boys from Roddick to leave with me at the end of term, and stay in Italy until the end of August. It would be a pleasure to have George with us, and I'm sure my parents will treat all the boys as part of the family.

I would of course encourage the boys to read and do necessary school work in preparation for the next academic year. Naturally, I haven't mentioned any of this to George in case you have other plans for him in the vacation.

I look forward to hearing from you, I hope in the affirmative.

George stares at Dawlish's large clear writing and flamboyant signature in total puzzlement. What is this Italian trip he knows nothing about? It's as if he is reading about someone else. He looks at the date on the letter: May. That was the year he was working secretly for Oxford, the year he did two days a week in the local garden centre during the summer holiday. Slowly the implications of the letter sink in.

'You forbade it, didn't you?' Geoffrey Warne's smug captain-of-industry face is turned towards him, as if watching him. 'You bloody forbade it! The last thing you'd have let me do is go and enjoy myself with a friendly family anywhere, let alone Italy! Miserable pathetic sod that you were. I can just hear you saying, No Lena darling, out of the question. We have no idea who this teacher is, and we only have his word for it the whole thing is above board. Dreadful things can happen abroad to young boys. You must write and refuse. I can hear you. And Lena would dutifully write and refuse on my behalf and poor Peter Dawlish would wonder why he seemed to have put his foot in it with glamorous Mrs Warne.'

George re-reads the letter avidly, looking at every implication. Tuscany, one of the family, visits to Florence, Arezzo, Assisi. To a boy as starved as he had been of any extra culture, the trip would have been true heaven. Even as he stands there the missed opportunity goes into him like a knife. He wonders who went – no one talked to him about it. He sits down on the sofa in the cold, cheerless room and lets a retrospective anguish fill him. Maybe Lena vetoed the idea without Geoffrey even knowing about it, turning down the invitation on the grounds that her darling son should not mix with people who might turn out to be 'not at all the Thing'. The unseen capital used to hang in the air when she used that phrase.

'Could you define the Thing?'

'Oh, don't be so tiresome, Jebs. You know exactly what I mean. People who aren't like us.'

People who aren't cold and manipulative in the name of what is good for you. George re-reads Dawlish's charming letter and tries to remember what he looked like. Curly fair hair, greenish eyes like George's own, but a smaller-boned body, softer facial features. Perhaps Lena had noticed the likeness when she met

Dawlish on an open day, and did not want to encourage further closeness. Pain fills him again. He is surprised at the strength of his own reaction to this long-lost opportunity.

All his vague thoughts about trying to find Dawlish again now crystallize: he will ring his college tomorrow, get Directory Inquiries looking for him, even advertise if those two channels didn't work. His affection and sense of debt had been based on the teacher he had known only in that relationship; this missed summer was no part of his feelings but now cannot help altering them. Dawlish must have liked him to have invited him to Italy, at least enough to risk his company for a month.

George gathers up all the letters and throws them in the box. He can't bear to stay in the house for another minute, and certainly wants no more revelations today. He will look through the rest of the letters in London. As he closes the empty drawers he hears a tapping on the window. There is Raj, forlornly pawing on the pane asking to be let in, mouth stretched in a faintly audible miaow. George ignores him, shuts the doors, locks up the house. The cat will have to get used to his new home with Dora Cunningham. All the same, despite his lack of affection for cats, George finds it takes some time to put poor Raj's despair out of his mind.

8 ∫

Greece. Marcia decides on Sunday morning that she needs to immerse herself in ancient Greece, and only one solution suggests itself – she will go to the British Museum today.

'Go and look at the Elgin Marbles as temple decorations, as aids to religious observance, not as art. Look at the carvings taken from the temple at Bassae. Look at all the temple sculpture but don't stand too close to anything. Try for a sense of awe and reverence.'

Marcia had had a drink with John Alsopp after he exhorted the cast early on in the course of rehearsals to go to the British Museum. As they sat in the pub below their rehearsal room, he gave her a postcard on which he had written out a quotation.

There is never equality between the race of deathless gods and that of men who walk the earth.

'Apollo said that in Homer, don't ask me where or in what circumstances because I don't know. I saw the phrase quoted and I grabbed it for you.'

'No equality. I had noticed.'

'Don't be judgmental. Just accept it.' Alsopp turns the postcard over. 'And look at this. That's the god you couldn't resist when you were eighteen.'

'Is it any wonder girls had fantasies about Apollo if there were fantastic sexy statues like that all over the place? Isn't he terrific!'

'Watch it, Marcia! Not the right reaction. This is a god, Phoebus Apollo, who rose out of the sea each day driving the horses of the sun's chariot over the world until they dipped out of sight again at sunset. A god, mysterious, beautiful, deathless – the rational and civilized god of prophecy. This statue is in Athens. It's a sixth-century BC bronze that was found not far from the city. If I remember, I'll bring another picture of Apollo for you. I've been collecting pictures of different statues of him for years. It's a private obsession.'

'How strange, John, that you should now be directing *Ion* – or perhaps it isn't the coincidence it seems.'

'It isn't. I've always wanted to direct the play Euripides wrote about my hero's son.'

'You're talking just as I did.'

'What do you mean?'

'"My hero's son." I don't think the god would appreciate being patronized as your hero!'

'You're right. There is never equality between gods and men – and we mustn't forget it. Another drink?'

'No thanks, John. And thanks for this picture. It will help.'

'Keep it. I've got another copy.'

Marcia tucked the image into the mirror in her hall, so that she saw it constantly. Some days later John had given her an envelope with PLEASE RETURN written in red above his address.

'Keep them for a bit, but I do want all these back.'

Inside was a series of personal photographs taken of a statue of Apollo, and a black and white commercial photo of the same statue. Marcia leafed quickly through them and took them home to look at again. Instead the envelope has stayed untouched for over a week on her hall table.

As soon as she's finished a leisurely breakfast in bed she lays out all the pictures of Apollo John Alsopp has given her on the bedspread. The sixth-century image on the postcard he gave her is remarkable: a perfect, full-sized naked body, one hand extended, head slightly bent, hair in almost-dreadlocks, a face of intense brooding beauty. The marble statue that John has photographed is quite different; it is badly damaged – arms broken off, hair chipped, face pockmarked. But its power is unaffected; Marcia stares at it until she feels hypnotized by the amazing figure. Larger than life size, the statue is clothed to his ankles in a thin cotton pleated tunic, the folds of which are not only as soft as muslin but also wet. They cling to his body, revealing but veiling his genitals, the muscles of his legs and torso, the cleft between his curved buttocks. Tightly bound round his chest is a sort of wide strap which Marcia examines with puzzlement until she realizes it is body harness, the sort a charioteer would wear who had many horses to control and needed to be linked to his chariot for safety. Phoebus Apollo has just risen out of the sea in all his godlike beauty, soaking wet, pulling with his right hand on the reins (only the stump of the arm is left but it implies strength and energy) while his other hand is resting nonchalantly on his hip (again, only a stump and a couple of fingers pressing into the flesh above his hip remain). His damaged face has an eerie calm that is both arrogant and meditative: his half-smile from some angles is almost mocking.

John has written a note on a post-it. 'Saw this statue on a little island off Sicily, known as Motya in ancient times. It was found on the sea-bed quite recently. Sums Apollo up in my opinion – quite fantastic.'

Marcia suddenly tucks all the Sicilian pictures back into the envelope as if she cannot bear to look at them any longer. She takes her postcard back to its place on the hall mirror, taking in afresh the peculiar intensity of the god's lowered gaze. His right hand is outstretched as if about to receive something from a devotee kneeling before him, his left hand clasps the broken end of a staff or similar cult object. His expression is concentrated, receptive, almost on the point of speech; Marcia imagines Xuthus before Apollo awaiting the answer to the crucial question.

So today she will go to the British Museum and see some more of ancient Greece. She knows that the museum is only open after lunch, but is nervous of staying at home in case Edward contacts her; she's not ready to be pressed to justify her behaviour of the night before. She will walk there, taking a slight detour across Regent's Park; it shouldn't take her more than an hour from Kentish Town. She'll find a pub and have a snack for lunch, or if the sun keeps out buy a sandwich and eat it out of doors. She puts on a pair of sturdy walking shoes she's had since she was twenty and lifts a hand to Apollo as she leaves the flat.

Marcia loves walking through London, particularly if she isn't in a hurry and has no timings to keep to. At some point in the afternoon she'll end up at the BM, but until then the streets are hers. Recalling Alexander Technique lessons, she lets her body move easily, poise without tension. Her mind focused on her feet, her knees, her loose arms and balanced head, she turns a corner and is almost knocked over by a group of people leaving a church.

'So sorry.'

'It's perfectly all right.'

All round her are chattering knots of the congregation, blocking the pavement and spilling out on to the road. She's noticed this Roman Catholic church before, but never seen it open. Curious, she puts her head in, inhaling the strong smell of spent incense. Near the door there is a vividly painted full-sized statue of the Madonna and Child. She finds it horribly garish, but as she leaves and walks on she remembers that John Alsopp explained Greek statues and temples were once brightly painted and would no doubt have seemed equally garish.

A few streets later she passes a synagogue, closed of course. She has hardly ever been inside a synagogue – Martin showed her one once at her insistence, but they did not linger. Even now, she feels no desire to go inside; her stirrings of interest in her family past don't encompass the religious side, and it puzzles her that this is so.

I'm more interested in what people used to feel about Apollo than about Jahveh. I'd really like to know how the ancient Greeks worshipped, what they actually did with the tripods that seem to be so holy, how they felt when they approached a temple, what they did there, what they did afterwards. That crowd outside St Mary's was off to eat a roast dinner at home, after a good gossip on the pavement; their minds were on someone's new clothes, or their badly behaved child, or who's doing the altar flowers next week, or what's for lunch; any sense of the numinous they might have felt earlier was gone, if it had ever been there. But I believe in the numinous, in the presence you can't explain. That's why I don't go to church myself: I never felt it in one, ever. I've felt it in unexpected places: at the tops of towers, at the seaside in winter, at sunrises and sunsets. Perhaps that's why I'm interested in Apollo. That amazing sunset I saw at

St Ives: great red and grey streaks in the black and purple clouds above a purple gold-flecked rough sea. Wine-dark – the only phrase of Homer's I know. He must have called it wine-dark because against a rising or a setting sun it is; but not at midday, never at midday. What time of day did people worship Apollo? Early? Late? In the heat of his sun? What did they do when there was an eclipse? How terrifying that must have been for his worshippers. How terrifying.

What did George say once? *We need the perspective of the past more and more as the future shrinks, because we all need vistas.* Global warming, pollution, overpopulation with resulting nationalism and wars – no hope for the poor old world whichever way you look at it. So if we don't have vistas ahead of us, then those behind—

'Marcia Fleckner, isn't it?'

Marcia is so lost in her inner monologue this voice jolts her considerably.

'So sorry to have made you jump. I walked past you sitting there on your park bench and I said to myself, I'm sure that's Marcia Fleckner.' The plump, grey-haired woman is smiling with proprietorial familiarity.

'It is.'

'I have to tell you how much I enjoyed your performance in *The Cherry Orchard* on television last year. And I saw you a couple of weeks ago in *Yours Sincerely* – only a bit-part but so funny.'

'Thank you. I didn't know they were doing a repeat.'

'I missed that episode first time round, and so I was particularly pleased to catch it.' The woman has perched herself on the bench and Marcia stands up, doing her best to dampen the cosy flood. It's a pitfall of an actor's life she hasn't come across very often because her face is not well known. The woman is repeating some of the lines from the sit-com and roaring with laughter. Marcia touches her arm lightly as she interrupts.

'It's nice to meet an admirer so unexpectedly. Would you like an autograph? I'll sign something if you like, but then I have to hurry off. I'd no idea how late—'

'Yes, please, what have I got, yes, sign this card. I was going to send it to my brother but now I'll keep it. How lovely, thank you.'

'Goodbye. Meeting a fan has made my Sunday.'

'Have a nice day—'

Marcia strides away at speed through Regent's Park, hoping her fan isn't going in the same direction. She feels mean, but knows her limits.

'How someone copes with being seriously well-known I have no idea.'

'I should enjoy it.'

'No, you wouldn't, Edward. Your public begins to think it owns you. You'd hate that.'

'Adulation. Lovely.'

'Admiration is what you need, not adulation.'

'I disagree. I'd like to try a bit of adulation for a change. Lots of people admire me but they're so damned restrained about it I'd love to know what screaming fans feel like.'

'Horrible.' Marcia thinks of this conversation she and Edward had early in their relationship as she crosses the pleasantly empty expanse of the Euston Road. She had tried to talk to him about her difficulties with the audience, about her sense of detachment when her part in the play was rapturously received, about her lack of need of overt praise.

'I love to play to a full house, I love good reviews, who doesn't, but the actual applause means nothing – I just wish I could switch it off as soon as it's got going. I've never had to deal with an ovation – thank goodness. And if I meet a stranger who enthuses I can't deal with it. I just mumble, I feel a fraud. And it's not false modesty, before you accuse me!'

'I wasn't going to.'

'It's as if I despise them for being so enthusiastic – which of course I don't, I'm delighted they've come. If they want to clap it's up to them, but I wish there was another way of showing appreciation.'

'How strange. I'd say you'd got problems, Marcia. Why be an actor if you feel like that?'

'But I love acting – I love to act with other good actors above all. I love it when everything comes right and the performance continues to change and grow. And of course the audience is crucial, I'm not saying it's not. It's just that my performance has nothing to do with them. A receptive audience is supposed to bring out the best in the actors, but I'm not even sure of that. I've been in wonderful performances when the audience has been small and half asleep.'

'I wouldn't be a director or designer if it wasn't for the audience.'

'Oh well, maybe I'm a freak. But I need the audience less and less.'

'Marcia, you're talking complete balls. Actors and audience depend upon one another and without that symbiosis there would be no drama.'

Did the Greeks care about the reactions of their audiences? They built huge theatres not only for dramatic use but as meeting places for the whole adult population of an area. Did they applaud at the end of a play in the time of Euripides? Or was the play more an aspect of worship, to be offered by the actors and witnessed by the audience? As Marcia weaves her way through the homogeneous streets of small eighteenth-century houses on her way to Charlotte Street, she thinks about the role of the mask in Greek drama – how they cut you off from the audience so that you became a cipher. Your real face would not have been known in the agora. Actors were perforce anonymous, there was no cult of the personality. For a moment, but only for a moment, she regrets John Alsopp didn't stick to his original plan to perform *Ion* in masks.

Marcia is particularly fond of this part of London; she finds the scale of the houses just right, and is enjoying the unaccustomed Sunday morning calm of normally busy streets. She cuts through a passage and finds a pub beyond where she stops for a beer and a sandwich. It's an ancient building, unspoilt, with quietly talking people and no juke-boxes or pinball machines. She picks up one of the newspapers on poles and stays for much longer than she means to, delighting in her peaceful haven.

She leaves in a hurry when she hears three o'clock striking, and crosses the unpleasant expanse of Tottenham Court Road full of Sunday shoppers. A window full of silver mannequins wearing gold body suits and wild white wigs holding a long chain of pink rubber sausages catches her eye, and as she slows down to look a man promptly sells her a copy of *The Big Issue*.

As she crosses Goodge Street she recalls Alsopp's remark about approaching temples by winding routes. Her route has been adequately circuitous. She is Creusa, on the last lap of her journey to the Sanctuary of Apollo at Delphi. She walks up the great sweep of steps before the classical frontage of the museum built to mimic a temple and has her bag searched by a museum employee with a severe cold. She's buffeted by a large crowd of Japanese following their flag-waving guide, and pushes her way into the bookshop to get a guidebook and her bearings, It's so long since she last came she's confused about exactly where the Duveen Gallery is.

Everything plays tricks. She remembers a temple with ruined pillars, and finds that she has muddled the Nereid monument in the room beside the Elgin marbles with the memory of the marbles themselves. It is noisy, there are crowds of people staring briefly before they move on, there's no sense of temple or sanctuary. She's approached the Duveen Gallery by going through the huge carved stonework from Egypt, and the contrast is disturbing. The Nereid monument looks mean and out of place, as if it's longing for the hillside in southern Turkey where it was first built.

Apollo – she searches for a temple to him, a statue, anything. Surely there must be something – then she goes through a door, looks behind a lump of stone, and is caught, is winded. Apollo has been lying in wait, hidden; the metopes from his temple at Bassae now ambush her. The dense series of carvings in deep bas-relief lining the walls of the small gallery are full of lively menace: Lapiths struggle with Centaurs, Greeks with Amazons. Marcia stares at the writhing bodies and lets allegory push out artistic appreciation – she goes below the surface to what is signified.

Civilization defeats barbarism, light banishes darkness, higher instincts rout the base ones. The lute, Apollo's instrument as god of music, its cool notes spiritual, wins over the coarser note of the reed pipe, that stirrer of the passions. Marcia hears the reedy notes of Rollo West's music and gazes in pity at poor flayed Marsyas, defeated in the competition with Apollo, before moving on.

'I'm going to draw this geezer.'

'Mum says we've got five minutes.'

'Tell her I'm here. This is the one I want to draw.'

Marcia watches the boy drawing a bronze head with clumsy assurance. He has a dinosaur on the back of his sweatshirt and huge unfastened trainers on his feet. He is drawing the head of what was once part of a full-size cult statue of Apollo; he peers closely at the straight nose, the blank eyes, the plump etched lips, the fillet binding the hair.

'He would once have had enamelled eyes, his lips would have been plated with copper, there would even have been eyelashes fixed to his eyelids.'

The boy looks quickly at Marcia to see if she is joking.

'He's the god Apollo. Do you think he's beautiful?'

'Nah. He's a bit fat.'

'He doesn't look fat to me.'

'Got a big neck.' The boy has exaggerated this in his drawing. 'Fat lips. Why did they put copper on them?'

'To make them look real, all pink. Copper's a pinkish colour. You've got his hair very well.'

The boy stares at his drawing. 'The ears are too small.'

'Why did you choose to draw him instead of those lovely birds over there?'

'That's my sister drawing them. I don't want to do silly birds too. I like men.' The boy shades in the two blank eyelids and his image suddenly acquires a sinister look. 'I got to go now. There's Mum.' He and his sister disappear and Marcia is alone in the gallery. She immediately backs away from Apollo and crosses to the other side of the gallery to look at the head from a distance.

An oblique approach is necessary to any oracle, and if this was the head of a cult statue, it would never have been seen by Creusa except from far away, too high in the shadows of the temple to be clearly visible. And any response from it would be cryptic, equivocal, covert; full of false signposts concealing the real way.

*   *   *

Edward is sitting in the kitchen, sipping a mug of instant coffee and reading a Sunday paper.

'How did you get in?'

'I've got a key.'

'I didn't give you one.'

'I saw your spare one on the hook above the fridge and had it copied.'

'This really upsets me, Edward.'

'It shouldn't. It's a compliment to you – I wanted to use it as a nice surprise.'

'I don't hand my keys around. I like to keep control. So this isn't a nice surprise at all.'

'You're not being very friendly, I must say.'

'I didn't expect to come home and find my flat occupied.' She continues to stand stiffly in the kitchen door. 'It was a shock. Can I have that key back, please?'

'Marcia, what is all this? Why are you being so touchy?'

'I want to have my key back. I don't like the idea of you ambushing me.'

Ambush. She turns to take her coat off and sees the postcard of Apollo stuck in the frame of the mirror. She takes it out and hides it. She can hear Edward laughing in the kitchen and wants to scream. He has moved and is now standing in the doorway, leaning against the jamb. He's smiling.

'I can see you want to get rid of me.'

'I—'

'Yes, you do. How unfriendly you are being to everyone. Your behaviour last night for instance. Rosie was very upset.'

'I was going to give her a ring.'

'And what about me?'

'Edward, don't let's talk now. I'm – I'm sorry, but I am just not up to a great in-depth discussion about our relationship. I need space until the play opens. You know that. It's a demanding part.'

'You're doing a real prima donna act about this wretched play.'

'It's not a wretched play. And I don't care if I am.'

The phone rings. Marcia picks it up, asks immediately she

hears Suzanne's voice if she can ring back and where she is, and puts the phone down. Edward is watching her closely.

'So who was that?'

'Edward, please stop asking questions. I don't pry into your life.'

'That's because you're not interested in anyone but yourself, Marcia. It's easy for you not to pry because you don't give a damn about other people.' Edward is still leaning against the doorjamb, still smiling and relaxed, still enjoying himself. Marcia knows he is trying to goad her, and doesn't answer. She moves into the sitting-room to draw the curtains and put on the lights, beginning to feel a little desperate. Edward in this mood could stay for hours; he thrives on tension and confrontation, which he likes to end in an energetic bout of sex. He holds that argument sharpens the nerve endings, and Marcia can see from the look in his eye that his nerve endings are sharpening nicely.

'Please give me my key back, and please go, Edward.'

'No. I came over specially to see you. Why should I go? Particularly since I came over with a bottle of bubbly to share with you. I thought we need it to make up our differences after last night.' He disappears into the kitchen and she hears the clink of a bottle coming out of her fridge, and immediately afterwards the pop of it being opened. He is singing 'misteriosa Marcia' as he brings the bottle into the sitting-room with the only two glasses he could find remotely resembling champagne flutes.

'You don't deserve me to come with champagne and good intentions when you're so unfriendly.'

'It's Napa Valley, not champagne, and your intentions aren't good.'

'Goodness, what a tongue we have today.' Edward sounds delighted, and tries to clink glasses with her. She evades him and puts her glass down.

'Edward. Why can't I get through to you? I don't want anything to drink. I don't want company. I'm feeling utterly anti-social and I want you to leave. I-want-you-to-leave.'

'I-want-to-stay.'

'I couldn't give a fuck what you want.'

'But a fuck is exactly what I want.'

'You're drunk.'

'Not very. Just nicely.' He closes in on Marcia, while she backs away and tries to laugh.

'OK, OK, give me my glass. I need fortification.'

'That's my girl.' This time she lets him clink glasses. His eyes are glittering, his pupils are large, his excitement is obvious. She realizes with a sinking sense of trepidation that she's never resisted him like this before, and that opposition stimulates him. He is standing close to her, tall, strong, intimidating; she can hear his roused breathing. Edward is often a rough lover even when she's willing, and has left her with raw skin and bruises on occasion. In the first weeks of their relationship this roughness was heady and new; it did not worry her because Edward was never violent. But she's worried now. She knows that his level of arousal directly affects his roughness, and she's never seen him looking like this.

'You don't want me to make love to you, do you? You want to throw me out!'

'I was joking.'

'Oh no you weren't, Marcia. You certainly weren't. You want me to go, and if I touch you you'll hit me, you'll fight me every inch of the way. You she-cat. God, Marcia.' The stem of his empty glass snaps in his hand without cutting him, and he tosses the two broken pieces on to the carpet as he bends his open mouth towards hers. Marcia ducks away from him, using the picking up of the pieces of broken glass as an escape route. She hurries into the kitchen with them, hoping to delay there and somehow defuse the situation. Her trepidation is turning to fear. Perhaps she ought to run out of the flat—

But Edward gives her no time – he's followed her, he's holding her from behind, pushing and rubbing himself against her. His whole body is hard, his grip on her arms is painful. Marcia forces herself to go soft, to relax and sag as if she's more than willing. She drops the cup of the glass in the bin but keeps the base hidden in her hand.

'Sorry, I'm feeling a bit faint and giddy—'

'Come on, Marcia, you were a killer shark two minutes ago. Kiss me. Bite me. Fuck me. I want to explode inside you. Come on, come on.' He laughs, he bites her ear, not gently, he lifts her bodily and pulls her on to the bulge of his penis. His regular hours in the gym give him the strength to carry her, floppy as she is, crushed against his body, to the bedroom. He drops her on the bed and starts to tear off her clothes and his. She controls all her resistance and remains soft, with her eyes and hands closed. Her mind is shrunk to the realization that if she is going to stop him she has to succeed in one gesture, because any struggling will simply excite him further.

'Rough stuff, I love it, let's hurt each other, hurt me, Marcia, hurt me—' He is panting above her, naked now, biting her shoulder as he forces his penis into her. With a sudden movement she jabs the broken stem of the glass base into his buttock and then using all her strength pushes him away, swinging her body to the side and off the bed. As he shouts out in pain she runs out of the room. She catches sight of her phone lying off its base on the hall table and grabs it as she heads for the bathroom where she locks herself in. While Edward starts to shout obscenities from the hall she rings her neighbours upstairs, Todd and Elspeth Reid. She knows they are in – she heard the rowing-machine earlier.

'Todd! It's Marcia. Come down and help me. Somebody's trying to rape me. Yes, I've locked myself in the loo. Bang on the front door and tell him you've got a key. He'll leave you alone. Oh, Todd—' Marcia is shaking so much she drops the phone. Edwards starts to hammer on the door.

'You bloody woman! I'm bleeding all over the place! I said hurt me, not try to kill me! I need a bandage, for God's sake.'

Marcia doesn't answer; she finds she's crouching on the floor as Edward shakes the handle of the door.

'Marcia!'

There is a heavy thudding on the front door.

'Who is it?' shouts Edward.

'I'm from upstairs—'

'Mind your own business and go away!'

'I'm coming in, Marcia needs help.'

'Leave us alone.'

Todd is a very large Australian, even taller than Edward. Though by nature a gentle, quiet man, he looks tough. Edward, completely naked, retreats cursing into the bedroom, blood dripping down his leg.

'I need a bandage. Tell that bitch in the bathroom to give me a bandage. I'm not leaving until she does.' He bangs the bedroom door shut, and Marcia puts her head out of the bathroom, elastoplast in hand.

'Todd. Give this to him. I'm staying in here.'

Elspeth's frightened face appears round the front door at this moment, and when she sees Marcia she runs to her.

'Are you all right?' She joins Marcia in the bathroom and they lock the door again. Elspeth hugs Marcia, whose tears turn to silent hysterical laughter as they sit hugging each other on the edge of the bath, listening.

'Who the hell are you anyway?'

'Todd Reid. Live upstairs.'

'So your habit is to pop in when you feel like it to check on Marcia's love life?'

'She rang me.'

'The bitch. Marcia! You are a bitch, you know that? There was no need to maim me. Bloody woman.' Edward's voice is still angry, but she can tell he's also enjoying himself.

'I think you ought to go.'

'Mr Todd Reid, I think you're right. I've no desire to stay anywhere near Marcia when she's in this mood. But I'm a generous man, Marcia, so I'll leave you the champagne. May you all choke on it.' The front door closes crisply.

Marcia and Elspeth join Todd in the hall, and there is an awkward pause. Marcia is wrapped in a towel, and she tells them to help themselves to the open bottle Edward has left in the sitting-room while she quickly gets dressed. There is blood on the bed and the carpet.

'Todd, did he leave a key?'

'Not to my knowledge.'

'That means he's still got one. I'll have to change the lock.'

On the Night •

There is another pause, which Elspeth breaks.

'If he's got a key to your flat he must be a friend of yours.'

'He had one cut without my permission.'

'When you said rape, Todd and I thought someone must have broken in and attacked you. I was ready to call the police.'

'He did break in. He let himself in while I was out. I call that breaking in.'

Todd and Elspeth are looking increasingly puzzled; because Marcia keeps her private life private, they have no idea who Edward is.

'I'm sorry you've been dragged into my messy life, and thank you both for being so wonderful. Edward is – was – my boyfriend, but this time he's gone too far.'

'If he tried to rape you, you ought to report him to the police.'

'The trouble is he wouldn't call it rape. He'd be outraged, he'd say I was mad. But it was rape, Elspeth, it was. I didn't want him in the house, I kept telling him to go but he wouldn't, he kept getting more and more excited as I got more antagonistic. He – he frightened me.'

'How did he cut himself?'

'It was my fault. I had to stop him. Did it look very bad?'

Todd shakes his head. 'I didn't see. Lots of blood doesn't necessarily mean it was deep.'

Marcia begins to cry helplessly, much to her fury, and blows her nose on kitchen paper. 'He's a bastard. Now I must change the lock. I can bolt the door while I'm in here, but he could let himself in while I'm out.'

'Here's some good news – the landlord is fitting an entryphone and a new lock on the street door next week sometime. Elspeth has been nagging them for ages and at last they're doing it. And I'll change your lock for you as well.'

'You are such good neighbours, you really are. Fill up your glasses, let's finish the bottle. What's the time, by the way? It feels like midnight.'

'Half-seven.'

'I am totally shattered.'

'I'm not surprised.' Elspeth takes her hand. 'Why don't you come upstairs and share our spaghetti? We were just about to put it on to boil when you rang.'

'It's really sweet of you, but don't worry about me – I've taken up enough of your evening. What I need is a hot bath and an early night. I have a long day of rehearsing tomorrow. I'm going to make sure you both have good seats for the opening as a thank-you present for tonight.' She kisses them both, and in a little while they return upstairs.

She bolts the door and gazes round her flat. It feels poisoned. She opens all the windows before shutting herself in the bathroom and pouring lavender oil into a deep hot bath. As she inhales the sweet aroma, she tries to empty her mind of the last two hours, but the sensation of the jabbing gesture with which she wounded Edward keeps returning to her. She would never have thought herself capable of cutting another human being with broken glass. Edward's violence bred her own. She hopes the wound is superficial and won't need stitching; she aimed at the soft flesh of the buttock, jabbed quickly but firmly and might have gone deeper than she intended.

She has the sickening fear that her violence could bring more from Edward. She hadn't realized he was a sado-masochist until this evening; she had taken his roughness as part of a powerful libido which made sex unsettling but always exciting. She used to crave it, but she knows that craving is dead. Permanently dead. She never wants to make love to Edward again.

The bathwater has cooled to the point of being unpleasant, and she stands up. Bruises have already developed on her arms; there is an old one on her hip-bone also caused by Edward. The marks on her arms are going to show when she wears Creusa's costume – she will have to cover them with body makeup.

You gripped my bloodless wrists
Dragged me shrieking for help into the cave
Bore me to the ground – a god without shame or remorse!—
And had your will

As she declaims this aloud she wraps a fresh towel round herself and goes out into the hall. She rescues the picture of Apollo from its hiding-place and tucks it back into the mirror-frame.

'Bastard.'

9

George finds Freddie Mentieth has not arrived when he reaches Chambers on Monday morning.

'As soon as he gets here, Douglas, ask him to pop into my room for a moment, would you?'

'I'll make sure he gets the message. By the way, sir, the brief has been delivered for the Feathers case. Seventeen ring-binders are sitting in your room waiting for you.'

'What a proper welcome back.'

'I hope everything went off all right for you, sir.'

'It did, thanks. The funeral was the easy part. I now have to live with the aftermath.'

'A sad time for you, sir. When would you like me to come and go through the diary with you?'

'Let me go through my mail and sort myself out first, Douglas.'

George shuts his door and stares at the boxes full of plump ring-binders stacked in a corner. The Feathers case is an intricate alleged fraud by the manager of a big family estate; George is acting for Lord Feathers and knows the case will be widely reported. He sighs and sits down heavily at his desk and goes absentmindedly through his mail. He can hear Paul whistling in the clerks' room, adding his usual cascades of trills round a basic tune. Patricia Saban puts her head in to say the advice he gave her about her medical negligence case was spot-on and she had a good win. Five minutes later Colin Simpson comes in and says how sorry he is about the death of George's mother.

'Patricia just told me. I've been out of London all week, otherwise I'd have said something before. When is the funeral?'

'It was last Saturday.'

'I hope all went well. Is your father still alive?'

'No.'

'My parents both died last year, and it left me feeling very odd. No more branches above me – I was now the top of the tree if you know what I mean.' Colin is clearly unrelaxed in George's company and leaves fairly soon, but George is touched he bothered to come in at all with his condolences.

When he becomes a judge he will say goodbye to all the unstructured camaraderie of Chambers which he so enjoys. His working life is completely self-centred, he can operate as separately as he wishes, yet connect with others when he needs or wants to. He has no responsibilities, unlike Freddie, and every advantage. He can come and go as he pleases within the limitations of his practice, he can take holidays when he wants. The self-employed status of the barrister is what he values; he's often said he would find it difficult to live in any other structure.

The bright certainty of yesterday has gone. He gazes round his familiar room with intense affection: it is arranged exactly as he wishes it to be, down to the small fridge installed in the fireplace embrasure which he keeps stocked with champagne. He looks at the piles of ring-binders and longs to read them. Not that there will be any lack of ring-binders and heavy reading on the Bench, but the rest will go. Instead of his freedom he will have a salary, a pension at the end, paid holidays, a highly structured existence as he goes out on circuit and presides for weeks on end far from London, staying in Judges' Lodgings run with an emphasis on formality by staff who are likely to be inflexible and resistant to change. But on the plus side there will be variety, new faces and places, new demands, and the undoubted comfort of not having to worry about any of the logistical administration. Cars with drivers will appear, ceremonies be performed, timings kept to. All this will be dealt with by clerks and marshals; all the irritations of organization will be suffered by others. He will be left to concentrate wholly on the trials coming before him; the workload will be heavy and relentless, but it will also be challenging.

'George old chap, sorry to disturb you. I'm just going round sounding a few people out on the thorny topic of the Chambers' Christmas party. Can't think why I've been asked to organize it again after all the flak I took over last year's effort, but there you go. People want a formal dinner this time, it seems – a black-tie dinner sort of do. What do you feel?'

'I'm easy, Simon. I thought the Tex-Mex restaurant and the square dancing afterwards were good fun last year. A refreshing change. Who's complaining?'

'Some people thought it was a bit too brash and noisy.'

'You can't win. I'd prefer it not to be black tie, but don't feel strongly.'

'It's the staff who like a black-tie do – makes it more of an occasion is the view.'

'Do what pleases them, Simon. Ignore us barristers – not one of us will agree with the other.'

'What a bunch of prima donnas. That's a heavy-looking case over there.' Simon's eyes have been darting about since he entered the room.

'It's the Feathers fraud.'

'Juicy stuff. Wouldn't mind being the junior on that one.'

'How is your practice going, Simon?'

'Like everyone else, I'm coming to the conclusion that crime doesn't pay. Legal aid is a nightmare these days – they're always chiselling down one's fees and then taking for ever to pay them. My brother's in a planning set, and he's on a grand more a year already, the bugger. Planners and builders rake it in.'

'Didn't know you had a brother at the Bar.'

'Twin. Not identical. Cheers, must go on with my intensely important research.'

Simon Hardy has a typical upper-class English face: long nose, big teeth, high colour, pale blue eyes under untidy straight brown hair. George wonders if it's the Norman influence on the bloodline – a name like Hardy is straight Norman French in origin. Looking as he did, he could have galloped beside William the Conqueror with no questions asked.

'George?'

Again his door opens, and this time it's Freddie.

'Hullo, Freddie. The person I really want to see—'

'Sorry about this, but I'm now tied up with a solicitor – shall we have lunch together?'

'Good idea. Not in Hall, if you don't mind.'

'Just tell me where and I'll meet you there at one.'

'Hodgson's?'

'Fine.'

Freddie is already sitting at a table looking through the menu when George arrives.

This is on me, Freddie. I insist. What shall we drink? White or red?

'Don't tempt me. Mineral water is wiser.'

'At least have an aperitif while we order.' George is conscious of the lack of ease between them. Freddie probably doesn't like him, which wouldn't be surprising given his reputation. This is the first time they have made an effort to spend an hour or two together on their own; though they meet constantly it is always in a Chambers context.

'Before I go any further, Freddie, I want to tell you how much I appreciate all you do for Chambers. The job of Head strikes me as being totally unrewarding in every way – no pay, no thanks, no appreciation. When things are going well we all take the system for granted, when things go wrong we complain like hell without a thought of where you stand. So right out of character, I'm saying thanks for doing such a thankless task so well.'

Freddie is looking surprised, and flushes a little as he smiles. 'How nice of you. I admit, it is a bind sometimes.'

'I'd hate to do it. In fact, I don't think I could – I'm too selfish.'

Freddie fiddles with his bread, eyes down. 'I take it there's no chance you'll ever be in a position to be asked.'

'I made up my mind yesterday to accept the Judgeship – everything was clear, I was happy to have decided. And this morning I'm as far away as I ever was from being sure. I feel ashamed of my vacillation, but there it is. The fact remains, Freddie, I have no one I can discuss it with except you. I can't spread the matter about, I have no wife to talk it over with. I wanted to discuss it with my mother but realized she would urge me to accept and then talk to all her friends about it. The sad thing is, she never knew. Now I regret not telling her – she'd have loved it. Ah, here comes our first course.'

Both men have chosen a fish soup served with rouille and croûtons.

'This smells excellent.'

'Doesn't it. I'm going to insist on a glass of wine to go with it – two glasses of the Sauvignon, Denise.'

'I knew you'd weaken, Mr Warne.' George appears to know the manageress well; Freddie sips his wine while they chat, and when they are alone again asks: 'What made you lose your certainty this morning?'

'Ordinary daily life in Chambers. I love the life, Freddie, and it hit me I'd lose it for good. It suddenly didn't seem wise to give up what I love for what I might well not love at all.'

'I see your point.'

'Some people really want and hope to go on the Bench – for them it's the culmination of their career. But I've never been one of them. I'm flattered I've been asked, of course, and honoured. But it's not what I've been longing for.'

'Turn it down then.'

'Do you really mean that?'

'No, George, I don't. I think you'd be mad. And don't forget how Chambers would bask in the reflected glory of a member going on the Bench.'

'I thought you might say it was my duty to accept.'

'That too. The Lord Chanchellor didn't ask you for fun.'

'I have to let him know today. His minions were aware I had Lena's funeral last weekend and haven't put any pressure on me. But I can't put it off any longer than today.'

'There's another aspect of all this we haven't touched on. It's – well, it's what I call the "if only" syndrome. You love the life of a busy silk and decide not to give it up. But you then might find that once the possibility of switching to a different existence had been permanently extinguished, the life you thought you loved could lose much of its appeal.'

'And I might easily find myself saying, if only . . . Freddie, here comes our turbot – why don't we have another glass of wine with it? Denise—'

'I suggest you have the whole bottle, Mr Warne, instead of messing about. You're paying more for it by the glass.'

'Words of wisdom. Bring the rest of the wine to the table. We don't need to finish it, after all.'

Freddie makes a cheerful helpless gesture, and the bottle is brought. Both men are enjoying each other's company far more than they expected, and both are aware that much depends on today's decision. George raises his full glass and pauses.

'I will admit I had not given thought to the "if only" feeling. And once felt, difficult to eradicate. Could poison the choice whichever way I decided, of course.'

'True. This is very agreeable Sauvignon. I'm glad I have an easy afternoon ahead. I wish drinking at lunchtime didn't feel so sinful – ten years ago I never thought twice about it, did you?'

'Puritanical, healthful, and political, correctness rules us all.'

'Natalie is very strict about it – she says it impairs my sense of judgement as well as making my nose go red. I admit, I sometimes feel a glass at lunchtime can free one's inhibitions about coming to decisions not entirely based on reason.'

'Like the one I'm facing.'

'Could be.'

'Perhaps I should simply toss a coin.'

'That will certainly induce a bad bout of "if only" syndrome.'

They both laugh, and there's an easy silence between them now as they eat.

'How is Nat, by the way?'

'Back at work. Went to Maidstone today on a drugs case.'

'Pneumonia isn't funny.'

'It certainly isn't. She gave me a fright she was so ill.'

'How did she get it?'

'She had flu, ignored it to do a case outside London, broke down driving back and got very cold and wet waiting for the AA in a storm.'

'Bill Sykes said he was very impressed by her when she appeared before him. A natural advocate, he said.'

'She is good.'

'The best of the women in Chambers.'

'Heather Somers wouldn't like to hear you say that.'

'I can't think how she got silk last year. It's almost as incomprehensible as the Lord Chancellor asking me to be a High Court Judge. Mind you, it is whispered that Heather is a cousin of his wife's, which could explain things.'

'Gossip, George, gossip.'

'I know. Don't I love it, and spread it too.'

'You do have that reputation.'

'You think I'm a shit, Freddie, don't you?'

Freddie meets George's eyes, and smiles.

'I'm beginning to think that you like to be thought of as a shit, but are not.'

'I'm selfish, cynical and not very kind. That probably makes me a shit.'

'It sounds like a description of everyone in Chambers. Actually, when I come to think about it, your reputation as a shit is mainly spread about by infinitely greater shits like Francis Bates.'

'Shall we have some more wine? This bottle's finished.'

'Absolutely not, George.'

'You may be right. Coffee, then, for two. Francis needs to think there are plenty of people as unpleasant as he is or he'd be lonely.'

Freddie laughs, and George goes on.

'My reputation hasn't been helped by the fact I can't keep a wife very long. I'm not very good at choosing them. Not that Sarah or Liz was driven out by me in dramatic circumstances – far from it. We parted very amicably – both of them said I neglected them so that they consoled themselves elsewhere. The strange thing is that I feel nothing now for either of them – to the point that I cannot imagine what possessed me to marry them.'

'Perhaps love blinded you.'

'Something certainly did. I thought it was love.'

'It's easy to delude oneself about love. Natalie has opened my eyes to my – my first marriage.' Freddie's voice is low; coffee arrives at this point and he waits, staring at his hands as if they are revealing something. George also waits, wondering what he is about to say, but it never gets said because Freddie suddenly rubs his hands together briskly and changes the subject.

'What do you think about the new junior clerk, by the way?'

'Trevor? He looks a bit like a ferret, and bolts into that clerks' room just like one. But he seems willing enough.'

'He's Douglas's brother's boy.'

'Nepotism on every level from the Lord Chancellor downwards.'

'I must go. Thank you very much for this lunch. I've greatly enjoyed it.' Freddie pushes back his chair and gets to his feet. 'George, you should accept. I think you would always regret it if you didn't.'

'As I probably will if I do.'

'Maybe. But not so much. And a change of career never harmed anyone.'

'I'll ring the Lord Chancellor's Department up as soon as I get back to Chambers. And I will accept, don't worry.' He smiles, all doubt banished. 'The choice is made.'

'You won't regret it.' Freddie raises a hand and hurries out. George sits for a while over another coffee, and thinks about his two marriages as he has not done for ages. Sarah. He knows the superficial reasons why he married her – she was attractive, she was sexy, she was clever, she was fun to start with. He was twenty-seven, beginning to do well at the Bar, and felt he'd like to share his success with a wife. Lena always disliked Sarah, said she was common and that her darling son would rue the day. She purred with righteousness when Sarah went off with an accountant.

But Liz, Liz was inexplicable on any level. He fell in love with her when he met her on a skiing holiday a couple of years after Sarah left him; he would have told anyone else that a holiday romance was not a good basis for a marriage, but he found Liz such a tonic – bubbly, bouncy, always laughing – that he ignored faint doubts. She was freckled, blonde, blue-eyed and wholesome-looking; Lena said she was pretty but her looks wouldn't wear well, and besides, people who laughed all the time had something to hide. In fact Lena was wrong this time – Liz had nothing to hide. Her laughter came from an empty mind; she was incurably stupid. After a couple of years she told George that besides ignoring her, he gave her such an inferiority complex she couldn't bear it any longer and was going back to her first love, who in the meantime had got himself divorced

and was free again. So George too became free again, now
aged thirty-five, and emotionally more or less untouched by
the débâcle of his two marriages. The only woman to touch
his heart since then was – is – Marcia.

'Not once but *twice*? George, it doesn't make sense.'
'I know. I think I liked the thought of being married for the
most selfish of reasons – to have somebody to keep house and
be there when I needed them. I gave very little of myself to
either Sarah or Liz, but Liz was essentially good and I expect
I'd still be enduring a marriage with her if she hadn't been
so dissatisfied with me. They both wanted more than I was
prepared to let them have.'
'Do you blame them?'
'Not at all, Marcia. They had plenty to put up with. They
said I was selfish and they were right, they said I was unkind
and they were also right.'
'Unkind?'
'Kindness doesn't come naturally to me.'
Marcia looked at him, her nearly black eyes assessing him.
'You've been kind to me.'
'I make an effort to hide my lack of it.'
'Kind. It's a funny, squishy word for a squishy quality. Kind –
a little more than kin and less than kind. Kindness for Shakespeare
meant natural, appropriate to the race, as well as kind in the
modern sense.'
'So kindness is appropriate behaviour given one is a
human being. Then if I am not naturally kind it follows
I'm unnatural.'
'That may be logical but I'm not sure it's right. You don't
strike me as unnatural.' She smiled at him. 'Were your parents
kind to you?'
'Not very kind. No, not kind.'
'Mine were overwhelmingly kind. But then I was their
Wunderkind after all.' Marcia laughed, and touched George's
hand lightly. 'I am sorry you had a hard childhood.'
'I didn't say it was hard. I just didn't experience kindness
very often.'
Kind. George stares into his coffee as he remembers this

conversation with Marcia, and lists the people in his youth who were kind. Aunt Cynthia. His uncle. Laura. Peter Dawlish. The list ends.

His mother was not kind, and perhaps the unkindest thing she did was to suppress or withhold information. His aunt's death. Dawlish's letter. Even keeping his real paternity secret could be judged unkind. George looks back at his young self and briefly aches for him.

Once back in Chambers, he looks up the name Dawlish in the telephone directory. To his surprise, there is not a single Dawlish living in London. He then rings Exeter College and is given an address in Gloucestershire which is recent: Dove Farm House, Tirley. They have no phone number listed. George decides to postpone ringing Directory Inquiries until he has made the call he cannot put off any longer.

10 ∫

Marcia enjoys technical rehearsals, tedious though they can be. It is the first walk-through on set in the theatre proper, and the smell of freshly constructed and painted scenery never fails to excite her. Her part in *Ion* is large enough for her to be on stage much of Monday, and when she is not she watches the others from the auditorium to see how they look as they move on set. It is a day of total concentration.

The play is being performed without an interval and lasts just over two hours. There are musical interludes before each entry of the chorus played live by a fiddle, clarinet and percussion from the nearest box. The young composer, Rollo West, has emphasized Greece's proximity to the Middle East in the music, and the chorus has to chant some of their strophes using the appropriate very nasal delivery. The rehearsing of all the entries, complexly lit, plus the extra time needed for the chorus to get used to live musicians rather than a tape, promises to extend the technical rehearsal into a second day.

'Try that exit again, Creusa. You have to hand over the poison as far downstage as possible – move right under that spot. More light, please, just until she's handed the phial over, and then a quick fade. OK. OK. That's better.'

Marcia comes off as the central musical interlude begins: the clarinet wails, strange and reedy, the violin makes a sinister churning, the hand-drums thrum tensely, and the hair rises on her neck as she listens. The music, full of menace, embodies an ancient, irrecoverable past. The chorus starts to chant using an alien sound made in the passages behind the nose which adds further menace to the words.

> *And if her plans miscarry*
> *She will die, killed by the sword*
> *Or strangled by the knotted rope*
> *Pain will make an end of pain.*

The music dies away, the chorus stop their nasal chanting and return to normal speech. Marcia stands frozen in the wings, her mind suddenly invaded by the feeling of broken glass in her hand making the jab into Edward's flesh. How could she have been so vicious? What a risk she took – she might have seriously hurt him. How dangerous. She covers her eyes with her hands. How dangerous.

Mechanical problems prevent the technical rehearsal from finishing on Monday; the entry of the goddess Athena and the last hundred lines or so of the play are postponed to first thing Tuesday morning, to be followed immediately by the dress rehearsal. (Athena was supposed to descend on the back of an owl with spread wings; the owl kept jamming in its progress downwards.) The cast bid goodbye to the technicians who have the air of people in for a long night's work; it's already after seven.

Marcia treats herself to a taxi home, and finds she cannot unlock her own front door. She is so exhausted she has a second try before panic hits her. Edward. He's let himself in and put the blocking lever down on the yale; he's in there, waiting for her. She creeps upstairs, her heart beating hard, and rings the Reids' bell.

'Todd! He's in there again. He's locked himself in. I can't turn the key.'

'But, Marcia, he can't be. Or have you given him the new key already?'

'What new key?'

'Marcia love, you asked me yesterday to change the lock, remember? I did it for you this morning, I put your key in your mail-box downstairs.'

'I didn't look in my mail-box. I'm a fool, Todd, I completely forgot you were going to change the lock. So no one's in there – what a relief, what a relief!'

'Are you all right?'

'Fine now I know why I couldn't get in! Just exhausted and spaced out after the tech. Dress rehearsal tomorrow. I'll be sane again when the show opens.'

'I'll run down and get your key for you.' Todd sets off before she can stop him, and lets her into the flat.

'Todd, you're an angel. Let me know how much I owe you.'

Once she has shut the door she cannot help checking the flat's emptiness. Then she throws her old key away, and while she struggles to thread the new one on her key-ring she listens to her messages. Rosie Amsterdam sounding annoyed; Christina Platt wondering how the rehearsals are going and would Marcia ring her at home this evening; then, after a pause, comes Edward's voice.

'Just to keep you up to date. I lost a lot of blood as a result of your little gesture, and ended up in Casualty having the wound stitched. It is extremely painful. I'd advise you to see a solicitor, because mine says I could take you to court for what you've done to me.'

The tape clicks and stops. Marcia replays it, numb. Then she draws a deep breath, and goes into the kitchen. Tea. Sweet tea. Toast. Scrambled eggs. Sweet tea.

Carefully, she prepares and lays out her food. Matching plate, cup, saucer. Aligned cutlery. Her best oil and vinegar for the small salad she assembles. Eggs done to the exact point when they are still gluey, and piled on to a perfectly browned piece of toast. With slow movements she eats her food, like a thirties advert for missish manners. She sips her tea, made in a pot. She concentrates on the taste of egg, of toast as its crispness wilts under the influence of egg and butter, of the sweet oily sharpness of each piece of lettuce, of tannin marrying with sugar. Her mind she keeps deliberately blank.

The phone rings and her answerphone clicks on. 'Marcia, if you're there pick it up. It's Christina. I need to talk to you. Where are you? I've been trying to reach you for days. Please ring tonight, it doesn't matter if it's late.'

Marcia can't move; she has no will to talk to Christina. The tea in her cup goes cold, her body goes cold, and on she sits until she finds she is shivering. Then she has a hot bath and as she soaks in it her thoughts slip their leashes. Edward – did she really hurt him so badly? One little jab? He would make a great song and dance about it however minor the wound. But loss of blood, pain, stitches. It sounds bad. As for his solicitor, she dismisses that threat – his brother Robert is a solicitor and she can imagine the two of them putting their heads together. Let's give Marcia a fright in return for the fright she's given you. Robert doesn't like her any more than she likes Robert.

Rosie could be annoyed for many reasons but it's also possible Edward went straight round to her last night and she took him to the hospital.

Christina does not have good news either; Marcia knows well enough that if there is good news she always implies it in her messages. She can't stop herself. Good news from Christina is sparse enough to require plenty of exposure. So probably Christina has heard from some helpfully malicious person (Rosie again?) that Marcia has been talking to Sedley Mortimer.

Marcia gets quickly out of the hot bath minutes after she has got into it, and after towelling herself roughly, puts on a bathrobe and rings Rachel.

'I'm sorry I didn't get back to you yesterday.'

'I was only going to say come and have a meal but you'd gone out anyway.'

'Rachel, I need a good sympathetic cheap solicitor.'

'If they're good and sympathetic they're not usually cheap. What for?

'You won't believe this story.'

'I believe anything these days.'

'Rachel, I can hardly believe it myself. But someone tried to rape me in my own flat yesterday, and I stopped him with the help of – of a broken wine-glass. Just a tiny bit of stem stuck out of the base – he'd just broken the glass. Oh, Rachel—'

'My God. You poor thing. Who was it?' There is a pause. 'I can guess. I've always thought Edward might have a violent streak. It was him, wasn't it?'

'Yes, it was Edward. He let himself into the flat while I was out, and then wouldn't leave. I hadn't invited him, I wanted to be on my own and prepare for a really heavy week, the last thing I wanted was champagne and sex. He was randy, he was in the mood, he wouldn't listen. When he started getting rough I was desperate, really frightened. I had to stop him somehow, so I went all limp to fool him and then gave him a jab and ran for it.'

'Marcia, it sounds terrible. The bastard. How bad was the wound?'

'I just pressed the glass into him once, one jab. I had to get him off me.' Marcia can feel tears coming and takes a deep breath.

'Did you get the police?'

'The Reids came down and got him to leave. Todd has changed my lock for me today – they have been marvellous.'

'You ought to report it to the police.'

'But Rachel, how can I? Edward's my boyfriend, or was, they'll just assume it's an argument. And Edward is bound to say I was encouraging him. Which I was in a way, because he loves it if people resist him or get angry with him. When I saw how things were going, I pretended to go with them too. Either way he wins.'

'I see your point. What's happened today?'

'I got back from the technical rehearsal late, and he'd left a message on the answerphone telling me he'd bled a lot, had to have stitches, and was thinking of taking me to court.'

'He's exaggerating, Marcia. He wants you to suffer. He probably never had stitches at all, just a dressing.'

'He said he'd been to hospital.'

'Do you believe him?'

'I don't know.'

'Have you wiped the tape?'

'No.'

'Listen to it again, really carefully. Analyse the intonations like the actress you are. Then ring me back – in the meantime I will go and get the solicitor's number for you.'

Marcia plays the tape three times. The message has been carefully rehearsed, that much becomes clear. Edward is reading it; normally he leaves messages full of hesitations, ums and ahs. There is an intake of breath at the very end as if he is going to say something else, but thinks better of it. The words 'extremely painful' are most unlike him – he'd be more likely to say it bloody well hurts. Cheered, she rings Rachel back.

'He's reading it. It was carefully put together, probably cooked up with his brother Robert, who's a solicitor.'

'Oh, well. You never told me that. Having a lawyer in the family makes you much keener on litigation. Don't destroy the tape, Marcia. It might come in useful. Keep any communication from him. Here's our solicitor's number – he's called Stephen Smith. He's a sweetheart, he's good, but I have to say he's not cheap. But you earn so little you'd probably get legal aid.'

'I won't contact him yet. Edward might let the whole thing drop.'

'Don't kid yourself, Marcia. You've hurt him and you've hurt his pride. He won't let it drop.'

'He could do me so much damage. He knows so many people. I feel sick when I think what he could do.'

'Don't think about Edward. Hang on to the play, give it your best, bury yourself in it and forget him for the moment. And you may be right – when his bum stops hurting he might forget it too! I can't help feeling pleased you gave him something to think about.'

'I shouldn't have attacked him with glass. I could have reached for the bedside lamp—'

'And risked killing him – I'm glad you didn't. I'm also glad you've changed the lock already, but if you want to come and stay here for a few days while Edward simmers down, you're welcome.'

'I'll be all right, Rachel. You don't want me around if you can help it this week – I'm subhuman at the moment and my hours are very antisocial once the run starts.'

'The offer stands anyway.'

'You've made me feel so much better. What would I do without you!'

'Survive. You're a survivor. It runs in your family.'

Ten minutes later the phone rings again, and this time it's Rosie.

'Why haven't you rung me back, you horrible woman? You've

been on the phone for ages to someone else. I've been trying to get through.'

'Rosie, I owe you a huge apology for leaving your party so early in such a bad mood—'

'Oh forget that. I didn't mind – if people don't feel sociable who am I to insist they should ruin it for everyone else? No, I wanted you to give me the update on Edward. He arrived on my doorstep yesterday pouring blood – said you'd cut him with a piece of glass.'

'Didn't you believe him?'

'Well, I didn't at first, I have to admit—'

'How bad was it, Rosie?'

'If you did it you ought to know.'

'I don't, so that's why I'm asking you.'

'Did you do it or didn't you? I'm getting confused now.'

'Did you take him to hospital?'

'Look, Marcia, this conversation is crazy. I'm telling you I know nothing beyond the fact he arrived here bleeding, said you'd done it, then Fenella – do you know Fenella Alberti? No? I thought you did – well, she happened to be here and she immediately whisked Edward away to have it seen to and I've not heard a word since from either of them. They've both got their answerphones on, as you had. I was getting worried.'

'So she might have taken him to a Casualty Outpatients somewhere.'

'Very likely. Is he all right? He seemed to be in a lot of pain. What on earth happened? He said it was an unprovoked attack. That's the bit I don't believe.'

Marcia knows that whatever she tells Rosie will be round London within hours, and hesitates.

'Well, did you attack him or didn't you?'

'Rosie, I hate to say it, but it's none of your business. As soon as I find out about how Edward is I'll let you know.'

'Sez you. Don't call me, I'll call you. You've got something to hide, Marcia, I can tell. Don't you want the truth to go round London rather than gossip?'

'I don't want anything to go round. Please keep it to yourself.'

'Heavens, I've just seen the time. I should have been at

Mervyn's place half an hour ago. Don't forget to ring when you hear how the great man is.'

'Goodbye, Rosie. You're going to get wet. It's just started to bucket down.'

A night of rain has washed London clean, and Marcia strides along the pavement to the Tube. The sky is clear, late leaves are falling, a milk-float rattles by, high heels tap on the opposite pavement. Marcia is wearing jeans, loafers, a heavy polo neck and an old donkey jacket. She has put her hair into a beret, and has no makeup on. The flower-seller at the corner of the station doesn't recognize her this morning. Marcia likes to go undercover during a show – anonymity is a comfort. Not that she expects any publicity yet, though there has been a piece in the *Guardian* about John Alsopp; it is just that when she is immersed in another character, she needs her own public persona to be as invisible and anonymous as possible. It is easier to shed this nondescript exterior to become Creusa.

As she waits on the crowded Underground platform, she takes George's letter out of her pocket and re-reads it.

It was lovely to see you at the funeral. Your red coat and your face transformed the church and turned the day around for me. Thank you for coming. I rang you yesterday to say all that and to tell you I was coming to see Ion *Saturday. Since I couldn't speak to you, writing this note seemed better. Can you come out for supper with me after the show?*

George's handwriting gives an impression of speed – there is a rushing to the right in the forward-leaning downstrokes and jet trails of ink between the words. Edward's writing is angular, spiky and disconnected, though the overall effect on a page is very attractive; her own is rounded and rather continental in feel – people have asked her if she was educated abroad.

The train arrives, she tucks her letter away and squashes herself in a corner of a carriage, and thinks of nothing much as she endures the journey.

*   *   *

'What have you been up to, Marcia?' Suzanne is in the dressing-room they share, eating a bacon buttie.

'What do you mean?'

'Everyone's saying you did a Bobbitt on Edward and tried to cut off his willy!'

Marcia throws her beret in the air and laughs. 'Oh false and wicked gossip!'

'I didn't believe a word of it, Marcia—'

'But you wouldn't have put it past me.'

'I wouldn't put it past any woman in desperate circumstances. So did something happen?'

'Nothing.'

'Why the rumours then?'

'Rumours start from nothing.'

'Do stop sounding like King Lear, Marcia.'

The five-minute call comes over the Tannoy for Miss Fleckner, Mr Frapp, Mr Obula, Miss Baker and the Chorus.

'Hurry up, Suzanne. The tech's about to start.'

'I'm going to finish my buttie. Two more bites.'

'So who's been spreading this wicked rumour?'

'It came to me via Penelope who'd heard it via someone with a name like a city.'

'Rosie Amsterdam.'

'That's it. Funny name.'

'Being named after a city adds allure. Think of Rosa Luxembourg, Jack London.' They start down the stairs.

'Irving Berlin. Isaiah Berlin.'

'Vittoria de Los Angeles.'

'Perhaps you ought to call yourself Marcia Madrid.'

'Right now I feel more like Marcia Maidstone. Or Macclesfield.'

They chatter on, but Marcia knows that Suzanne hasn't stopped wondering what happened to Edward.

The machinery works beautifully, the goddess Athena descends in her owl chariot without mishap. It takes about an hour to satisfy John Alsopp on the right levels of lighting, and the exact timing and balance of the music. He looks exhausted, but every director Marcia has ever worked with always is by this stage of proceedings. He comes up to her and Damian Frapp as they are about to hurry off to get into their costumes for the full dress rehearsal.

'I still feel unhappy about your last sentence, Damian.'

'*I take my honourable and just possession.*'

'The trouble is you don't think it's very honourable or just. I'm beginning to think we ought to go back to our first idea, and follow the editor that gives that line to Creusa.'

Damian nods. 'I'm the one who's been asking whether Apollo's oracles are truth or lies.'

'Quite. So you say it, Creusa, as the happy mother. You're ecstatic, after all – the god has told you you will have two more sons.'

'It'll change the feeling of the end.'

'I'll bring in the music earlier, so that you speak over it. Let's try that, Rollo. Change the music cue to "Come my son." Take it as slow as you can, so that what you've written lasts over the chorus to the end.'

They run through it and the music finishes too early. They move the cue until the timing is right; the musicians are looking as restless as Marcia feels by now. She knows her customary nervous diarrhoea is coming on; it usually starts after the dress rehearsal, but this time it's early. Her first-night nerves have always taken this form; it is as if the muscles of her bowels echo the tension in her brain. She takes some Imodium, and begins to dress.

Her costume is traditional and hieratic, in keeping with Alsopp's approach to the play. Her chiton is of a heavy red fabric with a black and gold key pattern along the edges and the hem, belted with an intricately twisted golden silk girdle; over it is a diagonal cloak fastened on her right shoulder with a row of jewelled buttons. It is also of red, with bands of gold. Her wig is made of long black hair bound and twisted into ringlets and plaited with stiff gold braid in a complex manner that reminds Marcia of Egyptian statues; a flat embroidered and jewelled pillbox of a hat crowns it. The whole headdress is heavy, as is the costume.

Marcia's face with its sharp cheekbones looks thoroughly foreign beneath the headdress; she extends her already long eyebrows in a curve and accentuates the shape of her eyes into an oval. She stares at herself: she saw faces like this in the British Museum. Suzanne stands behind her, helping her adjust the headdress to its least uncomfortable position, her eyes crossed with concentration as she adjusts ringlets and plaits. Then she looks up and stares at Marcia's reflection so that their eyes meet in the mirror.

'How well that suits you, Marcia. It's so right for your face. Or your face is so right for it. Is your family from that part of the world originally?'

'Not as far as I know. But Jews come from everywhere.'

'Well, it looks fantastic. It's got a funny smell, but that's probably all the adhesive and stuff they used.'

'It almost smells of rosemary.'

'Very appropriate.'

Jacynth, wardrobe assistant, comes in at that moment; she's wearing a smock covered with pockets, all of them full of implements and things she constantly needs. Scissors dangle on chains. She clatters as she moves, and Marcia half expects her little scraped-up bun of hair to double as a pincushion.

'How is it?'

'If you could tie a couple of these ringlets back it would be perfect.'

'No problem.' Jacynth whips off the headdress and crouches over it, busy with fingers and threads.

Marcia's own hair is flat on her head, squashed down by a cap made of an old pair of tights. She swirls round the dressing-room in her costume, testing its weight. Some costumes are easy to wear, others demand a shift of attitude and deportment to look good on stage, and Marcia needs to move with a gliding, controlled movement, sinuous but regal, for the heavy folds to look at their best.

'Not another problem with the headdresses?' John Alsopp is standing in the doorway, watching her. Jacynth straightens up at once.

'No – a tweak. It's done.' She puts the headdress back on to Marcia and bustles away. Alsopp gazes at Marcia.

'Yes. Your father was a king, you're Queen of Athens. You may be off duty on a pilgrimage but it's no more off duty than Princess Anne would be if she decided to go to Lourdes. Forget the memory of your teenage indiscretion with the god Apollo. I want your arrival at the shrine to be like a semi-official visit. There you are, a queen in full panoply. You've come the long journey from Athens in a litter lined with cloth of gold, carried by eight sweating athletes.'

'Over the top, Alsopp,' murmurs Suzanne, but if he heard he takes no notice.

'So when the audience sees you return after you've been sentenced to death, and you're only in your chiton with a simple wig, no big headdress, it's a big statement. What do you think of the set, by the way?'

'It's terrific.'

'Robin Klee has achieved exactly the effect I wanted. Don't you love the way the statue of the god in his colonnaded inner sanctum is so big you can only see up to his knees until the whole front of the temple splits open at the end! If I could bring in the smell of the roasting sacrifices and libations poured over the flames I would – we'll just have to make do with smoke. But Robin has got right away from the white marble purity of the usual Greek set – colour and barbarity instead.' He comes forward and kisses Marcia. 'As for you, you look fantastic, darling Marcia. And you are wonderful to work with.' His kiss smells of toothpaste, and there's fresh shaving soap in his ear. 'I can't think why we haven't worked together before.'

Because you're top of the tree, dear John, and I'm not.

'I'm glad you like the costume.'

'I just adore it. And the headdress. Xuthus's outfit hasn't worked so well for some reason. Andrew isn't very happy – says he feels a bit of a prat in it.'

And not very wise to tell you that. At that moment the five-minute call for beginners comes over the Tannoy system, and Alsopp races away to take his place in the auditorium. Andrew comes in when he's gone.

'I feel like a baby in nappies made of felt, and this bloody thing on my head is an instrument of torture.'

'Oh, Andrew.' He does indeed look a bit ridiculous. His face is pink with irritation, and he's still wearing his own socks and shoes.

'The sandals they made me don't bloody fit either. I could kill that designer – chop him up in little bits and sacrifice him on the altar of Trophonius.' Jacynth appears behind him and puts her arms round him.

'I'll take those extra bits off the wig and make it easier to wear.'

'That won't be difficult. I've never worn anything so effing uncomfortable in my life.'

'Come with Auntie Jacynth, there's a good boy.'

Marcia sits at her dressing-table waiting for the two-minute call. She breathes deeply, shuts her eyes. She needs to make her entrance ready to weep silent tears at the sight of Apollo's Temple at Delphi. She thinks of her mother, of that photograph of her breastfeeding, and by the time she is in the wings her tears are ready to fall.

Marcia sees Edward three times on the way home, and runs in panic from the sight of him.

'Rachel, I know it wasn't really him, just someone like him, but by the time I got home I was in such a state I'm beginning to think I will come and stay a few days.'

'I told you, you're welcome.' Simon is shouting stupid cow at Judith in the background, whose more distant voice screams back. 'Stop it, children. I can't hear myself think. Look, Marcia, let me ring you back when they've had their supper and gone for baths.' As she puts down the phone, Judith starts crying. Marcia begins to have an inkling of what life with the Kleins might entail, and decides she is being ridiculous. Paranoid.

She rings Christina, whose number is engaged. She rings George and finds he is out. 'We seem fated to communicate by answerphone. It's Marcia, just to thank you for your letter and say yes, I'd love to have dinner with you after the performance on Saturday. Come to my dressing-room or would you rather meet at the stage door?' She nearly adds she might need some professional advice but caution prevails. Then she lies down on the sofa feeling as if her whole life is kept taut by telephone wires, as if they pour from her fingers like Strewel Peter's fearsome fingernails and are wound round her body with every call she makes.

The phone rings.

'Marcia? It's Rosie. What's the news on Edward?'

'I have no idea and right now I don't care. Ring him yourself, not that it's any of your business.'

'What a lovely mood we're in. Goodbye.'

Marcia pours herself a whisky and pulls the telephone jack out of its socket so that she can't be rude to anyone else. With a slight sense of impending doom which she puts down to the first preview tomorrow, she switches on the television and passes the evening being mindlessly entertained.

'Is it possible to speak to Peter Dawlish?'

'It is possible but not advisable at the moment.' The woman answering has the clipped, precise voice of an academic.

'Ah.'

'He is in his eyrie, and I get no thanks for disturbing him.'

'I see.'

'Who is speaking, please?'

'Well, if it's the right Peter Dawlish, I'm a pupil of his from the past.'

'Unlikely to be the right one, since he doesn't teach.'

George is sorely tempted to give up on this unfruitful conversation.

'When he taught me he had just come down from Oxford. Perhaps the experience put him off teaching for the rest of his life.'

'Very likely. When was this?'

'About 1954.'

'Well before my time.' There is a silence. In the background George can hear the whirring sound of a busy household machine.

'Perhaps I may leave my name and details so that he can contact me if he wishes?'

'And if he's the right Peter Dawlish.'

'Quite.' George gives his home address and telephone number. The woman is so uncommunicative he is about to ring off, when she surprises him.

'Mr Warne, you can't have searched my husband out just for fun. Can I give him an inkling of what this is about?'

'It's about a debt.'

'Oh dear.'

'A debt I owe him. He opened crucial doors for me, and I'd like to thank him.'

'This is all very mysterious. I'm sure he'll be in touch with you out of sheer curiosity. Goodbye.'

George sits there half-wishing he had not made the call. But Peter Dawlish, if he is indeed the right one, will most likely have forgotten all about the twitchy fair-haired boy he once taught, and ignore it.

George finds himself in a strange and lonely limbo this Tuesday; his appointment to see the Lord Chancellor is first thing on Wednesday morning, after which he will be able at last to talk to his clerk about his future. The Feathers case will have to be returned: Douglas worked hard to secure that for him and might feel aggrieved. Perhaps Freddie could do it; it would be good to keep the case in Chambers. George sighs, and picks up a file. He has an opinion to write on a dispute over a complex claim repudiated by a big national insurance company which is raising interesting points of law. He has been mulling over the issue for some time, in fact since before Lena's death, and it is now completely clear to him. He takes up his dictaphone and records his opinion quickly and almost without hesitations, and decides to take it down to Jenny for typing himself.

He passes Francis Bates on the stairs, who notices the small cassette in George's hand. 'Still not using a word-processor, George? You should – you wouldn't have to chase after typists who can't spell. My printer turns out a perfect document – I haven't needed to use the pool for years, which also saves money.'

'It's sheer terror of failing, Francis.'

Francis's wily eyes go blank. 'Failing?'

'If I couldn't learn to touch-type at the speed I dictate, it wouldn't be worth all the hassle of setting myself up with a computer.'

'Well, you do need to practise—'

'Do you touch-type?'

'Actually no, but I'm a demon with two fingers and thumbs.'

'Failure, Francis. You should learn to touch-type.'

Pleased with this exchange, George bounces on down to Jenny's little room which she shares with the fees clerk. He is tired of being patronized by the computer-users, now the majority of Chambers.

'Jenny, you wonderful person—'

'What is it you're after then, Mr Warne?'

'I'm after you typing this opinion this very morning, if you would be so kind. It's super-urgent.'

'And what is Mr Mentieth going to say if I don't do his work next?' She's smiling at George; he's the only member of Chambers who can accurately mimic her Irish accent.

'You leave Mr Mentieth to me.'

He finds Freddie between meetings, and fetches them both a coffee from the dispenser.

'I'm glad you don't use a word-processor, Freddie. It seems we're both Luddites.'

'I'm not really – I can use one a bit, but I don't want to be shown up by Nat who of course is a dab hand.'

'It is the business of the wealthy man
To give employment to the artisan.'

'George, that's not very politically correct these days.'

'I have no interest whatever in being politically correct.'

'Nor have I, but being Head of Chambers has rather forced it upon me. But I take it you haven't come simply to tell me you've jumped Jenny's queue?'

'I'm seeing the Lord Chancellor tomorrow morning.'

'Congratulations.' Freddie's pleasure is genuine; his manner towards George has subtly changed since their lunch together.

'It's not in the bag, Freddie – don't forget I have to have a medical.'

'You're pretty fit, aren't you? You look it.'

'I feel it. But you never know – they may discover horrible things like high blood pressure and cholesterol levels. I eat well, I drink too much, and I don't take enough exercise.'

'That applies to most of us. But I'd say you had nothing to worry about. By the way, do you mind if I tell Nat about it? She's good at keeping her counsel.'

'Tell her, tell her. And of course after tomorrow I can tell Douglas. I don't get the impression he has any suspicions.'

Freddie smiles. 'Never underestimate Douglas Dean's inscrutability. Avoid talking to him about anything today, or he'll guess.'

'I'm sure he puts down my slightly odd behaviour entirely to the stress of my mother's death.'

'Don't count on that. He probably knows precisely what is going on – his antennae are uncannily sensitive. But he'll never say a word – I wish some members of Chambers were as discreet as he is. There can't be many senior clerks you could say that about.'

'He's certainly one aspect of life I'm going to miss – Douglas looking as discreetly impeccable as a permanent secretary.'

'In another life, with the full benefit of education, a high-up civil servant is exactly what he could have been.'

'I'll leave you in peace, Freddie. I've wasted enough of your time this week already. You've been very patient with my shilly-shallying.'

'It hasn't been wasted.' Freddie fiddles with the cap of his fountain-pen. 'We have got to know each other. A pity we didn't do it sooner. You—' He stops.

'I made it difficult by playing the role of professional shit so successfully. It's so easy for me I really must be a bit of a shit.'

As both laugh the telephone rings on Freddie's desk.

'You and Nat must come to dinner with me at Hereford Square.'

'We'd love that.'

'You might not love my pictures.'

As George goes down the staircase he wonders how Marcia would get on with the Mentieths. She'd surely like Nat – he stops on the stair as he hears Francis Bates's voice out of sight below him.

'George has got the Feathers case. Simon was rather hoping for a junior brief in it, but no go. There's probably a good reason for it – the solicitor wants someone else to do it – but George is not one to push the boat out for the rest of Chambers.'

'You really don't like him, do you?'

'He's the most selfish bastard in our set, and that's saying quite a lot.'

'I don't dislike him.'

Their voices die away, and George goes quickly down when he is sure they have not stopped at the clerks' room. I don't dislike him. Patricia's cool tone is more distressing than any of Francis's bitter remarks. She was non-committal, without emotion, despite the recent advice he'd given her about that case. Indifferent. It hurts.

George goes straight from Chambers to a Bar Council committee meeting on racial equality. He sits quietly during the topic under discussion – exclusive language – which normally would have provoked him into plenty of comment. He has no energy today, and this is a committee he will be leaving the moment his appointment is announced. He also feels his habitual sense of being alone in a crowd: everyone else seems to be so sure of what other human beings need and believe while he can barely guess what goes on in their brains. He puts this down to his impenetrable skin and lack of ordinary family life. Without exception everyone else on the committee appears to have partners, children, wide experience. He can't help feeling slightly inadequate. Helen Watts QC, in the chair, comments afterwards on his silence.

'Splitting headache, Helen. Couldn't think of anything useful to add.'

'Hope it isn't the flu. There's a particularly virulent strain going about. What did you think of the Lord Chief's statement?'

'He's getting very adept at sitting on the fence without appearing to.'

'Oh, did you think so? Pity you didn't say so. It might have livened up a bland discussion. Ah, Stanley, just the person I wanted to see to thank you for all your hard work—'

George slips out and queue-jumps for a taxi, hopping into one as an annoyed young man comes pounding up.

'He's not best pleased.'

'Guv, I pick up the person who catches my eye first. You

caught my eye – end of story. The peckin' order is for the punters to worry about. So where to?'

'Hereford Square.'

'Sometimes they get to fightin' and I leaves them to it. On a wet night they got murder in their eyes. Hereford Square? I was born in Hereford. Bleedin' borin' place. Give me London any day.'

His house smells musty. His current cleaner, a myopic thin woman called Michelle Masters, with whom he communicates by note, is less and less effective, unless he happens to be working at home when she comes to clean. Then surfaces shine and carpets stop smelling of dust. Michelle sings tunelessly while she works, and he wonders if the singing happens when she is alone. He opens the notebook they write in.

Dear Mr Warne, the sink is blocked again and I can't seem to shift it. Plus one of your studs went down that crack near your dressing table. Really sorry.

Can't come next week, got to take my Dad to the hospital. All the best, Michelle.

Michelle lets him down every six weeks or so, alternating the excuse between schools, clinics, hospitals. George sighs, and notices a line of dust along the wainscot. He switches on his answerphone as he goes through his mail. Laura's voice comes on first, thanking him for all his kind hospitality and hoping he will visit them at the farm one day, then a junior barrister to discuss a case on its way to the Court of Appeal, and then comes Marcia's voice. He replays her message, delighted she's agreed to dine with him after the show. Her tones are warm – more like the old days.

The final message, which must have arrived minutes before his return, is from his first wife, Sarah. 'George, so sorry to hear about Lena. I didn't know she'd died or I would have been in touch sooner. Someone has just sent me the death announcement. I hope I haven't missed the funeral – I was very fond of your mother and I'd like to pay my respects. You could have told me she'd died. Hope you're OK. It's a long time since I heard any news.'

A familiar plaintive sourness surfaces in her last remarks; George wipes all his messages and goes to change into old clothes before he tries to clear the sink. After he applies soda crystals and boiling water in copious amounts, there is a satisfying gurgle as the water begins to flow again. He watches the anti-clockwise swirl of disappearing water and thinks of his meeting with the Lord Chancellor the following morning.

The evening begins to feel quietly momentous. It reminds him of the eve of his first marriage, when a more comprehensive version of the same feeling filled him: hope, dread, anticipation, apprehension, but with a sense of new beginnings, new life uppermost. And of Sarah in her blue linen suit exactly matching her eyes, her laughter and ebullience outside the Registry Office. (She had refused to get married in church, much to Lena's disappointment.) He had taken her hands as they waited their turn to go in and laughed too: everything was possible, even happiness.

When the rings were exchanged, Sarah had winked at him: an inappropriate, knowing wink which turned a small part of him cold. *You're mine now – think of the fun I will have. Sex and money.* That wink lay like a cold coin against his heart, marking the moment when the new marriage, seconds old, had begun to end. Not that he allowed himself to acknowledge this: he continued to live with the signs that all was not well because he believed in the binding nature of the wedding contract, also because of Lena's antagonism towards Sarah. Then Sarah went off with her lover and the wink resurfaced.

George has occasionally noticed reports of bridegrooms and brides walking out on each other at the reception or on the honeymoon: he wonders whether fear or honesty drove them to it so soon after they had irrevocably committed themselves. And in his case, will that cold coin return again tomorrow, when he has said yes to the Lord Chancellor and shaken hands on it?

Since he cannot dispel the momentous feeling, he decides to celebrate it. First he looks out a fine bottle of wine: he knows he has several single bottles of excellent claret that he has not drunk because it never seems the right occasion. There is a 1947 Chateau Beychevelle which he fears might be undrinkable by now, but if it is not, then he will never drink finer wine. (He found the bottle in Geoffrey's cellar and stopped Lena throwing it out as too old to keep.) He puts the bottle out on the kitchen table, and as there is no food in the fridge, goes round the corner to his local food shop. He buys a pot of lumpfish roe, lamb chops, some courgettes, a fine bunch of grapes, a piece of ripe Pont l'Evêque, and some granary rolls.

When he gets back he stares at the narrow-necked bottle, at the elegant label, at the thin coating of dust. He won't open it yet: old wine can lose its taste and bouquet in minutes and he wants to be poised to catch what he can. He puts the chops on to bake with potatoes and garlic, and takes a glass of mineral water to his study; he's decided to sort through some more of Lena's letters while he waits for the food to cook.

He picks up the bundle from Aunt Cynthia, and takes out one of the most recent, written the spring before she died.

Yes, of course Jebs can come for the summer as usual – whatever made you think we didn't want him? He's part of our family – how could he be otherwise? This is his home from home, and I hope he will always find it so. And I can tell you, Lena, he's no trouble, unlike the girls. Sophie's latest effort is to announce she wants to leave school at sixteen and become an air hostess. She says she's tired of being a schoolgirl and wants a glamorous life! I ask you. Julian says she must stay on for two more years or he'll stop supporting her.

They're always arguing, those two. Oh the pleasures of parenthood!

His aunt's pleasant rounded handwriting hurrying over the bright blue Basildon Bond paper she liked to use brings back her kind voice. Pondering without rancour on what small betrayal lay behind her opening protestation, he looks at a couple of other letters from her, one about a small family inheritance, another thanking Lena for Christmas presents. All the letters arise from specific family business – there is no sign of a proper correspondence between the sisters, an outpouring of their hearts. Lena's only regular correspondent of any depth was a schoolfriend in Carlisle called Susan Beresford, who wrote a summary of her year each December, and clearly Lena did the same in return. They kept it up throughout the postwar years until George saw written on the last letter 'Susan dead' across the top.

George does not re-read the letter from Peter Dawlish but puts it away with all the others and then makes his way down to the kitchen. The telephone rings as he reached the hall, and he has the premonition it will be Dawlish himself. He is right.

'George Warne?'

'Speaking.'

'Peter Dawlish here. Are you the George Warne of Roddick Manor days?'

'I am.'

'Well, well. My all-too-brief spell as a schoolmaster.' Dawlish laughs.

George doesn't find the voice at all familiar, but the laugh is – a low-pitched, wheezing laugh. He remembers Dawlish laughing excitedly at the revels round the village bonfire all those years ago.

'Well, what has happened to you, George, since we last met? What have you spent the last thirty years doing?'

'I'm a barrister.'

'Are you. Are you. A lot of money in the law, they say.'

'And you, what did you do after the teaching?'

'A hundred different things. A full life.'

'You were a very good teacher, you know.'

'Not according to those creeps who ran Roddick Manor.'

'You were the only teacher ever to inspire me.'

'I think you must be muddling me up with someone else. I was only there for a year.'

'Not at all.' George finds the 'sir' nearly slips out. 'It was you.'

Dawlish laughs again, then coughs, a racking smoker's cough. When he gets his breath back, he says, 'My wife mentioned a debt.'

'Well, that's the debt I owe you. You came along just when I needed someone to wake my brain up, and you woke it up in a hundred different ways. Do you remember those trips to London?'

'I can't say I do.'

'You took a few of us to a gallery in Bond Street and then we had a spaghetti in a place called Paradiso – I've never forgotten it – Italian restaurants were the latest thing and the English had only just begun to realize that spaghetti didn't come out of tins. I'm not sure we didn't drink wine from a raffia-covered flask.'

'Banana juice. Dreadful stuff that early Chianti was. The Italians assumed we wouldn't know the difference.'

'They were right.'

'I don't recall any trips to London. But I do remember curious goings-on at a local bonfire night – did I go to that with you?'

'You did. You held forth about the Green Knight and the wild men of the wood.'

'Did I really! I'm not surprised they chucked me out – I was clearly seen as Bad Influence on the Boys. Teaching you to smoke and wicked things like that.' George can hear him lighting up a cigarette and drawing deeply on it.

'I used to pray you'd last until I'd sat my Oxford entrance exam, and you did. And I got in.'

'I remember you! Got it. Blond, lanky. You always looked miserable.'

'I was.'

'Yes, I remember you perfectly now. And you had a rather ritzy-looking mother. Yes.' There's a pause, during which George wants to mention the missed trip to Italy but does not know how to broach it. Then Dawlish starts coughing again, this time for longer. Eventually he wheezes, 'Look, I'm frightfully sorry, but I'll have to cut this short.'

'Can I ring you again sometime, and perhaps we could meet when you're next in London?'

'My dear fellow, you may wait years.' His voice is a squeezed whisper.

'I'm sometimes in Gloucestershire – perhaps I could drop in if I'm passing?'

Whether or not this is welcome George can't tell, because the next coughing fit is so extreme Dawlish has to end the call. But contact has been made. Elated, George opens the bottle of claret and enjoys every magic drop.

*　　*　　*

ACTRESS STABS LOVER WITH BROKEN BOTTLE. George, sitting in taxi next morning, sees this headline in the column of short news items in *The Times.* He has read the first sentence before the full weight of it reaches his brain.

Marcia Fleckner, about to open in John Alsopp's eagerly awaited production of Ion *at the New Fortune Theatre, attacked opera-director Edward Wintlesham with a broken bottle on Sunday night, giving him a wound that needed several stitches.*

George shuts his eyes and reads the sentence again in case he has mistaken Marcia's name. But there it is, linked with Wintlesham's in this gory snippet. He tells himself the press get everything wrong. It is unbelievable that Marcia would attack anyone with anything, let alone a broken bottle. There must be some mistake. There definitely must be some mistake.

He shoves the newspaper into his briefcase. His hands are shaking, but he puts this down to nerves about the interview ahead of him. The taxi is drawing up a couple of hundred yards short of the House of Lords; as he gets out he sees the time on Big Ben and realizes he's twenty minutes early.

He goes into the gardens that lie alongside the river between Lambeth Bridge and the House of Lords and strides across the grass to the Embankment. The wind shakes the tall plane trees hanging over the water, and ruffles the surface of the river. High tide. Feeling deadened, he stares at a row of barges sliding past, at the squat red-brick buildings of Lambeth Palace opposite, at the clouds rushing across the clear blue sky. Gulls wheel and cry as they circle above the barges, waiting for pickings; there's a strong smell of river water, not unpleasant. The windows of St Thomas's Hospital glitter in the sun.

Edward Wintlesham. He didn't know Marcia even knew him. He has seen a couple of Wintlesham's provocative productions and found them wrongheaded – Verdi in modern battledress, Mozart in an aircraft hangar. He's also seen Wintlesham on a late-night talk show and found him arrogant and humourless. But attractive – dark, tall, probably Jewish.

All the hurt of his rejection by Marcia surfaces as he stares at the gliding water. He thought his pain was dead, and he finds instead it was simply hidden.

Big Ben strikes ten, the sound bouncing off the water. A barge hoots as if in reply, gulls screech as they attack a package thrown in the river, a police siren wails down a nearby street. George walks out of the park and into the House of Lords.

12 ∫

Marcia wakes late and refreshed, having slept well. She has no pressures today; until she goes to the theatre for the preview, her time is her own. She breakfasts in bed with the sun shining through the window on to her face, she reads a recent copy of *The Stage* from cover to cover. There's an article about John Alsopp. A sentence catches her eye.

> *Alsopp is the most rigorous of directors, insisting that the cast do as much research as possible into the background of the play – he says he would have taken them all to Athens and Delphi had the budget permitted.*

Marcia thinks guiltily of her one rather late visit to the British Museum, and her scrappy reading. All her research skills seem to have atrophied, and she's read so little recently. Life with Edward has been such a rush . . .

Edward. She must ring him and see how he is. Later. Perhaps not today; she is afraid of upsetting him and of being upset – she needs no emotional distractions until the play has opened properly and the press night is past. But she should ring him anyway, find out how he is. The post has brought nothing from him; surely he's thought better of his threat?

The sun emerges from a cloud and dazzles her again. She shuts her eyes and thinks about the day ahead. I'm going to make a dress today, that's what I'm going to do, stay at home and make a dress for the last-night party.

Marcia is an inspired, quixotic maker of the occasional dress – she collects luscious fabrics and lets them sit in drawers for years, until mood and inspiration strike at the same moment and and she will construct a party dress. She pulls long-forgotten pieces of material out of their hiding-places and throws them all over the bed. Somewhere she has a piece of dark green crushed velvet she craves to use. She finds it at last, strokes it, drapes it over her arm, pleased that it is even more silky and beautiful than she remembers.

She takes her sewing-machine out of its case and searches through a collection of reels of thread she keeps in a biscuit tin. Dark green is a colour she's sewed before, and she finds what she needs. Absorbed now, she cuts a pattern from newspaper and begins work on the fabric. She has no distractions; the phone is mercifully silent, the street is quiet. Time passes so quickly she realizes with a shock it's afternoon and she must leave soon for the theatre. She hangs up her half-finished dress – bias-cut body, long sleeves – and quickly eats some bread and cheese as she gets ready.

Feeling at peace, restored, even content, she makes her way to the theatre wearing her usual drab disguise, her hair scraped back into a black beret, her glasses on. There's a crowd of press and photographers outside the stage door, and she pushes past them unrecognized. Willie the doorman grabs her as she signs in.

'Miss Fleckner, where have you been? Everyone's been trying to contact you today. Your phone's disconnected – I've got a dozen messages for you. It's been a madhouse here.'

'What is all this, Willie? Why is everyone looking for me?' Her well-being is immediately dispelled by his staring eyes.

'Oh dear dear me. So you haven't seen this?'

LOVER GETS THE BUM'S RUSH – OF BLOOD.
Actress Marcia Fleckner injured her lover Edward Wintlesham on Sunday . . .

Marcia pushes the tabloid back at Willie and puts her hands over her eyes.

'Oh, Willie.'

'I couldn't get through to you.'

'I unplugged the phone last night and forgot I had. I haven't been out at all today. Look, Willie, for God's sake don't let the rat-pack know I'm here, and don't let anyone, anyone at all, in after the performance.'

'But is it true you attacked Mr Wintlesham?'

'No comment, Willie. Tell everyone that. Marcia Fleckner has nothing to say.'

'The Press get everything wrong, we all know that. Still, look on the bright side – all publicity's good publicity.' Willie goes back to his cubby-hole whistling as Marcia bolts upstairs to her dressing-room. Suzanne's already in there getting ready. Marcia bursts into tears.

'Marcia, come here. Have a cuddle. What a bloody old mess!'

'It was a bit bloody.' Marcia's tears turn into hysterical laughter as she pulls away from Suzanne and falls into her chair. 'The bastard must have told the Press.'

'So you did do it!'

'Not a Bobbitt, as you all seem to think.'

'No, that was only the rumour yesterday. Now all the papers say is that you attacked him with a broken bottle – here's *The Times* and the *Independent* . . .'

'It was a piece of a broken wine-glass – the base. I can't take all this publicity in, Suzanne. It's ridiculous.'

'Don't be naive, Marcia. It's hot news. Top director has his bottom sliced by well-known actress while indulging in heavy sex session – perfect stuff for the rat-pack.'

'We weren't having sex, I was trying to fight Edward off.'

'They don't care. Don't give them any more details – whatever you say you will be shown as a sado-masochist or whatever.'

'Edward's the sado-masochist. Suzanne, what the hell am I going to do? Who informed the Press if it wasn't him? Yet I somehow don't think it could have been him – he despises the gutter Press, and is very unlikely to give them any statement about his private life.' She is going through the messages given her by Willie, and finds one with Edward's writing on it.

'Perhaps he's after vengeance.'

'He's certainly after vengeance, but not that way. Listen to this.

Dear Marcia,
I can't believe you would have been so unwise as to talk to the Press
about my injury. But I can see that somebody has, so I am refusing
to give any statements, and advise you to keep quiet too. A letter is
on its way to you from my solicitors, Peel, Cross and Thorogood.
Edward.'

'Marcia, this is getting serious.'
'His brother is a solicitor with that firm. Edward's just trying
to frighten me.'
'But did you hurt him badly?'
'I didn't think it was more than a small cut, not very deep,
though he told me it needed stitches. I should have rung him
today and found out how he was. I – I was too much of a
coward. Oh God. Why didn't I ring? I've been in a fool's
paradise all day.'
'Who has told the press, Marcia, if it isn't Edward? Could it
be Rosie Amsterdam?'
'He went straight to Rosie's after he left me. She heard a
version of what happened before another friend drove him
to a hospital. I wouldn't put it past Rosie, but she must have
known if she heard the story from Edward that I didn't do it
with a bottle.'
'I'm told that sometimes journalists deliberately get a detail
wrong to flush out comments from the people involved –
they know they'll get an angry phone call putting the mat-
ter right.'
'It wouldn't surprise me.' Marcia folds up Edward's letter and
puts it carefully into her bag, noticing that her hands are shaking.
'I'm surprised the Press didn't see you as you came in.'
'They did. But I'm looking so scruffy they didn't recognize me.
Even my friends don't recognize me when I'm wearing these.'
Marcia puts on her old National Health prescription glasses, and
Suzanne laughs.
'They don't do much for you, I'll agree.'
'They do a lot for me. They bring out all the worst features of
my face, the ones I usually play down. They're a great disguise,
and I'm very fond of them. Look at the time! We must get
going.'

'You amaze me, Marcia. You've gone all calm.'

'I feel calm suddenly because I can't do anything about all this press madness. And the more I think about it the more crazy it all seems.'

'You must get some good legal advice—'

'Suzanne, don't let's talk any more about it. I must do some exercises and get the whole nightmare out of my head and put Creusa and her problems in.'

Marcia starts to perform a yogic routine and Suzanne goes out to warn the gossiping cast that they must give her space.

By the time she has her costume and full makeup on, Marcia is focused only on her part. She has always enjoyed previews more than first nights; the audience is often more open, perceptive and responsive, no judgments have been made and no one is influenced by outside opinion; there's a freshness and generosity in the audience that disappears after Press night. Audiences have always fascinated her, despite her ambivalent feelings about them. Their collective effect can vary so greatly that she's always wondered about the extent of the power of each individual within it. Do some people give off a more pervasive aura of reaction than others? Why does a face sometimes stand out and catch the actor's attention? Why is one audience full of electricity, another as lumpish as a head-cold?

She goes down quickly when she hears her two-minute call over the Tannoy, and stands in the wings listening and sensing the silent audience in the darkness beyond. She hears her cue, Ion's query to the Chorus:

'Who is your mistress? Of what family?' As she enters there is a peculiar sussuration from the audience, and she's aware of flashes from small cameras, hidden until her entry and then held up for the few seconds needed to capture a good picture. There must be Press photographers everywhere.

She tries to blot out the realization that a large part of the audience will be seeing her as the notorious wielder of broken glass and not as Queen Creusa, despairing over her barren state, mourning the memory of a dead child. She can see that both Damian and Suzanne are staring at her in concern as she tries to regain her concentration. The flashes quickly stop, as does the rustling, and Marcia feels a sudden rush of power as Ion says his apposite first words to her.

Oh, my lady, what is the matter? Your cheeks are wet! The sight of Apollo's oracle has made you weep! The fortuitous aptness of the words in her reply enforce this sense of power:

When our oppressor is all-powerful, where shall we fly for justice?

Marcia gives thereafter a focused, subtle and commanding performance of her part and the audience explodes with appreciation at the end of the play. Alsopp rushes round to her dressing-room to hug her.

'Brilliant. And I love the ending now. It really works. As for the scene with Xuthus, it came alive for the first time. There was a real sense of sexual tension between you, even though the scene's so short.'

'Xuthus is such a prat – Andrew was excellent.'

'Prat he may be, but you like going to bed with him. That's what came over tonight. By the way, Marcia, on the subject of sexual shenanigans, thank you for all this timely publicity – the box office is humming.'

'Any time. I did it all for you, John.'

'Well, I can see how unpleasant all this is for you, don't get me wrong, but who cares what the Press say as long as they say something? And you are going to get sensational notices, darling, there's no doubt about that.' He kisses her on both cheeks before hurrying off to see other members of the cast. Marcia stands numbly in the middle of the dressing-room, staring at herself in the full-length mirror. Rollo West's haunting music fills her brain; he has promised her a tape, and she thirsts for it. Anything to blot out the growing storm.

Suzanne dashes in and they both start to take off costumes and makeup. 'Willy says you ought to slip out through one of the front-of-house exits.'

'I intend to. Thanks for keeping everyone off my back, Suzanne.'

'My pleasure. And by tomorrow it will be yesterday's dead story as far as the Press are concerned.'

'I hope so.'

'Willie gave me this note for you, by the way.'

Rachel's writing on the envelope is a relief.

If you need to keep away from the Press tonight and want to avoid your flat, come and stay with us – the bed's waiting. Just leap in a taxi after the show. We'll expect you unless we hear.

'I tell you something, Suzanne. I wouldn't survive without my women friends.'

'Tell me something new. Take care. See you tomorrow.'

Marcia slips out of the front exit in her beret and glasses, and gets into the taxi Willy has organized. It takes over half an hour to reach the Kleins' house in Hampstead, and she leans back with eyes shut, glorying in the warmth and comfort of a London cab. (Her Fiat has refused to start since it returned from Lena's funeral, and she has definitely decided to sell it and do without a car.)

Her mind goes back to the only taxi she ever remembers taking with her parents. Her mother had sprained her ankle, and could not walk as far as the underground station. She cannot recall where they were going, only that the three of them sat so solemnly in the taxi they might have been attending a religious service. Marcia sat on the jump-seat and could tell from the way her mother's eyes flicked from side to side that she was worried the taxi-driver was taking a long way round. Miriam's ankle was so swathed in bandages it looked like a bulb at the end of her leg; Martin patted her hand and murmured something in German.

'When I'm grown-up I'm going to go everywhere by taxi.'

'I see my Maüslein is planning to marry a millionaire.'

'I'm going to earn my own money. Lots and lots.'

Marcia thinks about that infant self, then about the fact she'd love some fish and chips but is sure that Rachel will have kept her some food, then about the heels on her shoes which are worn right down, about the tooth that is making signs of becoming troublesome, about anything in fact, rather than that paralysing moment when she walked on to the stage and nearly lost control. She should have expected that reception; she should have been prepared for it.

'There you are, love, number twenty-nine you said? Wakey-wakey.'

Marcia has to empty her purse to pay for the taxi, and laughs as she turns it upside down.

'I'm ten pence short – can I give you a postage stamp to make up?'

'Never write letters.' The man drives off with a wave, and Marcia hurries towards the Kleins' front door. Before she touches the bell she pauses; everything looks so polished and clean and well tended; there's a new car parked in the drive, lights shine brightly through the sparkling windows. There is a metal basket at her feet holding four empty milk bottles, just as sparklingly clean; the basket has a little clock on the handle with numbers 1–6 on it; Rachel has set the dial for 5. One extra for the guest. Marcia is staring fixedly at it, intimidated by this level of organization, when the front door opens.

'I knew I heard a taxi! Come in, Marcia darling, come in! What are you waiting for? You look tired, come right in and get warm, have a drink, something to eat. Jonathan, Marcia's here!'

Everything in Rachel's house shines with cleanliness: the cream walls, the light-coloured unstained carpets, the gleaming glass-topped tables, the all-white kitchen. Splashes of colour come from fresh flowers and from artfully placed cushions.

'Marcia, how good you've come! Long time no see. Sit down, sit down.' Jonathan, like Rachel, repeats his hospitable invitations until they seem almost like commands. 'Sit down and have a drink. What can I get you?'

'Whisky would be lovely.'

'Have you had a terrible day, you poor thing?'

'I had a lovely quiet, restorative day, actually.'

'But the Press – the papers—'

'I knew nothing about them until I got to the theatre. I didn't realize my phone was unplugged, I didn't go out at all, I had no idea. Then it hit me – there were press all over the theatre.'

'Water? Soda?' Jonathan has poured a restrained amount of whisky into a heavy cut-glass tumbler. He has changed over the last few years; the spare, wiry man with equally wiry black hair has become a plump-faced, stout person with a shiny pate.

'Just as it is, thanks.'

'*L'chaim!*'

'*L'chaim!*'

All three raise their glasses. There's a faint air of constraint which Rachel tries to dispel by bustling about.

'So tell us how the show went, Marcia?'

'Well, thanks, despite all the hassle. John Alsopp was pleased.'

'Is he upset by this scandal?'

'Not at all, Jonathan.'

'All publicity is good publicity.'

'Not really true, but yes.' Marcia has noticed his use of the word scandal. 'What aspect do you see as scandalous?'

'Sorry?'

'You used the word scandal.'

'Oh, Marcia, just a way of talking. It's a scandal the Press got hold of it, that's what I meant. Rachel, why don't you bring Marcia's dinner in here, so she can eat in comfort?'

'Just what I'm doing.' Rachel comes in with a tray laden with dishes.

'That smells good. Very good. I haven't had salt beef in ages.'

'Nor have we – I get worried about the BSE scare but this beef's organic.'

The Kleins eat kosher food in the home but used not to worry about it when they went out. Marcia has noticed a mezuzah up by the door which she doesn't remember seeing before, and asks if they always eat kosher food now.

'We try to.'

'So you're getting stricter?'

Rachel laughs, Jonathan wobbles his head, but neither denies it.

'You're my only *Jewish* Jewish friends, you know. I'm right out of it now, like most of the Jews I come across. Except you.'

'You can never be right out of it, Marcia.'

'You know what I mean.'

'It's having the kids that makes the difference. If we don't show them no one else will. So yes, we've got a little bit stricter for their sakes.' Rachel laughs again. It's becoming a nervous tic, her laugh, more noticeable in the home than in the public places where they usually meet.

'I can't remember the last time I came here. It must be at least two years—'

'Surely not so long, Marcia!'

'You've had the place redecorated since I last came. New kitchen too.'

'Then it is two years. My goodness. Yes, we had the kitchen redesigned two years ago – what a nightmare that was. Divorce, we were near divorce over that kitchen, weren't we, darling?'

'You kept changing your mind, that's why.'

As Marcia eats her wholesome and delicious dinner Rachel and Jonathan go on talking – about the house, the neighbourhood, the children. Marcia feels unreal. When she's finished, the dishes are cleared rapidly away and Jonathan goes off to lock the front door and check the windows. Bedtime is being signalled even though Marcia longs to unwind for another hour or so while her food settles. She stands in the kitchen doorway as Rachel wipes the clean surfaces cleaner.

'Have you been in touch with Stephen Smith, Marcia?'

'Who?'

Rachel freezes in mid-wipe. 'The solicitor I recommended.'

'Oh yes. No, not yet.'

'Don't put it off, Marcia. All this publicity is worrying. You could find yourself in deep trouble.'

'The Press will forget all about it in a day or two. I'll get in touch with Smith after the show has opened.'

'I can't understand you, Marcia. You don't sound bothered. I'd be on Stephen's doorstep by now if I was you.'

'Be grateful you're not!'

'You know what I mean.'

'I don't see any rush. If the shit is going to hit the fan, it will hit it whatever I do. And this week I have to be single-minded. The play, that's all I'm going to worry about. Once it's opened, I'll be able to look at the mess in my life.'

'You should get married, Marcia.' Rachel wrings the cloth out vigorously.

'Don't make me cross, Rachel.'

'It just seems hard for you to be bearing all these difficulties alone.'

'I'm used to it, and I'm fine. I'd rather bear them alone

than have a husband like Edward Wintlesham, I can tell you.'

Rachel comes across the kitchen and gives her a hug. 'Oh, Marcia. I'd just like to see you happy with someone, that's all. I'm an old friend – why shouldn't I tell you what I feel?'

'Time for bed, girls.' The women stare at Jonathan. 'Will I see you in the morning, Marcia?'

'I'll lie in until everyone's gone to work, school and whatever, otherwise I'll get in your way.'

'Till tomorrow evening, then.' He goes off, and Marcia waits for Rachel to finish her kitchen rituals before she shows her to Judith's room.

'Where's poor Judith sleeping?'

'In my workroom, there's a divan in there.'

'I could have gone in there, Rachel.'

'It's in a mess. It's better this way. You won't be disturbed when the kids get up. In case you need it, here's a new toothbrush and some moisturizer.'

'I don't deserve a friend like you.'

'Don't be silly. I know if I was in trouble you'd do the same for me.'

Marcia sits on Judith's pretty pink-covered bed and wonders not whether she would but whether she would ever be given the opportunity. The role she plays in the Kleins' life is that of their eccentric friend – she has actually once overheard Jonathan call her *meshugeh*, the Yiddish for crazy – a friend that needs their steadying influence. If they needed help, the last person they would ever ask would be Marcia Fleckner.

13 ∫

The House of Lords has a courtyard rather like an Oxbridge college, but of a forbidding height, each floor stretched beyond need or symmetry. These curious proportions strike George forcibly when he is led into the Lord Chancellor's own sanctum: the handsome heavy Victorian woodwork, the splendid view of the Thames, the huge overmantel mirror, all have their effect diminished by the extraordinary height of the room. As the tall, stiff figure of the Lord Chancellor, Lord Conwick of Moulton, greets him, George feels thoroughly dwarfed. They sit in red plush armchairs as coffee is promptly brought in.

'I'm sorry I had to postpone making my appointment with you, Lord Chancellor. My mother's sudden death rather disrupted my life.'

'Perfectly right and natural that it should. We all understood, and I hope my condolences were passed on.'

'They were, thank you.'

'I was interested to see you were born in India, Warne. Army or Civil Service?'

'Civil Service.' George has no idea if this is true, but felt his father was certainly not a soldier or Lena would have mentioned it.

'The Conwicks served in the ICS for three generations. Mainly in Bengal.'

'My family was in Rajputana, now Rajastan of course. But I left India when I was very young.'

'I was six when I was left behind in England to go to school. A mere six years old – it was so painful it feels like yesterday.' Piers Conwick passes George his coffee. 'I remember crying every night for my ayah – I missed her more than I missed my mother. Far more. Those awful school dormitories. Sugar?'

'No, thanks. I had no idea we shared a birthplace in common.' George is staring at the Lord Chancellor's pale, slablike face in surprise.

'My ayah was called Hannah. Like so many Indian girls she'd been abandoned at birth, and found and brought up by Welsh missionaries. She knew the Bible better than my mother, particularly the more gruesome tales from the Old Testament. She was a wonderful ayah, was Hannah, she used to stay and see me fall asleep every night of my life until that terrible day when I was brought home to England.'

'I missed my ayah too, though I was too young to remember her well. And luckily an aunt looked after me during the war, so I didn't have to endure school dormitories as young as you did.'

'You were indeed lucky. I think the ultimate betrayal for me was that my mother lied to me on the boat coming home, told me I'd be seeing Hannah again. I often wonder whether that iniquity was the root cause of my desire to become a judge one day.' Lord Conwick smiles at George, having adroitly led the conversation round to the point. 'I know you have been told why you have been summoned here. The Lord Chief Justice and I would be delighted to appoint you to the High Court Bench, and are equally delighted that you are minded to accept.'

The words lie heavy in the still quiet air between them, and George swallows before he manages to speak.

'It's a very high honour, Lord Chancellor, which I honestly feel I don't deserve.'

'We don't usually make mistakes.' Lord Conwick meets George's gaze while his fingers tap on the fierce red plush arm of his chair. 'We have two retirements looming, one of which has been brought forward because of ill-health, and therefore replacements have become a matter of urgency. I imagine you've already given a great deal of thought this next stage in your life and hope you are now in a position to give me your final decision. I don't know how you are placed vis-à-vis long-standing cases—'

'There is one particular case I'm due to start which will be difficult to get out of gracefully, but of course I haven't yet talked to my clerk. Neither have I had a chance to talk to my accountant who's away at the moment.'

'However, in the main, and with these things behind you, your answer is yes? We can expect your confirmation?' As the Lord Chancellor blows his nose with great vigour a tug hoots on the river, and George sees gulls circle high in the pale sky of the window beyond him.

'You can.'

'Excellent.'

'The only thing I ask is a few more days to put my house in order before that final moment.'

'Discuss the details with Jeremy Welsford. Of course, this appointment remains confidential until you've been sworn in, as I'm sure you realize. And of course, once your appointment becomes public you can no longer appear in court, as I'm sure you're aware—' As he talks, he goes to open a door and call through it. 'Ah, Jeremy. Warne has in principle accepted, so I will leave you to dot the i's and cross the t's.'

Jeremy Welsford, Permanent Secretary and Clerk of the Crown in Chancery, is a small, intense man with a cap of dark ginger hair of such depths of natural colour and thickness that it looks false above his lined white face. From the back he looks like a man of thirty, no more; his face shows all of his fifty-eight years. George shakes hands with the Lord Chancellor and follows Welsford into a room that is almost the twin of the first, furnished with the same red plush furniture.

'Do sit down, George. So the decision is not quite final?'

'I've had so much to assess and think about. It's a complex decision.'

'Yes indeed. Some people make it with ease, others need to think hard about it.' Jeremy Welsford is meticulously neat from his manicured fingernails holding his pin-striped knees to his highly polished black brogues with the laces tied in symmetrical bows. George feels a sudden piercing desire to run for it, to beat his way out of this apex of the establishment; he listens with increasing unease as Welsford picks up various sheets of heavy cream paper and gives him a summary of the next moves.

'I've made a provisional booking for your medical on

Friday – shall I let that stand? It takes place not far from here—'

The telephone rings and the creases on Welsford's forehead intensify as he answers it.

'I did say I didn't want to be disturbed – what is it? Oh dear, oh dear, when did this happen? One minute.' He turns to George and runs his hand through his hair, leaving it looking like a pile of straw that's suddenly been disarranged by a high wind. 'Sorry about this, George, but would you forgive me for a minute? One of my sons has broken his arm – it's my wife ringing from the hospital.'

'Go ahead, don't mind me.'

Welsford disappears into his secretary's office and George goes to the long windows on one side which look out on to the gardens he recently walked in. He watches a group of young people piling themselves round a statue for a photograph and hears their shouts of laughter as one puts a baseball cap on the statue's head. He takes a deep breath and stretches his arms upwards. He must stop procrastinating. Extra time will make no difference. He has accepted the offer in principle, he must do it in fact and not only live with it but like it.

Jeremy Welsford comes in, shaking his now wildly untidy head. 'The little horror is just over the river in St Thomas's right this minute, having his arm set. He fell off his bike on his way to school.'

'No other damage?'

'He's fine, full of self-importance, says my wife. Sorry to leave you – where were we?'

'Discussing the date for the medical. Friday will suit me perfectly. And if it helps, I can confirm my acceptance now.'

'Sure you don't want a little more time?'

'A leap of faith is needed.'

'Excellent. It makes matters much simpler. There are various things that need to be checked, consent forms to be signed, that sort of thing. The sooner all that is processed, the sooner your appointment can be announced.'

'When might that be?'

'We have to fit in with the Queen's schedule, but I'd say in late January. And of course the Lord Chancellor will have stressed the importance of confidentiality, beyond telling wife or partner and close family, your Head of Chambers, and naturally your clerk so that he can bring the flow of work to a stop.'

'Surely once the clerks know the news will be round the Temple in a trice?'

'They have to be extra discreet. There's another point I should raise on the matter of discretion. It is very important you inform the Lord Chancellor if there is any aspect of your private life which, should it become known after your appointment, could cause – er – difficulties and unwholesome publicity.'

'I've been married twice.'

'The Lord Chancellor knew that. Luckily for you and us, divorce is not a bar to going on the Bench. No, what he doesn't like to discover after he's made an appointment is any professional irregularity. But I'm sure this doesn't apply to you, George. And now, let me show you exactly where you have to go for the medical.'

When George arrives back in Chambers Paul is anxiously hovering on the lookout for him.

'Mr Warne. Tried ringing you at home, sir. They want you to come back into the Crédit Lyonnais case – you recall you advised on it a few months back, sir. Counsel is stuck in another case. The solicitors are getting restless.'

'By counsel you mean Alex Frith, I take it.'

'Yes, sir.'

'I told him he would need a leader. Why the bloody hell did he do it on his own, I'd like to know?'

Paul shrugs, eyes expressionless.

'Never mind, Paul. When is it listed?'

'Well, sir, it's set down for the High Court tomorrow morning, that's the problem. And Mr Frith's case has overrun—'

'So if I take it on I'm now going to have to read solidly until then – I suppose Frith thinks I've got nothing better to do.'

'He did say you were the only person who would be able to take it on at short notice, seeing as you'd already advised on it, sir. And Chambers doesn't want to upset those solicitors—'

'And I'm not in court on Wednesday. I just have the Feathers case to prepare, a mere bauble.' George is enjoying himself, making a busy QC's complaint as Paul would expect him to. 'What's the deal on the fee, Paul?'

'Half-shares with counsel, sir. Mr Frith has been working on this for months—'

'How much has been agreed on the brief?'

'I'll find out, sir. Douglas has been negotiating it.'

'It looks as if I have no choice. Get the papers to me at once.'

'I'll have the files brought down from Mr Frith's room right now.'

George shuts the door behind the scuttling figure of Paul and lets a smile of pleasure spread across his face. This is exactly the way he would like to spend his last weeks as a silk: to be dealing with an interesting legal point in the High Court, in a case that will need tough presentation. The adrenalin is already filling him. His smile fades when he thinks again of how much he will miss this life when his appointment goes ahead.

His internal phone rings; it's Freddie, to find out how his interview went. At that moment Douglas Dean puts his head through the door.

'Oh, sorry, sir—'

'Don't go away, Douglas. Freddie, can I come up and see you in ten minutes? Good.' He puts the receiver down and turns to Douglas. 'Now, Douglas, what's the real low-down on this case of Alex Frith's? Why didn't he have a leader on it to start with? Me, for instance?'

'He says the solicitors wanted him to do the case on his own, sir.'

'Pull the other one. He wanted to hog it, to do enough heavy cases on his own to increase his reputation so that he takes silk easily when the time comes.'

'I wouldn't comment, sir.'

'Well, his fingers are burnt this time.'

'Everybody's thankful you already know the details of the case, sir.'

'These brilliant young barristers get a bit above themselves.'

'You were just the same yourself, sir. Remember how you did without a leader whenever you could?'

'Touché. I love a bit of righteous indignation that's then punctured by my clerk. Not many clerks would be so honest.'

'Life is more interesting if one is honest. Not to say more amusing. Always bearing in mind one is also being discreet.'

'Douglas, if there was an equivalent of silk for barristers' clerks, I would award it to you. Now for the f-word: what is the fee on the frightful Frith's case?'

'To use a cliché, you are a caution, sir.'

Natalie is in the room with Freddie, showing him a fax; George hesitates.

'Come in, George, she knows.'

'Congratulations, George.' She kisses his cheek, then unexpectedly hugs him.

'No congratulations yet. I could fail my medical. What ignominy!'

'Of course you won't. How was old Piers Conwick?'

'Very friendly – in fact, knowing his reputation, quite exceptionally approachable. Told me he was also born in India, so we talked about our Raj background.'

'I didn't even know you were born in India, let alone the Lord Chancellor.' Nat is interested. 'Tell us more, George.'

'My family wasn't anything very pukka. I have a feeling, to continue in the correct idiom, my father was a boxwallah. In trade, in other words, but I told the Lord Chancellor we were Indian Civil Service to keep him happy. Like his family.'

'How old were you when you left India?' Nat rolls up the long trail of fax paper and taps her cheek with it.

'Under three. I was abandoned by my mother who returned to India at the outbreak of the war – she dumped me on my aunt. But being dumped was an expected part of the life of a Raj child. Conwick spoke very feelingly about his awful lonely years at prep school.'

'Shivers go down my spine when Freddie tells me about his. Being dumped at such a young age seems cruel to me in any circumstances. I must go and respond to this fax.' She goes to the door, and smiles at George. 'We're going to enjoy the reflected glory of Chambers' first High Court Judge.'

'What cases are you doing at the moment, Nat?'

'I'm about to start an interesting personal injury case led by Colin – it's a test case which could go all the way to the Lords.'

'So things are going well for you?'

'Yes, touch wood.'

'And you love the life, I can see.'

'I do. I really love it.' Her bright, alert gaze links with George's. 'You do too. You're going to miss it.'

'I know that only too well.'

'We'll miss you.'

'You sound surprised.'

Natalie laughs as a blush rises, then waves and disappears.

'You're bloody lucky, Freddie, to have Natalie as your wife.'

'Don't I know it. I sometimes can't believe my luck.' Freddie looks embarrassed and fiddles with a paperweight. 'When are they going to appoint you, George?'

'Late January I should think.' As they speak George notices that the item of news about Marcia's attack is uppermost on Freddie's folded copy of *The Times*. He freezes, then realizes that it would mean nothing to anyone in Chambers. No one has ever met Marcia or knows about his past relationship with her. His instinctive caginess, echoed by hers, he now sees as a blessing in disguise because the Press would love to link her with a QC, and go overboard if they knew he was due for the High Court Bench.

'I must go, Freddie, and start reading up this case of Alex Frith's which he now can't do.'

'When are you going to tell Douglas about your appointment?'

'After my medical. I don't like tempting fate.'

George sits down at his desk, which is now piled high with the Crédit Lyonnais case files. His mind is full of Marcia, and shock has given way to curiosity about the truth behind the news item. Perhaps Edward Wintlesham is neither a lover nor ex-lover, perhaps as usual every fact is wrong? He could ring her and ask her about it but he finds he can't bring himself to dial her number. He is beginning to see that whatever the truth behind the allegation, he will have to be extremely careful over his contacts with her in the future. Interception by the press of calls from an established Queen's Counsel and the resulting publicity would not go down well with the Lord Chancellor. If *The Times* has reported the attack, then the tabloids will have gone to town on it. Marcia Fleckner is hot news.

George knows that if prudence were uppermost, he would cancel his engagement to dine with Marcia after the play on Saturday. He is curiously upset by his predicament, and it is a relief to bury himself in his work and postpone any decision.

'Good of you to come, Warne. Jeremy Welsford tells me you are joining us on the Queen's Bench with a bit of luck and that I must try and encourage you rather than put you off!' Sir Bernard Markworthy gives his snort of a laugh. 'Did your parents call you George after George Bernard Shaw?'

'Not to my knowledge.'

'Mine did. George Bernard Markworthy. My mother was besotted by GBS but since she was Irish I suppose she had a slight justification. I dropped the George. Not that Bernard's much better as a name. They both hang round one's neck as rather pompous monikers.'

George laughs dutifully. Jeremy Welsford had recommended Mr Justice Markworthy as a good if eccentric source of information because he spoke his mind, and also, as a bachelor, would have a pertinent view of the way of life ahead. As a judge, he was known for his fearsomely sharp intellect and his impatience with counsel.

'Welsford told me you might have a lot of questions, so ask away, Warne, and I'll do my best.'

'None are very important, but since you, like me, are unmarried, I was wondering if this was a disadvantage?'

'Do you find it so?'

'I worded that badly. Let me turn it round. How much support do married judges get from their wives when they are on circuit for six weeks at a time?'

'Most of 'em don't show their faces at all. I don't actually blame them – in most lodgings they are there on sufferance. You can see the domestic staff thoroughly disapproving of matrimonial goings-on, and they make sure the wives don't feel too welcome. Why ask? Thinking of getting married?'

'No.'

'Good man. Overrated condition as far as I can tell. Damned hard work being a judge, best done on your own. Case-loads can be very heavy, you realize that?'

'The heavy work-load doesn't bother me – I expected that. But the way of life has many mysterious facets. What's your view, by the way, on the current suggestion that it would save the state money if judges stayed in hotels instead of what the Press call luxurious lodgings?'

'Luxurious is the last word you could use to describe some of them. Wait till you see the lodgings in Northampton! Bloody poky place, jammed on to the back of the courts. Ghastly. Chester's not much better – the zoo's right next door. Not only can you hear an elephant fart – you can smell it. Certainly we'd be better off in a hotel in those two places. But it's no good, Warne, to think of hotels – we can't function properly if we're surrounded by Joe Public. Privacy is crucial, complete privacy. If you're judging a really sensitive case, the less the public sees of you the better. You'd run across them all the time in a hotel, however private it said it was. Hotel bedrooms are not secure, so you'd never be able to leave papers around. I'm untidy, I need a good creative mess of paper to build up in my study when I'm working on a case, it helps me to think.' Mr Justice Markworthy swings a hand round to draw George's attention to the confusion in his room. 'Never be able to get anything done in a hotel. Two things are important in my view: privacy and mystery. A judge should be removed, apart. The wig, the robes, the whole rigmarole is important. You swish by behind bullet-proof glass. You're only visible when you're on the Bench. That's the way it should be. Sherry?'

'Thanks – just a small one. Which lodgings do you like best?'

'Lincoln, Winchester and Leicester.' Mr Justice Markworthy is on his knees rattling what sound like empty bottles in a cupboard. 'Could have sworn there was some in here.'

'Don't worry. Whisky would do if you have it.'

'I know that's finished – gave the last inch to the Master of the Rolls but yesterday. Aha, the sherry.' He produces an almost empty bottle of Bristol Cream. 'I won't join you – I'm allergic to any alcohol. I swell up like a red balloon.' He pours the cloudy remnants of the bottle into a small tumbler. 'There, that one's finished too.' He puts the bottle back into the depths of the cupboard all the same.

The sherry smells of vinegar. George finds a corner for his glass on a crowded table and hopes his host won't notice he hasn't drunk it. He has launched into a long analysis of a celebrated judgment given recently for which he was publicly criticized.

'You need a hide like an elephant's in this job. Have you got good hearing, Warne?'

'I think so—'

'You'll need that too. We are becoming a nation of mumblers. The young don't seem to have heard of good diction. I insist on people speaking up, but it's a tiring business sometimes. The court thinks I'm deaf, which I am not in the least. Just fussy. Anything else I can tell you?'

'I'm sure there is but I'm afraid I must leave you – I will be late for a meeting if not.'

'I hated life as a silk. All those ghastly Bar Council meetings. Couldn't wait to get on the Bench.'

'Thank you for your advice and comments—'

'You haven't drunk your sherry—'

'I'm afraid I can't. It's off.'

'Really? I didn't know sherry could go off. How interesting. I've had that Bristol Cream for quite a while, I suppose. Old Magpie Mactaggart gave it to me and he's been been dead five years.'

The walls are covered with faded prints of seventeenth- and eighteenth-century judges; the collection seems to have frozen sometime in the nineteenth century – perhaps the advent of photography discouraged Ede and Ravenscroft, Robemakers to the legal profession, from continuing the collection. George stares at the worried, craggy face of an early Master of the Rolls, and wonders how greatly the lives of the upper judiciary have changed since the eighteenth century. Certainly in terms of clothing very little.

'Out of interest, how much does having ermine trimmings instead of rabbit cost these days?'

'Three to four times as much, sir.'

'So we're talking about five thousand pounds or so for a scarlet cloth and ermine robe?'

'Indeed. But it does vary depending on the current cost of ermine – we only use the best ermine from Russia.' Mr Stockdale's practised, unctuous manner reminds George of his first visit, with his mother, to a tailor. Perhaps being a gentleman's outfitter causes this approach.

'What exactly is ermine, Mr Stockdale?'

'Ermine comes from the stoat, sir. Their coat turns white in winter so that they are invisible in the snow.'

'I'll go for the budget white rabbit, with its connotations of Lewis Carroll. Does anyone order the ermine these days?'

'Your judiciary abroad occasionally does, sir.'

'Hong Kong?'

'Exactly, sir.'

Scarlet robe trimmed with white fur, scarlet hood ditto, lightweight summer versions, black silk girdle, black silk scarf, lace stock and cuffs, full-bottomed wig, black tin wig-case with his name inscribed in gold paint. By the time George has finished ordering the necessary list the thousands have mounted well beyond five.

'I feel like the Right Honourable John Philpot Curran.'

'Sir?'

'The gentleman on the wall over there who looks as if he's had a nasty shock. I can't believe my wig is really going to cost me almost two thousand pounds.'

'There's a lot of work in a wig, sir.'

'Something must account for the cost, I agree. The tin box is splendid, though. I like this sprocket thing that pulls out so that you can hang your wig on it. Neat design. I wish the wig was as appealing.'

'We will make you look very good in it, sir.'

'Impossible. No one could look good in a full-bottomed wig. Even when they were in fashion, in my view they did nothing for the wearer.'

Stockdale gives a deprecating laugh as he finishes measuring George's head, and is called away to deal with a shop-floor problem before he begins to measure for the robes. George stares at his reflection in the full-length mirror: behind him is a phalanx of shadowy eminent legal faces, men of wisdom or of bigotry, one and all caparisoned in the wigs and gowns of their calling, proud in most cases of the air of distinction it gave them. The small room full of faces from the past seems suddenly a menace, a summation of former centuries of dusty, rarefied old courtrooms, hot in summer and freezing in winter, full of the strong smells of human beings who washed rarely, of their varied voices, high, low, querulous, growling, stentorian, inaudible, of their yawns, their stares, their weeping or rejoicing as sentence was passed. The past buffets George in the airless small room, and he sinks into the only chair.

'Sorry about that, sir. Now, where were we? Ah yes, the scarlet robe with coney trimmings, I believe. Yes. And of course you'll be needing the lightweight summer version, and—'

'Could I have a glass of water, Mr Stockdale? I'm feeling rather faint for some reason. Perhaps it's a lack of air in here.'

'These are very stressful days, Mr Warne, sir. You'll be glad when you're sworn in. I'll get you a glass of water, but I'm afraid I must keep the door shut because of confidentiality, you understand. You should not be seen in here or people might speculate.' Closing the door with irritating care, Stockdale bustles away again.

George lies back in the only chair, eyes closed to shut out all those faces. He can hear two shop assistants giggling in the showroom; the bells of St Clement Danes start to toll for a funeral in the Strand nearby.

The shop had *GENTS. OUTFITTERS. WE DRESS ALL SHAPES AND SIZES* written on the window in careful handpainted gold italics. Jebs followed his mother in, sure that his shape and size would defeat them: too thin, too lanky, too tall for his narrowness. In his mother's hands were enough clothing coupons to buy his first sports jacket and grey flannels. Lena had told him several times she had made up the amount with some of her own. He watched her charm the shop assistants, he had to follow one of them to a fitting room.

'Now, young fellow, we need to take some measurements.'

'Can't I just try some of those jackets outside—'

• Peggy Woodford

'They're men's sizes.' The assistant, a Mr Spooner, had Brillcreemed black hair and a strange waistcoat that was hung with tape measures, pins, scissors, and a piece of tailor's chalk on a string. 'Yours will have to be made up specially for you.' His breath smelt of tobacco and rotten teeth as he stretched the tape round Jebs's skinny body and called out the figures to his assistant, a boy who looked very little older than Jebs.

'Get these figures down correctly, Jim. Seventeen-and-a-half. Thirty-seven. Twelve-and-a-quarter . . .' The long list of figures clearly gave Mr Spooner no pleasure. Jebs was sure his body was abnormal and utterly to be despised. 'That's all done, young man, so let's go and find Madam and see what cloths we will be selecting.'

Lena had every bolt of tweed in the shop laid out. A large-bottomed woman was busy delving for grey flannel. At the sight of the choice ahead of him Jebs wanted to run.

'Now, darling, what about this Harris tweed? Pre-war, I am told. Very special.' She was holding out some scratchy brown stuff that looked to Jebs more like the pelt of a Yorkshire terrier.

'It'll be itchy.'

'Of course it won't. Anyway, you'll have lots of layers between you and it – lining, jersey, shirt, vest – layers and layers. Don't be silly.'

'It's very brown. What about that greeny one over there?'

'This one?'

'No, the other green one.'

'That will make you look like a bookie, darling. No, too green. Here's another Harris tweed I think is very suitable.'

'It looks scratchy as well.'

Miserable with intense embarrassment, Jebs endured the unrolling of bale after bale while Jim sniggered in the fitting-room door; every time Jebs rejected a fabric, Jim put his hand over his mouth to hide (vainly) the extent of his amusement. Jebs longed to plunge the fat-bottomed lady's pair of scissors deep into him.

'This herringbone then, Jebs. Now, this won't be itchy or scratchy at all. Feel it.'

It wasn't, but it was a dull grey colour, it made his skin look grey, it was absolutely safe and boring. He settled with relief for the herringbone, with dark grey flannel trousers. His mother would keep calling the trousers 'slacks', much to Jim's merriment.

'A very good choice, Madam, if I may say so. Years of wear in those. See him through his schooldays. Shall we leave a good allowance in the sleeves and trouser bottoms for future elongation, or has the young man done his growing?'

At this Jim collapsed with delight and disappeared into the fitting-room. Mr Spooner glared in his direction and sent the large woman to 'sort Jim out'.

'I think you should leave room for growth, Mr Spooner. After all, I'm quite tall and his father's very tall. Oh dear, is that the time? I had no idea we'd taken so long!' Suddenly flustered, she hurried Jebs out of the tailor's. 'Well, are you happy with the herringbone, darling?'

'It's not too bad, but I liked the green. And Father isn't *very* tall, Mum. He's not much taller than you.'

14 ∫

Marcia is woken by a rhythmic screeching, and struggles out of her deep sleep to realize it is one of the Klein children practising on the violin, and that it is only six o'clock in the morning. She pulls the pillow over her head but nothing will keep out the laboured progress through a well-worn tune that she can't quite place even though she has ample opportunity to hear it many times through the thin wall. She is also aware of the sound of a piano beneath her being played with confidence and some skill. Almost simultaneously, both piano and violin players start running through scales; Marcia clamps her fingers in her ears as she vainly courts a return to sleep. Then silence descends, sleep seems a possibility, but within five minutes the piano starts up again, played at a much lower standard, and from the room next door comes the sound of a clarinet picking its way hesitantly through 'Greensleeves' with many a harsh reedy squeak.

Marcia can now also hear parental murmurings and heavy footsteps going downstairs. At seven o'clock sharp the concert stops. By half-past the front door has banged shut once, after cries of 'Goodbye children, be good' from Jonathan. At twenty to eight it bangs again and there is no further sound for the hour it takes Rachel to deliver her children to two widely separated schools. Marcia lies in bed feeling stunned and rather chastened by the Klein early-morning ritual, and falls asleep again just as she decides it would be a good idea to have a bath before Rachel comes back. Rachel wakes her with a mug of coffee some time later.

'I thought you might want to get started on your day!'

'My God, what time is it?'

'Half-ten.'

'Oh, that's all right. Coffee, how lovely. You are spoiling me, Rachel.'

'I hope we didn't disturb you earlier.'

'I – no, of course not. I sleep like a log.'

'The children do their practice before school – it works better that way. I meant to warn you.'

'I was vaguely aware of an orchestra at one point.'

Rachel laughs. 'Simon's just started the clarinet – he decided Judith wasn't going to be the only one to play two instruments.'

'They must be mad. Surely one's enough? Can't you stop them?'

'I think it's a rather good idea, actually.'

'But practising at six o'clock, Rachel!'

'I don't force them to. What would you like for breakfast?'

'Just this coffee is perfect. Don't worry about breakfast.' Marcia pulls the duvet round her naked body. 'Get yourself some coffee and come and talk for five minutes.'

While Rachel is downstairs Marcia finds Judith has hidden a pile of *Sweet Valley High* romances with lurid covers between mattress and bedhead. Marcia pushes them back into their hiding-place as Rachel returns and kicks the bean-bag nearer the bed. Both Rachel and bean-bag sigh as she subsides into it.

'It sometimes takes me all morning to recover from the school run. There was a broken-down bus causing havoc this morning, so Simon was late, which he hates. So stressful – he's complaining away and there's nothing I can do to hurry us up. I wish his school wasn't so far.'

'Couldn't he have gone to the one on the corner near here?'

'It's a dump, Marcia. A dump. He'd never get into a good secondary school from that place.'

'I'm right out of all this. I had no idea educating children was such hard work. Music practice at dawn, school runs in all directions. I admire you for your dedication.'

'Don't be snide, Marcia.'

'But I do. Honestly. It would be beyond me.'

'Not if you had children.'

'I'm not sure. I couldn't be so driven, somehow.'

'What do you mean, driven?'

'I don't really know.'

'You think we drive our children harder because we're Jewish—'

'No, no, that hadn't even entered my head.'

'Well, it's not true anyway – compared with some kids ours have an easy life. Some of Judith and Simon's friends – goy friends – do karate and fencing as well as two instruments.'

'Unimaginable.'

'No, normal. Well, in middle-class North London it's normal.'

'Poor little sods. What happens to their childhood? I used to spend hours messing about doing nothing in particular with my friends before and after school – we had a real imaginative life in that gap between school and home.'

Rachel stares at the poster-covered walls of her daughter's room. 'Marcia, things have changed since your day. Life is more competitive, plus the streets aren't safe—'

'Oh dear, I've spilt a drop of coffee on the sheet.'

'Don't worry, I'll be changing them when you go.'

There is a small, full silence.

'I'd better get dressed.'

'Feel free to have a bath – my cleaner's just arrived but she won't be coming upstairs yet awhile.'

Marcia stops herself saying 'But this house is spotless already', and goes for a bath in the children's bathroom. It is reassuringly messy – toothpaste tubes ooze, lids afar; underclothes and shoes litter the floor; half a glass of milk sits on the washbasin. Marcia tips this away and lowers herself into the steaming water.

Wednesday. The second preview tonight, and the Press night tomorrow. And the pleasant prospect of supper with George after the show on Saturday; she will ask his advice about what to do . . .

Marcia sits up suddenly in horror. George knows nothing about Edward, and he's bound to have read the unfortunate publicity. He'll see it as a scandal – she tries to avoid the word but can't. She covers her face in shame. She can picture George's expression as he sees the report in *The Times* or the *Independent* – she knows he reads both.

She dries herself and dresses hurriedly, wondering whether she ought to write to George cancelling their dinner, and then deciding against it because it would probably only make matters worse. How could she not have thought sooner about him seeing the item and being upset by it?

'Rachel, would you say I was very insensitive?'

Rachel laughs and shakes her head. 'Oh, Marcia, yes and no, but aren't we all!'

'Then would you say I'm very bad at seeing the result of my actions?'

'Perhaps. You hurt me sometimes, but I always know you don't mean to.'

'I seem to be incapable of any kind of foresight at the moment.'

'More coffee? I've just made a fresh pot. And Mrs Smith has just brought me these bagels fresh from the baker. Have one.'

'You are so good to me.'

'You always did rush into things without thinking about the consequences. Remember the time in college when you took up the carpet in your room and it got thrown out by accident?'

'Whatever made you think of that?'

'You were surprised the Dean was so angry. "Did it not occur to you that other people are going to use that room after you, Miss Fleckner, who might prefer it carpeted?"'

'This bagel is bliss.'

'Take a couple with you for your lunch.'

'No, Rachel, one is plenty. I have a tight-fitting costume to wear and it doesn't give an inch.'

'Oh, go on, the one thing that hasn't changed about you is your waistline – you're so lucky.' Rachel pulls at her skirtband and sighs. 'Are you coming back here tonight? You're very welcome.'

'No, really, I must go back home and face the music. Not that there will be any more publicity – Edward doesn't want it and I don't. The rat-pack is probably fed up already and on to better things.'

'There's nothing in my paper today.'

'Thanks for everything, Rachel. You and Jonathan are my salvation.'

'We're just your good friends, always here.'

After they part Marcia hurries down the street, breathing deeply. She knows that Rachel is as glad to be rid of her as she is to go – no friendship can stand too much proximity. She skips along the pavement in the November sunlight towards the Tube.

She's still wearing her drab clothes but hasn't put on her beret or glasses yet. Before she dives into the station she does so, and takes a detour when she arrives at Kentish Town so that she approaches her flat from an unexpected direction. There is no one lying in wait on her doorstep; the street is empty, cars have no patient watching occupants. She slips through the outer door with relief, and collects her mail from her locked box. Nothing of interest except a postcard from a friend working in Glasgow with the Citizens' Theatre. She reads this as she climbs the stairs and therefore doesn't see that someone is sitting on them until she reaches his feet.

'Good morning. Miss Fleckner?'

She freezes. The man looks more like a travelling salesman than a reporter but he can't be anything else.

'Isn't she there? Have you tried her door?' Marcia adopts a cold-ridden Glasgow accent. 'She's usually there in the mornings.' She carries on up the stairs past her own door.

'No reply, I'm afraid.'

'I can give her a message, if you like.' Marcia fakes a terrible sneeze in the direction of the man and makes great play of blowing her nose. 'I hope to God I'm not going down with the flu.' She sneezes again. 'Who shall I say called? And it's a bit strange to find a man sitting on the stairs like this . . .'

'It doesn't matter, I'll call again.' He starts to move downstairs, but not with much conviction. Marcia, beginning to enjoy herself, moves down after him.

'No, look, leave me your name and phone number and I'll make sure she knows you were waiting here.' She gives another dreadful sneeze. 'Sorry, they always come in threes.'

He's moving away fast now.

'Mind you shut the street door after you.' She follows him

down as if to make sure, and hears a heavy bang. Still acting the part of the nosy neighbour, she goes so far as to stick her face out through the door in the street. The man is hovering on the pavement but at the sight of her he hurries off. Delighted, Marcia lets herself into her flat with the triumph of repossession.

'Och, that gave him a wee run for his money.' She addresses the photo of Apollo as she takes off her glasses and beret. She replaces the phone-jack into the wall but leaves her answerphone switched on. She cleans the flat, makes some lunch, and then spends an hour working on her green dress. When she sews her brain idles; snipping and stitching, fitting and shaping, are actions that calm her more than any drug could. She pins the hem and tries the dress on: it looks good. As she stands checking the hem, the phone rings.

'Marcia, this is Christina. If you're there pick up the bloody phone – what's got into you? I've been trying to get hold of you for days—'

Marcia picks up the receiver. 'Christina.'

'I knew you were there, I just knew.'

'I've been avoiding the Press, staying elsewhere. Sorry for the silence.'

'Whatever made you carve up poor Edward?'

'I didn't carve him up. If you've only rung to discuss that, I don't want to talk about it.'

'No, no, Marcia, don't ring off. I rang originally about something else. But you never got back to me so I'm afraid the little advertising job had to go elsewhere.'

'This week has been incredibly stressful.' She doesn't fully believe Christina saying that there was a job for her.

'How did the preview go?'

'Well, actually. Pity you couldn't come. When are you coming?'

'Tomorrow if all goes well, but anyway soon, soon. So tell me more.'

'It's the best thing I've ever done. I'm happy with my performance, the director, the cast, the music. Rapture all round. It's been a lovely experience.'

'You talk as if it's over.'

'There's always a change of gear when the show opens and starts its run, you know that. I have loved the preparation.'

'Good. Let's hope Alsopp uses you again. I think he's definitely in the top five.'

'Thank you for landing me this part, Christina.'

'You landed it – I am just there to open doors.'

Marcia knows from Christina's tone that she's heard a rumour Sedley Mortimer is tempting her away.

'This is the best door you've ever opened.' Pins are dropping out of the velvet on to the floor. 'The best.'

'Let's hope your career will take off now, Marcia—'

'Never say things like that. Don't tempt fate. What was it you rang me about by the way, if it wasn't the carving up of Edward?'

'To ask you how the play was going, of course. What's Rollo West's music like?'

'I didn't like it much at first but it grows on you. It's amazingly addictive. I've asked him for a tape.'

'I heard Sedley Mortimer say he's the hottest new composer around.'

'Really? Oh well, if the great Sedley says so he must be. I didn't know you knew Sedley Mortimer, Christina.'

'All agents know each other to some degree. I met him recently at a do at the Press Association.'

'What do you think of him?'

'He's very pleased with himself. Arrogant.'

'I must stop chatting, Christina. I've suddenly realized the time and I must get on. I'm standing with pins dropping out of a dress I'm making.'

'You're mad, Marcia. Why on earth are you making a dress this week of all weeks?'

'Therapy. See you tomorrow. Let's have a drink together after the show.'

'I might not be able to make tomorrow.'

'Whenever.' Whenever you can be bothered to get yourself to the theatre. Marcia reflects that Christina seems to have an aversion to going to performances of her clients. 'Och, that gave her a wee run for her money too,' she says to Apollo as she passes him, and then goes on with making her dress. The neckline is a little lower than she'd planned, and she searches in a drawer full of old stoles and scarves for something that she might be able to drape over her shoulders. She turns out the whole drawer and sees at the bottom, long hidden, her father's prayer shawl, his tallit. It still smells faintly of his skin and of his pipe smoke, a habit he acquired in England and which Miriam constantly deplored.

His tallit. To her knowledge she never saw him use it, yet it smells of him. Did he use it as a scarf inside his clothes? She presses it to her own face, her eyes shut, her heart pierced by sudden longing for her parents.

'She had nightmares, you know. Even long after Hitler was dead, she used to dream that his troops overran England and rounded up her Wunderkind with all the other Jewish children. If she could have changed your blood for Anglo-Saxon and wiped your DNA profile clean of Jewish genes she would have. And there you are looking just like your Cohen grandmother! Nothing to do about it except have nightmares.'

'I have a Jewish dream about once a year. I know it's Jewish but I can't explain it.'

'What do you dream about, Maüslein?'

'It's always the same – a sort of noise of voices, rows of people chanting something strange, chanting Hebrew I suppose, but I don't understand a word. I dream I get out of bed to see better and it stops. A silly dream.'

'Maimonides.'

'What?'

Martin's gaze had gone blank, his mouth soft and shapeless.

'I used to play a tape of Arabic chanting when I was working on Maimonides, after you'd gone to sleep. You were no more than three or four.'

'What's Maimonides?'

'Who. Moses Maimonides was a twelfth-century Egyptian Jew of immense learning – he was part of a burst of learning which marked the end of the Dark Ages, a small Renaissance of its own as remarkable in some ways as the one everyone knows about.' He stopped.

'I've never heard of him.' Her father's obvious unwillingness to talk about this arcane subject made her curious. 'Tell me more.'

'He lived and worked all his life in Cairo, but he was known throughout the Jewish Diaspora. He was a late starter, became a doctor in mid-life, and wrote extensively on diet, medicines, treatments – with an extraordinarily modern emphasis on psychosomatic diagnoses. He was a profound thinker, a rationalist, heroic in every aspect of his busy life. He's always fascinated me, he's my hero in Jewish history.'

'Why haven't you ever mentioned him to me before then?'

Martin ignored her remark. 'I tell you, Marcia, when I discovered soon after Miriam and I arrived here that large numbers of original documents about him found in a synagogue attic at the end of the nineteenth century were stored in Cambridge, it was like a miracle. I decided to write a book about him, but I couldn't get any funding so I had to do my research in my spare time and in school holidays. Maimonides became part of our family – Miriam and I used to discuss him as if he was in the next room.'

'Where does the chanting come in?'

'In Maimonides' time all public learning was by heart – the whole of Jewish history and teaching was handed down without any change to the pronunciation and punctuation through the centuries, and somebody lent me a tape of Yemeni Jews chanting because they've preserved the ancient Arabic pronunciation. It was probably the same pronunciation used by Maimonides himself. My friend lent me his recorder with the tape, and I had it for about six months and played it often. Very haunting. You must have heard it when you were in bed in the next room.'

'I don't remember it.'

'Your dream-mind does.'

'And your book on Moses M?'

'It was never written.' Martin stared beyond her. 'After I'd finished all my research and was about to start the easy part, the book itself, I wrote to an American university hoping to interest them in publishing it. I'd kept in touch with a Berlin friend who emigrated to New York, and he was certain I'd get a contract for it, an advance, the further funding I needed. It was an important subject, with wider implications beyond its relevance to Jewish and Islamic history. My friend was a top academic; with his recommendation I felt sure I'd get a publisher. Would you make some tea, Maüslein?'

Marcia remembers how bleakly blank her father's face was as he asked – unusually for him – for tea so late in the evening. It was the blankness of the traumatized. While she boiled a pan of water on the gas ring, she heard rustlings and the opening and shutting of drawers as Martin searched for something. When she returned, he had a letter in his hand, still folded crisply as if it had never been read. Marcia tried to look over his shoulder as he opened it out and saw it was from the Department of Jewish Studies at Harvard before Martin folded the sheet up again quickly.

'This is only the second time I've ever looked at this letter, and it still hurts.'

'Can't I read it?'

'You don't need to. Every word is still burned into my memory.

Dear Mr Fleckner,

I was interested to hear of your researches into that important figure in our history, Moses Maimonides, and you are right in assuming that publications on his life would be welcomed by our Press as well as by other American academic institutions. But alas, you are too late. There are at least six publications in the pipeline on all aspects of Maimonides's life and works by eminent scholars – S. D. Gostein, Alexander Marx, Arthur Hyman, to mention three of many. Of course there is nothing to stop you completing your book, and it may throw its own special and valuable light—'

Martin stopped again.

'Dad, let me read it. Please.' Marcia took the sheet from his fingers and read the last paragraph first.

I am sorry if this is rather a blow. Scholars are by nature secretive, and some, like you, pay the price of this secrecy by wasting years on a subject being covered by others adept at concealing their traces. My advice to you is wait, read the publications as they appear, and discover if you have a fresh angle.

After skimming through the rest of it – he had indeed remembered it word for word – she gave the letter back to Martin who promptly put a corner of it in the gasfire and watched it burn up in his fingers.

'That professor sounded like a nice man. Did you follow his advice?'

'What was the point?'

The grey crinkly ashes fell from his fingers on to the tiled hearth.

'Life was very hard for you and Mutti.'

'No harder than for all the others.'

'This must have been such a disappointment after all those years of research.'

'Marcia, we continually fool ourselves. Perhaps it hurt me so much because it was really only a delusion that I could write a definitive book about Maimonides. Not long ago I read the book on him by Gostein. I could never have done anything so good. At the time I thought I could, of course I did. But no way. I see it now.'

'But you never tried.'

'No. It was beyond me. You see, Miriam and I, but particularly Miriam, saw ourselves as victims of fate and could never shake that off. Others turned themselves around and flourished and enriched everyone else who came in contact with them. Forced emigration can have a wonderfully creative and productive effect in the long term, but not for everyone and not for us.'

'It would help me a lot to know why.' Marcia watched a draught make the letter's ashes lift and quiver. Martin stirred sugar into his tea with one of the Woolworth spoons that replaced the stolen silver ones.

'If we had known why it would have helped us too.'

'You have given me such a good start in life.'

He looked up in surprise at her.

'You have. What a sacrifice you both made to make sure I was a good little English girl. Don't look at me like that, I'm not mocking you. I loved my school, I loved being an adopted gentile, I was proud to be baptized like all my schoolfriends. You made the right decision.'

'We did it out of fear.'

'I don't care why you did it. It gave me freedom. School, university, drama school, what fun I've had. It's not your fault I've chosen this risky profession. I love it, so never think of it as a bad choice for me the way I know your friends do!'

'I'd like to see you happily married.'

'Ah, Dad, don't hope for that too hard. I'm not sure I'm the marrying type.'

'I liked your Neil.'

'I liked my Neil. But look what happened the moment we got engaged!'

'I got ill and you came home to nurse me.'

'No, no, before that. Neil seemed to change, he began to take our relationship for granted, to assume he'd call the tune. Of course he didn't really change, it was me who came to my senses – I stopped kidding myself I'd be able to change him and saw him as he really was. I expect he saw me differently too. Anyway, you falling ill and needing me was a perfect excuse for moving back home, out of that relationship for ever. Never blame yourself for that, Dad. I like living here with you.'

'I feel it cramps your style.'

Marcia laughed. 'Not at all. I live the way I want to.'

'You don't bring boyfriends here.'

'I don't want to. There haven't been any real ones since Neil anyway.'

'You must feel free to leave me any time you like, Mauslein.'

'I do feel free. I will leave when I need to.'

'Good.'

Marcia fetched a dustpan and brush and swept the ashes off the hearth. As she returned to the kitchen she kissed her father's cheek.

'Thank you for telling me about Moses Maimonides.'

'I should have burnt that letter long ago.'

'Now was the right time.'

'I have let my Arabic go completely.'

'It's a pity you couldn't have taught it instead of German. But I suppose there was no demand.'

'Not in England. Not much in Germany either, come to that. My father couldn't understand when I decided to concentrate on Arabic instead of Hebrew. I remember telling him there were countless Jews who knew Hebrew but only a few knew Arabic. And our history is so tied with the Middle East, it seemed important to learn it. Maimonides only wrote in Arabic, for instance; he didn't know Hebrew. He had to be translated into it. My father couldn't believe that a great Jewish thinker existed who didn't know Hebrew.' Martin was smiling as he talked about his father; Marcia stood in the doorway, dustpan in hand, unwilling to move. He so very rarely talked about the family. 'And think how he would have despaired if he'd known how many hours I'd spent studying Maimonides, and all in vain, all in vain.'

'Would he have been proud of you if you'd done the book?'

'Yes, of course. Jews are always proud of sons who write books. In a strange way, he was even proud of my Arabic.'

'What did he feel when you had to leave him behind in Germany?' Marcia had never been able to ask this question before.

'He thought we were panicking unnecessarily. He was one of those people who can shut their minds to what they don't want to see.'

'Sounds like me. Did you try to persuade him to leave with you?'

'Of course I suggested it, but it was pointless. You can't imagine the solidity, the stability, of his existence until then. He was an established German banker; even the First War hardly affected him. The world needs bankers during wars – if another war came he'd be just as useful. That was his view. And he couldn't leave the house my mother died in, I'd been born in, he'd been born in. Miriam and I both knew we couldn't force him to come with us. So we left him. He was rounded up early in the war, and was certainly dead by 1942.'

'This is the first time you've ever talked to me about him.'

'It's such a long time ago, Marcia, and I don't feel any pain now. He'd have hated it in England, he couldn't have changed his good life, the memory of his good marriage, for the makeshift existence he would certainly have had here. He chose to stay, and we respected his choice. There wasn't much else we could do.'

'But you must have felt guilty you didn't persuade him—'

'Of course we did. Of course we did. And Miriam's parents too.' Martin looked at his daughter. 'I suppose, looking back, that was why Miriam – why Miriam gave up on her life. Even the arrival of our Wunderkind didn't counterbalance that heavy weight of guilt and grief. The last thing Miriam's mother said to us was: don't feel guilty if anything happens to us. But guilt is involuntary, Marcia. Guilt is involuntary.'

Guilt is involuntary. Marcia puts the tallit away again and stares at her bed. Guilt is involuntary. If I'm honest, there was a minute element of sadistic glee in me as I pressed the glass into Edward's backside, just a flicker, and I am feeling guilt. But he frightened me, I had to do what I did . . . or did I? Did I need to hurt him to stop him?

Marcia dials Edward's number. She imagines his movements round the flat as he comes to answer it – too long, he can't be there—

'Hullo?'

'Edward. It's Marcia. I thought you must be out—'

'I can't move very fast at the moment, as you should well know.'

'I'm sorry—'

'So you bloody ought to be. It's very painful, every movement pulls at the stitches.'

'I really am sorry.'

'I can't sit down properly, I can only lie down in comfort on my front. Not a lot of fun.' Marcia listens to further details of his uncomfortable and restricted life and knows that she is being manipulated.

'Why did you do it, Marcia?'

'You frightened me.'

'Come off it.'

'I only rang to apologize for hurting you. I must go.'

'Since when did a little sexual horseplay frighten you!'

'Goodbye.' Marcia unplugs her phone again and goes to the window, her face between her hands. The call has achieved nothing, even done harm.

She sees the time and gets dressed to leave for the theatre in a long drab old coat, her black beret and her glasses. Her head throbs and she takes a couple of painkillers before locking up her flat.

Todd is outside talking to two reporters. When he sees her she says quickly in her best Glaswegian accent, 'Todd, have you seen Marcia today?'

'Marcia—'

'Just tell her if you do that a man was asking for her earlier. Could have been selling insurance, could have been anything. Wouldn't leave his name.'

'Oh, yes, right—'

'See you, Todd. I'm off to my yoga class.' Marcia hurries away in the opposite direction to the station and ducks down a side street when she is out of sight. She decides to walk as far as Camden Town, even if it makes her slightly late.

It is beginning to drizzle and she turns her collar up to meet her beret. She shouldn't have rung Edward; she grows more angry with herself at every step. She should have lived with her guilt. Guilt is involuntary, after all. As Martin said: *You can't prevent it and you can't banish it. All you can do is face it and learn to live with it. And it goes away one day of its own accord, like a wart.*

Creusa must have felt terrible guilt. However young she was when she abandoned her baby to the mercy of the god, and however blindly faithful to the belief Apollo would look after his child, she must have felt guilt. And then to be childless for all those years of marriage would have seemed like a judgment on her for her misdeed. Creusa was probably about sixteen when she was raped, and in her mid-thirties by the time of the play's action. In her prime. Seventeen years of regular menstruation (the despair at the ever-regular arrival of blood), seventeen years of remembering the sensation of tingling in the nipples, the full breasts of pregnancy, the unused milk leaking from engorged breasts after the birth.

Marcia sits with her eyes shut as the train rattles between stations, running through her part. She opens them to find a man staring fixedly at her from the opposite seat, wonders if she's been muttering her part aloud, and shuts her eyes again.

If she were better off she'd have taken taxis to the theatre during this crucial week, and particularly today, the press night; she longs to sit in a capsule, internalized. But she also knows that the journey amongst crowds, in a jolting train snaking through tunnels under London in the required winding manner is no bad preparation either for Creusa's own journey from Athens to Delphi.

She enters the theatre past the box office and goes backstage through the stalls, popping her head in on Willie before she disappears into her dressing-room.

'How are tricks, Willie?'

'There's still a small reception committee outside. I told them to go away but it's useless. These flowers just came too.' He passes her a bunch of richly scented white lilies. 'I put all the others upstairs.'

'Heavens. What a little publicity will do for one's image.'

The lilies are from the Kleins; there's a bunch of carnations from Christina, and a pot-plant, a dazzling blue cineraria, from Todd and Elspeth.

'Everyone is sorry for me, Suzanne.'

'Don't tell me you never get flowers when you're playing the lead.'

'Not like this from old friends.'

'Moan, moan, moan.'

'What's the matter, Suze?'

'My father was rushed to hospital last night. He's had a stroke.'

'I'm sorry.'

'And he's in Yorkshire so there's no way I can see him until Sunday. Luckily he's recovering better than expected. Isn't it strange how crises always seem to develop when I'm in work?'

Marcia puts her arms round Suzanne and they stand hugging until they hear John Alsopp call from outside. 'Can I come in?'

Marcia opens the door and John comes in. 'Just to say good luck for tonight and to give you the Alsopp remedy for instant energy.' He kisses Marcia and Suzanne and gives them each a box of Bendick's Bittermints before hurrying off.

'That man is such a dear. I'd work for him anywhere.' Suzanne sounds quite tearful. 'Just give me the chance.'

'Me too.'

They are both now undressing and preparing themselves at speed for the performance.

'Oh, Rollo left this tape for you. It's the music.'

'Do you mind if I put it on?'

'Go ahead.'

As the reedy sound of the Greek *clarino* begins, Willie knocks and hands in a basket filled with fruit.

'Fortnum's no less.' Suzanne puts it on the battered armchair under the window, and hands Marcia the envelope lying on the fruit. Inside there is a postcard of a red-figure Greek vase, with a message from George:

This is to wish you the very best for the opening tonight. I'm bringing a guest on Saturday and in case he suggests dinner and it becomes awkward afterwards I shall be seeing him home. The last thing you need after the performance is to make smalltalk to a stranger! So I've ordered a car to collect you – you can come when you're ready – the driver will wait outside the stage door and will bring you straight to Hereford Square. I'll be there by the time you get there. All the best, George.

Marcia tucks the card into the edge of her mirror, obscurely bothered by it but in no state to consider why. The process of dressing and making up takes all her attention; Rollo's music is drawing her into her part and by the time she is waiting in the wings for her first entry her personal life is forgotten.

15

Does Euripides denounce Apollo? Is he expecting the audience to assume that Ion is in truth Creusa's son by Apollo? Or is the true explanation he is an all-too-human bastard? Are, therefore, the goddess Athena's remarks at the end of the play that though Ion is Apollo's true son this must be hidden from Xuthus and from the rest of the world, simply an equivocation?

George sits in his dress-circle seat reading the programme as the theatre fills up around him. He's alone (he had been lying about the friend) and nervous. He hasn't seen Marcia act for a while, and never playing a central part like this one. He'd expected a low-budget, fringe feel to this production and is surprised to see the quality of the cast, director and producer, and the big names amongst the sponsors. Alsopp clearly has pull; even the programme has a lavish feel. He's written the introduction George has just read, but does not give his own views about the questions he raises.

The play, like all good plays, resists a final and definitive interpretation. You, the audience, are as right as I am.

Humility or cowardice? Irritated, George looks at photographs of the actors in rehearsal; one of Marcia's face shows it vivid with fear as a young man – Ion? – threatens her. Another shows her alone, with her face thrown back in some internal epiphany of feeling. He is afraid he will find her acting too emotional, even embarrassing, from these two images, and closes the programme. Three minutes to go. It's a full house. The reviews he saw were excellent, with particular praise for Creusa and Ion. The production was also praised for its otherness, its emphasis of the strangeness of the ancient world. The house lights fade and the expectant buzz dies.

The play opens in the darkness before dawn, with thin wailing music permeating the words coming from the almost invisible figure of the god Hermes. His voice echoes eerily as he tells the audience the story of Creusa's rape by Apollo, and how the child was brought to Delphi to serve the god, in ignorance of his origins. As Hermes fades the dawn breaks slowly to the sound of birds, a vociferous chorus of birds from all sides. A young man places a burning tripod before the sanctuary and announces:

The dazzling chariot of the sun now lights the earth.

The simplicity of his diction, his naive energy as he sweeps the sanctuary, his shooing of the wild birds away from the temple carvings, his unselfconscious sweetness, immediately enchant the audience. He is the perfect son, the dream of any childless woman. Damian Frapp is almost naked, with the curled plaited hair of a typical *kouros*. The contrast with Creusa's elaborate headdress and costume is marked; she is an hieratic figure as she enters, but her face is awash with ordinary tears.

I have no child – Apollo knows how true that is!

The hairs rise on George's neck. There is a quality in Creusa's tone, in the movement of her lips, that evokes in him the terrible night Marcia ended their relationship. It is not a personal but an archetypal female cry. From that moment he watches the play utterly gripped as the Queen moves towards the central crisis and through it to the final denouement which, though expected, is still fresh, still moving. Mother and son embrace but Ion asks for himself and for everyone: *Are Apollo's oracles truth or lies?* There is no answer, only a happy resolution based on concealment, manipulation and deception.

George is so drained he finds it difficult to get out of his seat. Almost the last to leave the dress-circle, he hurries home and goes straight to his desk. He takes out the letter Lena wrote the day she collapsed and re-reads it.

Your father's name is Philip Symes ... He never knew that I became pregnant, because I decided to move away from Jodhpur. I met Geoffrey on the train to Delhi – it was the luckiest train I ever took. He took care of me from that moment on, and married me as soon as I'd had you. We left you with your ayah for a few months, and then moved with you to a new posting. No one in India ever knew you were Philip Symes's son and not Geoffrey Warne's, but I think it's just possible that Philip might have guessed who you were. I have never contacted Philip since I left India, and I have no idea even if he's alive.

Lena did not abandon her baby in a cave, she left him for months with an unknown Indian wet-nurse. And the baby grew up with another equivocation: that his parents were Lena and Geoffrey Warne . . .

George stares out into the dark street and the square beyond through the uncurtained window. He had paid no particular attention to the sentence about his being left for a few months with an ayah; he had focused only on his father's name, Philip Symes, and his relief that at last his mother had confessed it.

The first betrayal was no doubt Geoffrey Warne's idea. Leave him, let's go and get married, we'll collect him later, we'll move to a far part of India, no one will ever know. What else could Lena do? Like Creusa, she was trapped, and the abandonment of the baby was the easiest solution. And after those months, how did she feel? How much had she missed her son? Was she tempted to leave him forever, child to a woman who would surely have also abandoned him, had funds dried up, at the doorway of a Christian mission for the white man's god to save?

George holds his hands out and looks at them. Soft, white, well-cared for, the hands of a Western urban sophisticate. As a baby, these hands had pounded at brown breasts as he sucked at dark nipples; his life had been surrounded by Indian faces and Indian voices, Indian children fighting him for the woman's attention, in surroundings light-years from anything he ever experienced again. Unimaginable. And if he had been left there? He sees himself momentarily as an attendant at a shrine to Krishna, sweeping the sanctuary, scaring away the birds – tears run down his cheeks until he shakes himself, puts the letter hurriedly away, tries to restore calm by splashing his face with cold water and then breathing deeply.

The door-bell rings. It can't be Marcia already. But it is, he can see her through the frosted Victorian glass panels on his front door, bending to peer through the glass as she always did. It is her first visit here since they parted.

'What a wonderful play.' He takes her coat as they stand uneasily in the hall. 'Wonderful.' He kisses her cheek.

'You really liked it?'

'Profoundly.' He turns away to hide his emotion, and leads her to the kitchen where he takes a half-bottle of Bollinger out of the fridge.

'How nice your house looks, George. That's a new picture – another of your art-school buys?'

'Got it at last summer's Royal College degree show.'

'Magic realism.'

'I suppose so. Like tonight.'

'Tonight?'

'The production was in the same style. Magic realism.'

'I'm not sure I know what you mean.'

'I think I mean the presentation of "real life" by exaggeration and distortion of chosen characteristics which then become symbolical. This of course emphasized the strangeness of the "real life" of two thousand years ago.'

'I hadn't thought of it like that.' She watches him ease off the champagne cork. 'Very perceptive of you. Did you like the music?'

'It was all of a piece with the production – marvellously evocative of an unimaginable past. A contradiction in terms, because it has to be imagined, but so is magic realism.'

'I'm going to pass all that back to John Alsopp.'

'He'll think I'm being very pretentious.' They both laugh. 'As for you, Marcia, you were also wonderful. You deserved your rave reviews. I'm glad you got them.'

'It's been amazing. I feel outside it all – quite oddly detached. Damian Frapp accused me of being blasé but I'm not. Why is everyone so surprised that I'm good? I've always known I could pull off a big performance if I was given the chance.'

'Here's to many more of them. Come and sit down for ten minutes – unless you're desperately hungry and would like to go and eat now?'

'It takes me a while to unwind after a performance. Hunger doesn't come until I have.'

She follows George into his sitting-room and they sit down at right-angles to each other and sip their champagne in silence for a few moments.

'I thought the actor playing Ion was excellent too. He really grew up as we watched.'

'Our Damian will go far. He thinks he's God's answer to the English theatre but as he probably is, it's hard to dislike him for it. And he's good to work with – as they all are. I could face a long run with this lot.'

'But it's only on for a couple of weeks, isn't it?'

'There's a good chance it might transfer to the West End.'

'What excellent news, Marcia. It deserves to.'

'I can't really believe it yet. We were only told today.' There's a glint of tears in Marcia's eyes, which she blinks away as she smiles and gives her head a shake.

'This is a real celebration, then. A real celebration.'

'Why, have you just had a big win or something?'

'Or something. But that's for later. I'm still shaken up by the play, so let's talk about it – it's honestly the best thing I've seen for ages. Euripides writes so well – no one has really improved on him in all these centuries. It gave me a dose of catharsis, you know. Doesn't often happen to an old cynic like me.'

'I'm surprised in a way it appealed so much to you.' Marcia thinks of Rachel's intensely emotional reaction to the first night. 'I would have thought it was more of a woman's play.'

'I recently learned from my mother that she abandoned me at birth for the first few months of my life. So the play was all rather near the bone.'

'Oh, George. Oh dear.'

'I'd also guessed long ago that Geoffrey Warne wasn't my real father, but it was only just before she died that Lena told me who it was.'

'Did your adoptive father know the truth? Or was he treated like Xuthus and kept in the dark?'

'He knew from the beginning. He rescued Lena when she was illegitimately pregnant and married her as soon as I was born, then later took me in so that I could be passed off as their son in a new job far from my birthplace.'

'Is your real father alive?'

'I have no idea, Marcia.'

'You ought to find out.'

'It might unleash all sorts of trouble.'

'True. Digging about in one's past sometimes does.'

'Have another glass?'

'I'm starting to feel very hungry.'

'It's only a half-bottle – let's finish it.' George picks up his glass and raises it. 'To the West End transfer!'

'It's not definite.'

'Then may it happen!'

'And your good news?'

'It isn't good news in the way yours is.'

'You've been made Head of your Chambers?'

'That would be cause for despair!'

'I thought being Head of Chambers was an honour?'

'Unpaid hard work. Come on, let's go.'

George helps Marcia into a drab long coat, wondering why she isn't wearing the red one which so caught the eye at the funeral. She pulls on a beret that does nothing for her. They leave the house in silence, just as it starts to rain. George darts back for a large umbrella; in order to share it, they have to walk close together but Marcia doesn't take his arm.

'Did you see the papers?'

'Your reviews – a couple—'

'No, earlier this week. The report of my attack on Edward Wintlesham.'

'Yes, I did.'

'And you were horrified?'

'I was a bit shocked when I first saw it. Then I told myself that the Press get everything wrong and tried to forget about it.'

'George, Edward's been my lover for quite a while.'

'So I gathered.'

'It's over now.'

'I wondered about that.'

'Did you make me come in a hired car alone so that you wouldn't be seen with me in public?'

'I'm afraid I did.'

'You old devil! I guessed. No one recognizes me anyway with this old coat and beret—'

'I'm sorry, Marcia. I hated myself for doing it.'

'Doesn't matter.'

'The thing is, I suddenly have to be extra careful. This is absolutely confidential – I've been asked to tell as few people as possible – but I'm going on the High Court Bench.'

'Congratulations!' Marcia gives a little skip. 'How exciting, particularly since I remember you telling me it was something you never expected to be! Sir George Warne!'

George groans. 'Don't.'

'You'll have to stop mixing with unsavoury characters like me.'

'Marcia, I've missed you. I didn't realize how much until I saw you at Lena's funeral. I know you've been involved with someone else and I'm not expecting you to have missed me, but I wanted you to know I've missed you. Why should one keep these things hidden? Enough. This is the restaurant.'

'I remember coming here with you before.' Awkwardness returns as she follows him in, his words ringing in her mind. They take off their coats and then are taken to a table in a bow window. 'It's such a pretty place. I love the real fire. I can smell the wood.'

'I've ordered dinner already, do you mind? They like you to do that here, particularly if one is eating late.'

'I love surprises. And I couldn't concentrate on a menu after hearing your big news. When is it all going to happen?'

'Too soon. Within a couple of months. They have to be quick about it once you've accepted, in case the news gets out.'

'I can see why you didn't want the Press to see you with me.'

'Mr Warne, nice to see again. Welcome.'

'Michel! We're ravenous and ready to start.'

'I changed the menu a little. First you are having the wild mushroom ravioli with slivers of white truffle, then I give you borscht, then you don't have the two grouses, you have grouse pudding with oysters. And with it the good Barolo as you asked. I just open it ten minutes ago.'

'The borscht is an excellent idea. It sounds perfect, Michel.'

'It is perfect. Good-balancing meal.' Michel is a strange-looking man with long bony wrists protruding inches from his cuffs, and a permanently lugubrious expression. His French accent is heavy. As he goes round the tables he never smiles, but his clients shine with contentment.

'You're a great foodie, George.'

'Blame it on my mainly single life.'

'Nonsense. I know lots of single people who think of food simply as fodder. I'm a bit like that myself.'

'That's not the impression you've given me.'

'Ah, I'm a chameleon. I become a foodie with you. With Edward I might find myself happily eating at McDonalds.'

'Happily?'

'Well, not unhappily.'

The first course arrives at this moment and George can hide his hurt at the easy familiarity with which she mentions Edward. He wonders if the affair really is over, and what exactly happened to excite the Press to report the incident so widely.

They eat the ravioli in appreciative silence until George breaks it. 'A minor worry about life as a High Court Judge is the food I'll have to put up with. One has to live in Judges' Lodgings, you know, and be ruled by the prevailing regime. It can be stultifying for a free spirit.'

'What's your definition of free spirit?'

'In my book, a free spirit is usually self-employed and therefore only answerable to themselves for what goes right or wrong with their lives. Someone who does what they want to do not too selfconsciously and without caring what other people think of them. Someone who lives daily with uncertainty and who has the courage to ignore the prevailing current. Someone like you, Marcia.'

'No, I'm an actor, I'm by nature selfconscious. Too selfconscious to be a free spirit. I fit the bill in some of the other ways, I suppose. So do you.'

'I'm not as immune as I was to other people's opinion of me. And I'm about to give up being self-employed. I'm going to have a salary and a pension. I'll lose the edge of uncertainty, everything will take its appointed course. Oh dear.'

'But surely you'll have plenty of uncertainty – think of the decisions you'll have to make in really tricky cases? Like that recent case of the little girl who had treatment withheld by the NHS? Were they right or wrong to do so? How could anyone have been certain which way the judgment should have gone? The poor judge would have been criticized whatever he decided!'

'That was a very difficult decision, I agree, and I've no doubt at all I'll have some equally testing ones to make.'

'Lots of lovely uncertainty! You are funny. Most people long for the opposite. Oh, George, this is the most delicious meal I've eaten since – since the last time you took me here!'

'I suppose I am a foodie.' A waiter removes their well-cleaned first-course plates, smiling as he hears that remark.

'By my standards you certainly are. What are we having next?'

'Borscht.'

'My mother used to make borscht.'

'I'm a foodie partly because I don't have much in my life besides work and food and drink.'

'Don't talk like that, George.'

'It's true. I'm not complaining or asking for sympathy, but it's a fact. Most of the time I work, and I interrupt the passage of my days with good food and wine. I go to the opera, to concerts, to the theatre. I look at beautiful things in exhibitions. I travel in a manner that mirrors my home life bar the work. It's all very predictable and will get more so when I'm on the Bench.'

'But isn't a free spirit an inner thing? You could lead any life, however constricted, and be a free spirit, it seems to me. Maybe your new existence will give you a new dimension as well – I don't know, I'm just burbling. But on the subject of freedom, George, I can tell you I don't feel free most of the time. When I've got no work, or lost a part to an actress I think is worse than me, and my overdraft gets to flash point, I certainly don't feel free. Trapped would describe it better. You can talk about freedom because you have no financial worries – if you have a problem you can just throw money at it. Not an option I've ever had.'

'I've always admired the way you cope, Marcia. I don't know how you do.'

'I just wait until problems go away.' Bowls of clear vivid purple-red soup arrive, curls of sour cream suspended in the liquid.

'And if they don't?'

'Ay, there's the rub. George . . .'

'What is it?'

'I've never asked you for legal advice . . .'

'I wouldn't mind. Go ahead.'

'I might have an awful problem looming. Edward Wintlesham has gone to his solicitor about my attack. He threatens to take me to court over it.'

'Have you had a letter before action yet?'

'What's that?'

'Have the solicitors written to you outlining Wintlesham's position?'

'Not yet. Actually the solicitor in question is Robert Wintlesham, Edward's brother. He's a very smooth piece of work – I don't like him and he doesn't like me.'

'His firm?'

'Cross and Thorogood and something?'

'Peel, Cross and Thorogood. It's a good firm. I've acted for them in the past.'

This remark upsets Marcia so much she stops sipping her borscht.

'Oh God, George. This is going to be serious. I wish I hadn't mentioned it. I'm beginning to feel sick.'

'These things never come to much. I'll sort it out for you – the moment you get a letter let me know and I'll help you. Relax and finish your soup.' He takes her hand.

'I haven't taken any of this seriously enough. I've refused to face the truth.' She withdraws her hand gently and picks up the spoon again.

'What do you see as the truth?'

'Edward is a vindictive man. I've hurt his body and worse, I've hurt his pride.'

'Forget the pride. The body is the important aspect. How badly did you hurt him?'

'I cut him. I gave him a jab with – with the base of a broken wine glass. Edward had just broken it, I picked it up to throw it away, he started to attack me, I dug it into his buttock.' She drops her spoon in her soup as she rubs her forehead and starts to laugh. 'It sounds so stupid and messy. So silly.'

'Stop laughing, Marcia. You'll become hysterical.'

'I am already, just thinking about it.'

'No, you're not. You're on a high after that marvellous performance. Come on, do try and finish that soup. Michel is not impressed by people who leave good food uneaten – it will ruin my reputation with him.' He watches her finish the borscht, noticing how her hand shakes as she carries the spoon to her mouth. 'I don't want to hear the details now, nor do I wish to pry into your private life, Marcia, but I do advise one thing which could help future developments enormously. Sit down tomorrow or as soon as you can and write an exact account of what happened. Try not to make any judgments, don't edit, just write down exactly what was said and what was done in what order. Bald and clear.'

'I hate to think about it.'

'I'm sure you do, but you have to. Even if nothing further happens and any actions against you are dropped, you'll find it is curiously therapeutic to write it all down.'

The waiter takes away their plates and George pours some wine.

'You're the first person to talk sense to me, George.'

'Who is your solicitor?'

'I haven't appointed one yet. Someone has recommended Stephen Smith, but I haven't done anything about him yet. Solicitors cost money.'

'He's good. But wait for a few days and see what happens. People change their minds. You may hear nothing more.'

'Let's hope so.' Marcia blows her nose. 'Do you mind if I disappear for a moment? I need to recoup.'

As she walks away George notices she's lost weight. The black skirt she's wearing is not the tight fit it should be. Her face is always angular, her arms and legs slim and wiry, but he remembers her body being more solid, more rounded, in the past. He shuts his eyes to blot out the intensity of his desire to see her breasts again, her accentuated waist, the whiteness of her stomach above intensely black thick pubic hair, the two deep dimples above her buttocks. Snatches of remembered love-making flash through his mind, the feel of her vagina, her sounds when—

'There, I feel much better.' Marcia sits down opposite him, her makeup refreshed, her expression much calmer.

'You look beautiful.'

'Don't, George.'

'Why not? It's the truth, and I'm just being appreciative and honest.'

'I wasn't very good to you.'

'Forget the past.'

'I've never been much good at that. The past seems to stick to me and intrude all the time whether I like it or not. Never mind. Tell me more about your future. I'm fascinated. You've only talked about your lodgings!'

George is aware she is steering him away from emotion and lets himself be led. He tells her about his robes, about the ceremony of swearing in and taking the oath, and realizes how much he would like her to be there with him. Wives and family are welcome. As he wonders whether ex-mistresses with colourful reputations would be equally welcome, the grouse pudding arrives and is cut in half before them, releasing its delicious contents.

'With this pudding there is navets and potato purée and a little steamed kale.'

'Michel, this looks wonderful.'

'Bon appétit.' Michel slithers off, face funereal.

'And then you go to Buckingham Palace to be knighted?'

'Afraid so.'

'How grand you will be. As I said before, you won't be able to mix with riff-raff like me.'

'Don't talk nonsense.'

'Actually I'm not talking nonsense. You honestly can't risk your name being linked with mine. The Press love a scandal. They've been thick round my door all week – the good reviews have kept their interest going. You were wise to send a car the way you did.'

'I refuse to talk about it now. It will spoil my dinner.'

'You and I seem to have several topics that upset our digestions!'

'Life's little problems.'

They eat without talking for a while; the silence is easy.

'Did Lena know about your news?'

'No, sadly.'

'She would have loved it. She'd have been so proud. What a pity she didn't know.'

'I do regret not telling her about my appointment.'

'And your unknown father, George? Are you going to look for him?'

'I don't know. He was older than Lena, so he's probably dead. He may never have known of my existence, so why disturb him? And he was last heard of in India, in Jodhpur.'

'But aren't you curious to find out more about him?'

'Of course I'm curious. Curious is the correct word – I don't burn to find out. Though of course if I started to look I would no doubt get hooked on the search. And then, if he was alive, I would have to see him. Actually, searching for people who were important to me in the past seems to be part of my life at the moment. I had a teacher once who changed my life, got me thinking, got me into Oxford, and I've just traced him. Spoke to him a few days ago on the telephone.'

'Did he remember you?'

'Eventually. Peter Dawlish was a meteor who streaked across the ghastly tedium of my minor public school, and like meteors didn't last long. But in the short time he taught me he influenced my life more than any other person before or since.'

'Did you tell him?'

'I said I owed him a great debt. He didn't seem particularly impressed. I'd love to see him again – he lives in Gloucestershire somewhere, not too far away. I said I'd drop in sometime but he had a coughing fit at that point – he always smoked a lot – and it wasn't very clear whether the idea was welcome before he had to ring off.'

'You must go. I haven't got anyone like that in my life – my teachers were a uniformly uninspiring lot on the whole. My father was my guru. Full of ideas and wisdom. I think you'd have liked him.'

'Marcia. It's Sunday tomorrow. Come with me to Gloucestershire. Let's make a day of it.'

Marcia's dark eyes meet his in surprise. The waiter comes up to clear the main course at that moment, and neither of them speaks until he has left.

'It's a mad idea, George. You'll regret it.'

'Why?'

'You certainly will if the Press get hold of it. Say we have an accident?'

'You're not saying no, though. I can see you'd like to go.'

'It's exactly the sort of impromptu outing I love and you know it. To whizz out of London after the tensions of the last week would be bliss.'

'Then let's go. Who knows you're with me?'

'Nobody. I know what you're thinking – that someone could shop me to a reporter. No one knows. And your note is here in my bag.'

'That decides it. We'll go. I'm in between two lives, everything is strange, and impulses must be heeded. The idea came out of the blue.'

'I could see.'

'I'll ring Dawlish when we're on our way and if he's willing for a visit we'll go and see him. If not, we'll have a day in the country.'

'I'd love a good walk. Just coffee, thanks. No dessert. I've eaten superbly.'

Michel puts a small dish of petits fours in front of them, his glum expression at odds with the caressing gesture he uses to nudge the sweetmeats back into the centre of the dish. He brings a pot of coffee with the two cups, and goes. The silence at the table has changed again, and Marcia swallows as she breaks it.

'George, you're not hoping for anything to start again between us, are you?

'No. Yes. There's been no one else.'

'There will be. But not me.'

'Friendship then.'

'That we definitely have.' Her smile is so warm he feels faint. 'We always did – it would be lovely to have it back. But caution should rule you in your new life, and I'd completely understand if even friendship was too risky.'

George ignores her last remark. 'We ought to leave fairly early tomorrow. How are we going to plan this escapade?'

'I need to cover my tracks. And you mustn't be seen anywhere near my flat. The best thing would be for me to meet you at a convenient point somewhere tomorrow – say outside a Tube station.'

'Or I could give you a bed for the night—'

'On every level that would be folly.'

'I had no ulterior motives—'

'I know. But what if anyone knows we're here, dining together, and sees us return to your house for the night? Someone in this restaurant could have recognized one of us, put two and two together. I'll ask Michel to call me a taxi now, and leave before you. That way we won't be seen outside together.' She catches Michel's eye and organizes the taxi. 'Where shall we meet tomorrow?'

'Aren't you being over-careful, even paranoid, about the Press?'

'They've made me paranoid by their behaviour all week. You can't imagine what it's been like.'

'This cloak and dagger stuff still seems a bit extreme. All right, let's meet at Lancaster Gate station, since I'll be taking the M40 out of London. Nine o'clock?'

'Ten. All right, nine-thirty. I'll be unrecognizable.'

'Not to me.'

'You wait till you see me in my green bobble-hat, pink anorak, and trainers.'

What Jebs most liked doing to help his aunt, besides collecting the eggs, was de-podding the dried beans in the autumn. Aunt Cynthia would cut down the stems and put them to finish drying in a conservatory; then they would pull all the pods from the tangle of beanstraw and take the shiny beans out and put them in separate bowls. There were grey beans with red flecks, dark almost black beans, pale green beans, fat butterbeans. He loved removing the papery casings and running his hands through silky heaps of different beans, stirring them, holding handfuls up against his face.

'I like the flecky ones best to look at but the green ones are best to eat.'

'Don't you like the butterbeans?'

'Not so much. And they don't taste of butter.'

Jebs adored butter, and would watch his aunt making it to supplement the butter ration. She would shake the milk solids in a Kilner jar, on and on, rhythmically, as she walked about the kitchen. Jebs stayed close because it was always the best time to talk to her, since the shaking didn't take up her attention. She shook and shook until the whey had separated and then would mix salt into the yellow mass of butter before she pressed it into a wooden mould. Sometimes there was a little too much to fit comfortably into the mould, and Jebs would have it on hot toast. The taste and smell of hot melted butter, rare in wartime, entranced him.

'Your little Jebs loves helping me. He follows me round like my shadow . . .'

George puts Cynthia's letters away again; he's been sitting reading them for an hour since coming back from the restaurant. He's cold now because the central heating has long been off; he feels heavy, weighed down by good food and wine, by desires, by memories.

16

A car alarm wakes George just before his clock goes off; the meshing of the two bells is highly unpleasant as he struggles out of sleep and extinguishes one of them. The other drills on and on, driving him from his warm bed to the bathroom. He runs a deep bath and shaves while the tub fills, his red-rimmed eyes blankly intent as the razor purrs over his skin. He needs more sleep.

The jaunt to Gloucestershire seems utterly inappropriate to him this morning. He hasn't warned Peter Dawlish, who may not like such short notice and may even not be at home. He doesn't want to make this crucial visit in anyone else's company, even Marcia's. He can't imagine why he thought it was such a good idea last night.

But the sun is shining and he hasn't anything better to do. He should go down to sort his mother's house but knows he cannot face it. He needn't take Marcia as far as Gloucestershire, he could simply find somewhere pretty for a walk and a pub lunch. They could perhaps stop in Woodstock and visit Blenheim, they could walk in the Chilterns, forget about Dawlish entirely. By the time George has had his breakfast he's feeling cheerful; he collects maps and guidebooks together, he makes a note of Dawlish's address and phone number just in case, then he is ready, fittingly rural in corduroys, a thick jersey, strong leather boots.

The woman standing on the pavement outside Lancaster Gate station can't be Marcia. She's in a bright pink jacket padded like a Michelin man, and a Russian-style black fur hat with the flaps pulled down over the arms of heavy spectacles. And she's too short, surely . . .

But it's Marcia. She waves.

'I was looking for a green hat.'

'It looked too awful with this pink. How do you like my charity shop coat – amazing colour, isn't it?'

'Blinding.'

'I look such a fright. You're brave to have me anywhere near you! But if you don't mind, I'll keep the hat and glasses on until we've reached Westway.'

'I really think you're taking caution a little too far.'

'I'm protecting you as much as me.' Marcia sounds amused. 'Cheer up, this coat has the advantage of reversing to black, and once the hat and glasses are off I'll be me again. I've enjoyed perfecting the art of simple disguise. Luckily most people, and certainly the rat-pack, expect actresses to look like actresses, full of glamour, so it's not difficult.'

'Perhaps when I'm a judge I'll have to master the art of disguise too.'

'You'll find it harder. You're tall, you've got a distinctive profile, you move in a particularly characteristic way. You've got some noticeable habits—'

'Goodness. What do you mean?'

'Well, you toss your head in the air when you're considering something. I bet you do that in court all the time. You stand very straight, again with your head in the air. I'd know you in any crowd, whatever you were wearing. You're always you.'

'And you're not always you?'

'No. I shrink or I stretch when I play parts – it's only an impression but most actors seem to do it. They seem able to change physically.'

'I suppose it is true that in all my court performances I am only playing myself – in fact, you could say, for what it is worth, it is my stamp on the material I am presenting in court that has made me into a successful silk. As a judge I'm going to have to absorb all the time and project little. It's not a change I've given any thought to.'

'You'll still be you, with your own authority. Surely that's what the system is looking for and needs. A bit of duende, a bit of charisma.'

'I shouldn't think the ad hoc old boy network you kindly

call the system ever considers such qualities as duende or charisma.'

'You're laughing at me.'

'I'm laughing at the thought of Lord Conwick saying to his Permanent Secretary, "How's his charisma?"'

Marcia laughs too as she takes her glasses and her hat off and shakes out her hair. 'These hats are so snug. I thought it might come in useful if we go for a walk – there's a bitter wind despite the sun. What's the programme for today?'

'I haven't rung Dawlish yet. I thought we'd stop for coffee in Oxford and I'd do it then. After that we can plan accordingly.'

'I don't expect to come with you to see him. I'd be perfectly happy going off on my own while you're there.'

'Let's play it by ear.' But George can't help feeling a surge of relief at this as he puts on a Haydn trio into the cassette-player. When they reach Oxford he parks in St Giles and settles Marcia in the Randolph Hotel with coffee before going off to ring Dawlish. He spends a while rehearsing what he is going to say. Happen to be passing? Staying with friends nearby, suddenly realized how near it was?

'Hullo.'

'Mrs Dawlish? George Warne here, your husband's old pupil—'

'Peter's out at the moment fetching the paper, he'll be back soon—'

'I'm nearby and wondered—'

'Oh, drop in, do. Peter's tickled pink you got in touch. Come any time, take us as you find us.'

'Perhaps this afternoon?'

'Any time.' She rings off abruptly, leaving George in mid-sentence.

As he crosses the foyer on his way back to Marcia, a voice calls his name.

'It is George Warne QC, isn't it?'

'Yes, but I'm sorry I don't—'

'Richard Stenton. I interviewed you for a piece I did on civil rights for the *Observer*.'

'So you did – of course – so sorry not to recognize you.'

'Are you here for the Human Rights Convention too?'

'No, just passing through Oxford actually.'

'I'm covering it. I'm about to have some coffee – do come and join me.'

'I'm afraid I can't. Are you still with *the Obsever*?'

'Freelance now. One of the tabloids has commissioned me this time – I have to confess their interest is more in Bob Geldof than any wider issues, but I'm trying. Well, nice to meet you again.' He starts to move towards the room where Marcia is sitting.

'You too.'

George hurries out into Beaumont Street, sweating with panic and wondering how to alert Marcia to the turn of events. He goes to the car and writes her a note.

Marcia, a journalist I know has just sat down for coffee somewhere near you. Could you finish on your own and pay the bill? I think it would be better if I waited in the car. Sorry about all this.

He then writes Miss Fleckner on the envelope, disguising his writing. Darting back to the Randolph, he asks the receptionist, oiled by a fiver, to deliver it to her table, describing Marcia precisely, and explaining it is all a surprise for her birthday. He then returns to the car and waits in frustration and helplessness. At last Marcia strolls up, glasses on. She leans towards him, holding a map.

'Excuse me, but could you tell me the way to the Bodleian Library?'

'Get in.'

'Check if he's around first. If you see him, I can easily meet you at the end of this street.' She continues to hold the map up, which in fact is of London's Underground.

'I can't see him anywhere.'

'How nice of you to offer me a lift. Are you sure it's not out of your way?'

'Just get in, Marcia.' He starts the car.

'George, you've got to learn to ad-lib.'

'You're being melodramatic.'

'I'm not. All sorts of people are around, overhear. And look at you – you meet a journalist you know and go into a flat spin!'

'Are you blaming me? He's here covering some convention for a tabloid—'

'Not at all. You did the right thing not to join me. But you should have kept the whole thing going when I pretended to be a tripper. Just for practice if nothing else.'

'This has been a bit of a shock. I didn't realize how vulnerable I was.'

'I did.' Marcia has not taken off her glasses, and has put her hat back on.

'It's such a coincidence there's a convention which I might very well have attended—'

'There's always a coincidence. Edward took me to Paris soon after we first met and thought no one knew about us, and we promptly ran into three friends of his who were over for a funeral.'

They drive to the end of the Woodstock Road in silence, then head for Cheltenham, and George begins to relax. 'Let's find somewhere for a walk fairly soon, have a pub lunch, and then go on to the Dawlishes. Mrs Dawlish said drop in any time, but cut me off before I could mention you were with me—'

'I meant it when I said I wouldn't come with you. This is your reunion. I'll find somewhere to have tea and read my book.'

Another silence descends and George puts on more Haydn. They stop short of Cheltenham and walk in some nearby woods, commenting on the beauty of the autumn trees in the stilted way even friends use when a problem has arisen which preoccupies them. Each feels a distance developing; Marcia looks strongly foreign in her black hat and now black coat, her high cheekbones accentuated, her urban skin and long fingers pale against the dun vegetation as she prods about looking for good specimens of dried fir-cones. Her idea of a walk is obviously more of a forage; she has a plastic bag in her pocket for her finds. He longs to stride out and feels hampered by the ambling speed she adopts.

'I'm getting hungry, Marcia. Shall we get going and walk to the pub in the valley?'

'Poor George, you didn't have any coffee. I just adore fir-cones – aren't they beautiful? I love their shape and the way the scales lap into each other.'

'I've never given much thought to fir-cones, to be honest.'

'They're like acorns and chestnuts, so satisfactory.'
'You've got mud on your jacket.'

George leaves Marcia at a hotel on the edge of the Severn river, about two miles away from the village where the Dawlishes live. The weather has turned cold and grey.

'Stop fussing, George. I'll be fine. We've had a lovely walk, I've got a good novel to read, I can easily pass the next couple of hours.'

'I'm sure I won't be longer than that.'

'This lounge is very comfortable, there's a nice view, and my tea is arriving already. Off you go.'

Bell Farm House is a rather mean brick building of no great age on the edge of the village; it sits in a small walled front garden as if trying to take up as little room as possible, there on sufferance because the farm it was once part of now clearly belongs to someone else. A large climbing rose in need of pruning is dangling half off one wall of the house; the garden is full of the dying remains of annuals and perennials. The windows have untidily pulled curtains but the panes gleam. Someone has polished the toby jug brass door-knocker. When George uses it a dog starts barking frantically.

'You must be George Warne. Be quiet, you bloody dog. I'm Hope Dawlish. Do come in.' Mrs Dawlish has a large square face above a tall thin body, and a marked gap between her front teeth. George finds his eyes drawn to the unusual stretch of pink gum.

'I'll give him a bell. Peter has a hideout in the garden.' She leads George through to the back of the house where a long room looks out onto the garden. She picks up a handbell and rings it out of one of the windows towards a shed a hundred yards away. 'The old school bell. I rescued it when they closed down the village school. It's been very useful.'

'It certainly makes a fine noise.'

'It had to be heard all over the school.'

'What a pleasant view of the river.'

'There was floodwater right up to the end of our garden last week. Sit down and be comfortable. Peter never appears until he's good and ready.'

'Perhaps you ought to warn him it's me who's arrived.'

'Oh, he'll know. We weren't expecting anyone else. Tea?'

'How kind.'

'Not particularly. We always have some at this hour.' She stares at him, twisting her tongue so that an edge of it peeps through the gap in her teeth. It's clearly a habit. 'You aren't at all as I expected you to be. I thought you'd be much younger.'

'Sorry to disappoint you.'

She grins at him. 'I'll get the tea. I'd ring the bell again, but it makes him twice as slow. You could call my husband a cussed man.' She disappears.

George paces up and down the room, gazing out at the garden for signs of movement. The shed is a comic-looking place, encased like a parcel in badly applied roofing felt. There are no windows on this side. On the roof is an incongruous weathervane in the shape of a cat, swivelling briskly in the sharp wind. The dog is sitting in the middle of the lawn waiting tensely for his master to appear.

'Not as tense as me, however.' George wriggles his shoulders and breathes deeply.

The wedding photographs on the mantelpiece show a Dawlish George recognizes – the curly hair starting by then to recede, the eager look. Hope Dawlish stares at the camera in surprise, her arm clamped into her husband's, her mouth firmly closed. They appear to be in their mid-thirties. George scans the room for clues about their lives and jobs, but it is curiously uninformative – few books, some dull water-colours, worn chintz-covered chairs, a bentwood rocking chair, an untidy dog-basket.

Nothing happens. Ten minutes pass, the dogs waits, George waits, the shed door stays shut, the tea doesn't appear. Take us as you find us. He hadn't quite expected to be ignored, and thinks of Marcia curled up with her book and a tray of tea.

Then the dog jumps up and starts to race round in circles barking; it is obviously possessed of some special early sign because the shed door doesn't actually open at once. When it does, a tall figure wearing a black trilby, a plaid blanket over his shoulders, and mittens, wanders across the lawn looking like an extra from a Victorian costume drama. He is coughing.

Minutes later Hope Dawlish comes in with the tea followed by

Peter Dawlish divested of his outer coverings. He is cadaverously thin and fairly bald, but George would recognize his eyes and smile anywhere.

'I remember you! You haven't changed that much, George Warne.' His palms are warm, his fingers ice-cold as they shake hands.

'I'd know you too, sir.'

'Sir. No one calls me that except the postman. At long last, bring yourself to call me Peter. And you've met Hope of course.'

Mrs Dawlish has poured orange tea into three mugs and is now standing at the door holding one of them. 'I'm going to leave you two to talk.'

'All right, dear, but I thought there was some cake.'

'It's rather stale.'

'Cake's better when it's stale.'

'If you insist.' She comes back with an end of ginger cake still in its paper wrapping, and cuts it into four small pieces before disappearing again. George refuses the cake, and Dawlish wolfs down the lot.

'She starves me, you know. She thinks food is rather wicked. Lives on nothing herself. Anyway, here you are, unexpectedly soon.'

'I hope you don't mind. It seemed an opportunity not to be missed.'

'My only successful pupil. I never taught again after my experiences at Roddick Manor. Is it still going?'

'There was a disastrous fire and it closed down.'

'Burnt down by a desperate pupil I should imagine.'

'You're probably right. I was certainly miserable there.' He looks at Dawlish, who is picking up ginger cake crumbs with a dampened finger. 'Until you arrived, and then suddenly school started to have some point.'

'Goodness me. Are you sure you're not muddling me up with someone else, George?'

'No one else encouraged me at all. It was as if my father had commanded them to stifle whatever talent or potential I might show. They certainly obeyed.'

'They told me when they sacked me that I'd brought anarchy and mayhem to Roddick Manor. I was rather proud of that letter, I remember.' Dawlish lights a cigarette having waved the pack at George. He inhales deeply, his fingers stained an ancient yellow.

'You encouraged me to try for Oxbridge, you took me on dubious but delightful excursions, you were kind to me. I have a lot to thank you for, because my life changed course – I got into Oxford, and then I was free.'

'From your remark, I take it your father was bad news. Your mother was memorable – or perhaps she still is?'

'She died very recently, in fact. My father's been dead some time.'

'Ah, I see. Often when one becomes the oldest generation, one does a bit of assessing. And you remembered me.' He is staring at George through the smoke rising from the cigarette which he holds cupped in his hands.

'I've always remembered you. No, it was a letter I found amongst Lena's papers that shook me into action.' George takes it from his wallet and passes it to Dawlish, who reads the letter carefully.

'What an unctuous little squirt I was, trying to charm her into letting you come. It didn't work, though I can't remember why. The boy who did come was an absolute disaster. Can't remember his name either.'

'Mackie? Stubbs?'

'Mackie. That sounds ominously familiar. I've wiped him from my mind from that day to this. Why didn't you come? You'd have enjoyed it far more than the miserable Mackie.'

'I never knew about it. My parents refused on my behalf and never told me.'

'The hell they did. What pigs parents can be.' He hands the letter back. 'I expect they had their reasons – suspected I would corrupt your innocence in wicked Italy.'

'My father more likely was afraid I might enjoy myself. He made a point of ensuring my life had no pleasure in it. He saw it as for my own good, of course.'

'And your beautiful mother didn't fight your corner?'

'No. So I fought on my own by building a wall round myself. Then you came along and I saw an exit to my *hortus conclusus*. Whether you like it or not, Peter, and unknown to you, you were my salvation.' George laughs, and Dawlish laughs with him. 'God knows what would have happened to my life if you hadn't whizzed through it when you did.'

'Thank goodness I was unaware of my daunting role. The burden would have sent me running.' They laugh again, and Dawlish then has a coughing fit. Wheezing as he recovers his voice, he points to a water-colour above the fireplace.

'That's the place in Italy,' he whispers. 'Casa di Lello. Sold now.'

George gets up to look closely at the picture. A long stone house set against a hillside, umbrella pines and cypresses, far-off faint cupolas and campaniles between a distant fold of hills, a foreground of terrace, olive press, a vine running along a pergola. Golden light from a dropping sun. George feels a dull pain deep inside.

'Rather a rose-tinted view of it painted by my mother – didn't show the drains that were always getting blocked, the leaking roof, and the mosquitoes that descended in enthusiastic hordes.'

'It looks beautiful.'

'It was. But I had to sell it. Hope and I live on the proceeds. I wanted to sell this and live in Casa di Lello, but Hope can't stand heat.'

Both men stare bleakly at the painting. Hope puts a head round the door.

'More tea?'

'What a good idea, darling. And more cake.'

'There isn't any.'

'Toast, then. Talking about the past is hungry business. We need hot buttered toast, don't we, George?'

Hope shuts the door and George wonders why Dawlish doesn't go and make some toast himself, particularly since she returns within minutes with a saucer bearing a few Marie biscuits.

'No hot buttered toast then?'

'It will leave us short of bread for breakfast.' She pats him lovingly on his bald head, and leaves again.

'Hope runs a very tight ship. Biscuit? Don't blame you. They've seen better days.' He proceeds to eat all of them. 'We tried spending the winter in Italy and the summer here, letting each house when we weren't in it. But that didn't work out. Tenants are terrible people. So-called friends were the worst.'

'I've sorted out enough landlord and tenant problems in my early life at the Bar to know the truth of that.'

'Of course, you're a barrister. I'd forgotten. Did you read law at Oxford?'

'No, history. I converted later.'

'Sounds very religious. I know little about the workings of the English Bar – my brush with the Italian legal system when I sold the house was a life-shortening experience I don't want to repeat. Tell me, George, are you married?'

'I'm not. My two efforts were singularly unsuccessful. No children resulted, luckily.'

'Do you know, I honestly think marriage is a matter of complete luck. I had no idea what I wanted of marriage when I got spliced to Hope, and it's worked out a treat. Pure luck. We suit each other. Neither of us has ever met anyone else remotely tempting. Don't suppose we're very tempting ourselves.' He laughs and coughs again.

'I thought I did know what I wanted, and it turned out I was wrong in both cases. It's impossible to know what you want. You only think you do.'

'Are you a successful barrister?'

'Yes, I suppose you could describe me as one.'

'Then you probably asked too much of your wives. You thought you knew what you wanted and they couldn't provide it. I didn't know what I wanted and most of the time Hope wouldn't provide it if I did. No hot buttered toast—'

'What are you saying about me, you awful man?' Mrs Dawlish comes in with fresh tea.

'Moaning about the lack of toast.'

'You've had cake and biscuits! I don't know.' She sits down close to her husband and looks roguishly at George. 'I bet he ate more than you.'

'I—'

'I was telling George about Casa di Lello, and how sad it was to lose it.'

'Sad for you, dear. Not for me. I couldn't stand the place.' She fixes her gaze on George. 'Miles from anywhere, down a lethal track that gave you a puncture regularly, took hours to get to Florence or Siena, no electricity, no telephone, and a neighbour who prowled around with one of those Italian mastiffs with odd ears ready to tear you to pieces if you put a toe on their property. I was terrified every time I tried to go for a walk.'

'Instead you've got bulls and Alsatians round here.'

'Ah, but we've also got public rights of way and the Italians haven't.'

'It is a better system.' George wishes she would go away again but fears she won't. She spends some time telling him about a right of way dispute she has had with a local farmer. Peter Dawlish stares into the distance, not listening to a word, a happy smile on his face. He suddenly interrupts her.

'I messed about in Soho for a couple of years after I got the sack from Roddick Manor. Sowed my wild oats.'

'I never like these stories. That dreadful Francis Bacon.' Hope Dawlish takes her mug and disappears again. George wonders if Peter has changed subject on purpose but he gives no sign of even noticing his wife's departure.

'Actually I didn't really know Francis Bacon very well, though I often saw him. All his friends were queers like him, as you probably know. We once had a good chat though, standing outside the Caves de France on a hot evening. I'd corrected someone who'd said "the *hoi polloi*" – it should be *hoi polloi* without "the", no need of another article – and he pounced on me. Ah, he said, so you know a bit of Greek. When he found I'd done a year of classics before I switched to history he made me quote some Homer in the original. I declaimed splendidly, I was just drunk enough to lose all inhibition but not too drunk to remember the words. My moment of glory. Then his friends swept him off to dinner. He liked good food, you know. He always ate at Wheelers. He asked me to go too but I knew I'd be unwelcome with his friends.'

'So you weren't seduced.'

'I was too much of a coward, George. The invitation to take things further was there, I'm sure of it. But despite the totally louche life I was leading, sleeping on people's floors and spending all day every day going from one drinking place to the next, I still couldn't take the leap from hetero to homo. Yet I was surrounded by people who did, and then eventually went back to their wives and girlfriends.'

'A bit of a change from Roddick Manor.'

'I sometimes used to go into fits of manic laughter when I considered what the headmaster would have made of my daily Soho routine. Soho was a paradise in the fifties, you know, for anyone who wanted the bohemian life. Everyone spent their time drinking and talking all day. My favourite hole was the Caves de France in Dean Street, gone now alas, I went to look for it once. It was full of extraordinary people – eccentrics, rejects, failures, all sorts of riff-raff, all ages, all colours, all sexes, all with some tenuous toe-hold in the arts. You could drink all afternoon and talk and talk and talk. Real Bohemia. How I loved it, I was addicted to Soho. Sordid, drunken, licentious but joyful and fascinating too. The French, the Colony Club, the Caves, Wheelers, Old Compton Street, Berwick Street, Rupert Street, Dean Street – my universe for two whole years.'

'Then what happened?'

'My mother died, my father stopped the allowance she'd been paying me unbeknownst to him, and I had to earn a proper living again. I'd been pretending to be a poet and it had to stop.' Dawlish stares at his thin veined hands. 'But I was so glad I had those two years. There was nowhere like the Caves, then or now. It was a much better education than Oxford. Where do you live in London?'

'South Kensington.'

'A very proper area.'

'It is rather. But I bought my house because I liked it, liked the square, liked the shops and restaurants around. It's like a village, but then London is full of them.'

'We may have all known each other, but Soho was not like a village. We were all too selfconscious, too edgy. Too many poseurs.' Dawlish looks nostalgic. 'I fell for every act and posed the whole time myself. What fun it was.'

'Well, you were a tonic to a miserable introverted seventeen-year-old like me, desperately looking for role models and seeing only second-rate teachers in a second-rate school.'

'I've never been thought of as a role model before. You're

unique in my life, come to think of it. Unique. First time anyone's ever said they owe me something.'

'You said marriage was a matter of luck, and so are one's teachers. For some people it doesn't matter that they are never given impetus by someone who inspires them, because they've had plenty of stimulation in their upbringing. But to others teachers are crucial.'

'George, I wish you wouldn't go on about my teaching. As far as I remember I didn't teach you much – we just did a lot of talking when we should have had our heads down.'

'You've just said Soho was better than a university and all you did there was talk and get drunk! I'm sure the secret of good teaching is more than imparting knowledge – it's talking and taking an interest. I used to watch you getting excited about something and feel I was learning for the first time.'

'Goodness! The responsibility of all this! I'm so glad I was totally unaware of my talents.' For a moment he looks like the young Peter Dawlish, his eyes bright but ironic as he lights another cigarette. A short coughing fit ensues.

'I'm sure I've been nobody's inspiration in my life. But you were definitely mine.'

'Only on a very lowly level. Don't exaggerate.' Dawlish's voice is hardly more than a whisper. 'A little squirt inspiring a slightly younger little squirt.' They both laugh again, and Dawlish wheezes on. 'No one uses the word squirt now – I looked it up not long ago and saw it was now described in my OED as dialect. But when I was a boy it was a common form of gentle abuse. Not unconnected with the old slang word for diarrhoea – the squirts.'

'I thought that was the squits.'

'Originally squirts. Both good words either way. So you live in South Ken. So did Francis Bacon, you know. Had a mews house there.'

'I didn't know. Seems an unlikely part of London for him—'

'No, no. He liked its contrast to Soho. South Ken was for working and Soho for fun. He seemed to spend most of his time in Soho, I always thought he couldn't have had much time or energy over for his work. Most of us did very little creating and I assumed he was the same. When I saw his first big retrospective it gave me such a shock. I had no idea what his work was like, nor its scope, nor its sheer mass. Very humbling.'

'Do you like his painting?'

'Like is too pale a word, George. Love is wrong too. He's the greatest painter England has produced since God knows when. Ever. I'm knocked sideways by his stuff. All that red. It invades me.'

'I hate a lot of his work, but I agree, he's the giant of this century.'

'He used to end a conversation with the phrase: "We are meat." Then he'd lift his glass and say "Cheerio." No one said, "Cheerio", quite like him. *We are meat, Peter. Cheerio!*'

Hope Dawlish put her head into the room. 'Not still talking about Francis Bacon!'

'On and off. What about something stronger to drink, George? A whisky?'

'I'm driving straight back to London, so I won't, thanks. I had no idea it was so late already. I must go, I'm afraid I've overstayed my welcome.'

'Of course not. Join me in a small one. Please do.'

'Well, a very small one. Then I must go . . .'

But as he drinks whisky with the Dawlishes he feels so guilty about Marcia he wishes he hadn't given in. As soon as he can, he takes his leave. Peter Dawlish stands in the front doorway with glass and cigarette in hand.

'Come again, George.'

'I will.'

'I'm so glad you dropped in.' He lifts his glass and gives a wheezy laugh. 'We are meat. Cheerio!'

Marcia is not in the hotel. George searches all over the public areas and even the car park but there is no sign of her. He asks the receptionist if she has a message for him.

'I've just come on duty. Let me ask Susie, she's been here all afternoon. She's still out the back.'

She returns and takes a folded piece of paper from the key-rack. 'If you're George Warne, this is for you.'

Dear George, I've been offered a lift back to London so I'm taking it. You're an hour late, and I need to get home. Thanks for the day out. Obviously Peter Dawlish wasn't a disappointment. Marcia.

Bereft, George speeds back to London, looking in vain into every car he overtakes. He can hear Marcia's fir-cones rolling about in the boot at every corner.

17 ∫

'We are instructed by Edward Wintlesham whom you assaulted on Sunday, 15 November last by severely cutting him with what he believes to been glass or some cutting weapon. This attack was unjustified and unprovoked, and we have advised our client that he is entitled to substantial damages for assault and battery.

His injuries are not yet healed and we are therefore unable to quantify his damages. Our client is unable at present to follow his profession, and the wound continues to give him considerable pain and discomfort.

We are instructed to invite you to acknowledge your liability towards him immediately, to save the costs of otherwise inevitable litigation, and we will revert to you when the full quantum of his damages is established.

'It makes me sick to read it out to you.'

'It makes me sick to hear it.'

'Has Edward's wound gone septic or something?'

'Rachel, I have absolutely no idea. He could have gangrene for all I know. He could be healed up and pretending not to be. We're not on speaking terms, so how could I know?'

'You sound as if you find it funny.'

'It's so terrible I might as well laugh. Unjustified and unprovoked. I have to laugh or I'd scream. The bloody man was trying to rape me.'

'It's a pity he didn't, and then everyone would have been on your side.'

'That is not funny.'

'It's not meant to be. And you're not taking your situation

seriously enough. You still haven't been to a solicitor and I gave you Stephen Smith's name right at the beginning.'

'I didn't really believe Edward would go this far.'

'Ring Stephen now. Make an appointment to see him. Get yourself sorted out, Marcia. No one can do it for you.' At this point Rachel is interrupted by the doorbell, and Marcia waits for her to return, resenting her bossy tone.

'I have to go, Marcia. It's the window-cleaner. I'll ring you later.'

'Thanks for listening.'

Marcia wanders round her flat holding the crisp letter from Peel, Cross and Thorogood, reading it out loud. 'Pompous gits. *When the full quantum of his damages is established.* Why can't they say "When we see how long he takes to heal and how much work he has lost." Oh God, what am I going to do?' She folds up the letter and puts it on the shelf in front of the photo of Apollo. She tries to remember what work Edward had lined up; she recalls him talking about a new opera by Harrison Birtwhistle and he also mentioned some work in New York. The full quantum of his damages – his wound could develop complications and prevent him working, and his earnings are considerable. Fear paralyses her until the street doorbell rings and Rosie Amsterdam's voice crackles on the new intercom.

'Marcia – I'm just passing – can I come in for a chat?'

'Rosie! Yes!' Marcia presses the release button and quickly hides the solicitor's letter. She hugs Rosie delightedly and takes her into the kitchen.

'Tea? Coffee?'

'What stage are you at?'

'I was about to make myself a sandwich with some coffee before I leave for the matinee.'

'I'll join you in the coffee.' Rosie is looking at her most polished, but sounding very tired. Her voice, always husky, today is hoarse. 'Saw you in the play last night. I couldn't come backstage because I was with a gang who were in a hurry.'

'Black? Sugar?'

'Both. Lovely. Darling Marcia, you were wonderful. I didn't like Damian Frapp but then I never do.'

'He grows on you.'

'I'd rather not give him the chance. But I really liked your performance, Marcia – we all thought it was strong stuff. Really powerful.'

'Don't sound so surprised. Do you want a tuna sandwich? I can easily make you one.'

'No thanks, and I am certainly not surprised. I knew you were capable of a performance like that, I've just never seen you deliver it before.' She narrows her eyes over her steaming coffee. 'Sedley Mortimer was in my party.'

'You seem to be very friendly with him all of a sudden.'

'I've known Sedley for years. *Years.*'

'What did he think?'

'He was very quiet. I know that's a good sign.'

Marcia snorts and takes a huge bite of her sandwich.

'Yes it is, with Sedley. When he goes silent on you he's impressed. He was watching you with that look on his face—'

'I wouldn't leave Christina.'

'I didn't mean he wanted to take you on, Marcia – don't jump to conclusions.'

'Sorry. Edward kept going on at me about joining Sedley's stable and I'm a bit sensitive about it.'

'How is Edward?'

'I was going to ask you the same question. More coffee?'

'Please. No one seems to have any up-to-date info – he's lying very low. Someone said he wasn't at all well—'

'Who?'

'I can't remember, somebody last night. Not Sedley, but it could have been Sonia, Sonia Masters.'

'Who's she?'

'That woman with red hair who works for the Arts Council. I remember now, she said he was supposed to attend some meeting and had to cancel because of illness.'

'Perhaps Edward's just got flu on top of everything else.'

'Marcia, you sound like someone who's trying hard not to be worried. Admit it.'

'I can't believe a small cut would incapacitate him for ordinary life, that's why.'

'And I can't believe you haven't been round to see him to judge for yourself, instead of worrying away about it.'

'I'm not worrying away about it.'

'Just a little bit concerned then, shall we say?' Rosie is smiling and Marcia itches to scream at her in frustration. She jams the remains of her sandwich in her mouth instead and chews busily. 'Tell you what, darling, would you like me to go and see him for you? I have every reason to pay him a sick-bed visit, after all. Then I can report back in accurate detail.'

'Don't go and see him on my behalf.'

'Then I'll go on his and mine.' Rosie gives a sly little smile. 'And if I'm feeling very kind I'll give you a ring even though of course you're not *really* interested.'

'Oh, for heaven's sake, Rosie, of course I am. He was my lover until this happened. Communications at the moment have broken down, that's all.'

'Do you miss him?'

'No. I must go. I need a long time to get into that costume and headpiece.'

'It all looks fantastic on you, I have to admit. Is the headgear heavy to wear?'

'I'm getting sore patches on my scalp. They're going to make a new one for the West End run.'

'So the transfer is definite then?'

'Yes.'

'Everything's going well for you, darling.'

'Everything?'

'I'll give you a ring.'

Marcia needs exercise and walks down to Camden Town. She still hasn't rung Stephen Smith to make an appointment, and though she knows she can't procrastinate much longer, at least she can wait for Rosie's update.

Consulting George is not an option. After that dismal day out with him, she's decided it would be better not to see him again. It wasn't simply that she minded being left for nearly three hours in the hotel, it was more his behaviour towards her in public after the incident in the Randolph. His voice and expression had that shadow in it, the shadow she'd encountered before when she'd been with a celebrity and realized they would rather not be seen with her. Throughout their walk in the woods, she kept imagining George on the Bench, in wig, in robes, outlined against the autumn trees, a huge public eye looking on. There is no future in their friendship; she will simply be a liability and, worse, he will feel she is.

The painful thing is that she minds. She loved being in his company again at dinner, and anticipated a happy day together in the country. How nice, she'd thought as she woke to the winter sun coming into her bedroom; I'm going to spend the day with someone I like and used to love, and might one day love again. Someone who understands my tough skin because he's had to grow one too, someone who never tried to own me and didn't need me to own him, someone with whom the minutes and hours pass with their full weight but never drag. No hype, no pressure to be what one isn't . . . Everything seemed possible that Sunday morning; the thought even flicked through her head that getting married would remove George's problems with publicity. She wouldn't have been an appropriate wife for a High Court Judge, but at least she would have been legal.

How stupid I am! Marcia finds she is muttering this aloud in self-embarrassment as she walks along the busy streets. What a ridiculous thought. How could I have even given a second's brain-time to the idea of being Lady Warne? Her cheeks burn.

She decides to walk on through Regent's Park – she still has plenty of time in hand. A fast walk past the zoo and down the central avenue through the park will help to blow away her angst.

As she passes London Zoo a crowd of small children boil past her heading for the Zoo, their chatter a match for the noise from the aviary. A little ginger-headed girl trips and falls flat right beside Marcia, her teeth hitting the path with a sickening crack. A minute fragment of tooth lies on the rough tarmac as the child raises her head, chin and nose grazed, eyes blank with pain and shock, and starts to scream. Marcia lifts her, cuddles her, smells her clean hair and the synthetic raspberry smell of her lollipop (it lies in the dirt), holds the small shaking body close. A teacher hurries up.

'Cecilia! Poor little thing – show me what's happened. Oh dear, you've chipped your tooth. Is it a baby tooth?'

Sobbing, Cecilia shakes her head.

'Never mind. It's only a tiny little chip. Thank the nice lady for helping you, Cecilia, and come along to the Zoo. We'll find the first-aid post and clean up your grazes.'

'Fank you.' Extraordinary bright green eyes magnified by tears meet Marcia's. Dribbles of blood are running down the child's chin.

'Here's a clean tissue.'

'Fank you.'

'Come on, Cecilia.'

Marcia watches the stubby plump legs hurrying to keep up with the teacher's rapid steps, giving the impression that the held hand is being dragged rather than supported. Briefly, Cecilia looks back, searching the path for her lost lollipop.

Marcia suddenly wants to cry. She loved holding the trusting softness of the child's body, her small bones, her sweet-smelling hair, her smooth freckled skin, within the circle of her arms. She hurries blindly across the open grass, wrapping those empty arms around herself.

'Do you love me, Mutti?'

Marcia paces across the grass, trying to bring a clear image of her mother to her mind's eye. It is difficult. She is ashamed that she can only recall grave, attentive eyes, a clamped mouth, facial hair that could easily have been plucked out, clothes that were tidy and dull and unloved.

'Do you love me, Mutti?'

How did her mother answer? Marcia remembers asking the question more than once because she wanted to be smothered in hugs and kisses in reply, as she had seen happen to her schoolfriend Angela.

'Do you love me, Mum?'

'Come here and let me eat you up!' Angela's mother would chase her round the playground before the hugging started.

Whatever Miriam did it wasn't the affirmation she longed for or she would have remembered it. Angela had an inexhaustible supply of kisses and cuddles available on demand. Miriam's supply of love was rationed.

'But rationing is a device to save things so that there is enough to go round. There was never enough of her smiles or love to go round even her family of three.' Marcia watched Rachel cuddle Judith.

'Perhaps she was saving them for all that big wide family she lost. Perhaps she found it impossible to stop thinking that one day she'd need it all when she saw them all again. Even though she knew she never would.'

'What about your mother, Rachel?'

'You forget, she came over unmarried, found a nice Jewish boy here and married into his lovely big family to make up for what she had lost.'

'My parents were very isolated. They didn't join in the Jewish community life at all. They turned in on themselves.'

'That was sad.'

'They didn't seem to think so. I think they considered their isolation a strength. My parents were quite arrogant in their way. That generation tend to think they had a monopoly in suffering. I had a gentile landlady once who told me she'd lost all her family and her house in the Blitz, and was trapped herself in the rubble for two days as well. When I told my father about her, he said it was different for them. Honestly, Rachel, I can't see too much difference. Pain and loss in war is pain and loss in war.'

As Marcia marches across the grass towards the Marylebone Road, she wonders whether, had her family passed their lives in comfort and prosperity in Berlin, with no war and no Shoah, there would have been the same restricted giving of love, the same ultimate frustration between them. Mothers and daughters. Rachel doesn't hug Judith so much because these days she has started to push her mother away.

Where was Creusa's mother when she needed her? Her pregnancy would have been visible to any woman who loved her and spent time with her. Silence. No mother stepped in. Creusa coped alone.

Marcia imagines her young self hiding swelling breasts and stomach under baggy clothing, always locking the bathroom door, avoiding situations which would give away her secret. Would her mother, had she been alive then, have noticed that her daughter was not simply overweight? Could she have had a child and left it in a skip or dustbin, an offering—'

'Marcia Fleckner?' A man touches her arm as she waits by traffic lights.

'You gave me such a shock! I was miles away!'

'You were in such a complete trance you missed the pedestrian light, so I thought I'd better bring you back to the present.'

'It's Sedley Mortimer, isn't it? What a strange coincidence! Rosie Amsterdam told me you'd been to *Ion* last night with her.'

'I was going to write and tell you how much I'd enjoyed your performance. Now I can tell you face to face. Congratulations – can I offer you a drink, or even a late lunch, to celebrate?'

'Late is what I'm going to be for my matinée, so thanks but no thanks. Are you going to the Tube too?'

'I've just come out because there's a delay on the line, so share my taxi? Our route coincides more or less. I'll be hopping out first.' Sedley gives a startling powerful whistle and a taxi on the opposite side of the road does a U-turn for them.

'I pride myself on my whistle but yours is in another league. How do you do it? You didn't use your fingers.'

'I roll my tongue into a sort of funnel and then force the air through against my front teeth.' Sedley gives a toned-down demonstration as they settle themselves in the back of the taxi. 'How do you do yours?' Marcia puts two fingers in her mouth and makes a small pure sound. 'Oh, high-quality stuff, not a big boomer like mine. Can you waggle your ears? Oh, superb. You certainly win there.'

'This is a ridiculous conversation—'

'What about burping to order? No expertise there? I remember how my sister and I worked on our burp for days but never got the hang of the extended performance. I had a cousin who could fill himself with air and burp for minutes on end. Admirable.'

'I must have had a deprived childhood – I somehow missed out on burping.'

'Farting? My sister was pretty good, but nothing like the Frenchman Poujart le Pétomane who used to be able to play tunes with his farts. Trust the French to make an art of it.'

'I feel quite unreal – riding through London discussing the art of farting with the great Sedley Mortimer who's just picked me up in the street.'

'I really enjoyed your Creusa. I particularly liked the way you dealt with her ambivalence – the fact she was immediately attracted to Ion as the ideal son, and yet when given the chance to be his stepmother, decided to kill him.'

'For political and dynastic reasons.'

'Not entirely, I felt. Your reactions were complex. Rich and messy.'

'Rich and messy?'

'It's a compliment. I felt there was layer after layer of Creusa superimposed and kept in precarious balance, with her inner chaos only hinted at. Rich and messy. And moving.'

Marcia stares out of the taxi window, unable to speak she is so pleased.

'Have I upset you?'

'No.'

'You're giving a good impression of it.'

'You've just said the most wonderful thing about the way I act. Try to act.'

'Good. It's praise you deserve. I can't think why you haven't become better known.'

'Perhaps I haven't always acted so well.'

'Maybe. Or perhaps your agent hasn't been as assiduous as she ought to have been, putting you about.'

'When we last met, I was really impressed you didn't say a word to knock Christina Platt.'

'I hadn't yet seen you in a big part.'

'I thought it was professional of you not to imply a criticism of her, whatever your private views.'

'Ouch.' Sedley is laughing. 'Pax.'

'You think I'm being over-loyal to Christina, don't you? Misplaced loyalty at that.'

'Don't put thoughts into my head I haven't had yet.' Sedley stops smiling and points a finger at her. He's got pale yellowy-brown eyes, thick black lashes, and a heavy afternoon shadow on his chin. His full, dry lips are pursed until they open to say: 'All right. I'll admit one thing, since we met by pure chance and are sitting here together only until I get out in a couple of minutes. I have a low opinion of Christina Platt, for reasons I won't bore you with. I had no idea until I saw you last night in *Ion* how good you were. No idea. I never poach by making offers, but if you ever made a move towards me, I have to admit I'd enjoy being your agent. Stop at the next corner, driver, please.' He hands a note through the sliding window. 'Take my companion to the New Fortune Theatre as fast as you can. Bye-bye, Marcia. I enjoyed our ride together.' He grins at her. 'Sock it to them, and don't forget to practise your whistle.'

As he lopes off laughing, Marcia leans out of the taxi and gives a full and earsplitting demonstration of her whistling ability.

18 ∫

'The Lord Chancellor has decided, since your medical is all clear, to announce your appointment in mid-January. I thought it important to impart this to you without delay.'

'Thank you for ringing me so promptly, Jeremy.'

'The Lord Chancellor hopes you'll be able to take a good holiday before you begin your duties. Go away somewhere warm with your wife and forget about the Bar for a couple of weeks.'

'You forget I'm not married.'

'I'm frightfully sorry, George, how remiss of me. You don't come across as the bachelor type.' Jeremy Welsford's cool, precise voice becomes flustered.

'How's your son, by the way? The one with the broken arm?'

'Mending well, back at school, can't wait to play rugby again. No sense. He's the youngest of my four boys, but quite the wildest. We never know what he's going to be up to next.'

'Four sons? What a responsibility!' George stares into the coloured swirls of a heavy glass paper-weight given him by his first wife Sarah.

'People keep telling me they keep me young but in my view they speed the ageing process considerably.' Jeremy's level tones don't change; do his boys see him as a dry stick or does he play football and cricket with them, get muddy, exchange jokes?

'Enough of my sons. I'd rather talk about your elevation to the Bench. Is there anything you'd like to discuss?'

'There are one or two minor points.' As they talk about other matters, George thinks of Marcia, of the sense of danger in their renewed liaison. All week he has been obsessed with thoughts of her, of their past affair, of the whiteness of her body, the darkness of her hair and eyes, of the contrasting reds and browns of mouth and nipples and cunt, of their love-making. The fact she has not returned any of his calls since the outing has simply increased this obsession.

'I hope that's helpful, George. Anything else I can advise you about?'

'Not really. Well, perhaps you could say what you think about a small personal problem I have at the moment. An old friend of mine has suffered some adverse publicity recently, and since she's rather in the public eye—' George pauses, and Jeremy ums encouragingly – 'it's possible the gutter press could link her name with mine. It's also possible that an action might be brought against her, and since this is over an incident of a rather colourful nature—' he hates himself for talking like this, but he doesn't want Jeremy to take it all too seriously – 'she'd then be hot news, and her whole life would be raked over.'

'Forgive my asking, George, but the question is rather crucial – are you emotionally involved with this lady?'

'I am not in the process of having an affair with her, if that's what you mean.'

'Just good friends as they say?'

'You know as well as I do what innuendo lies in that sensible phrase.'

'Indeed I do. Indeed I do.'

'We are not only friends, but as a friend I would like to be able to help her in her current difficulty.'

'Of course, quite natural. But if, as my sons so elegantly put it, the shit hits the fan, do you foresee a lot of publicity?'

'Yes. All going well, the problem will be settled out of court, well away from the public eye.'

'I can't see anything wrong with the friend in question seeking your advice in a purely professional capacity as long as it's well before your appointment. After all, you are still practising as a silk.'

'I have to admit I feel rather exposed about it, Jeremy. I don't suppose the Lord Chancellor would appreciate one of his judges being in any way linked with a scandal.'

'Ah. A scandal. You didn't quite put it like that.'

'Because it isn't, but it will be presented as such by the Press.'

'Can't a friend advise her, and leave you out of it?'

'Of course they can. But if she approaches me for help I need to know where I stand, and I don't want to hurt an old friend.'

'Naturally, George. Naturally. You should do your best to help. Just keep a very low profile – you are right to be cautious.'

The call ends and George picks up the paperweight and shifts it from hand to hand, a habit he has when thinking. The swirls of trapped colour seem to revolve as he turns the cold mass of glass. It's a beautiful object, the only thing of beauty Sarah left in his life.

Douglas taps on his door.

'Well timed, Douglas. Come in and sit down. We need to discuss tactics. I've just been told that the appointment will be announced in the middle of January.'

'Good, sir, now you can do that arbitration. I'm glad I didn't return it at the same time as the Feathers case.'

'But I think that's about all I can fit in. The Lord Chancellor's Department suggested I should take a good break, so keep my diary clear after the arbitration. Do the junior clerks suspect anything yet?'

'I doubt it, sir. I handle your diary – they don't think about it. They wouldn't have noticed it's blank after Christmas.'

'You're a veritable clam, Douglas.'

'I never like to chatter.' Douglas picks a tiny piece of fluff off his perfectly cut jacket. 'Waste of energy in my view.'

'I'm going to miss you.'

'This may be presumptuous, sir, but have you considered who your clerk will be when you are on the Bench?'

'To be honest I've no idea. I haven't given it a thought. I'll presumably be allotted one, won't I?'

Douglas looks as near to coy as George has ever seen him. 'You wouldn't be setting a precedent if I came with you, sir. It's happened before.'

'Heavens, Douglas, Chambers wouldn't survive without you—'

'They're going to have to some day soon, sir. I always promised myself I'd retire at sixty, and I'm sixty-one. Time to give up the hassle of the clerks' room and start something less demanding.'

'But you wouldn't be retiring—'

'It's not full retirement I'm after. It's a change and an easing of the tension, sir.'

'I'll happily ask the Administrator of the Royal Courts if it's a possibility.'

'Strangely enough, they have just advertised for more judges' clerks, sir. I have the ad here – I was waiting for an opportunity to discuss it with you.' He passes the cutting, which George looks at in bemusement.

'I had no idea they advertised in this way. You amaze me as usual, Douglas. Word-processing skills – what a good thing Freddie insisted you all did that course a few years ago.'

'Indeed, sir. I think I would have every chance of being selected, and then it is a simple matter for you to make sure I am allotted to you.'

George tips back his head and laughs. 'Douglas, you've made my day! You'd be happy to be away on circuit for six weeks at a time?'

'No problem. My wife's so busy in her dress shop she'd hardly notice I wasn't there. My son would be only too delighted with my absences.'

'I am concerned about Chambers, though. It has never crossed anyone's mind you wouldn't die in harness, so to speak, like your father. Mr Mentieth is bound to be upset about your leaving.'

'No, sir, he's expecting me to give up soon. I told him when he became Head of Chambers not to count on me after I reached sixty. He won't be surprised if I go with you, that is of course, if I am taken on.'

'I'm sure you will be, Douglas. I'll give the Court Administrator a ring later on today and alert him to the fact you'll be applying. It will make all the difference to have a familiar face with me on circuit. And I'm glad my Head of Chambers won't regard it as the basest treachery on my part to steal you away!'

There is a pause during which Douglas clears his throat. 'I know you will realize the remuneration is low compared with what I'm

used to, but I've done well here, sir, and a less pressurized life
will give me a chance to pay attention to my investments.'

George laughs again. 'You've got it all sorted out, Douglas. I
envy you. I wish I was as well organized.'

'I'll go and clarify the date for the arbitration, sir.'

'Remind me where it's taking place?'

'Geneva. Estimated one day.'

'That will do me nicely in the run-up to Christmas.'

George watches Douglas make his dapper exit, and then stands
up to pace the room. He cannot understand why Douglas wants
to leave the lucrative life of a senior clerk receiving a percentage
of the income of a successful set of chambers, but the man seems
convinced. He rings Freddie.

'Have you got a moment, Freddie? I'd like a word. Right, I'll
come up in half an hour.'

He then rings Marcia's number; she's forgotten to switch on
her answerphone, and he cuts off after ten empty rings. He tries
the theatre, knowing that today is matinee day, but she hasn't
arrived yet. He does not leave a message. Ever since Sunday
she has avoided contact, and he seethes with frustration. He
will send a note over by courier.

Dear Marcia

*I'm truly sorry for leaving you alone for so long on Sunday –
you were right to take off without me. I felt dreadful when
I arrived at the hotel and found you had gone. But please
forgive and forget, and give me a ring. There are developments I'd like to tell you about, and I'm also wondering
whether you've heard from Wintlesham's lawyer yet. My offer
of help stands.*

With love, George

With love. So anodyne and slack in meaning. His emotions are
in turmoil and all he can put is 'with love'. It says nothing or
everything.

'I was thinking of India, Freddie.'

'Now is the best time of year to go.'

'I haven't been back since I was a small child.'

'Are you planning to join a group? India can be quite intimidating on a first visit if you're on your own.'

'I only thought of India as I came up the stairs just now, to be honest. I've no idea how or where I'll go. Or if I really will.'

'You must, George. Take this opportunity. Go for three weeks if you can. I went there with my first wife Anthea, and we stayed in wonderful hotels which were converted rajah's palaces. You would enjoy them. Some were very eccentric.'

'I'll have to come to you for tips.'

'And when you come back, Chambers will give a dinner for you to celebrate your appointment. Where would you like it to take place?'

'I'll leave that entirely to you, Freddie. I'm not fussy. Surprise me.'

Natalie comes in, waves at George, and throws herself into an armchair. 'One of these days I will murder Francis Bates.'

'I admit that the thought of a future without Francis Bates is the sole advantage of leaving Chambers.'

'Oh, George, you won't escape him that easily. He is bound to come before you, and drive you mad with his witty circumlocutions and prattish comments.' Natalie shuts her eyes. 'He is an absolute master of the pretentious periphrasis.'

Freddie laughs. 'What has the poor fellow done to deserve this!'

'You've never had the bad luck to be led by him. A constant daily diet of Francis is finishing me off. I must tell Douglas never to do this to me again.'

'Ah, Douglas. I hadn't got round to Douglas.' George fidgets awkwardly. 'Freddie, he said you might not be surprised if he decided to join me as my clerk. He always planned to retire soon after his sixtieth birthday, he says—'

'What are you talking about?' Natalie shoots upright in her chair.

'No, it doesn't surprise me. He had warned me he might do something like this.' Freddie sighs. 'We'll have to advertise at once for another senior clerk. Mid-January is not very far away.'

'What is all this?' Natalie is horrified. 'Douglas can't be leaving.'

'I was as surprised as you are, Nat.' George touches her stiff shoulder. 'It was entirely his idea to follow me. His mind seems made up.'

'What on earth will we do without him? My practice is mainly due to Douglas – he's built me up brilliantly. It could all fall to pieces if he leaves.' Natalie ignores George and stares in despair at Freddie. 'This is a disaster, Freddie.'

'Darling, don't be silly. Clerks come and go – you're good, your solicitors will stay loyal. You probably won't notice any difference.'

'But aren't you upset about it?'

'Of course I am. But he has his reasons, and he told me long ago he wasn't going to do what his father did, go on and on. Yes, I'm upset because he's one of the best senior clerks in the Temple, but he won't change his mind and I wouldn't try to make him. This move will suit him. We'll find a good replacement.'

'Everyone's going to be as upset as me when they hear.'

'Don't tell anyone yet. Let Douglas do it his own way.'

'I'm just praying he's going to change his mind.' Natalie leaves the room and Freddie shrugs ruefully at George.

'If everyone reacts as strongly as Natalie has, I think I'd rather Douglas did change his mind and stayed put.'

'Too late, George. Douglas doesn't waver. And some people will be pleased to have a change. Patricia Saban for one. No, it doesn't surprise me he wants to go with you. He's always had a soft spot for you.'

'Really? I hadn't noticed.'

'He likes tough eggs like himself. You'll make quite a team.'

'I'm not sure how much of a compliment that is.'

Freddie notices George's slight smile and smiles too. 'You will find him invaluable.'

'Of that I am quite sure. Thank you for being so understanding.'

The phone rings on Freddie's desk and George takes his leave and hurries downstairs, asking Douglas to follow him as he passes the clerks' room.

'Douglas, are you absolutely and totally sure you want to leave Chambers so suddenly for my sake? It's going to cause them all a lot of pain and upset, if Natalie Harper's reaction is anything to go by.'

'I'm having a drink tonight with a person who might be ideal to take over from me. He's blocked in his present set, looking for promotion. If he decides to come, no one will miss me for long, I assure you, sir. My mind is made up.'

It is a clear, crisp evening and George decides to walk home. He hasn't done this for years, but all the norms binding his life together have changed to such an extent that the habitual hardly feels comfortable. As he strides across the heart of the West End – Covent Garden, Leicester Square, Piccadilly, Knightsbridge – all freshly decorated and lit for Christmas, he experiences a burst of joy. The pleasure of walking on a fine cold night, the exhilarating feeling of his life moving into uncharted areas – these two emotions hold his mind in a kind of thoughtless stasis. Into this trance suddenly intrudes a poster of the Taj Mahal above the byeline *'Indiahhh'* and he stops at the open door of a travel agency.

'I would like to spend Christmas and the New Year in India.'

The tired, heavily madeup woman who is in the process of locking a cupboard stretches her face in a smile. 'The brochures are all on that rack over there.'

'I thought more of a tailor-made holiday, not a group affair.'

'Before we go any further, sir, I have to warn you that flights to India are very heavily booked throughout the festive season, particularly in economy.'

'I'm prepared to pay for better seats.'

'Let me take your name and phone number, and I'll contact you tomorrow about availability. I'm just about to close – all the other staff have already left.'

'Two seats. Try for two seats, please.'

India. He does not want to go alone – the very thought of it intimidates him. Would Marcia come if he asked her? He remembered her saying that the transfer to the West End was not immediate – there would a hiatus of a few weeks. He'd invite her as his guest. They'd have separate rooms, even travel separately if necessary. And if she refused to come? There is no one else he could or would ask. He stares unseeingly at the bulk of the Natural History Museum as he marches down the Cromwell Road, and feels afraid. These years of working at full stretch, the cushioning structure of his agreeable life, his position as a Bencher of his Inn, his membership of various clubs, his busyness, all have hidden the central dearth of intimate friends. His pain after Marcia ended their relationship made him fill every spare minute of his life with some planned activity or meeting. With Lena's death, with the change in his future, the structure has collapsed. And now Marcia is back, and because his life was a vacuum, she is reinstated as – as the apple of his eye.

Keep me as the apple of your eye: hide me under the shadow of your wings . . . A couple passing by give him a sharp look and he realizes he's said this resonant phrase from the Psalms out loud. The apple of the eye: the pupil, without which the eye cannot see.

Marcia. Now she's back, he cannot conceive of life without her. There is only one way out of their situation: he will ask her to marry him.

The little square of red light indicating the presence or absence of messages is flat and unwinking. George presses the play-button all the same and a series of clicks and whirrs echo in the quiet house. The post on the mat contains only a circular and a letter from his insurers. He stands in the hallway considering this silence from Marcia.

He undresses and takes a long hot shower to wash off the sweat and grime, and as he switches off the pounding water he hears the extension in his bedroom ringing. Grabbing his towel, slipping on the wet floor and painfully stubbing his big toe, he runs to answer it. His cleaner's cold-ridden voice says she's very sorry, but she's got the flu and won't be able to do his house this week.

George subsides on the bed cursing life and rubbing his sore toe. Pale hairs cover his legs and arms except where clothing has worn bare patches on knees and elbows. All his body hair is in shades of pale ginger; when he occasionally used to find one of Marcia's pubic hairs entwined with his, it looked like a black thread. He would leave it where it was until it disappeared of its own accord.

He dresses himself in the same cords and jersey he wore on Sunday, and goes to the kitchen to make himself something to eat. Nothing attracts him, and he ends up eating a cheese sandwich. As he prepares some coffee, he comes to a decision. He knows it's not a wise decision, but in his present state of mind he does not care.

He reaches Marcia's street at about ten o'clock, the earliest possible time she could arrive home after the show, if she hurried through her cleansing and changing and took a taxi straight back. He parks some way from her door but has it in clear sight, though she is unlikely to pass him on her route from the station. Her flat is in darkness, but the windows in the flat above and below are lit.

He opens up a copy of *The Lawyer* but his eyes flick constantly up and his attention is thin. He continues to hold the paper open, but hardly reads it. An hour passes.

A couple walk past the car, sagging into each other as they kiss. The woman is dark-haired and although she is too short to be Marcia, George's heart contracts as he watches her eager response to the man. They stop in a doorway nearby where they begin to kiss frenziedly, hands grabbing at buttocks or disappearing to touch genitals. George hides behind his paper, roused, but trying to ignore them. They are hard to ignore; from the sounds they are making they are reaching a climax.

Then George becomes aware that Marcia's lights are now on. He's missed her; she's slipped in from the other direction so quickly that, distracted as he has been by the lovers, he hasn't noticed.

He leaps out of the car and disturbs the couple, who tug at their clothes and walk on. Otherwise the street is empty. He sees that Marcia now has an entryphone, and pauses. This isn't wise. He could ruin everything. He stares at the brand-new bell and can't stop himself pressing it.

'That was quick, Rosie. Come on up.' Marcia's voice accompanies the buzz of the releasing mechanism. He cannot speak, and finds himself inside, at the bottom of those familiar lino-covered stairs. They smell as usual of polish, dust and nearby cooking. He starts to climb them, hearing as he reaches the second flight the sound of Marcia's own door opening. Then Marcia looks over the bannisters and sees him.

'George! What are you doing here? Where's Rosie?'

'I'm alone. I came in when—' He stops, frozen on the stair.

'I can see you came in.' Their eyes stay linked for moment until Marcia rolls hers. 'This is madness. And Rosie will be here any minute.'

'Marcia—'

'Oh, come upstairs, George. You know this is madness.'

'No one saw me.'

'It's crazy. You must go.' But she lets him into her hall though she does not shut the front door.

'I had to see you. Why haven't you answered any of my messages?'

'It was wiser not.' She does not look at him. He can hear a kettle come to the boil and switch off in the kitchen behind her.

'Did you get my letter today?'

'Yes. You must go, George. I don't want you to meet the friend who's about to arrive. She's – she's a dreadful gossip.'

'Wait, Marcia. Please. Seeing you again has opened everything up – I can't get you out of my mind.' George wants to touch her, but knows she would push him away.

'I should never have agreed to have dinner with you.'

'But why not, Marcia? We had a lovely evening – you enjoyed it, you said so, and I could see you did. I'm sorry about the hitches on Sunday—'

'Sitting waiting in that hotel made me think about the future. It's no good George – your life and mine just can't mesh. You have to be so careful, and I'm a real liability at the moment. Your face in the Randolph Hotel said it all. I was an embarrassment.'

'No, no, never an embarrassment. I admit the whole encounter threw me because it was so unexpected. I should have just brazened it out—'

'Of course you shouldn't have. You did absolutely the right thing. Listen to me, George, listen to what I am saying. I *am* an embarrassment to you, and with all the trouble brewing over Edward it's bound to get worse. I was keeping out of your life for your sake. You can't risk being seen with me. You shouldn't have come here.' She is white-faced with exhaustion, and stands so stiffly she is rocking on her feet. 'There's no future for us.'

'There would be if we got married.'

Marcia crumples against the wall, her eyes shut.

'Don't say no now and rule it out. Give me some space. We have both changed in two years, but I find my feelings for you haven't. I've come to a crossroads in my life and I've been taking stock. Marcia, I didn't realize how much I'd missed you until I saw you again. I love you.'

Marcia's eyes are still shut. Near her head is a postcard of Apollo; the god's confident eyes gaze at George; his erect, challenging body is in direct contrast to her slumped confusion. At that moment the door-bell rings three times.

'Rosie. I'll have to let her in.' Marcia opens her eyes but doesn't move.

'Marcia, I'll go now. Come to my house after the show tomorrow. I'll send the same car for you. We can't stop talking now.'

'Yes. No.'

'Come.'

'I've had a letter from the solicitors.'

'Bring it with you. Come.'

'All right.' The doorbell rings again imperiously. Marcia presses the release switch and tells George to go quickly to the landing above out of sight. He hears running footsteps on the flights below which mask the sound of his own feet.

'Were you asleep or what?'

'Sorry, Rosie. On the loo. Come on in.'

The door shuts on the two women and after a few minutes George quickly leaves the house, his heart still beating hard.

19 ∫

'I brought some whisky, Marcia. Only half a bottle, but I'm skint. If you don't need a whisky now, you'll need it when I tell you about Edward.'

'Let's pour the whisky then. Big ones.'

Rosie is glimmering with her unsaid news; she goes to the fridge to find ice as Marcia puts two highball glasses with chipped rims on the kitchen table.

'Oh. You didn't fill your icetray last time you used it.'

'Shit. I thought I had.'

'There's one piece each. I'll refill, shall I?'

Marcia flops onto a kitchen chair as Rosie fills the icetray to the brim with water and carries it in slow motion to the fridge. 'Well, go on, Rosie. You're clearly the bearer of bad news. Creusa would have had you put to death for bringing it.' Marcia takes a swig of whisky. 'So how is Edward?'

'He's back in hospital.'

'What!'

'He's got an infection in the wound, apparently. When I arrived at his flat he was groaning away feeling terrible. The whole area round the wound was red, he had red patches coming up all over his body, so I said get the doctor, Edward, don't mess about. And the doctor sent him straight to hospital, and he's now having antibiotics intravenously from a drip. I'm so glad I dropped in when I did.'

'But this is awful, awful. Poor Edward. Oh God.'

'I was afraid he'd got that killer disease they keep talking about – you know, when the infection races through the cells too fast to stop. You've lost a leg before you know it.'

Rosie takes a first sip of whisky. and follows it at once with another.

'It's unbelievable. All I wanted to do was give him a fright in return for the fright he'd given me. Oh, Rosie, it's a nightmare. Poor Edward – he'll hate being on a drip, he's so squeamish.' She bursts into tears. Rosie comforts her, and they both drink deep from their glasses.

'A top-up?'

'Yes, but with lots of water. I'll be legless otherwise.' Marcia takes a length of kitchen paper and blows her nose vigorously. 'Did you see him in hospital?'

'No, I had to go off to an appointment. But I rang Fenella to tell her and she's been, and apparently this infection was boiling up for a couple of days but he'd done nothing about it. He's in the Chelsea and Westminster, by the way. I'll go and see him tomorrow.'

'I've never felt so guilty in my life.'

'It's just bad luck, Marcia. A cut doesn't usually behave like this. Even the doctor said that. Don't blame yourself too much.'

'Edward is definitely going to sue me now.'

'What are you going to do?'

'I've actually made an appointment to see a solicitor. I did it after the matinée, and felt so much better I wish I'd done it days ago. And now this. How long is Edward going to be kept in, did Fenella tell you?'

'Just until they'd controlled the infection and could take him off the drip, she said.'

'Edward was supposed to be going to New York, to work on a co-production at the Met. He's been negotiating it for months. He'll be beside himself if he has to cancel.'

'Just pray he doesn't have to.'

'Have a Ritz biscuit.'

'Half a bottle goes nowhere, does it?'

'When this is gone, I've got a bit more whisky somewhere. I need to go to bed drunk tonight or I'll just lie there and worry.'

'Your answerphone's still on, and you've got three messages.'

'I'll play them tomorrow.' Marcia switches off the answerphone.

'I could never do that. Far too curious.'

'I'd rather not run the risk of any more complications. At the moment my life is over the top, right over the top. I don't want anything else to happen.' Marcia bangs down her glass. 'Nothing.'

'My life's been dull for months. I gave that party to liven things up.' Rosie looks glum, and takes another swallow of whisky. 'All it did was put me in the red. The man I was after didn't even bloody come, damn it. I thought I'd lure him to a big do with premises of Sedley and others being there, but no. Men are basically bastards. Nothing changes. Whisky's great.'

Marcia hacks up some cheddar and puts the pieces approximately on top of six biscuits. 'One two three for me, one two three for you. I must go and see Edward. I'll come with you when you go.'

'Not a good idea, Marcia. Let me go on my own and report back.'

'I feel so bloody guilty.'

'Don't keep saying that. It's boring.'

'I could come with you and wait outside, then you could come and get me if it was a good idea.' Marcia's voice is slurred, and she pushes the plate of biscuits towards Rosie. 'Have a cheese and biscuit. I mean a biscuit and cheese.'

'No thanks, darling, you eat them. I ate earlier. Why don't you ring me in the morning when we're sober and we'll see how we both feel then about you coming with me?'

'Must see Edward. Don't want to but must.'

'We'll talk in the morning.'

'It was self-defence, Rosie. He was starting to rape me.'

Rosie puts her empty glass down. 'All finished. The trouble is, Marcia, that's not what he will say. He'll say you wanted sex. He is your lover after all.'

'Was. WAS. It's over. I'm not going to see him because I want to start it all up again.' Marcia hiccups. 'I'm going because I feel guilty. Guilty.'

'Edward might not see it that way.'

'He never sees it my way.' She hiccups again. 'I need water.' She stands up and sits down again. 'I'm pissed, Rosie. Truly pissed. Truly, truly pissed. That whisky went straight into my bloodstream. I think I'll go and lie down.' She does not move, and hiccups again.

'Drink some water first.' Rosie pours her a glass of water; she is at the super-careful stage of inebriation, and succeeds in not spilling a drop. 'I must go, Marcia, or I won't have the strength to walk home.'

'Has it been one of those days! Yes, it's been one of those days. A little girl with ginger hair fell in the park right at my feet. I cuddled her, Rosie, I cuddled her because she was crying. She was so sweet, she cracked me up. Oh God, here we are, two childless women—'

'Go to bed, Marcia. I can't take people who get maudlin. I'll ring you tomorrow morning.'

'She had a lovely name too, Cynthia, Celia, oh what was it? Don't you long for children, Rosie?'

'No. Come on, the bedroom's this way, remember?'

'Christina. Clariss—'

'Goodnight, Marcia. Sleep tight. Which you surely will.'

'Cecilia. She was called Cecilia.'

Marcia wakes up still partly clothed at nine o'clock, to find she's lying in sunlight and has no hangover. She stands gingerly, but it is true: she has slept solidly for eight hours and has no headache. She has a bath, tidies the flat, and puts a much-needed load of clothes on to wash. Then she sits down with toast and coffee to ring Rosie.

'Hullo? Oh, Marcia.'

'You sound bad.'

'I have the mother and father of a hangover.'

'Did I wake you?'

'Not quite. How come you're so bushy-tailed?'

'Are you going to see Edward this morning?'

'I doubt if I'll be going anywhere this morning. I've just taken two Alka-Seltzer and I'm waiting for them to reach my brain.'

'I've decided it would be better not to go and see Edward yet. I'll send him some flowers and a card. When you do get there, you can ask him if he'd like to see me. If he does, I'll go.'

'That's what I think. Not that I can think yet. I was up half the night drinking water I felt so dehydrated. Whisky never used to do this to me.'

'It's most unfair I'm feeling so well this morning. Anyway, thanks a lot, Rosie, for your immoral support, and we'll speak later.'

'Who was that little girl you were burbling about last night?'

'What little girl?'

'You kept going on about some child called Cecilia.'

'God, I must have been very drunk. I do vaguely remember mentioning her. She was just a child I saw in Regent's Park, that's all.'

'You were lamenting us being childless women.'

'Well, we are. I felt sad about it yesterday, but today it feels like an advantage. Bye, Rosie. Good luck with Edward.'

Marcia rings the hospital for an update and is told he is comfortable and improving. She makes a note of the ward on the bottom of the solicitor's letter, and puts it in her bag ready to show George. She shouldn't be seeing him, but it's a comfort to know she can ask his advice about what to do next vis-à-vis Edward.

'You're looking very chipper, Miss Fleckner.'

'I feel better today. But you, Willie – what on earth have you done to yourself?'

'The story I'd like to tell is that the missus hit me with the rolling-pin, but really what I did was walk straight into a lamp-post. Just wasn't looking where I was going. I've got a box for you, came just now.' Willie has a bandage on his forehead and his hair sticks up around it. He passes over what looks like a shoebox wrapped in brown paper. It's very light. Marcia's name is written in large unfamiliar black-ink handwriting.

'Take care, Willie. No more violent encounters with lamp-posts.'

She shakes the box as she climbs the stairs to her dressing-room. Nothing moves inside it. The removal of the paper reveals a man's shoebox; she lifts the lid and sees inside an old tin whistle sellotaped to a card in the base of the box. Round it in the same large script is written: *Come to dinner next Sunday evening?*

There are two phone numbers underneath, but no name. Marcia laughs. She knows it's from Sedley. She tests out the whistle just as Suzanne comes in.

'Goodness, you made me jump. Is that a safety device to deter would-be rapists?'

'Hardly. It's a very feeble noise. I can make more unaided.' Marcia demonstrates her own whistle and Suzanne laughs.

'So you can.'

'Everything all right in here?' Andrew puts his head through the door.

'Just practising.'

'Thought you needed help. Got me worried.'

Marcia puts the whistle and the piece of card with the telephone numbers into her handbag next to the solicitor's letter, and starts to get ready for the performance.

'Talking of would-be rapists, how is Edward getting on?'

'Bad news. He's gone back into hospital with some infection, but is responding to treatment well, I am told.'

'Oh dear. Let's hope the press don't get hold of the latest.'

'Edward won't tell them, and I won't, but no doubt some helpful friend will. By the way, Rosie swears it wasn't her who spilled the beans in the first place. I suspect she talked to too many people, and one of them decided to have some fun.' Marcia scrapes her hair into its cap ready for the wig, and tucks cottonwool into it carefully. 'I wish this thing didn't rub me so badly. I'm looking forward to something that fits me better when we transfer.'

'Let me help you get it in the right places.' Marcia watches her friend's fixed gaze of concentration as she repositions the pieces of cottonwool.

'It's going to be great doing a West End run together, Suze.'

'It certainly is. And my bank manager can hardly believe his good luck.'

'I'm still in the red, but those lovely little rows of black figures are in sight. I must resist a fatal temptation to throw a party to celebrate. Thanks, that feels much better.'

'I don't know a single actor who is sensible about money.'

'I don't know any actors who have money to be sensible about.'

*　　*　　*

'We are meat! Cheerio!' George lifts his glass to Marcia. 'Apparently, that was a toast of Francis Bacon's.'

'Perhaps it explains why all his pictures are in red meaty colours. Who did that picture over there, by the way? The one in the red range too.'

'One of last year's Royal College finalists. Sandra something. I wish they'd sign their works.'

'So you still go to shows and pick up bargains?'

'I've filled up all my walls, so I only go now if I get fed up with a picture and want a new one.'

Marcia and George talk about collectors, collections and museums as they sit in the kitchen consuming the cold supper George has prepared. They are both aware they are simply making conversation before they broach the various other matters on their minds. Marcia cracks first.

'This letter came from Edward's solicitors. I also heard that Edward has been re-admitted to hospital with an infection in the wound.'

'Ah.' George skims through the letter. 'Well, it's a good letter, making all the points I would expect.'

'I'm frightened about it all now, George. Mainly because Edward can't be malingering, as I thought – hospitals don't give people beds unless it's serious. I feel extremely guilty.'

George gets up to make coffee without commenting, and Marcia tells him about the job in New York that might be missed.

'His solicitors will milk this latest setback for all it is worth, quite correctly. You would expect them to do so if you were in Edward's position. Always put yourself in the opposition's shoes, Marcia. It's a useful exercise. Have you written down your statement about what happened?'

'No.'

'You must.'

'I keep putting it off. You know what a great procrastinator I am. It's like the prospect of writing an essay. And I'm nervous that when I start writing I'll remember something I'd rather not.'

'All the more reason to do it soon. If you're deluding yourself over any aspect of this sad business, it's better to discover it sooner than later. You can bet that the opposite side will know what you've hidden from yourself, and will use it. Face up to those shadowy details you're shirking, Marcia.'

'You sound very stern.'

'I'm giving you good advice. Do you want me to recommend a solicitor, because you ought to see one as soon as possible—'

'I've made an appointment to see one.'

'That's a relief.'

'I feel I ought to visit Edward in hospital.'

'See your solicitor first. A little more wine?'

'No more, thanks.'

'Look, there's half a glass each left.'

'If you insist. Your wine is always lovely.'

'Leave it if you don't want it.' In silence they watch the reddish-brown liquid being poured into the two glasses. Then their eyes meet.

'I'm sorry I came round unannounced last night like that. But I'm not sorry I asked you to marry me.'

'It was the last thing I expected – I didn't know how to react.'

'You could say yes?'

'No, George. It would never work.'

'I think it would work very well.'

'Can you really see me as Lady Warne?'

'Why not?'

'I can't, I honestly can't. And your world would be shocked at mine.'

'That's nonsense, Marcia, and you know it.'

'No, I don't – I can only guess what your world is like. I still think I'd be a fish out of water – an unknown, rather dubious actress with a law-suit pending isn't going to be good company for judges—'

'Don't be naive—'

'I am naive. I am a bad risk. I am a mess. You should avoid me like the plague, not ask me to marry you!'

'It's the best solution.' He takes her hand. 'Marcia, listen to me.'

'Solution. That word is wrong.' She squeezes his hand lightly and slides out of his grasp. 'Marriage shouldn't be seen as a solution to problems. I may be naive, but surely marriage ought to happen despite problems, not to solve them?'

'It's only another way of putting it.'

'You said solution. You're playing with words.'

'So are you. Please take me seriously, Marcia.'

'I do. I wouldn't have come here if I didn't. But I can't marry you.'

'Then come to India with me instead this Christmas.'

She is wordless.

'I've got until mid-January before I go on the Bench, and I'm determined to have a good holiday. I want to go to the land of my birth, and this is the best time of year to go to India. Come with me.'

Marcia gets up and paces about the kitchen. 'You're confusing me.'

'I'm confused myself at the moment. All the changes happening to my life are unsettling. New beginnings in all directions. When the idea of going to India came to me it seemed absolutely right. I know you have a break coming up before the play transfers, so have the trip as a Christmas present from me.'

Marcia stops pacing and puts her hands over her face. 'Of all the places in the world I've most longed to see, India is first. Ah, George.'

'Nothing to stop you seeing it at last.'

'Everything to stop me. If I say I'll come, you'll assume there's still a hope I might agree to marry you. I'd be coming under false pretences—'

'I promise not to assume anything. We'll have separate rooms, we can even travel on different planes so that no one knows we are going together. We'll simply travel together when we get there, as friends.' George stands up and starts to clear the table. 'I don't want to travel alone in India, Marcia. I think I've lost the knack of solo travel. Please come with me.'

'You're confusing me by tempting me to do something I desperately want to do, but for the wrong reason. I'd be using you as my air ticket, my meal ticket.'

'So what? I can afford it.'

'There could be a risk of the press finding out we'd gone together—'

'Why? Don't tell anyone where you're going, just go. I'll say I'm going alone. I'll fly alone, you'll fly alone, we'll meet at the hotel.' His eyes are alight. 'I'll find out about visas—'

'Don't rush ahead like this. It's a crazy idea.'

'You've always liked crazy ideas.'

'I can't decide tonight. Give me some space and time, George. You're crowding me. I've got a massive problem on my hands over Edward, and I just can't think about India as well. Give me time.'

'Of course you've got time. Let me do some research into what's available at this short notice, and you think hard about coming. And I promise there'll be no strings attached. No pressures on you. I promise.'

'I'm exhausted. I have to go home and sleep on all this. Let's call a cab.' Marcia picks up her bag awkwardly, and its contents spill out. The tin whistle rolls several feet. and George pounces on it.

'Good Lord. I had one just like this when I was a boy.' He gives it a blow. 'Mine had a better sound, I have to admit.' He hands it back to her. 'Funny thing to carry round in your handbag.'

'I know.' Marcia tucks it away. 'Could you ring your usual minicab service?'

As George does so, Marcia takes out the whistle again. She hasn't yet rung any of those numbers to see if they are Sedley's, but who else could it have come from? She looks up when George returns and knows her expression has softened and lightened. He remains stiffly in the doorway.

'How much time are you going to need?'

'Time?'

'To consider my suggestion about coming to India.'

'Give me till next week. Tomorrow I'm seeing the solicitor, then it's the weekend, so let's say by the beginning of December.'

'The first of December is next Tuesday.'

'I'll let you know by then.' They hear the sound of the doorbell.

'That will be the taxi.'

'They were very quick for once.'

'I'll tell them to wait.'

'Please don't.' Marcia has slipped on her coat and is ready to go. 'Thank you for a delicious supper. And all your good advice. I'll write down my version of events in the morning, before I see the solicitor.'

'Marcia—'

'Don't see me out. It's better if I open the door and go alone. I promise to let you know by the first.' As she pulls the door open he leans forward to kiss her goodbye. She moves away muttering 'Careful.'

'Goodbye.'

'Goodbye.'

George watches her run down his front steps, his eyes bleak.

When I came home that Sunday, 15 November, I was shocked to find Mr Wintlesham in my kitchen . . .

Mr Wintlesham's unexpected presence in my kitchen that Sunday was a shock. He had secretly had a key cut without my permission . . .

I was tired and needed to rest and be alone to prepare myself for the week ahead, but Mr Wintlesham had other ideas. He wouldn't listen to my protests that I didn't want to make love . . .

Edward Wintlesham clearly had let himself uninvited into my flat with the express idea of making love to me whether I wanted to or not . . .

Marcia groans as she puts a line through each version and starts again. The statement is agonizingly difficult to write; every sentence seems woolly, stiff, inaccurate. She shuts her eyes, trying to recall exactly what happened, what was said, and in what order.

She pushes the pad of paper aside and fetches the tape-recorder she uses when she's learning her lines. She talks into it without worrying about repetitions and bad English, and finds it much easier to reconstruct what happened.

'Then I said something like wanting to keep control of things, and Edward said he wanted to destroy my control. I think that's exactly what he said: "I want to destroy your sense of control."'

Or was it? Certainly he'd said something almost like that, and his face had shown his pleasure in the idea. Marcia continues trying to describe how Edward enjoyed both domination and roughness, and how excited he was becoming at her resistance.

'He broke the stem of a wine-glass he was holding – damn.'

She switches off the machine again. She's forgotten to describe the champagne he'd brought and which she hadn't wanted to drink but he'd forced on her. Never mind.

'Then I picked up the pieces of broken glass to throw away, and he followed me to the kitchen. I kept one piece of glass in my hand, I suppose out of fear. Since I was now deliberately not resisting him because resistance only increased his excitement, I was beginning to feel scared. Edward is very strong. He's hurt me in the past.'

She switches off the small machine and freezes its turning tape. She tries to recollect exactly what happened next. How did Edward actually get her into the bedroom? Did he drag her? Did her carry her? She can only remember precisely the feel of the base of the wine glass in her hand; it's as if it has erased the sequence of full recollection. Real clarity only returns when her hand jabs the broken stem into Edward's buttock. Just a little jab, a short jab that punctures flesh but does not go deep. She puts her hands over her eyes as she recalls his yelp of surprised pain, her quick escape, his rage as she locked herself in the bathroom, her foresight that caused her to grab the portable telephone. But between the moment when she decided to hang on to the piece of glass to the using of it, her memory falters. She imagines a cool rational voice cross-examining her.

'And why did you agree to go into the bedroom at all, Miss Fleckner?'

'I think he carried me there.'

'Exactly, because you were more than willing. You allowed him to undress you, and he describes you in his statement as langourous with desire.'

'I was pretending. Edward is excited by resistance. If I'd fought him he'd have loved it, and won anyway. I could only escape if I took him by surprise.'

'Mr Wintlesham says you were aroused, as aroused as he

was, and your attack was a vicious outcome of perverted desire.'

Marcia makes herself a coffee as she replays the tape. It's better than her written efforts, but still confused. She's tempted to leave the whole enterprise to another day, but stops herself. She puts a fresh tape in and starts again, and this time her statement flows better; she includes the champagne, Edward's explanation of how he had a key cut, and more about his fondness for rough sex.

Stephen Smith is a surprise. She expected someone bland, serious and quietly dressed, and finds instead a short, ebullient man wearing a bright red shirt and a sharply cut hound's tooth suit. His office is pleasantly untidy and dominated by a spectacularly large rubber plant. He has hung his scarf on one branch and his umbrella on another.

'Your plant is going to go through the ceiling.'

'My triffid. Yes, another six inches and then I'll have to make a decision about its future. My secretary hates it and suggests sawing it up. Do sit down, Miss Fleckner. Rachel Klein tells me you've been friends since college days.'

'Poor Rachel, I think she feared I'd never get my act together and come and see you. But here I am, bearing a tape of my statement even. And I'm so glad your secretary told me about the green form – she said if I fill one in I get £100 worth of advice on legal aid. As she instructed, I've brought my tax figures for last year, and here's the pathetic total so far for this.'

'And the famous green form is all ready for you to sign.' Stephen Smith watches her sign from under heavy lids; his large mouth is pursed, he looks forbidding. But this fades the moment he looks up to reveal his lively dark blue eyes. 'Excellent.'

A fax machine rings briefly and then starts spouting a long tongue of paper. Smith ignores it, though Marcia can't keep her eyes off the spewing paper.

'I'd love one of those. So much better than an answerphone. By the way, I remembered to bring this tape of the message Edward left.'

'Let's start at the beginning, Miss Fleckner. What I'd like you to do is to tell me in your own words now what happened. I will be noting everything you say, and I'll correlate this with your tape later to make a final statement. So you returned on Sunday, 15 November last to find Edward Wintlesham in your flat . . .'

As Marcia tells the story again she begins to feel she's reciting a speech she has learned from a play. The impression is intensified by Smith's silent, intense concentration on the narrative. He does not interrupt her, but she notices he makes several quick marginal signs that look like a Q.

'That was an admirable summary. You sounded as if you were watching yourself on stage.'

'I was.'

'Just a few questions spring to mind. One in particular.' His keen blue eyes are friendly and unthreatening. 'Why, when you had already picked up the broken glass and were presumably free to move about because you went into the kitchen, didn't you rush out of your own front door and escape upstairs to your friends who you already knew were in?'

'Edward was between me and the door. He stuck close to me as I went into the kitchen. I could have dashed past him, I suppose, but I thought I could control the situation. Besides, he would have tried to stop me and my struggles would have excited him. He wanted resistance, he wanted to fight me. He wanted violence.'

'Did he interpret your passivity as acquiescence?'

'Probably.'

'His statement will no doubt make much of that point.'

'His statement—'

'He has already made one. I haven't seen it.'

'He's going to say my attack was unprovoked, isn't he, because I was passive and let him take me into the bedroom?'

'Very likely.'

'He terrified me by this stage. He was more excited than I've ever seen him. I'd several times told him to go because I was exhausted and had a hard week ahead, and he'd simply ignored whatever I said.'

'He could suggest that you changed your mind, that you became aroused, that you went willingly to the bedroom.'

'You think I did, don't you?'

'Not at all. I'm simply playing devil's advocate to alert you to the most dangerous part in your statement, so that together we can make sure you are absolutely clear about your thought processes and actions.'

'I can see how my passivity will be twisted in court.'

'With luck, Miss Fleckner, we won't get that far. What happened to the piece of glass, by the way?'

'I threw it out at once. I couldn't stand the sight of it. It never occurred to me it would be needed.'

'Pity. Describe it very precisely.'

'It was the base of a wine-glass. Since Edward had brought champagne – well, sparkling wine – got out two glasses which were the nearest thing I had to champagne flutes. I gave him the nicest one – finer, with a thinner stem.'

'Have you got another like it?'

'It was the last of a set of six.'

'Tell me exactly how he broke the stem.'

'I honestly think he did it deliberately. As if to show me how roused he was. He held it like this, he pushed his thumb one way and his fingers the other. It snapped and he didn't cut himself. The glass was empty, and he dropped the pieces on the carpet and came for me. I had to duck down to avoid him so I pretended I was doing it to pick up the bits.'

'How long have you known Edward Wintlesham?'

'Over six months.'

'Did you realize he had a violent streak?'

'Yes.'

'Did you say anything to him about it?'

Marcia shuts her eyes. A sense of hopelessness is enveloping her as Stephen Smith's questions underline the feebleness of her case.

'No,' she whispers. 'Not clearly enough.' She remembers how at the beginning of their relationship she had found Edward's decisive ways in bed arousing and exhilarating; he sometimes took her to the edge of pain but not, at first, beyond. He could see that she enjoyed it; when he began to go a little further, his roughness still seemed under control and she felt no particular alarm. When rubbed and roughened skin became bruised and broken, she did ask him to go more gently. Sorry, sorry, Marcia, you're so exciting I get carried away. Flattery to warm her should have warned her.

'It looks as if I asked for it, doesn't it?'

'It could do. We have to be very careful.'

'Because I was passive, he's going to say the attack was unprovoked and everyone will believe him. It's pointless fighting this.' Marcia starts to get up.

'Not at all, Miss Fleckner. Courage. It's good to air the difficulties. What about some tea or coffee? Tea?'

'With milk. No sugar, thanks.' Marcia watches him dispiritedly as he rings through to his secretary. His black hair is wild and stands on end, and his ears and nostrils sprout hair; it creeps out of his shirt and tries to cover the backs of his hands. He grins at her and she can't help smiling back.

'Another question I have to ask is this. What does Mr Wintlesham expect to get out of you? He presumably knows you have no money, and earn what little you do on an irregular basis, so money can't really be what he's after.'

'He wants to humiliate me, make life hell for me. And you have to remember that his solicitor brother Robert is also behind this. Robert doesn't like me or I him, and I'm sure he's as much behind this letter as Edward is. They become a pair of horrid schoolboys capable of tearing the wings off butterflies when they're together.'

'Robert Wintlesham has a reputation for being tough and clever. I don't know him personally.'

The tea arrives and while it is being put out Marcia picks up the solicitor's letter again. 'This was done mainly to scare me, and now Edward's back in hospital it's succeeding.'

'The fact he's had a relapse is not relevant to your position – Mr Wintlesham is going to have to prove there wasn't an intervening cause which has nothing to do with the original wound. So don't worry about the fact he's gone back into hospital except from a humanitarian point of view. How bad is he?'

'It must be a serious infection – he's receiving antibiotics intravenously. I want to go and see him – do you think I should?'

'Have you tried to build bridges?'

'I've only spoken directly to him once, since that Sunday. I rang him to say I was sorry he was in pain.'

'Can you recall the exact conversation?'

'Edward started to complain the moment he heard my voice. He was fed up with the pain, the discomfort, the fact he couldn't sit down, the restrictions to his life. Then he asked me why I'd done it – I told him he'd frightened me into it and he didn't believe me. So I rang off. I didn't justify my actions or start arguing with him because there was no point.'

'And that was all?'

'I knew if I said any more it would only have made things worse.'

'What do you feel now?'

'I'm beginning to want to talk to him again, to sort this whole thing out as friends.'

'Well, it does seem to me that there's some scope for appeasement. You were wise not to argue your position further, particularly since your remark about being frightened might have stayed in his mind and affected him later. People sometimes shift ground quite radically before they can bring themselves to admit it.'

'He's a proud person, with a trouble-shooting brother. I don't have a lot of hope, but what do you suggest I do? Make a visit to the hospital, try and talk to him there?'

'I think there are better solutions. You need to have time to talk to him without being interrupted, and neither of you will be able to control privacy in a hospital. The best thing would be for you to meet on neutral ground, not his territory or yours, so your flats wouldn't be suitable either. And I think you may find he'd insist on his solicitor being with him, so I also would need to be there.'

'But I was thinking of something informal – just to put my side of things . . .'

Stephen Smith looks straight at Marcia as he shakes his head. 'That's what I am afraid of. You see, you might say things you didn't really mean, and implicate yourself in ways you didn't really intend. If you're alone with him, with no one around as backup, emotions could take control again.'

'Our relationship is over—'

'Does he know that? You need to look very carefully at your motives for this meeting – what do you want to gain from it?'

'I want him to see sense and drop the idea of criminal charges against me.'

'Anything else?'

Marcia stares out of the window before replying. 'Perhaps it's too much to hope for, but I'd like to be on speaking terms again. We live and work in the same milieu.'

'Anything further?'

'What are you leading me towards saying?'

'Are speaking terms all you want to return to? Are you hoping, in your heart of hearts, for a complete reconciliation and a return to the status quo? It helps me to know.'

'No. Absolutely not. No. I should have made that clear. I don't want to go back to him. Our affair is over as far as I'm concerned. I just want him to understand how much he frightened me, so that he sees his violence for what it is.'

'Does he want the affair to continue?'

'He can't. He must realize it's over now—'

'He might not. Perhaps this letter is part of a strategy.'

'You're making me feel nervous. I don't want to know about this.'

Stephen Smith shrugs, leans back in his chair and swings his arms up, patting his hands on his stiff hair. Clearly its springiness gives him satisfaction and the habit releases tension. Marcia watches his lightly bouncing palms and wants to shake him. Instead she gives an explosive sigh.

'Say it anyway. What strategy?'

'A deal, Miss Fleckner. You come back to me, be my lover again, and we'll forget about the whole thing. Otherwise—'

'Shit.' Marcia gets up and goes to the window. 'Excuse my language, but shit sums it up.'

'May I make a suggestion?'

'Not if it's going to make me feel as sick as the last one.'

Smith laughs. 'I suggest you invite Mr Wintlesham and his solicitor here, to this building, to meet you. We have a pleasant conference room at the back where you can both talk to each other in privacy, and both solicitors will be on hand to be called in should the temperature rise.'

But Marcia is hardly listening. Surely Edward does not want her back? Surely he just wants to humiliate her, crush her, make her suffer? It can't be money he's after. It's the power to hurt. But the best way of hurting her would certainly be for them to become lovers again. That can be the only reason he would want her back.

20

'George?'

The hesitant voice is oddly familiar yet unplaceable. George frowns.

'Is that George Warne?'

'George speaking.'

'I thought I had a wrong number for a minute. It's Laura.'

'Laura! How nice to hear your voice.'

'Don't be too surprised—'

'I'm pleased. What can I do for you?'

'Father asked me to ring you. He's not very well. Ever since the funeral he's not been himself.'

'He's a good age, Laura.'

'I know, but I can tell he's upset about something. He says he wants to see you. He's mentioned it several times, and though I told him I thought you'd be too busy to come down here, he won't accept it. Oh dear. He's such a burden sometimes.'

'It must be hard for you.'

'Only sometimes. He's still got his sense of humour – we often have a good laugh.'

'How ill is he, Laura?'

'You mean, how long has he got? That's why I've rung you now. He's become very weak. The doctor says it's elective starvation. He's had enough of living.'

'I'll come down and see him as soon as I can.'

There is a pause, during which he can almost hear Laura thinking. 'If you don't come down *very* soon, I'm afraid it will be too late. He's asked for you every day the last few days. This morning I was quite frightened suddenly, he looked so weak.'

'I'll unscramble my plans for this weekend and come down, Laura. Can I beg a bed for the night?'

'Of course. Father will be thrilled to see you. Oh, thank you, Jebs, for saying you'll come.'

'Will Sophie be there?'

'Whatever gave you that idea? She hardly ever comes to see us.'

'Expect me around tea-time tomorrow, Saturday.'

'Do you remember the way to Bellwether?'

'Of course. As if I could forget.'

But he finds that he has. The last visit he paid to Bellwether Farm was before the death of his aunt at least thirty-five years ago. No motorway existed, and he remembers the crawl through Taunton. As he takes the Wellington exit off the M5 and reaches the village, nothing is familiar. He drives through it until he sees the church. It has shrunk, as has the rectory next door, once so shabby and untended and now in spick and span condition with carriage lamps and white paintwork and two new cars parked in the drive. A white fence separates it firmly from the churchyard; it no longer houses the vicar. There is no village shop next door to it, but the pub is still there and beyond it that road he had taken so often when he'd walked to the village to shop for his aunt and buy sweets for himself. There are new houses on the road, the verges have been tidied up and made into pavements, but yes, this is the way . . .

He drives straight past the turning to Bellwether Farm and only realizes he has done so when he reaches a corner and sees familiar barns down in the valley. His uncle's barns; the house is hidden by a fold of hill. He retraces his route and finds he missed the turning because it is narrower than he remembered, and that old green board with white letters hand-painted by Aunt Cynthia has been replaced with a smart black and white strip fixed to the open farm gate. Bellwether Farm. In anticipation and in trepidation, he drives slowly down the bumpy track. That at least hasn't changed. He remembers the care with which Geoffrey used to navigate the ruts, frowning when brambles whipped against his precious car.

Laura has heard him approach and is standing waving at the gate of the front garden.

'Leave the car here, just tuck it in well so that the tractor can get past.'

'I could put it in the yard—'

'Too muddy.'

The sight and smell of the farm, so much part of him yet so long ignored, move him unbearably, and he knows tears are close. Laura stands beaming as he parks the car and takes his time getting his grip out of the boot. He turns to greet Laura and a peck on the cheek turns into a long hug.

'Laura. Why haven't I been back before!'

'I don't know.'

'You look well.'

It is true. She looked at her worst at Lena's funeral, constrained by her dated best clothes. In jeans, a checked shirt, and a worn old tweed jacket of Julian's with the sleeves turned back to show the striped black and white cotton lining, she looks sturdily handsome. Her well-polished and well-worn short brown riding boots are exactly like the ones she wore as a girl. Perhaps they are them. George follows her towards the house, looking up at the attic windows of his old bedroom. The glass is very dirty, and there are no curtains any more. The room looks unused.

'I've put you in Sophie's old room – it has the best view. Do you remember where it is?'

'Top of the stairs and turn right – down at the end of that corridor.' His voice is a little husky.

'I'll put the kettle on while you go and settle in. Bathroom's where it always was.'

And unchanged as far as he can see, except that the old geyser has gone and the lino is newish. But the old bath, the washbasin, the ample taps, the long, crookedly mounted towel-rail, the row of aged hot-water bottles on the back of the door, are all there. The rubber bottles are so stiff with age they look as if they haven't been touched for years; in fact, the whole back of the door reminds George of many works he has seen in art students' degree shows.

He has nothing to unpack, and turns to go downstairs. A trick of light coming through the window behind him caused by motes of dust in the beams from the setting sun makes him see his own boyish form ahead, swinging round the newel post as he always did.

'We're in the kitchen.'

His uncle is sitting by the Aga, heavily muffled. Two armchairs have been moved in there from the sitting-room, and clearly they are in constant use. When Julian Roper sees George he tries to stand up and drops his mug of tea.

'Oh, Father. Oh dear.'

'Hullo, Julian. Please don't get up for me.' George takes his uncle's bony hand in both of his.

'Sit down, Jebs, sit down. She'll mop up.'

'I can't believe I haven't been back since I was a boy, and find it all so familiar and unchanged.'

'After Cynthia died, we rather let things slide.'

'Father, don't be silly, we kept things going remarkably well considering.' Laura is on her knees with an old-fashioned dishcloth.

'I mean over people. We didn't invite you here, Jebs, and we should have.'

'If you had, I'd have come. As I've come today.'

'We didn't expect you to invite us to Lena's funeral.' Laura throws the cloth into the sink and sits on the kitchen table near George.

'Why ever not? You're family.'

'You didn't invite us to your wedding. Father saw the announcement in the paper. Not that we really expected you to – don't look so guilty! No reason why you should have even though we were family – we hadn't met for years. Then we heard you'd got divorced.'

'And married again. And divorced again.'

'Gracious.' Laura looks less taken aback than he expects. 'How busy you've been. Do have a piece of cake. It's Mum's recipe for chocolate cake – I remember how you used to love it. Mine isn't as light as hers. You too, Father. Just one piece.'

The grandfather clock in the corner whirrs and strikes five.

'I remember that clock so well – it always sounds as if it's not quite going to give us all the strikes it ought to. You can only have four – oh, all right, five then.'

'I never even hear it.'

'Are you going off in a minute, Laura?' Julian's hands pick at the shawl wrapped round his shoulders. It's a cheap Kashmiri shawl, with rather violent embroidered flowers. It looks wildly out of place in a farm kitchen.

'No. Why should I? You're not eating your cake.'

'You always have plenty to do on the farm after tea.'

'Not when Jebs is here.' Laura laughs and pours more tea.

'I need to talk to Jebs.'

'What's the hurry, Father? He's here all weekend. You can talk to him tomorrow when I'm at church. Unless you want to come with me, George—'

'I might, for old times' sake.' George can see distress is building in his uncle's eyes.

'Please leave us alone, Laura. You know this is my best time, between tea and bed. I might not feel so good tomorrow.'

'Can't I clear the tea things first? You are in a mood, I must say.' Laura noisily piles the cups and plates in the sink, and marches out of the kitchen, winking at George as she goes out of the back door. The dogs in the yard start barking excitedly and she walks off with them to the line of barns.

'She's been a good daughter to me.' Julian pulls the lurid shawl closer. 'I expected her to marry and leave me but she never has. She'll inherit the farm. Sophie will get a bit of money, of course. But Sophie has been lucky in life. Don't tell the girls I've done that, will you?'

'If you don't want me to. Won't Sophie be upset?'

'Yes.' He gives George a little smile. 'I won't be here to see it. I take it Lena left you everything?'

'She did. I'll be selling the house in due course. There isn't much else – she lived on her capital, she'd had to borrow against the house.'

'I should have thought Geoffrey would have left her well provided for.'

'He was surprisingly inefficient in that way.'

'Your father—' Julian stops and lifts a shaking hand towards George, then drops it again. 'I was fond of Lena. Very sorry to hear she didn't have a good death. I'm determined to die here in my bed.'

'I was upset I wasn't with Lena when she died. I wasn't far away, I could have easily been there. Instead she died with strangers around her.'

'I have to tell you something, Jebs. About your father.'

There is a quality in Julian's tone which pierces George with an extraordinary flash of hope. 'About Geoffrey? Or about my real father?'

'So you know.' Julian's eyes are cloudy; his irises are ringed with a milky aureole. He blinks his virtually lashless lids. 'So you know.'

'Lena left me a letter telling me his name.'

'I always thought it was very cruel of her not to tell you right from the beginning. It was perfectly clear you had nothing in common with Geoffrey Warne, and you always looked terrified of him when you were young. Cynthia longed to tell you, but she was sworn to secrecy. She only told me because I kept going on about the fact you didn't look like Geoffrey, nor much like Lena.'

'So Aunt Cynthia always knew.'

'Always. She told me after they'd come back – you must have been about ten.'

'What did she know about my real father?' George waits on edge.

'His name is Philip Symes.'

'That is all Lena told me. Just his name. What else did she tell her sister?'

'Not much, but not long before she died he resurfaced.'

The kitchen spins. 'Before who died?'

'Before my Cynthia died, of course. Lena was in a great state because he'd traced her and turned up in the house in Harrow unannounced.'

The clothes hung on the slatted dryer above their heads quiver in the rising heat from the Aga and the cross-draught between the back door and the window. The dogs bark in the distance as they accompany Laura on her rounds. George waits numbly for his uncle to continue.

'After Lena's funeral I went through her letters to Cyn, and found the one about Philip Symes. It's been worrying me that you mightn't have known about your real father, and I didn't

want to die without telling you, even though I'd promised Cyn
never to tell anyone. Some promises have to be broken when
circumstances change and the people are dead. If you hadn't
come down this weekend I'd have had to write to you and that
would have involved Laura since I can't hold a pen any more.
It's not something I could have discussed on the phone.'

'Does Laura know?'

'Of course not.'

'I would love to see my mother's letter.'

'It's here, in my pocket.' He fiddles inside his cardigan and
pulls out a blue envelope, the same bright blue Basildon Bond
both sisters liked using. 'You keep it now. In fact, you can
have all Lena's letters to her sister. They're all sorted. I did
that years ago.'

George holds the neat envelope and looks at its purple 3d
stamp bearing a young head of Elizabeth within an oval
plaited shape.

'Would you forgive me if I went and read it alone upstairs?'

'Not at all, Jebs. I'll have a little nap.'

'I won't be long.'

'I catnap all the time, night and day. Haven't had a solid
night's sleep in years. Don't seem to need it any more.' The
garish shawl has slipped and George tucks it back round Julian.
'Dreadful thing, isn't it – Laura picked it up in a jumble sale
and keeps saying how bright and cheerful it is, bless her. Ah
well. When I shut my eyes I don't see it.' In fact, his eyes are
already closed.

George goes up to Sophie's old bedroom and sits on the bed.
Night is falling, the sunset has faded, and he switches on the frilly
bedside light. The cabinet still contains a china chamber-pot; he
used to use one himself when he lived in the house.

'How life has changed.' He says this out loud before he makes
himself pull out the folded sheets inside it.

11 Feb 1952

Dearest Cyn
You won't believe this and I can hardly write it. But HE has
re-appeared out of the blue. Just rang the doorbell, no warning
... Mrs Waley said it was a Mr Symes, but I was a million miles

away from thinking of that *Mr Symes. When she showed him in
I nearly died.*

*'Hullo, Helena,' he says as if he'd seen me yesterday. 'I was
passing by and dropped in.'*

*Of course, thinking about it afterwards, he couldn't have been
just passing by – he'd obviously tracked me down specially, and
come on purpose. Cyn, all I could say was how nice to see you,
do have some tea, playing it all as normal as possible though my
heart was going pit-a-pat.*

'Life seems to be treating you very well,' says he.

*'I can't complain. What about you, Philip? Are you home
for good?'*

'On leave. I go back to India next week.'

*It was easier to be friendly after that, I can tell you! He told me
his wife Madge had died, and that he hoped to found a school in
Delhi. A prep school for Mayo College was how he described it.
Then I saw him looking at a photograph on the piano of George
in his Roddick Manor uniform. There was nothing I could do. He
just stopped in mid-sentence, got up, held the photo up and said,
'That has to be my son!!'*

What could I say? They are alike as two peas.

'I want to meet him, Helena.'

'No.'

'He's the only child I've ever had.'

'He's my son and he doesn't know anything about you.'

'But you admit that he's mine, not Geoffrey Warne's.'

*I couldn't deny it, Cyn. They really look too alike. He knew. So
I said: 'I don't want George to be upset, Philip. Leave him alone.
It's better this way.'*

*He took no notice to start with, as you can imagine. He kept asking
me where George was at school, but luckily nothing was written on
the photo. Of course I wasn't going to tell him. And I was terrified
Geoffrey might come home early and then I don't know what I
would have done. They never met in India. I had to beg Philip to
leave us in peace, I burst into tears and then he took me seriously. I
made him promise not to contact us again. He didn't want to agree
to that, he wanted to meet George one day. Only when I appealed
to his good sense as a teacher of boys did he then promise.*

'This is breaking my heart, Helena. But I promise. You won't

see me again. I don't plan to make my home in England, particularly now.'

I cried and cried when he'd gone, I had to go to bed pretending one of my migraines which I had anyway by then. I wish I'd taken Philip's address from him before he left. He's gone for ever now.

I know you're not very well, Cyn, but if you had time to visit us for a few days it would be lovely. You're the only person I can talk to about all this. Geoffrey doesn't even know he came here, and I am not going to tell him. Do come and stay. You and I can have a good laugh and take in some matinées.

The bedspread is green, a grassy-green shiny brocade. George stares at it and his mind fills with more green, the green of hedge and field as he sat in his mother's Austin A40 and tried to take in his aunt's death while Lena sobbed beside him. That was the end of the summer term, 1952. She had received the visit and written the letter only a few months before. Perhaps those tears were not only for Cynthia.

He sits for some time in the unheated bedroom, as numb as he was that dreadful summer day when his childhood ended. The implications of this letter are too much to take in. He can only feel a curious pity for his mother, for her inability to embrace the results of her actions, for her consequent lack of emotional growth. Anger over this last betrayal will come in time; now he only feels desolation.

'Jebs? Come and join us for a drink?' Laura's voice carries up the staircase, echoing in the sparsely furnished and uncarpeted farmhouse. There are a few rugs dotted dangerously about, but mostly the floors are of polished boards. Not so polished as once they had been, but still fairly slippery.

'Lovely. Just coming.' He has been up here for an hour: time has not existed. He puts the letter in his pocket and hurries downstairs. Julian is drinking whisky from a plastic beaker with a shaped top, like a baby's, and George sits down beside him.

'What about a whisky? That's what we're both drinking.' Laura has taken off the jacket and put on a red jersey. The colour suits her well. Again, George is surprised by how much better she looks now than she did at the funeral.

'Whisky would be wonderful.'

'I've got a stew in the Aga, and if it's not too early for you we'll be eating at seven.'

'That's fine by me. I brought some wine to go with it, but it needs to warm up a bit.'

'How kind. Goodness, two bottles. We'll be squiffy.' Laura sounds exactly like her mother; when Cynthia said how kind, both words had the same focused weight.

'Keep one for another day.'

'Isn't it nice having Jebs here again, Father?'

Julian is sucking at his whisky with more enthusiasm than he showed for his tea, and just nods.

'The house hasn't changed at all – I'm so relieved you haven't covered all your wooden floors.'

'Jebs, that's not so much choice as necessity. I know it's now the fashion to have bare boards, but believe me I'd love fitted carpets. Much snugger. This place is so cold and draughty, but tonight I've warmed the sitting-room in your honour, lit a big log fire, so let's move in there now. Being in this kitchen all the time gets me down sometimes.'

'I'll stay here, Laura.'

'Oh, come on, Father—'

'It's such a business moving me anywhere else.'

'Don't be silly, Father, we want you to come—'

'No. Leave me here.'

'Please yourself then. Come on, Jebs.'

'Why don't we just stay here with Julian?'

'I need a break from the kitchen. Father won't mind.' She picks up her glass of whisky and leaves.

'You go, Jebs. I'm used to my own company.'

'Julian, thank you for giving me that letter.'

'I hope it hasn't upset you too much.'

'It has, but I'm not going to think about the implications yet.'

'You go and talk to Laura, Jebs. She gets very lonely here, never has anyone but me to talk to. But give me a drop more whisky before you go. Just a drop. With water.'

George puts a generous inch into the beaker, and tops it up with a little water. Julian takes it and grins at him.

'Don't tell Laura. I'm only supposed to have one.'

'I won't breathe a word.'

'Whisky's the one thing that makes me feel better, despite what the doctor says.' He sucks contentedly at his beaker, and George touches his shoulder before he goes to find Laura. She's playing the piano as he goes in, but stops immediately.

'I thought you were going to desert me.'

'I'd forgotten you played the piano.'

'Playing the piano keeps me sane, that and my riding.'

'This room isn't at all as I remember it.'

'Not surprising. We put in the french windows. Mum always wanted to do it, and eventually Father did it as a sort of memorial to her. It's magic in the summer – there's the terrace just outside and the hills beyond.'

'There used to be a leafy-patterned wallpaper with a top border of flowers in here.'

'You have got a good memory. That went when we did the french windows.'

'I remember a great deal about this house. It was my home.'

'Home?'

'Even after my parents came back and set up house, the farm remained home to me.'

Laura is staring at him, frowning. 'But you hardly came to see us after they took you away, Jebs. You just came for the summer holidays for a bit.'

'I lived all year for those weeks.'

'We were told you stopped coming because you'd got bored with the countryside now you lived in London.'

'We didn't live in London, we lived in Harrow. It's pure suburbia. I hated it. My parents stopped me coming to stay here after your mother died. The implication was that with Aunt Cynthia gone I wasn't really welcome any more.'

'What nonsense. One shouldn't speak ill of the dead but Aunt Lena was not always a kind woman. She told us you didn't want to come, Jebs.'

'She did what Geoffrey told her to do.' He sips his whisky, to hide the tremor in his voice. Laura doesn't notice – she's drawing the curtains and straightening a picture. Logs hiss and spit on the fire. 'It's really very good to be back here.'

'I hope you had a useful talk with Father.'

'We did. Very useful.'

'And you're not going to tell me what it was about?'

'I'd rather not.'

'People are always surprising me. What could Father have to talk to you about that was so important? He's a farmer, stuck here all his life, you're a sophisticated London barrister.' George laughs uneasily and is grateful the phone out in the hall starts ringing at that moment. Laura looks annoyed and goes to answer it, leaving the door open.

'Oh, it's you, Sophie. No, he's fine considering he won't eat anything, he's getting thinner every day, but what can I do? Yes, of course I've tried mashed potato. You must think I'm an idiot. Come and look after him yourself if you're going to take that tone. No. Yes.' There is a long silence from Laura, and George can hear her kicking the wainscot. 'Look, Sophie, I'm really sorry about all this, but you married him with your eyes open. No, of course I'm not being unsympathetic, just realistic. Well, it may sound like it but it's not meant to. Look, I must go. I can hear Father calling. Yes, I'll ring. Bye.'

There is a complete silence from the kitchen, though George hears Laura open the door and call in, 'All right, Father? Good, good.' She returns to the sitting-room looking smug.

'Sophie doesn't know you're here and I'm not going to tell her. I couldn't give a damn about that stupid husband of hers. It makes me thankful I'm not married when she tells me all her troubles. Let's have the other half – I'll go and get it. And I'm sure Father would like another drink too, poor old sausage. He deserves a treat.' She takes their glasses away. George pulls the blue envelope from his pocket.

I want to meet him, Helena. He's the only child I've ever had.

Why did Lena keep from him the knowledge she'd seen Philip Symes again? Why couldn't she hand him the small comfort that his real father had recognized him, wanted to meet him? Because she knew George would have been so angry at what he had missed, the mother–son relationship would be affected for ever. As it is, his memory of her has altered irrevocably. He's tempted to burn the letter, but puts it back in his pocket after all when he hears a door open and shut.

Laura returns with their drinks, her face flushed by dealing with hot ovens. 'It's most unlike me, but I forgot to put the potatoes in to bake. So now they're boiling, it's quicker, but dinner is going to be late. Father says he couldn't eat anything, so I'm going to put him to bed now. He likes to be in bed by eight o'clock.'

'Do you want some help getting him upstairs?'

'He'd hate you to see him struggling. Just come and say goodnight and leave me to it. By the time I've finished the potatoes will be done.'

George follows her to the kitchen, where Julian is lolling with his eyes shut, the shawl on the floor beside him. Laura picks it up.

'Right, Father. Beddie-byes.'

'I'm sorry to desert you, Jebs. I'm feeling very tired. It's all this excitement.' He gives George a little wry smile.

'What about a nice mug of hot milk?'

'It would make me sick.'

'Oh, you are impossible.'

'Goodnight, Julian. I so enjoyed our talk. We can continue it tomorrow.'

'I wish I had asked you to come here long ago.'

'I wish you had.'

'Off you go, Jebs. The *Telegraph* is in the sitting-room if you want to look at it. Put a log on the fire when it needs it. Come on, Father. Put your arm round me.'

Laura's face is set, her expression staunch but her eyes despairing. George leaves them, humbled by her burden of care. Through the closed door he hears the slow and painful process up the stairs, and wonders why she hasn't converted a room downstairs for her father. The noises go on. To the bathroom. To the bedroom. He thinks about the intimate nursing she has to do for her father; he hears her light footsteps moving about on the bare boards.

She taught him to dance. Where did they dance, always to the same Glenn Miller record: 'Little Brown Jug' on one side and

'Chattanooga Choo-choo' on the other? Of course, in Sophie's room, to her new gramophone, grabbing the opportunity if Sophie was out.

'You're a better dancer than Neil Roundhouse . . .'

'What happened to Neil Roundhouse?'

'Whatever made you think of him! He joined the army, and was killed in a stupid car accident in Cyprus, poor Neil. His family still live in the village.'

'Still running the pub?'

'No, it's been taken over by a couple from London. It's been tarted up, but not entirely ruined, I am told. More stew?'

'Yes, please. It's excellent. Do you know, that pub was Mecca to me as a boy. I dreamed of the day I'd be old enough to go through that nice heavy door and order myself a pint. I never did. So let's walk up there after dinner and rectify that – would you like to?'

'I can't leave Father.' The grandfather clock ticks, the dogs bark from their kennel. 'You go on your own.'

'Of course. But surely you could leave him for just an hour? You must leave him during the day when you go riding or shopping?'

'Somehow the day is different.' Laura gets up and starts clearing the table. George is aware he has pushed against a subterfuge for survival, and keeps silent.

Yet later she comes downstairs with her hair brushed and some lipstick inexpertly applied, and says, 'Off we go to the pub, then, if you still want to go. Father's asleep, and I've left a note on his pillow telling him where we are and saying we'll be back about ten.' She has a large torch in her hand and keeps its light on the track in front of them as they walk towards the village. 'I haven't been to the pub in ten years. They're going to drop dead with surprise.'

George has his childhood memory of a warmly lit quiet scene through leaded windows so clearly in his mind that he doesn't recognize the pub at all. It has been enlarged, it has more windows, the whole building is floodlit, as is a new car park full of cars. The old door is still there, however; when George swings it open the noise, the crowd, the loud music and the heat are overwhelming. Laura steps backwards.

'Jebs. Oh dear—'

'Come on, there's a relatively calm area over there.' He takes her arm and drags her through the shouting mass of people. 'Now, what will you drink?'

'Bitter, please. Just a half.'

'Look, grab that seat while I get the drinks.' As he waits at the bar, he sees her dismay grow. She is clearly conscious of her thick working clothes in contrast to a group of women near her who are in their Saturday best – high heels, makeup, artful hair. Laura has crossed her legs and is staring fixedly at her old leather boot, her big torch on her lap.

'Here's your beer, Laura. We forgot it was Saturday night.'

Laura stands up beside him. 'This is hell, Jebs. I had no idea it would be like this.'

'A change from the peace of Bellwether Farm.'

Laura has a froth of beer on her upper lip. 'I live the life of a recluse. I expected to find a couple of farmers and a sheepdog on the hearth.'

'So did I. I never go into pubs in London, either. This will teach me to indulge in nostalgia.' They both laugh, as clapping develops in the far end of the room and shouts of encouragement urge a plump blond woman on to a platform. She takes a microphone as a new tune blasts forth.

'Jebs, do you realize we've hit karaoke night?' Laura is staring in fascination at the woman on the platform. 'I know her face. She's on the till at the supermarket.'

'Come on, Betty, give it to us!' Everyone near the woman is shouting at her, but they fall silent when she begins to sing. She has a powerful, harsh voice which she uses cleverly, varying the tone and volume; her eyes are on the crowd, not the prompt-screen – she does not need any help with the words of 'I will Survive'

> *I should have changed that stupid lock*
> *I should have made you leave your key*
> *If I'd known for just one second*
> *You'd be back to follow me.*

George is caught despite himself by her controlled depth of feeling, and finds that, like Laura, he is joining in the chorus when Betty urges the crowd to sing with her.

> *I will survive*
> *As long as I know how to love*
> *I know I'll be alive.*

The crowd make her sing the whole song again, after which she is given an ovation as she fights her way off stage screeching at her friends.

'I'm getting very hot.' Laura's face is indeed bright red.

'Another bitter?'

'I really can't take all this noise any longer, Jebs.'

Someone has turned up the volume, and a man is now at the microphone, swaying in an awkward imitation of a pop singer.

'Off we go then, I've had enough too.'

They raise their faces in pleasure at the cold air outside and head down the quiet road.

'That woman Betty was extraordinary.'

'A bit of wish fulfilment to alleviate life on a supermarket till.'

'But Jebs, didn't you think she sang well?'

'Yes. Indeed she did.'

They turn down the farm track and the silence is now complete. Stars are out above them, the sky has completely cleared, the moon is full. Laura switches off the torch and they walk back in the moonlight.

'The tune of that song she sang was very familiar, but I've never consciously heard the words before. *As long as I know how to love I know I'll be alive.*' Laura's voice sings a wavery approximation of the tune. 'The trouble is, knowing how to love and loving don't always coincide.'

George doesn't answer. He has just realized he hasn't given Marcia a thought since he arrived at Bellwether. Only their footsteps now break the silence until the dogs hear them and start barking.

'Shut up, you stupid animals. It's only us.'

'I think I'll head for bed, Laura. The fresh air and the beer have done for me.'

'Goodnight, Jebs. I won't wake you in the morning – just get up when you like.'

But she did wake him. She stood in her pyjamas in his bedroom doorway, eyes flat with shock, bare toes curling in the morning cold.

'Father's dead. He died in his sleep. He's smiling.'

21 ∫

Marcia has a dream in which she is being shown a building by George. He keeps telling her it is the most beautiful building in the world, and that she must shut her eyes until he says she can open them. He pulls her along stumbling and when she is allowed to open her eyes all she can see are rows of structures, confusing and shifting, and she has no idea which one he is talking about. The dream peters out as George disappears, presumably into one of them, and she wakes up. She lies in bed for a while, pondering on the dream. Clearly her unconscious is as undecided as she is about the trip to India.

Saturday. On her way to the matinée she must drop her letter to Edward and the chocolates into the hospital; she should have done it yesterday, but decided to rewrite the final paragraph of the letter.

> *Could we meet when you're feeling better, and have a talk? My solicitor Stephen Smith has offered the use of a conference room in his offices in Southampton Row. He'll be getting in touch direct with Robert in the hope of fixing it up soon. Please say you'll come.*

As she re-reads this for the last time, she smiles. If Edward is hoping to resume their relationship, he will come. If he thinks she is, he will come. He will refuse if vengeance with destruction of her reputation is his main, or sole, aim. At least she will know where she is.

'What a fabulous place you have up here, Sedley. Two minutes from Saint Martin's Lane – who would know these buildings contained such wonderful flats? How did you hear about them?'

'I bought the lease off one of those old bachelor theatre-goers who never miss a show. His legs started playing up, he couldn't manage the climb any more, and he'd promised if he ever moved he'd let me know. So here I am.'

'I love it.'

'But of course you would, Marcia. You're a thesp – to lots of people it's full of disadvantages – noisy streets, nowhere to keep a car, pollution.' Sedley, almost unrecognizable in his sweatshirt, jeans and weekend of stubble, hands Marcia some wine.

'There's no noise in here.' Marcia looks round the starkly elegant top-floor conversion.

'I've double-glazed everything, even those windows above us.'

'I can see you're a perfectionist. There's nothing out of place.'

'It can be rather a fearsome attribute to possess.'

'I wouldn't know, because I'm the opposite. What did you describe me as? Messy? I'm certainly messy.'

'I said rich and messy. But you're a perfectionist over your performances, I suspect. I couldn't see anything wrong with your interpretation of Creusa. Perfection.'

'Goodness me, Sedley. What praise, coming from you.'

'Don't be bitchy, Marcia. There's no need.'

Marcia opens and shuts her mouth. Her voice had sounded more acid than she'd intended.

'I wouldn't have asked you to dinner if I had thought you belonged to the usual band of bitchy actresses.'

'I do, so shall I go?'

They stare at each other, both surprised at the rawness of the moment. Then Sedley suddenly laughs.

'That was a bit pompous, I admit. Forgive me.' At that moment the street doorbell rings, and Sedley goes to the entryphone. 'Pippa, Gareth, come straight up. You know the way.'

Marcia is filled with relief that she is not the only guest, then the relief is faintly tinged with disappointment. She watches Sedley get two more fine wine-glasses out of a built-in cupboard that is invisible until he touches its flush white door. He also brings out a small Victorian chamber-pot filled with crisps.

'Proof that I have lapses in taste. Have a crisp.'

'I'm not sure I dare.'

'I love watching people get the courage to overcome their distaste. It's perfectly and gleamingly clean, and I doubt it was ever used for its proper function.'

'How perverse you are, Sedley.' Marcia takes a handful of crisps.

'I work at it.'

'I feared as much.'

'Meet Pippa and Gareth Norwood. Get to know Marcia Fleckner while I tinker with dinner.'

For the next hour or so the three guests discover and inspect each other's boundary posts in the way complete strangers have to when the host is present only spasmodically.

'You're the first actor we've met here who is not a client of Sed's. I was beginning to think he had cornered the London stage.'

'I'm not grand enough for Sedley's stable.'

'Don't play games, Marcia.' Sedley has slipped in to refill their glasses. 'She's playing the lead in *Ion* at the New Fortune, if she hasn't already told you.'

'We've just booked to go. The reviews were excellent.' Pippa's slightly crossed brown eyes stare assessingly at Marcia. When Sedley disappears again to the kitchen, she adds: 'I bet Sed's planning to steal you.'

'Pippa, really.' Gareth is eating the crisps by handfuls. He's large and solid, and his wife, equally tall, is pole-thin.

'I was just stating the plain truth. I'm off to keep the chef company.'

'What sort of buildings do you build, Gareth?'

'None. I teach people how to. Or how not to. I'm rather a fraud, I sometimes think. I haven't built anything myself for years.'

'Lots of people teach acting who have never done anything on the stage. They're sometimes better at seeing what is needed. I've learnt most about acting from good directors who've often never acted themselves. John Alsopp, the director of *Ion*, is a case in point.'

'How precisely does he help you?'

'It's difficult to pin down. He has an uncanny ability to bring out tones and inflections in one's voice one didn't know one had. But in the end, he helps you simplify your performance without losing the depth. He strips away. He doesn't add.'

'Sounds like me when I'm faced with too much fussy post-modernism. I wish Sedley wouldn't use a po to put his crisps in – I've finished them all and it bloody emphasizes how greedy I've been.'

Though Marcia is interested in discussing the nature of the good director, she senses Gareth is not. He yawns, quickly covers his mouth, and gets up as he hears Pippa laughing in the kitchen.

'Let's go and tell them we're hungry.'

Marcia is left alone in the calm room under its skylight of darkness. She stares upwards, examining the mechanism which opens and shuts the great sheets of glass. She wonders what the room would be like in a rain-storm, or under a heavy weight of snow. She touches a switch and there is a gentle growling sound as blinds begin to unroll. In horror, she touches the switch again but only speeds their progress.

'If you touch the next button, they'll start retracting.'

'Sorry, Sedley. My curiosity undid me.'

He has a splash of grease on his sweatshirt and he smells of freshly chopped garlic. They both watch the blinds sneak back into their holders.

'Brilliant design, isn't it?'

'The whole room is wonderful. It honestly takes my breath away.'

'Good. In my world, first impressions are crucial.'

'How nerve-racking. In my life they inevitably go wrong.'

'Try harder.'

'I don't think it would make much difference.'

'What you really mean is that you don't think first impressions are worth putting effort into.'

'Could be.'

'Don't you like giving people surprises?'

'Of course. But I don't think a good first impression is about surprises.'

'What a cool one you are, Marcia.'

'Sedley! The gnocchi are done.'

The kitchen is urban farmhouse style as interpreted by the 1990s, and in complete contrast to the other room. The dresser is covered densely with mixed colourful china; ropes of onions, garlic, and chillies and bunches of herbs hang from a rack. A metal basket full of eggs is suspended near the window. They are there for effect, Marcia is sure. Even a large family could not use so many.

'This is divine food, Sed darling. You never fail.'

'Just as well Camisa's is round the corner, and Italian food is what my friends like.'

'The best cuisine in the world.'

'Oh, come on, Gareth, how do you know!'

'Lots of people agree with me.'

Marcia eats but says little. The other three are arguing about the best way to cook polenta when she notices the basket of eggs jerk slightly as if twitched by an unseen hand, before it crashes to the floor followed by a hail of plaster. There is a terrible smell as rotten yolks and whites ooze over the cork tiles.

'Oh my God.' Sedley stands staring at the mess swinging his arms in distress. 'Oh my God.'

'Let me help you.' Pippa is up already.

'Absolutely not. Everybody takes their glasses and their spoons and goes through to the other room. Let's go. Take the pudding, Marcia, please, and I'll bring the wine.'

'At least let's put some newspaper over it to mop it up—'

'Pippa, I said let's go.'

'Great meal, pity about the omelette.' Gareth, fairly drunk, stumbles down the corridor, laughing at his joke. Marcia follows Pippa, holding the tiramisù and waiting in the corridor for Sedley. The smell is disgusting, and she thinks she hears him retching. She hovers, unwilling to join Pippa and Gareth without him. He bangs the kitchen door and pushes past her. He is tense and his jollity has evaporated.

'My cleaning woman can sort that disaster out in the morning. I'm not going in there again. Let's eat the dessert.'

But the tiramisu has raw egg in it, and the faint eggy smell means no one can do it justice. They clatter their spoons noisily to cover their lack of enthusiasm.

'I can smell it in here. Can you? God, what a thing to happen.'

'Don't worry about it, Sed.' Pippa gives him her widest smile.

'I remember when I was a small boy being given dozens of bad eggs to throw at a wall. The pong was indescribable but it didn't last too long—'

'Shut up, Gareth.' At his wife's steely voice, Gareth finishes his glass of wine and pours himself some more. 'I think we ought to go home. Monday tomorrow and all that jazz.'

'The thing about really bad eggs, I mean seriously old ones, is they almost explode. Terrific.' Gareth laughs and spills some wine on his jacket. 'Yours weren't in that league. Old but not explosive.'

'We're going home, Gareth.'

'One last swigeroo. What about a lift, Marcia? Don't worry, I'm not driving. Taxi going to Hampstead – are you interested?'

'A lift would be good—'

'Don't hurry off, Marcia.' Sedley rouses himself from his gloom.

'Whoops.' Gareth has pressed the switch to activate the blinds, and all four watch them close. They are dark blue with a thin white stripe and give a curious nautical air to the room.

'I want some coffee. Let's all go out for some coffee together before you all disappear.' Sedley stands up, his expression lightening at the thought of escape from the smell. Coats are rapidly collected and Sedley leads them off towards his favourite café. They pass several suitable places, but he ignores Gareth's cries.

'What about here?'

'My place is nicer.'

'A coffee is a coffee is a coffee and I'm drunk and I need one now. Let's stop here. This will do.'

He has stopped outside a basic sandwich bar, quite the least appealing place they have passed. Two skinheads are drinking coffee at the counter out of plastic cups.

'Not here, Gareth. Come on.'

'Here. Pippa, Martha, in you come.' He trips over at the entrance and bangs his head against the door. 'Coffee is on me.'

'Gareth, you're being a bloody nuisance.' Sedley tries to take his arm and lead him on, but Gareth pushes him away.

'Fuck off, Sedley. I'm choosing the place and I've chosen. Four coffees for my friends.' He knocks into one of the skinheads and sends his plastic cup flying. 'Sorry, sorry.'

'Fuck sorry.' The other young man pours his coffee over Gareth. Pippa starts twittering, Sedley tries to calm the situation, the barman is threatening to call the police.

'Four coffees, I asked for four coffees.' The second time Gareth shouts this, Pippa slaps his face. Sedley takes his arms and the two of them begin to drag him out of the coffee bar. Marcia decides she has had enough, realizes that if she hurries she will catch the last Tube home, and runs.

'Christina? Have you been to see the show yet?'

'Marcia, forgive me, I had to cry off the day I planned to come, and life has been hectic ever since.'

'This is my biggest performance to date and my agent hasn't yet been to see me.'

'I grovel. Let me look at my diary – actually I could come tonight – I like going to the theatre on Mondays. Everyone seems more relaxed after the weekend.'

'I doubt if I will be after my experiences last night. OK, come tonight and let's have a quick bite together afterwards. I want to talk about the West End transfer.'

'What happened to you last night then?' Marcia had fully intended to tell Christina about her disastrous dinner with Sedley Mortimer, but promptly decides not to, annoyed at this example of Christina picking up on the least important aspect of her remark.

'Never mind. I want you to get a better deal for me from the management. Tugwell is offering me the same as Damian Frapp and I don't think that's on.'

'He is the male lead—'

'Christina, he's at the beginning of his career, it's the first lead part he's played, I'm in my prime and this is not my first lead.'

'Have you been going to assertiveness classes?'

'No. But I think you should. It's time you pushed me more, and got me more money.'

'A little gratitude for this break wouldn't come amiss.'

'Christina, I'm grateful. You know I am. It's the future I want to talk about. See you after the show tonight.'

'Let's hope nothing crops up to stop me.'

'Don't let it.' Marcia doesn't quite bang the phone down, but shouts out loud to herself: 'What's the bloody use of an agent who doesn't go to see her clients' shows?' Immediately the phone rings and it's theatre to warn her Damian Frapp is ill and the understudy will be playing for a couple of days. She will have to go in early to rehearse.

As she is about to leave, Stephen Smith rings.

'I've had a word with Robert Wintlesham, and we've fixed a provisional date next week for the meeting with Edward.'

'I haven't heard from him at all. Are you sure he'll agree?'

'Nothing's sure. Just hope. Wintlesham said his brother was out of hospital, and he was sure we could come to an amicable arrangement without darkening the doors of a courtroom.'

'He really said that?'

'Those were his very own words. I do try to eschew clichés.'

'Stephen – do you mind if I call you Stephen? Call me Marcia. Don't underestimate what a nasty piece of work Robert is. If he's being all pleasant, it makes me very suspicious.'

'That makes two of us, Marcia.'

Damian Frapp's understudy, Mark Milbourne, is excited, pushy and edgy. Marcia struggles to keep control of the shape of her performance, but the subtleties she has built up with Damian are gone. She has to respond to what she is given.

Mother – to have found you is a dear happiness; to be Apollo's son is beyond all my hopes; but there is something I need to say privately to you alone.

Damian at this point draws Creusa gently downstage, building it into a quiet, tense moment charged with shame-faced affection.

Are you certain that you didn't – many a young woman might, they can't help it – fall in love and give yourself to a secret lover, and then put the blame on the god? Did you say Apollo was my father when he wasn't, to avoid disgrace?

Mark's tone is tougher, more insinuating. He is confronting Creusa with a developed suspicion, not nervously postulating a possibility. Marcia's response turns from a passionate, convincing reiteration of her story to a vigorous denial, almost on the edge of bluster. Ion's worries about why Apollo should then give his own son to Xuthus become in Mark's mouth antagonistic, so that her explanation that Apollo is establishing Ion in a royal house for his own good is greeted with derision:

This is too far-fetched. I need a better answer. I will go into the Temple and ask Apollo himself.

Damian plays these lines as a petulant teenager, half-believing his mother but keen to test her to the end. Mark's crude approach distresses Marcia but there is nothing to be done in the short time available.

'Mine is a perfectly justifiable reading.'

'Oh, I agree. Good luck, Mark. When did Damian think he'd be back on his feet?'

'Not before Wednesday.'

'The understudy's dream opportunity.'

'I'll say.'

'My worst performance yet, and Christina's here to watch me tonight. Isn't it typical?'

'Oh, come on, Marcia, she knows you're playing with the understudy, she'll make allowances. Actually, Mark's doing very well. Pushy little bugger, though.' Suzanne is bent over her *petit point*, her needle creeping across a pile of apples in a basket. 'At least he hasn't dried.' She sighs. 'Rollo's music is beginning to get on my nerves. But then I never did like it much.'

'I still love it.'

'Sedley Mortimer's taken him on, by the way.'

'Taken *Mark* on?'

'No, Rollo.'

'I didn't know he handled composers.'

'As far as I can see, Sedley Mortimer takes on anyone who is on a rising curve. He seems to catch them as they enter the fast lane. He must have been to see the show.'

'He has.'

Suzanne anchors her needle and looks up. 'How do you know?'

'Rosie Amsterdam told me.'

'Do I detect a hidden agenda? Are you joining him too?'

'Absolutely not. I've got Christina and I'm sticking to her.'

'Despite the fact she's a rotten agent?'

'Suze, be fair. She's not that bad.'

'She may have been good once but she's not good any more. An agent is only as good as her contacts, and Christina has lost it.' Suzanne has gone back to working on a deeply satisfying patch of red apple. 'If you have the slightest chance of being taken on by Sedley Mortimer, go for it. Don't mess about with misplaced loyalty.'

'Can I come in?'

'Christina! I'm nearly ready – come in. You know Suzanne Baker, don't you?'

'Of course. Haven't seen you in a while, Suzanne. How's David?'

'We split up ages ago.'

'I'm sorry. Shows you how long it is since we last met. Well, Marcia, congratulations. What a performance! Damian and you really bring out the best in each other! First time I've seen him. Both of you were terrific. So pleased I came.'

'But you saw Mark Milbourne, Damian's understudy. There should have been a slip in the programme about it. Damian's ill.'

'My slip must have fallen out. Actually I missed the beginning, when they might have made an announcement. Anyway, what does it matter? – it was a great evening. Excellent acting all round, good set, didn't like the music much though. Mind if I smoke, girls?'

'Go ahead. I thought you'd been using nicotine patches to give up?'

'Useless.' Christina blows smoke through her plump, moist lips. Her eyes are moist too, as is her handshake; it's as if the moisture in her body is keen to escape.

'Which bits of the play did you particularly like?' Marcia is cleaning off the last of her makeup as she watches Christina closely in the mirror.

'What did I like? Well, it's hard to pick out bits, it's such a short, dense play. I liked all the tension and excitement when you were taking cover in the sanctuary. That was very well done. I really thought Ion was going to kill you, in the usual Greek style. They were keen on killing their mothers, you have to admit!' She gives a husky smoker's laugh. 'Mind you, I'd guessed by then whose son Ion was.'

'But Hermes tells you that at the beginning—'

'I told you, I missed the beginning. I was let in when Ion came on to sweep. It wasn't my fault I was late – a whole bunch of faxes arrived just as I was about to leave and had to be dealt with. Can I use this as an ashtray?'

'No. Use the window.' Marcia yawns widely. 'I am totally knackered. Playing with an understudy kills me. Do you mind if we don't go out now, Christina? I think I'm only fit for my bed.'

'You were the one who wanted to eat out. I'm perfectly happy going straight home.' There's an edge to Christina's voice as she turns to drop ash out of the window. Suzanne rolls her eyes at Marcia and makes for the door.

'I'm off now, Marcia darling. See you tomorrow. Bye, Christina.' There is a knock on the dressing-room door as she puts her hand out to open it. She reveals Sedley Mortimer. 'Hullo, Sedley, and goodbye, I'm just off. Suzanne Baker, we met once at Nicky Lloyd's.'

'Suzanne—'

'Must rush. Bye, everyone.' She goes, ignoring Marcia's anguished expression as Sedley comes into the dressing-room.

'Hullo, Sedley. What a surprise. I didn't know you and Marcia were acquainted.'

'Hi, Christina.' Sedley gives Christina a wide smile but his eyes like hers are cold and wary.

'I hope you haven't come to woo my brilliant client away from me.'

'I don't woo clients. They woo me.'

Marcia is silently getting ready to leave, without both of them if need be.

'I didn't see you in the audience tonight.'

'I wasn't there. I saw the play ten days ago.'

'Wonderful performance.'

'I agree.'

'I'm going home. If you two want to go on talking, I suggest the pub. They'll be closing the theatre any minute.' Marcia opens the door to show out her prickly guests. Christina goes past first, and Marcia is able to frown at Sedley and put a finger to her lips. They go down the stairs in silence.

'Can I give you a lift home, Marcia?'

'I'm fine, thanks, Sedley. I've got a Tube pass.'

Christina lights up another cigarette as she stands beside them, eyes solid with suspicion.

'I was passing in a cab, knew the show ended about now, so here I am. You can take the cab on home after it's dropped me. There's my cab. What about you, Christina? Hop in too if you like. Where's home?'

'Ealing, so no thanks. I've got my car, actually.' She does not move.

'Come on then, Marcia. You're surely not serious about preferring the Underground to a taxi.'

'A lift would be lovely, I admit.'

'Let's make a date, Marcia. We haven't had our talk. Why don't you come into the office this week and I'll give you lunch? Let's fix a day.' Christina takes a diary out of her jammed handbag, and searches through it with her cigarette hanging between her lips. Various loose bits of paper cascade out of the diary and Sedley retrieves them.

'Thanks. What about Wednesday? Or do you have a matinée then?'

'Wednesday is fine. Matinees are Thursdays and Saturdays.'

'Twelve-thirty, then.'

'Thanks for coming to see the show.'

'A pleasure.' As Marcia and Sedley get into the taxi, Christina tries to jam her diary back into her bag, misses and drops it in the gutter.

Sedley breaks the silence in the taxi. 'I came to say how deeply sorry I was for the fiasco last night. Gareth was terrible. He was much drunker than I realized.'

'He came tanked up. I noticed.'

'Pippa says he's drinking too much, but he won't listen to her.'

'I got the impression he had to.'

'She gives a tough impression, but she's a softie really. Anyway, I wanted to say sorry for such a dreadful dinner party. Everything went wrong after those eggs crashed down.'

'And I'm sorry I ran away – very cowardly of me, but I'd had enough of Gareth and decided to catch the last Tube.'

'You're a confirmed user of the Underground, I see.'

'No choice. My car died a little while ago, and I can't afford a lot of taxis.'

'So your career has not been all that lucrative.'

'But you know it hasn't. Most actors are broke most of the time. If I earn ten thousand in one year it's a cause for great celebration.' Marcia's tone is sharp. There's another silence before she goes on. 'Sorry to snap, but I'm on my knees. I had to do the show with Damian's understudy, and it was a strain. Plus the fact I knew Christina was watching. tonight.'

'I could see her mentally knifing me.'

'Well, you can understand her suspicions.'

'Can I give you some supper? You haven't eaten, have you?'

'Thank you, Sedley, but no. I just need to unwind on my own, have a bath, eat an omelette—' She stops and gives him a quick grin. 'Your cleaner must have had a lovely time this morning.'

Sedley groans. 'She threatened to hand in her notice, so I had to give her a bonus she couldn't refuse.'

'How long had the eggs been up there?'

'A year at least. What a disastrous dinner party that was. And I was out to impress you!'

They both laugh, and Sedley takes her hand and holds it lightly between his. She leaves it there for a while, then moves it to open her bag and take out her keys.

'I'm sorry you met Pippa and Gareth on a bad evening. I've known them for years and spend a lot of time with them. For instance, I always join them for a week over New Year in their house in Northumberland. It's a stately pile Gareth inherited. If you're not doing anything, why don't you come too? Huge walks, huge fires, huge meals, huge fun. I never miss it. Come.' He tries to take her hand again. Marcia can see from his expression how much he would like her to join him. She knows life with Sedley would be lively and amusing, but he is too like Edward in his awareness of self, of image, of all the latest things to do and see. Too much part of her world. George's apartness is increasingly precious to her.

'How lovely that sounds, Sedley, but I'm going to India for Christmas and the New Year with some friends.'

'I didn't really expect you to be free at this short notice.'

'I'd love to join your stable some time soon, though, if that's all right?'

'Done.'

That was how Marcia finally made up her mind.

22

Dawlish stares round the Groucho Club, his hand shaking slightly as he lights a cigarette.

'I don't recollect this place at all.'

'It was only founded about a dozen years ago, so it's not surprising.'

'There was a snack bar round about here, a very cheap meat pie sort of place. Baked beans and two white slices sixpence, meat pie a shilling.' He lifts his glass towards George. 'Cheerio. We are meat. Everything changes.' He inhales deeply and coughs for some minutes.

'How did your visit to the specialist go?'

'Not well. He says I must stop smoking, and alcohol's not good news either. I said to him, then what's the point of living? He said try and get your pleasure from eating well – you're too thin, Mr Dawlish. Spend the money you save not buying fags on delicious food.' Dawlish laughs, which sets off another bout of coughing.

'It's good advice, though. Let's have some delicious food now – they do beautiful calves' liver, and the soups can be very good. When you're through that cigarette we'll order.'

'It may be good advice, but can you see Hope getting lots of expensive food into the house? It would make her miserable, absolutely miserable.'

'But if she knew your health depended on you eating well—'

'I can't upset Hope, and I can't give up fags.'

'I'm going to have haricot bean soup with garlic croûtons and the liver. What about you?'

'I'll keep you company. No wine though, just another whisky. Can't drink wine any more. So who belongs to this club? Is it like the Colony?'

'Not at all. It's a sort of alternative Garrick Club, though no one would thank me for saying that. But it has the same sort of mixed arty membership – publishers, actors, agents, literati, barristers. And unlike the Garrick, women can be members.' The dining-room is still empty; he has had to meet Dawlish early because of problems with trains back to Gloucestershire. Dawlish only rang him three days earlier, the Sunday evening of Julian's death, and suggested meeting after his appointment with the specialist.

'It's very kind of you to invite me here. You know how much I love Soho.'

'That's why I did. I hardly ever use the club, so I'm glad you've given me the opportunity to justify my membership. Ah, the soup. Smells good.' George has deliberately ordered a substantial lunch in order to encourage Dawlish to eat, but Dawlish shows none of that enthusiasm for stale cake and biscuits for the food in front of him. He eats some of the croûtons but hardly touches the soup.

'I can see you're doing well, George. Funny to think of anyone from Roddick Manor doing well. It struck me as a school for no-hopers staffed by the second-rate – and that included me.'

'My parents chose Roddick very carefully.'

'I find it hard to believe anyone in their right mind would have actually chosen it!'

'They – well, my father at any rate – wanted me to shine, but dimly. A glimmer at most. He wasn't my real father, he'd been landed with me, and he didn't like me.'

'I'm not sure blood-ties are that important, you know. I expect he would have behaved just the same if he had been your real father. When someone's as disagreeable as that, they're not going to change much for true sons.'

'You're probably right.' The dining-room is filling up with noisy articulate people. Dawlish is staring about him with interest, another cigarette burning as they wait for the liver to arrive.

'They look like the same sort of crowd that used to frequent the Colony in my day, just better dressed and better off. Mind you, one or two, like Francis Bacon for instance, always dressed well and had money to throw around. Perhaps the difference is that this lot look a bit more proper somehow. I can't see them having a stand-up row with the people at the next table and pouring wine down their necks. Ah, the liver. Now, that looks good.' Dawlish leaves his cigarette burning as he attacks the liver, bacon and onions. 'I love a good fry-up.'

'Shall I order some chips?'

'What an excellent idea. Hope won't allow them through the door.'

'Do you mind stubbing out that cigarette?'

'Of course not.' Very carefully, Dawlish eases the burning end of the cigarette off with his knife, before going back to his liver and bacon.

'If Hope doesn't cook you the things you like, why don't you cook them yourself?'

'Never learned how to cook, and she'd hate me to hang about in the kitchen. She's delighted I leave her in peace and spend the days in my den.'

'I meant to ask you. What exactly do you do in your den?'

'I'm translating Dante. I've finished Hell, I'm nearly through Purgatory and Paradise is in sight.'

'I didn't know you were an Italian scholar. Is this a commission?'

'I'm not and it isn't. Ah, chips. Chips. Or French fries as the waiter insisted. What a pleasure.'

'Go on about your translation.'

'I wanted to do something that was valuable in itself, but with no pressure on me because if I fail it doesn't matter. There are plenty of translations, some of them very good. Mine won't be missed if I never get it published.'

'But you'll try to publish it?'

'Hope thinks it ought to be, so I'll leave the submitting to her.' Dawlish has cleared his plate already, and is eyeing the remains of his cigarette. 'You're wondering what we live on, I expect.'

'Well—'

'Old age pensions, a bit of money Hope has, and what's left

from the sale of Casa di Lello. Not a lot, I have to admit. Actually
– do you mind if I light up again?'

'Go ahead.'

'Well, actually at the moment things are a bit desperate. The
roof of my den nearly blew off, and it's going to cost a lot more
than we've got to put right. Then Hope has made me spend all
this money going to see a specialist – totally wasted, I knew
what he was going to say and he said it.'

George stares at his finished plate and re-adjusts his knife and
fork. It never occurred to him that Peter Dawlish might want to
borrow money when he suggested a meeting, though perhaps
it should have. He swallows some water while inner areas of
his being slip and slide. He can hear Dawlish trying to reach
the point, and helps him out. 'Of course I will help you out.
How much do you need?'

'I feel bad about this.' Dawlish has still not lit his cigarette;
the match he struck burned away unused. He strikes another
and draws on the tobacco. 'Hope would not like it at all if she
knew.'

'Don't feel bad about it. I owe you a great deal. Here's one
way of paying some of it back.'

Dawlish looks up, his gaze stricken. 'No. No. Forget I asked.
Not a good idea.'

'But you have asked, you need the money, and I'd be happy
to help you out.'

'I shouldn't have asked.' Dawlish finally gets his cigarette
going. 'I shouldn't have asked. I'm a bloody fool. You seek
me out after all these years and I touch you for money. I am
a bloody fool.'

'Did you go to a specialist this morning?'

'No, of course not. The NHS is all I've ever used and ever
likely to.'

'Well, it might have been on the NHS, I suppose. Miracles do
happen.'

'George, please forget I asked you for money. I am longing
to undo what I said, I've spoiled whatever I stood for, but we
can't step in the same river twice, and there we are. I am a
bloody fool.'

'What would you like now? Some pudding? Coffee?'

'Just coffee. And you're being very kind to an old scrounger.'
A waitress clears their plates; the dining-room is full now and
the noise level is high. Suddenly George tips back his head and
laughs. Peter Dawlish joins in, before a coughing fit develops.

'Let's go and have coffee downstairs in the bar. Come on.
And a malt whisky to go with it.'

Dawlish lights up yet another cigarette when the whisky
arrives. 'Everyone's so stuffy about smoking nowadays, it's a
pleasure to find this place upholds the good old Soho traditions
of laissez faire. Or perhaps one should say laissez mourir.'

'Have you any idea how much the roof of your den is going
to cost?'

'Please forget I mentioned it.'

'I can't.'

'Hope and I tick over all right, you know. It's only the big
sums we can't manage.'

'Tell you what. Get your den repaired and have the builder
send the bill to me direct.'

Dawlish does not looked overjoyed at this suggestion, and
George remembers how he once bought a tramp a meal instead
of giving him money and got much the same response. He has
removed the element of choice that lies in money in the hand
or pocket or bank, and the possible guilty pleasure of misuse.
He quickly writes Dawlish a cheque and leaves it folded on the
table between them.

'That will cover the roof, and save hassle and postage.'

Dawlish picks the cheque up without looking at it and puts
it in his breast-pocket.

'Thank you, George. I shouldn't take it, but what the hell.
My chap needs ready cash up front to buy materials, you know
what it's like. If I win the lottery I'll pay you back.'

'It's a gift. Don't think of paying it back.' And don't play the
lottery either, he nearly adds, but stops himself.

'Soho has always brought me luck, always. There must be
something about the air in Dean Street. Is the Gents downstairs
or where?'

'Through there and down.'

George signs for their food and drink, and stands waiting,
wondering what Dawlish felt when he saw the size of the

cheque. But Dawlish gives no sign he has looked at it when he returns, though he does promptly buy two packets of cigarettes at the bar.

'I think if you hurry you'll catch your train.'

'Coach. I came by coach. Much cheaper.'

'Very wise.'

'George, thank you for lunch. And everything. I realize I've fallen off my pedestal, revealed my feet of clay, generally ruined any image you had of me. But your image was wrong anyway – I've always been a selfish scrounger; if I hadn't married a good woman with a bit of money heaven knows where I'd have ended up. My father used to say that the phrase ne'er-do-well could have been coined for me. At least he didn't cut me out of his will!'

They are standing on the pavement in Dean Street; there's light drizzle falling which Dawlish ignores. George puts up his umbrella.

'I must get back to the Temple. Have a good journey home.'

Drops of rain are collecting on Peter Dawlish's eyebrows as he stares enchantedly about him.

'Do you know, I've decided I'm going to take a later coach. I'm feeling very nostalgic. I think a visit to the French is in order.'

'Enjoy it, Peter.'

Peter. Sir. It has been difficult to say his Christian name. He watches his former teacher move off down Dean Street, his familiar loping gait unchanged, the tilt of his head as jaunty as ever.

George walks briskly back to the Temple as the rain grows heavier and starts to beat on his umbrella. When he is back in his room he rings up the travel agent and confirms the final arrangements for the trip to India. Three first-class seats return on the flights, and a single room for him and a double for Marcia and Laura in Delhi.

23

'You're looking very cheerful tonight.' Suzanne is lying on the floor semi-supine, with a book under her head. 'I'm feeling depressed. I don't want this run to end, it's been such a good experience.'

'Hasn't it.' Marcia joins her on the floor. 'Just five minutes before I put that heavy costume on and my back starts to ache.'

'I know most of us are staying in the cast but it's never the same after a transfer. Mind you, I'm not really complaining, I'm just having an attack of the pre-Christmas blues – December only has to start and I feel miserable.'

'I hate Christmas too. There we are, women on our own, people being specially kind, all that. Grim.'

'What are you doing to survive it this year?'

'Suze, I'm so lucky. I'm going to India!'

'India?' Suzanne sits up.

'It's a very cheap deal.'

'You never mentioned you were even thinking of India.' Suzanne stands up, sounding quite put out. Marcia stays on the floor with her eyes shut.

'It's all blown up rather suddenly. I didn't know for sure until this week.'

'Are you going with a tour group?'

'Yes.' Marcia doesn't yet know the details of George's arrangements – she's agreed to have a drink with him after the show that night – but it seems safer to say she's in a group. 'What's the matter, Suze?'

'I honestly thought we were good mates – I share all my

plans and problems with you but there's not much in the way of vice-versa.'

Marcia rolls over and springs up. 'Please don't be hurt – you are one of my very best friends – I don't know what I'd have done without you the last few weeks. It's been bliss sharing a dressing-room.' She hugs Suzanne. 'I've told you all about Edward, and you've really helped me through the whole messy business.'

'You're not going to India with Edward!'

'No, no, of course not! Nor is that business over yet, but we have a meeting lined up next week and I hope it all gets sorted out sensibly. Thank God, Edward has agreed to meet me and talk. I got a letter only today.'

Both women are starting to put on their makeup, sitting beside each other without the usual easy warmth.

'I'm glad about that. So who are you going to India with then? Sedley Mortimer? I got the distinct impression he has the hots for you.'

'No, not Sedley, but he did ask me to join him at some do in the New Year so you could be right. I'd rather go to India – you've been, haven't you?'

'Backpacking when I was twenty. I found it pretty tough going and then got such a bad bout of giardia I had to come home early. I wasn't really ready for India – I'd hardly been out of England when I went there and it certainly was a culture shock. I'm sure I'd love it now. Pity I can't afford to join your tour. Could I borrow some tissues? I've run out.'

'Have the box. I've got another.'

'Marcia, Suzanne.' Andrew Lockwood follows his knock. 'I'm collecting funds for the last-night party. If you could let me have a tenner each ASAP I'd be grateful.'

'Make sure you get plenty of vodka. What are we going to eat?' Suzanne starts looking in her purse.

'The chippy on the corner is going to make up packets of fish and chips for everyone at a special price, three quid a head. So seven goes on the booze. And John Alsopp has put in £200 for champagne so it should be a good party.'

'That man is an angel.' Marcia gives Andrew her ten pound note, Suzanne promises hers tomorrow, and Andrew continues on his round. 'I'll have to get my green velvet dress finished.'

'I wish I could dress-make, I'd save so much money. Mind you, the charity shops get better and better as post-Thatcherite Britain chucks out its clothes with increasing rapidity. I got a fantastic black designer suit to go to Rick Loredano's funeral. Cost me a tenner, same price as this party.'

'Rick's dead? I didn't know he'd died.'

'He developed pneumonia. Mind you, he'd done well – it was a long time ago they first diagnosed Aids.'

'I'm really sorry. I liked Rick a lot.'

They chatter on until they hear their call, and Marcia is thankful she hasn't had to lie about George.

Suzanne has left by the time Marcia goes out, suitably disguised as usual, to find George's car. To her surprise she sees that the passenger seat is already occupied; a solid, plain-looking woman of George's age is peering out at her, smiling nervously.

'Marcia, you haven't met my cousin Laura Roper.'

'Hullo, Marcia. I saw you at Lena's funeral, but we didn't meet.'

'I had to rush away. I was rehearsing this.' They shake hands awkwardly through the open car window.

'Hop in, Marcia. Laura and I have eaten, but if we go to a brasserie I noticed on the way here, we can have a drink while you eat something.' George accelerates away and there is a silence. Marcia can smell mothballs; Laura Roper's coat obviously doesn't go out much. Her hair is so unevenly cut she probably did it herself. She turns her head, showing a fine profile and a creamy freckled skin.

'Jebs tells me your play is wonderful. I wish I could see it.'

'Come. I can always get you a seat.'

'I can't. I've got to go back to Somerset tomorrow. George whisked me up to London today after the funeral to take my mind off things.'

'We've had another death in the family, Marcia. Laura's father died in his sleep recently. I just happened to be staying there for the weekend when it happened.'

'Thank goodness you were, Jebs. I don't know how I'd have coped without you.'

'Was he Lena's brother?' Marcia is confused.

'Brother-in-law. I spent my childhood with the Ropers while my parents were in India during the war.' George gives Marcia a brief explanation of the family structure, while Laura looks out of the car window and blows her nose after dabbing her streaming eyes.

Marcia is puzzled by George this evening. Why should he ask her to join an unknown cousin for a drink when it looks as if poor Laura would much rather be letting her grief out in private with him somewhere? He is also looking very cheerful despite the death, and in some subtle way different from the George she thinks she knows. More vulnerable? Younger?

When they finally reach the brasserie Laura says all she'd like to drink is tea and disappears to find the toilet.

'I'll have a beer and a toasted sandwich. George, what are you plotting?'

George laughs. 'You'll see. What do you think of Laura?'

'That she's feeling very sad, not surprisingly, and would rather not be out with a total stranger.'

'She thought this was a good idea.'

'You mean, you thought it was a good idea. She looks absolutely drained, poor thing.'

'Don't judge me too harshly, Marcia. Ah, here she comes.'

Laura sits down, her red nose freshly powdered and her lips pink. 'Sorry about this, Marcia, but I find I suddenly need to cry even when I don't want to.' She smiles and moves the cutlery about. 'I can't stop myself.'

'When my father died it was the same – I'd be walking along thinking of other things and the tears would come seeping out. I think the body does a lot of its own grieving and needs to let off pressure.'

'I'm sure you're right.' Laura's shy hazel eyes look forlorn until the smile reaches them; her eyebrows are bushy and untidy, her hands are a farmer's hands, rough with battered nails. 'I'm so glad to meet you, Marcia. When my sister and I saw you in the corner of the church in your red coat and dashing hat, we all speculated madly about you! Particularly as you then disappeared!'

'It was a great shame Marcia couldn't stay for lunch afterwards. Ah, here comes our waiter.' George is clearly relieved that he can interrupt a description of the speculations. 'Are you sure tea is all you want, Laura?'

'Well, you can put a drop of your whisky in it if you like.'

'Another whisky please, waiter. I remember how Julian used to lace his tea after a cold day at the farm.'

'It's a family addiction. Sophie does it too.'

'I'm glad Sophie was able to come over for a couple of days. She was on good form.'

'She's going to be hell when we start going through the house.'

Marcia watches them chatting comfortably together and feels a flash of envy of their long association, all the edges rounded by time and consanguinity.

'Please forgive us, Marcia. Very boring for you. But Jebs has been out of my life for so long I can't stop talking to him about the family. And did he tell how strange it was – Father suddenly insisting on getting Jebs to come down to Bellwether because he had something to tell him, and Jebs coming at once on his first visit in a hundred years, and then Dad dying that very same weekend.'

'It's not so strange, Laura. He told me what he wanted to get off his chest, and he'd practically starved himself to death. He was ready to die.'

'I know. I thought for a moment when I found him that he'd killed himself. Don't worry, I'm not going to cry. I've had my weep for the evening.' She gazes at George. 'I'm dying to know what he told you, Jebs. Is it tellable?'

'Why not? He wanted to tell me Geoffrey wasn't my real father, which in fact I already knew.' As George explains, Laura's stare grows increasingly fixed. Marcia gets on with finishing her sandwich until George pauses and glances at her. 'Marcia knows part of this already, but I did learn something new from him, quite new. He told me my real father Philip Symes had dropped in unexpectedly on Lena when he was home on leave from India. While he was with her, Symes caught sight of a school photo of me on the piano, and since I look very like him, he knew at once who I was. But Lena refused to let him meet me, and he disappeared back to India and was never heard of again. No one told me about this visit until now.'

'My goodness. You've really winded me, Jebs. I had no inkling of any of this. Mum never let on, nor did Father.'

'He might have told you if I hadn't come down in time.'

'No, never. A son he might have told, but not a daughter.' Her voice is momentarily bitter. 'But Jebs, I'm getting excited, is your real father still alive?'

'No idea. He said to Lena he was returning to India for good, and he'd also told her he was going to found a prep school in Delhi.'

'Aha, that's why—' Laura's face is alight. George interrupts her.

'Marcia, let me explain what has happened. I've asked Laura to join our Indian expedition, I hope you don't mind. She needs a break from the farm, and has a good farmhand she can trust to keep things going. So I persuaded her to come – it took some doing.'

'But why should I mind?' By their faces, they feared she would. 'You're free to ask whoever you like, George. It's your party. And I think it's a brilliant idea, I really do. I don't mind sharing a room with Laura if she doesn't mind sharing with me, and I'm sure we'll all have a lot of fun together.'

'There you are, Jebs! All sorted. Of course I don't mind sharing. We can gossip and drink gin out of toothmugs.' Laura's sore nose is now red from excitement and the whisky in her tea 'I don't snore, I'm happy to say. I do wake rather early, but maybe in India that's rather an advantage. What are we going to see when we get there, Jebs? Are we staying all the time in Delhi?'

'We'll have a week there, and a week based in Jodhpur where I was born, and then travel about – there's a lot to see in Rajasthan.'

'Are we going to look for Philip Symes?'

'I don't know, Marcia. I'm tempted to try, but not too hard. No more than looking in the telephone directory, and ringing the British Embassy, but that's all. I imagine he's been dead a long time. After all, he was older than Lena, so he would be well into his eighties. All this has come too late.'

'You found your former teacher. I always think the same sort of things seem to happen in clusters in one's life.'

'Two deaths came close together, coinciding with your visits.' Laura touches his hand briefly.

'Searches for father-figures. Uncoverings of secrets.' Marcia finishes her beer.

'What did you feel, Jebs, when you learned you might have actually met your real father if Lena hadn't forbidden it?' Laura drains the last of her tea.

'Anger, frustration, heartache, regret. Then later I had a clear picture of a man who looked like me turning up unannounced at Roddick Manor, out of the blue, asking to see his son. I saw myself as I was in my midteens, spotty, selfconscious, agonizingly shy and lacking in confidence. I would have found it very hard to have had my fantasy that Geoffrey wasn't my father confirmed like that, with no chance of a private adjustment to such a shock. It wouldn't have taken much to destabilize me completely. So perhaps Lena was right to decide as she did. Maybe she also saw that Symes wanted to meet me as much for his own benefit as mine.'

'*Those ends we pursue against the will of the gods can do us little good when we gain them. What they grant us willingly will bring blessing,*' murmers Marcia. 'Ion says this to his mother when she is pressing for an answer from the oracle of Apollo. Sorry to interrupt, George, but it seemed rather appropriate.'

'You must both stop me from getting obsessive about Symes when we're in Delhi. If we find out easily, then I'll follow the lead up. If not, no searching. Keep me to that, won't you?'

'We will, Jebs, don't worry. Gracious, I can hardly keep my eyes open all of a sudden. My battery's run flat.' Laura's flush has gone, and her freckles stand out on her now greyish skin. 'I'm pooped.'

'I must get home too.' Marcia stands up. 'I'll have to get myself to the Indian High Commission tomorrow first thing and get my visa under way.' She smiles at the cousins. 'The excitement is beginning to get to me.'

As they walk down the street, George puts his arms through theirs.

'Let me drive you home, Marcia.'

'Absolutely not. Laura needs her bed far more urgently than I do. There's a station right here – I'll be home in half an hour. Goodbye, Laura. I'm very pleased you're coming too.'

'I'm so relieved you're not terrifying after all. A successful London actress – I had jelly knees at the thought of meeting you! Jelly knees!'

All three laugh, and Marcia kisses Laura on both cheeks. 'Roll on December the twentieth!'

'Gossip and gin!'

'Gossip and gin.' Marcia turns to George. 'Thanks for everything, Jebs.' Their eyes meet, they hug, and Marcia darts off to the Tube.

Marcia stands in the window of Stephen Smith's conference room trying to calm herself. Quiet colours – soft greys, oyster – surround her, and the room has a light, airy feel; the only picture is a large calm water-colour of this very building, carefully placed to remind those in the room exactly where they are.

Stephen Smith comes in. 'They have just arrived. Edward Wintlesham, his brother, and Sarah Pengelly, a solicitor in the same office.'

'I feel sick and slightly faint.'

'Not surprising. Have some mineral water? I'll pour you some. There's a decision you have to make, Marcia. Edward Wintlesham has just said to me that he wants to talk to you alone to start with. What do you feel about that?'

'Panicky.' She sits down in one of the chrome and leather chairs. 'To say the least. I have no idea what I'm going to say to him.'

'You could insist on all solicitors being present throughout as we planned, you know.'

'It seems melodramatic to say I won't see him alone at all. Why don't you all come in for the first few minutes and then leave us for a while? If I can't cope with that, I'll come and get you.'

'You don't have to. Sit in this chair, Marcia, because there's a bell to press under the rim of the table. If you need help, tea, or whatever, just press it.'

'Give me a couple of minutes before you bring them all up.'

'Don't forget – sit in this chair.'

'Oh God, Stephen, this is worse than any audition!'

He laughs as he leaves her, and she tries to laugh too. She concentrates on the word audition and finds it oddly helpful to think of the period of time ahead as a performance which could win her a part.

Edward is very pale, his hair and beard have been trimmed, and he seems thinner. He is wearing his familiar black leather jacket, with new-looking black corduroy trousers and a mustard-coloured polo-necked sweater. Marcia can see he has dressed with even greater care than usual; she, on the other hand, is in one of her drab outfits, but at the last minute she mitigated the frumpish effect by adding large silver earrings.

As the introduction take place between those who need them, Edward engages Marcia's gaze. Neither smiles, but there is a quality in Edward's expression that gives Marcia hope.

'Thank you for coming here.' she says as they all sit down.

'A meeting was a good idea.' Edward drums his fingers nervously on the table. 'But don't read too much into it.'

'I'm not going to.'

Stephen Smith gently takes charge of the meeting and with admirable clarity and tact outlines the reasons they are here.

'Now, before we discuss matters further, are you happy, Miss Fleckner, to grant Mr Wintlesham's request that the two of you talk alone for a while at this point?'

'I suppose so.' Marcia shuts her eyes for a moment. 'Yes.'

'Then shall we leave you for, say, twenty minutes?'

'Yes.'

'You can always summon us if you finish talking sooner.'

'We won't.' Edward's arrogance is re-asserting itself, and the little spurt of hope in Marcia withers. She waits for him to speak first when they are left alone.

'Rosie Amsterdam has been telling me amazing stories about you, Marcia.'

'You surely don't believe everything Rosie says.'

'She was very good to me in hospital, which is more than I can say of you.'

Marcia does not answer.

'Anyway, tell me if there's truth in the rumour that you've ditched Christina Platt and joined Sedley Mortimer's stable.'

'We haven't come here to talk about the state of my career, Edward.'

'How can we be open with each other if you take this line?'

'We're going to talk about what happened that Sunday, and what it led to. That's all.'

'Marcia. My darling. Now listen. Let's see all this in its full context – I can't believe you've forgotten that we were lovers until this happened.'

'Of course I haven't.'

'And still are as far as I am concerned. There's no way I regard our relationship as over just because of this painful interlude. Painful for me, that is.'

'And for me.'

'Come off it, Marcia. I am the one with the wound, remember!'

'Wounds don't always show. And Edward, we have to get one thing absolutely clear, absolutely, or we'll be talking at cross-purposes. For me, our relationship is over.'

'I thought you'd say that. But you change your mind very easily, Marcia. You always have. Quicksilver, that's you.'

'Edward—'

'I know I shouldn't have had that key cut without asking you. I'm sorry.'

'Edward, I—'

'I'm asking you to forgive me. Here's the key.'

'I've had the locks changed. Throw it away.' The key lies on the table between them. Marcia takes a deep breath and stares at him. 'Having the key cut is not what this is all about, Edward.'

'Yes it is. You were furious with me, and you were right. No one should invade privacy like that, and I mean it when I say I'm sorry.' He gives her a half-smile. 'But you are quite something when you're angry like that.'

'This conversation is getting nowhere. I think the others should come in again—'

'Marcia! No! Not yet – we need to talk, just you and me. Why are you being such a hard bitch suddenly? This isn't the Marcia I know. What's happened to you?'

'I've done some thinking in the last few weeks.'

'So have I. There hasn't been much else for me to do.'

'Oh, Edward. I never asked – how is your wound doing now? Rosie has given me updates of course, but—'

'Look for yourself.' Edward unzips and lowers his trousers before Marcia can stop him. He turns round and pulls up a leg of his boxer shorts. She sees raw, barely healed star-shaped scar tissue surrounded by inflammation. 'It's looking good, don't you think? Almost healed. That infection was a blessing in disguise. It grounded me in hospital and gave the wound a chance to heal properly at last. I have to take care, but at least life is getting back to normal. I don't have to lie on my front all the time cursing you!' He pulls his trousers up gingerly past his scar. 'You're a devil, you know. You ought to have to go through something like this. It's such an ignominious place to have a wound.'

The affection in his voice upsets Marcia greatly. She drinks some water because she's unable to speak, and watches him lower himself into the chair.

'Ahh. Painful, but at last possible. Not for too long, though – I can't sit for too long, which is why I haven't been to see *Ion* yet. Tell me about it, Marcia – what a success it has been by all accounts! I can't wait to see it – I'll get to the last night come what may!'

'Don't—'

'Why not? I feel better every day. Everyone says your Creusa is the best performance in London at the moment – of course I'll come.'

'I mean, don't talk as if nothing's happened between us, as if nothing's changed.' Marcia takes a letter out of the envelope in front of her, and skim-reads it out loud. '*We are instructed by Edward Wintlesham whom you assaulted . . . by severely cutting him . . . He is entitled to substantial damages for assault and battery etc.*' We've met to talk about this, not to pretend that nothing has changed. I did severely cut you, I'm appalled by the size of the wound and the pain it has caused you. I'm very sorry I did it. But Edward, let's not forget *why* I did what I did.'

'I'm not at all clear why. First you were playing hard to get, then you were saying yes all the way, all soft and yielding, and then wham, I find blood pouring from a cut in my bum and you've gone berserk and rushed off and locked yourself in the bathroom. That's the way it looked to me.' Edward looks at her in simple injured innocence. She takes another big breath.

'All right. This is the way it was for me. I told you I didn't want to make love, I was tired, and I pushed you away. I meant it. You like resistance so you went on. You said you wanted rough stuff, and I could see you were really going for it when you snapped that glass. You frightened me. I realized that by resisting I was making things worse for myself, Edward, so I started to go with the flow. But I kept back that piece of glass because I was frightened.'

Edward laughs. 'You're as good as I am at reinterpreting what happened to suit yourself. You melted, Marcia, you melted. I know the difference between playacting and passion. After all your resistance, I couldn't miss the signals you were giving me. You wanted violence too.'

'Do you really believe that?'

'Would I say it if I didn't?'

'Yes.'

There is a long pause as they look at each other. A soft tap on the door breaks the silence, and Stephen Smith comes in.

'We agreed I'd see where you were after twenty minutes—'

'We need longer.' Edward is curt.

'Yes, a little longer. I'll call you.' Marcia doesn't quite meet Stephen's eye, because she's nervous she's saying things he wouldn't approve of if he heard them.

'What about some tea?'

'Could you bring some for everyone, Stephen, when I buzz that we're ready for you all to come back?'

'Sure thing.'

'You seem very pally with your solicitor.'

'You seem very pally with yours.'

Edward laughs again. 'Marcia, I've missed your acid tongue along with other things.'

'You know plenty of people with tongues as acid as mine. Please, please understand I mean it when I say, our relationship is finished. *Please*. I am not going to change my mind.'

'Marcia—' He tries to take her hand.

'No!' She snatches it away. 'No! Watch my lips, Edward. It's-all-over. I-am-not-going-to-change-my-mind!'

'Rosie's right then. She saw you with Sedley Mortimer, both looking very keen, she said. You've fallen in love with him, haven't you? I can sense there's someone else in the picture.'

'Damn Rosie. She's completely wrong. Yes, I've been out with him. Yes, he's going to be my agent. No, I am not in love with him. Satisfied?'

'No.'

'You never are and you never will be.'

'But Marcia, I don't think you've quite appreciated your position, Sedley Mortimer or no Sedley Mortimer.'

'What do you mean?'

'You see, if you don't come back to me, I will be seriously tempted to go on with this action.'

'Go on with it then. You'll lose.'

'I don't think I will. Robert doesn't either.'

'But I've got no money. It's pointless.'

Edward gets up slowly, pursing his mouth at the spasm of pain. 'Oh yes, it is pointless. The publicity will be unpleasant and do you no good. So why not see sense and return to how we were? Your mark's on me, Marcia. It will be there for life. So exciting.'

'I'm beginning to think you're mad. What are you suggesting? That I spend my life with you to avoid nasty publicity, and because you think this wound which I gave you in pure self-defence has some permanent significance? Is a bond between us?' Marcia is standing up now, her pulse racing as her emotions build. He nods. 'You are mad.'

'Perhaps I am.' Edward is watching her with appreciative intensity.

'This is a nightmare.'

'Either way I win.'

'Not if you lose the case.'

'My view of events is as convincing as yours. It has to be,

because it's the real one. And you know it, Marcia, you know it.'

Marcia paces to the window and back, twice. Edward doesn't take his eyes off her. It is becoming horribly clear there is only one way out of the impasse.

She sits down again at the table, and gives the bell a quick press before covering her face with her hands. 'Oh, Edward, what a mess this is.'

'It's a mess of your own making. And your undoing.'

'I'm starting to see the truth of that.'

'I knew you would, even though you're the most unpredictable person I know.' Edward sits down beside her this time, again with a little moue of pain. 'But you've got a heart and a conscience.'

Marcia is afraid her hands will shake and reveal the strain she is under, so she puts them on her lap as she smiles at Edward.

'I was beginning to wonder whether I had either.'

At that moment the solicitors walk in, plus a secretary with a tray of tea. All notice that the couple are smiling.

'I hope you've had a useful talk.' Robert Wintlesham sounds wary.

'I think so.' Edward exchanges an unreadable look with his brother. 'Very useful.'

Tea is distributed and Marcia uses the pause to gather her thoughts. She has to complete her performance; it's going to take all her acting skill, and it won't be pleasant.

'I'd like to make my position very clear.' Marcia keeps her hands on her lap and she looks from face to face, letting her gaze linger on Sarah Pengelly, who has clearly been imported by Robert as a female make-weight. 'And I'd be grateful if it was either recorded or taken down word for word. First, I still see myself as provoked into action on that fateful Sunday, but I accept now that Edward could have genuinely misread my signals as encouragement.

'Second, I think we should do everything in our power to avert a court case. It would be pointless, unpleasant and destructive.'

Edward starts to interrupt her, not much liking the fact she has taken control.

'Please, Edward. Let me finish. I called this meeting and I'm going to have my say. You said yourself that a court case would be pointless and unpleasant – your very words. But you also said you would go through with it unless our relationship was reinstated.'

'Hang on, Marcia, that was a private matter. You sound like a bloody solicitor yourself the way you're talking.'

'I'm sorry, but I need everything to be clear between us and be heard by witnesses. Well, I'm prepared to give it a try because you're right, Edward, I can't pretend you don't mean anything to me. You do. I thought my love was dead, but love is hard to kill.' She stops; this time Edward says nothing. No one else moves. 'However, since we've both been through quite a lot, you more than me of course, in the last few weeks, let's have a moratorium over Christmas and the New Year. The run ends this week, the West End transfer doesn't open until the end of January, and I'm taking a long holiday in between. When I come back, let's take stock and start afresh.' She smiles at him and drinks some tea, her cup knocking against her teeth. Edward also drinks some tea, frowning.

'I wish we'd discussed this alone, Marcia.'

'Please understand I needed to say all this in front of witnesses.'

'I do of course, but why don't we go off on holiday together and give ourselves a real chance?'

'I've committed myself to something else, and I can't get out of it. But it's best this way.' She flicks her gaze to Stephen's and sees his eyes are totally expressionless. 'I can't let my friends down at this late stage.'

'Who?'

'A couple you don't know, not that it's any of your business.'

'Not Sedley?'

'Of course not.'

Edward stands up slowly. 'I can't sit any longer, it's too painful.'

'I think we should call this meeting to an end.' Robert Wintlesham stands up too, and collects together his papers. 'Thank you for hosting this, Stephen. Sarah, shall we go?'

Sarah Pengelly's expression says openly that the whole exercise has been a complete waste of her time.

'We'll speak tomorrow, Marcia.' Edward touches her shoulder.

'Not tomorrow – it's the last night of the run. Let's talk on Sunday.'

She stands stiffly by the table while Stephen shows the party out. When he returns he finds her with her face on her arms, weeping.

'Marcia, what's the matter?'

'Just reaction. Give me a few minutes. I feel as if I've been through three auditions on the trot.' Stephen slides a box of tissues at her and waits quietly as she regains some composure.

'Were you surprised by the turn of events?'

'I confess I was. It was the one outcome you hadn't considered possible. And he's won.'

'He thinks he has. I'm an actress, don't forget. I didn't mean a word of the scene you all witnessed. Love may be hard to kill, but my love for Edward is dead. All that was an act.'

'I'm deeply confused.'

'When the moment is right, after I've had a holiday and things have cooled down between us, I'll tell him what I did. I'll tell him I was acting today just as I was when I pretended to be all melting and submissive that dreadful Sunday. He was completely taken in both times. I think he'll get the point.'

'Isn't he more likely to be angry and to reinstate his action against you?'

'I'll risk that. I could have had the scene now, with all of you as witnesses, told him now I'd been acting. But I know Edward. I know his feelings for me will cool down when he thinks I'm no longer resisting him. Let him think he's won for three weeks – it will make a lot of difference. Anyway, I have no choice but play him along.'

'Pardon me, but you have. You could let him take you to court and in my opinion you'd win.'

'The Press exposure could ruin more lives than just mine.'

'Please forgive me if this sounds intrusive, Marcia. I prefer out of court settlements but the way you've settled this worries me deeply. It could backfire.'

'I hope not.' Stephen's obvious concern touches her. 'I need to tell you about a few recent developments in my life which meant I had no choice but to act as I did. A very good friend who wishes me well and even wants to marry me, though I can't honestly see why, has asked me to go to India with him. He's got some weeks of holiday before he becomes a judge. I can't for obvious reasons tell you who he is until it is announced. I've been resisting him for a mixture of reasons, selfish and unselfish, but I suppose mostly selfish. I've let my own life take precedence, been too immersed in the play and my own problems.' She stops, drinks some water, rubs her eyes. 'He's a good man, Stephen. I can't allow a risk of scandal to damage him or his career. It's simply not on, whatever price I pay. If I have to live a lie with Edward for a while, so be it. And with Edward in a good mood going round saying all is well and we are together again, the gossip will die and the Press will forget.'

'It could be tough on you—'

'Heavens, look at the time! If I don't leave soon I'm going to be late.'

'I'll call you a taxi – on my account. I insist.'

'You've been very kind to me. I'm sorry to land you with this sorry business and have it all end so uncomfortably.'

'I can understand your reluctance to risk damaging this friend of yours. Either that, or you'd have to give him a wide berth until the litigation was over.'

'Once I am tarred there will be no untarring. I'm not risking anything – when the Press got news of the wounding it was bad enough.'

'You mentioned you were going to India with a couple. Was that to pacify Edward?'

Marcia laughs. 'No, it's true, but it did, didn't it! My friend has asked his cousin to join us – she's the daughter of the uncle who died recently – and she and I will be sharing a bedroom so it will be most proper.' Marcia's eyes glint. 'She's a real farming country type, and I like her a lot. Edward couldn't be jealous of the set-up for one second. I really must go now – isn't that the taxi? Stephen, forgive me for wasting your time.'

'The time hasn't been wasted. You needed to arrive where you are by going through each process. You couldn't hurry it or foresee what would eventually happen. Nor could I. And you completely took me in. Some actress!'

'If I ever need a solicitor again, I know where to come.'

Stephen gives a little bow and opens the front door. 'When do you leave for India?'

'The twentieth.' She shakes his hand, then kisses his cheek. 'We're going to look for my friend's father, last heard of in Delhi. He's probably dead, but if he's not and we find him, it will be the first time father and son have met in their lives.'

'Your life is certainly full of drama, Marcia. And risk.'

'What's the point of living if you're not aware of the edge?'

Marcia picks up the basket. It is lacquered with bright red paint, and contains a white cyclamen in full and perfect flower. The note buried in the leaves says simply: *Good luck. SM.*

'You have this, Suze. I've only got to look at a cyclamen and I kill it. Besides, I'm going away.'

'It's ravishing. Thanks.'

Marcia drops Sedley's note in her bag. The dressing-room is full of flowers: she has never had a last night like it. She gives bunches to the chorus and keeps for herself the yellow roses from George. His note simply says how thrilled Laura was to meet her and that she planned to see the play when it opened in the West End.

'So that's the famous green dress. You've got thinner, Marcia.'

'Have I? Must be the strain of life. I think I've made it too low at the back – what do you think? It feels distinctly unsafe.'

'It looks wonderful.' Tears start to course down Suzanne's cheeks, then she slumps into a chair and breaks down completely.

'Suze! What on earth's the matter, darling Suze?'

Suzanne shakes her head as her sobs build. 'I'm not going to be doing the West End run.'

'Suze! But I thought it was fixed?'

'No contract, and now someone else has been put up for my

part. It's more than rumour, Marcia. I know I'm going to be ditched.'

Marcia hugs Suzanne. 'I'll talk to John.'

'I already have – there's not a lot he can do. West End management politics rule.' She gets up and rinses her face with cold water. 'Ah well. It's been a marvellous experience, too good to be true.'

'Anyone else for the chop?'

'Possibly Peter Newman.'

'Well, I've never thought he was that good, but you were. Are. I'm really upset about this, Suze.'

'I must put my glad-rags on, though I couldn't feel less like a party.' She shakes out a long red skirt. There are sounds of shouting and laughter on the stairs, and the faint thump of dance music.

'Don't let people see.'

'As if I would.'

'Attagirl.' Marcia hugs Suzanne and then both women put fresh make-up on to their clean faces.

'When things go wrong I think of David and how badly that bastard treated me and how I climbed out of it just the same. I'll hang in there, Marcia. I'll be all right.'

'I know you will.'

'You were specially good tonight, by the way. I could feel the weight of a thousand years of Greek male domination when you said: *"Life is harder for women than for men. Good and bad, we are lumped together and judged by men, then despised."'*

'That is the fate we are born to!' They say this together and laugh.

'It's as if the ancient Greek woman was considered incapable of full moral stature by her menfolk.'

'Euripides didn't think so, luckily for us.' Suzanne finishes her makeup and stares without enthusiasm at her reflection. 'I love the way he writes. I shall miss not saying his words every night.'

Marcia is busy applying lipstick and doesn't answer. She puts an arm round Suzanne when she's ready and leads her downstairs to the stage where the party is already in full swing. A shopping trolley full of paper parcels of fish and chips is wheeled in as they arrive, and everyone is handed their packet. The stage reeks of vinegar reacting on hot oily food and warmed paper.

John Alsopp carries a parcel to Marcia and pulls her down to sit beside him on the steps of Apollo's sanctuary. They talk comfortably about the success of the production and the ways they can improve it while they eat their fish and chips. Marcia is waiting for the right moment to bring up the subject of Suzanne Baker when John does so himself.

'I'm sorry Suzanne isn't transferring with you – I know what good friends you are.'

'Then it is definite.'

'I've done my best, Marcia. The main backer has a new wife who is a fairly well-known actress – don't guess, you'll find out soon enough – and she wants a part in the play. She was after Creusa. Yes, I never told you. I sent them both complimentary tickets, sat with them, and was going to make sure they saw that the success of this production was in a large part due to you. To give them their due, they agreed your performance was special. So that left the next woman's part of size, the Priestess.'

'Is this woman a good actress?'

'As good as Suzanne.'

There is a pause as Marcia rolls up the remains of her rapidly congealing chips.

'What a nasty old world it is, John.'

'Without this backer there'd be no West End transfer.'

'I sometimes wonder how many knocks an actor can take without giving up.'

'It sounds callous, but if a setback like this knocks Suzanne over, then she shouldn't be in the theatre business. End of story. I think she'll survive. I must go and talk to Timothy Tugwell before he slips off.'

'I didn't notice he was here.'

'Just for ten minutes, he said. Come and say hullo.'

'Marcia, what a success story for you. Congratulations.' Tugwell, as messy as ever in his expensive clothes, bends over to kiss her. 'Love the outfit. Reminds me of Scarlett O'Hara's green velvet dress.'

'I confess mine's also home-made, but not out of curtains.'

Timothy Tugwell hugs her, gives a noisy laugh, and slides

off to talk to Rollo West, John Alsopp in tow. Marcia returns
to the sanctuary steps, leans back against the hollow painted
altar, badly scuffed now, and watches the company letting its
hair down. Suzanne is being embraced by Ron, one of the
stage-hands, and by the look of her back-view she's in tears
again. The noise level continues to rise. Marcia shuts her eyes,
feeling rather full of battered fish.

'Marcia.'

The familiar voice is close to her. She is so tired she wonders
if she's hallucinating.

'Marcia!'

Her eyes open. Edward's voice is real and he is right beside
her.

'Don't look so shocked, it's only me.'

'I'm not shocked, I'm appalled – this is the last-night party –
what on earth are you doing here?'

'Timothy brought me in. I met him at the stage door and he
just swept me in.'

'But outsiders shouldn't come, you know that—'

'I wanted to see you, Marcia. I tried to leave you a message,
but you don't seem to use your answerphone these days.'

'It's broken. I must get a new one.'

'I'll give you one for Christmas. I was wondering what to
give you.'

Marcia looks at her hands, at her velvet-clad arms, at her
knees, and sees a slight quiver of shock still present in her
body. The sanctuary step is hard and uncomfortable under her
thighs, but she cannot move.

'Would you like that?'

'Thanks, Edward, yes, it would be a good present. I'll get
yours in India.' Her voice is flat and formal.

'I thought you might have invented the India trip as a way
of avoiding having to see me, to be honest—'

'I leave on December twentieth. I've had my jabs. I've even
got my visa. I can't wait – I've always, always, always wanted
to go to India.'

'You didn't have enough money to mend your car but you
can afford India?'

'The fruits of success. Overdrafts become easier to get.'

Edward is holding a tumbler of neat vodka which he is drinking rapidly. He notices her glance and raises his glass.

'It's wonderful to be off drugs and on the sauce again.' His eyes hold hers; the pupils are dilated. 'And it's equally wonderful to be sitting beside you here on stage. You were terrific, by the way.' He leans forward to kiss her. She can smell the depth of vodka on his breath – everyone else smells more of fish and chips, so he clearly hasn't eaten anything. 'And I love this dress.'

'One of my cut-it-out-and-hope-it-works efforts – for once it did—'

'Stop gabbling and kiss me.'

'Whoops!' Suzanne trips over Edward's feet and lands in his lap. 'Who have we here?' She tries to focus on Edward – she's also got very drunk very quickly. 'Mr Edward Wintlesham no less. He of the sore bum. *Bonsoir*. Rollo, come here. Look, strangers in our midst. Not on, is it?' She grabs Rollo's arm. 'Let's dance, Rollo, you gorgeous man. Why are all the most gorgeous men gay?' She prances unsteadily off with Rollo to the area of the stage where a few couples are dancing.

'Suzanne Baker is nearly legless already.'

'I won't be a minute, Edward. I promised I'd have a glass with Willie.' Marcia is already on her feet and running through the crowd on the stage towards the staircase, which is blocked by a technician voraciously kissing Jacynth. Marcia pushes past them down towards the stage door where Willie is entertaining a front-of-house crony in his little sanctum. His cat is staring down disapprovingly at the gathering from his customary place on the shelf above the switchboard.

'Have a drink, Miss Fleckner.' Willie never eschews the practice of old-fashioned formality. 'Can I compliment you on your dress?'

'Thank you, Willie. I seem to have hit lucky with this dress.'

'Scotch suit you?'

'I'll finish my wine first, thanks. The night is still young.' They can hear Jacynth now being chased up and down the staircase shrieking and giggling.

'I was just saying to Vera here what a good crowd you've all been. Lovely atmosphere.'

Vera waves a glass at Marcia. Normally Vera's face behind the crush bar is stern enough to put tentative drinkers off trying, but now she beams. A heap of congealed chips lie between her and Willie, and she shoves another in her mouth.

'Always liked a cold chip.'

'Willie, how come you let outsiders in? Mr Wintlesham's up there. He's nothing to do with the production whatsover.'

'He came in with Mr Tugwell, so I thought to myself he might have been a backer or the like.'

'It's bad luck to have outsiders at a last-night party.'

Willie is frowning at Marcia's agitation, and pats her arm. 'There, there, Miss Fleckner, drink up and forget about him. He won't stay long. I'll personally ask him to leave if you like. Now have some Scotch after all and relax. Pass the bottle, Vera. Let's drink to the leading lady. Bottoms up.'

'Oh, Willie, I wanted to relax and let myself go and have a really good party, and now I can't because he's here and I don't trust that man.'

'There, there, drink up. Take no notice of him is my advice. And certainly don't go anywhere near him with a broken glass.' Willie crumples at his joke and Vera gives a great neigh. Marcia joins in despite herself, and the three of them become rapidly hysterical with laughter. Edward appears at the foot of the stairs.

'So that's where you are.'

'I couldn't leave poor Willie on duty without coming to see him.' Marcia hugs the doorman's shaking shoulders; Vera's neighs increase, and tears are spouting from her eyes.

'Careful with that glass, Vera. You might break it waving it about like that.'

'You are a one, William. Ooh, this is too much.'

'I'll come up soon, Edward. Give me five minutes.' By this time the volume of noise from the small cubicle is so overwhelming that Edward smiles stiffly and retreats up the stairs again.

'Fancy him appearing just as I'd made my crack, Vera—'

'Water! This'll be the death of me.'

Marcia pours a glass for Vera, whose face has indeed become alarmingly red. Slowly the laughter subsides into half-laughs and groans.

'What you got to realize, Miss Fleckner, is that if the gentleman gives you trouble, I will personally throw him out.' Willie nods his head several times, having had trouble getting his tongue round the word personally. He tries it again, with more success. 'Personally.'

'You're a darling, Willie. You've cheered me up.' Marcia finishes the whisky, doubting Willie's ability to walk up the stairs let alone get rid of a difficult guest. Yet this little encounter has released something in her, let her see Edward's presence as an extra dimension rather than a threat. She kisses both Willie and Vera and returns to the stage.

The feeling of the party has changed: an element of wildness, of unstoppered frenzy, has crept in. Most members of the company are dancing with bacchic abandon to powerfully rhythmic music. Spots light up the dance area, leaving most of the stage in relative darkness. Marcia sees Edward sitting on the sanctuary steps with Alsopp and decides to dance rather than join them. One of the stage-hands, a shy young Welshman called Mickie, is standing watching the dancing, and Marcia takes his hand and leads him into the scrum. He turns out to be an excellent dancer and Marcia can feel her body moving better and better as she gives herself to the beat. She has always loved dancing, but rarely does it these days.

A hand grabs her, taking her from Mickie.

'Hail Xuthus, my dear husband.'

'Come dance with me, my sexy wife.' Andrew Lockwood is a manic dancer, lurching about and totally ignoring the prevailing rhythm. But his glee and energy are catching, and they end up leading the entire body of dancers all round the columns, across the sanctuary and over the altar.

'This is how I imagine Dionysiac rites to be.' Andrew hangs some plastic grapes over Marcia when they finally drop exhausted against a corner of the altar. 'Fabulous frenzy.' He kisses her.

'Unfortunately this is an altar to Apollo.' Edward is standing above them; he has been watching the dancing from a corner of the stage, alone, drinking steadily. He glares at Andrew, who pulls Marcia into the crook of his arm and hangs more plastic grapes around her neck.

'So what? Who cares?'

'Dionysos and Apollo are diametrically opposed – the dark,

passionate and irrational against the civilized, rational and controlled.' Edward takes Marcia's free hand. His voice is so slightly slurred it hardly gives away the fact he is very drunk.

'Poor old Apollo isn't going to get much of a look in tonight then, is he!' Andrew kicks his legs in the air and whoops. Suzanne catches a leg and pulls him off the sanctuary steps, dislodging Marcia who rolls after him. A fresh burst of music has drawn most people back to the dance and feet are beating dangerously close to Marcia's head. Edward bends over her and cradles her. She tries to struggle out of his arms to her feet, but he prevents her. Instead he picks her up to lay her on the altar, where he kisses her.

'My sacrificial victim.' He kisses her again, pushing his tongue inside her mouth.

Rollo has started dancing round the altar playing a clarinet, picking up the time and beat of the disco but transforming it with the reedy, wailing sound of the Greek *clarino*. Another of the musicians has a fiddle and is following him, another is beating a tabor.

Marcia lies on the altar intoxicated by alcohol and noise, and an ancient terror starts building in her. Edward is now staring down at her intensely, his hair wild, his eyes black, as if assessing her. She is limp, mesmerized by his gaze at the axis of the vortex of noisy music around them. He raises his arms into the orant position, like a priest consecrating the altar. The tabor is beating madly at Marcia's head. Edward's arms move and Marcia sees the flash of a knife in his right hand. She tries to scream but only a strangled sound emerges through tensed vocal chords.

The bucket full of ice-cubes and water hits Edward in the face, soaking him and Marcia. He staggers back and Suzanne drops the bucket before pushing at him violently.

'You bastard! I saw you!' She grabs his wrist and the base of a broken wine-glass drops out of his hand. 'Bastard! You were going to give her what she gave you!' She hits him across the face.

'Suzanne! Steady on!' John Alsopp is pulling at her arms while Marcia struggles to her feet, water and ice-cubes pouring off her.

The dancers, unaware of the scene in progress, come thumping and chanting across the stage in another long line following the faun-like prancing of Rollo with his clarinet.

'Get that maniac out of here before he hurts Marcia!' Suzanne is screaming at Alsopp, her eyes staring and hair on end, a maenad *in extremis*. 'Out! Out!'

Edward turns to Alsopp. 'Interesting party.'

'OUT!!' Suzanne has to be restrained as Alsopp walks off stage with Edward. Marcia picks up the piece of glass which is now on the altar and stares at it; a lethal prong of glass glitters at her.

'Give that to me, Marcia.' Suzanne takes it with a steady hand; exercise and emotion seem to have sobered her. 'I'm going to give it to Willie to keep safe. It might come in very useful one day as evidence.'

'Oh Suzanne. Thank you for noticing what was going on. No one else did.'

'He probably wasn't really going to use it but I didn't like the look in his eye.'

'Oh God. Oh Suze.' Marcia leans against the altar, plastic grapes at rakish angles.

'Just let me give this nasty little object to Willie.'

Marcia folds up into a ball and shuts her eyes. The musicians and dancers circle her, their beating feet raising dust, their faces rapt in the rhythm of the dance. Remorse and relief fill her. She lets her face drop on to her wet velvet-covered knees, her heart beating as if in time to the music while the party rages round her.

24

'So *bagh* must mean garden.'

'I suppose so.'

'I do find Delhi confusing. I can't help feeling overwhelmed at the moment, Laura. I'm loving it and hating it at the same time – my skin feels so thin I swing from one emotion to the other in the space of a second. Let's sit here for a minute.' Marcia flops down on a bench in the shade of a tree; Laura stays standing as she watches the antics of some small squirrel-like animals.

'They are so sweet – I think they're chipmunks. Look at that baby one – so naughty.' Laura scrabbles in her rucksack for her camera but by the time she has got it out the chipmunks have disappeared up a tree.

'There's a heavenly scent wafting down on me – do you think this is a neem tree?' Marcia lies back on the bench and stares up through the mesh of narrow leaves at the blue sky. 'They keep mentioning neem trees in *A Suitable Boy*. Neem trees and ashok trees. Have you read it?'

'No. I keep meaning to.'

'What little knowledge of India I have comes from that book. I just feel so ignorant now I'm here. I know nothing about the history, the languages, the religions, nothing about anything. No wonder I feel confused.' Marcia shuts her eyes as Laura sits beside her. The traffic of Delhi roars and rattles in the surrounding streets, distant car horns blare endlessly, autorickshaws honk and beep.

'I think you're trying too hard, Marcia.'

'What do you mean?'

'Well, I'm as ignorant about India as you are, if not more

so, but I'm just letting everything wash over me. It's obvious one can't be an organized visitor armed with a guidebook, as one can in France or Italy. Nothing goes quite as we plan it, nothing turns out quite as we are led to expect. Everything challenges us, takes longer, is a hassle when you think it will be straightforward, and easy when you expect it to be difficult. Very confusing, I agree.'

There is a silence before Marcia murmurs, her eyes now shut: 'Like this morning. Who would have guessed after the dreadful day we had yesterday trying to extricate ourselves from the rickshaw accident in Connaught Place, that it would take George two simple phone calls to find his father!'

'Precisely. It was like a miracle. But George didn't realise his father was quite a well-known figure here.'

Through the gates of the Railway Museum comes a flood of young boys in white turbans, red jerseys and white trousers. They chatter in high voices as they line up tidily before being marched off into the main museum building.

'They were talking English. Wouldn't it be an odd coincidence if those very boys went to the school – what did George say it was called?'

Marcia sits up and watches the tail-end of the queue of boys. 'Chana something Preparatory School. Named after this part of Delhi, I thought he said.'

'I wonder how it's all going.'

Marcia does not answer. The leaves rustle above them, releasing a faint, delightful scent. Laura takes a photograph of the schoolboys.

'Tell me what his parents were like when George was living with you at the farm.'

'Aunt Lena was one of those grown-ups children feel uneasy about. They blow hot and cold. She'd seem thrilled to see us, ask us lots of questions about our lives, half-listen to the answers and then ignore us completely. Particularly if Geoffrey Warne was there: she seemed to be totally under his thumb. Sophie and I couldn't stand him, by the way. We thought he was awful!'

Marcia grins. 'So the newly found father isn't up against any competition!'

'It would be difficult to be more off-putting than Geoffrey

Warne was. Always terribly stiff and pompous, no sense of humour as far as we could see. Father used to say he'd been born with a coat-hanger instead of shoulders. Quite good-looking, I suppose – and Aunt Lena obviously thought he was wildly attractive. She was always touching him. I bet he hated our beady eyes.'

'George has changed a lot since Lena died, and also since your father died.'

'I haven't seen him for so many years I wouldn't know. How has he changed?'

'It's very hard to pin down. When he came back from that visit to the farm he seemed younger – rejuvenated. As if he'd found wings he didn't know he had. It could simply be that he'd learned all the nasty secrets there were to learn about his mother, and having hit bottom could only go up. But I think he also gained something from seeing Bellwether Farm again – he clearly loves it in a way he loved nowhere else. So I can't help asking myself why on earth he didn't go down and see it and you all before this?'

'Because he was told he wasn't welcome at Bellwether after Mum died. Then time passed, and he never dropped in to see if it was true.'

'How unkind of Lena to let him believe that. More than unkind, wicked.'

'I would call her selfish rather than wicked. It seems rather fitting, now I think about it, that her cat Raj should end up at Bellwether. George is going to bring him down when we get back. George says he's a very touchy cat, just like his mistress.' They laugh, and stare at the leaves during another easy silence.

'Something else puzzles me – why didn't he ask any of you to his weddings? At least let you know he was getting married? He seems to have cut himself off completely.'

'Oh, I don't know – why should he invite his boring country cousins? Particularly if he just had a registry office wedding, which I expect he did. And if Aunt Lena didn't approve of the wives, I can see her not being keen to show them off to her in-laws! I expect if he'd married a title she'd have made sure we were all invited.' Laura stands up abruptly. 'Shall we wander round this place, see what there is to be seen in case George is longer than he expects? I adore trains. I once wrote an essay on the Indian railway system when I was doing colonial history at school. Not that I remember much about it.'

Marcia follows Laura, content to be led. As they enter the museum building they see the turbaned school boys exiting at the far end. Marcia and Laura are now alone in it; Laura bounces in delight from exhibit to exhibit.

'Oh, listen to this, Marcia. Can you believe it – the first locomotive was put on the wrong ship and sent by mistake all the way from England to Australia instead of to India! I somehow thought the Victorians never made cock-ups like that – they come across as super-efficient empire builders. But look at the speed with which the railways covered India after that rather unfortunate start. Best thing the British Raj did for this country.' The two women stare at maps, at charts, at blown-up grainy photographs of gangs of workers cutting through jungle and mountain, at carriage furniture, at portraits of whiskered worthies in wool suits and topees. Marcia's eye lights on different things from Laura's, and at one point she calls her over.

'Oh Laura, you must come and listen to this – I don't know whether to laugh or cry. The letter's dated 1909.

Dear Sir.
I am arrive by passenger train Ahmedpur Station and my belly is too much swelling with jackfruit. I am therefore went to privy. Just I doing the nuisance that guard making whistle blow for train to go off and I am running with 'lotah' in one hand and 'dhoti' in the next when I am fall over and expose all my shocking to man and female women on platform. I am got leaved at Ahmedpur Station. This too much bad, if passenger go to make dung that dam guard not wait train for five minutes.

Poor Mr Sen! But it says that as a result of his letter all compartments on the railways were fitted with loos, so his suffering wasn't in vain.'

Laura is so taken with this item she tries to photograph it, after which they leave the museum and head for the old trains lined up on tracks in the museum compound, having checked that there is no sign of George anywhere. They ask the surly ticket clerk to look out for him and tell him they are looking at the trains if he appears.

'That's the first person who's been rude to us. Everyone is so enthusiastically cheerful and friendly on the whole.' Marcia puts her arm through Laura's. 'And the other thing that has surprised me is how so many people speak English. I had no idea it had remained such a permanent part of everyday India.'

'I remember how I claimed with great confidence in that long-ago school essay that the railways and the use of English had unified India. Then I heard someone say in a talk on Radio 3 that the continued use of English in India has impoverished Indian languages and stood in the way of the growth of an indigenous national language. So it's not all for the good.'

'Do you regret not going to university, Laura?'

'Bitterly.'

'Nothing to stop you doing an Open University course.'

They pause as a small steam train goes past them, pulling diminutive carriages packed with the shouting schoolboys, their turbans, teeth and eyes gleaming.

'I know. I probably will. Everything's possible now. Everything and nothing. I can see me staying buried at the farm and going on just as before.' Laura laughs. 'Let's go and look at the little train that went all the way up those loops to Darjeeling. I wish we were going into the foothills of the Himalayas. Simla, Darjeeling – they sound so romantic. I know what you're going to say – nothing to stop me coming back one day and going.'

They wander companionably round, inspecting luxurious saloons fitted out for rajahs or royalty as well as doughty steam engines retired after up to 100 years of hard work. As time passes both are keenly aware of George's continued absence, but don't refer to it until they sit down again under the tree.

'This place closes soon. He's been gone a long time.'

'I'm glad we looked round.' Laura is turning the ill-printed buff pages of *Exotic Indian Mountain Railways* which she extracted with some difficulty from the ticket clerk whose subsidiary job – clearly regarded as an imposition – was to run the meagre bookstall. 'Jebs isn't going to have time to see it, because I noticed they don't issue tickets after quarter past and I have a feeling the rules have to be obeyed.'

'I admit I'm beginning to feel quite tense about his meeting with Philip Symes.'

Laura dwells on a blurred photograph for a minute, and suddenly speaks in a rush. 'Marcia, can I say something? I – I can see that Jebs loves you. I don't blame him either!' Her eyes are still down, her hair hangs over her face. 'I wanted to say that I wouldn't mind at all if when we went to Jodhpur you and Jebs shared and I had the single room. There, I've said it. I couldn't have said it to Jebs!' She looks up, her face pink.

'Oh, Laura.' Marcia puts her white thin hand over Laura's farmer's fist. 'Laura.'

'Life's so short. You two should be together.' There are tears in her eyes.

'I'm enjoying sharing a room with you. And I think George wouldn't agree to your suggestion – he'd hate to offend the Indian sense of proprieties apart from anything else.'

'People are so silly.' She blows her nose energetically. 'Do you love him, Marcia?'

'Yes.' Marcia looks very surprised at the speed with which this little word has escaped. 'Yes! I didn't really admit it even to myself until I came away, but I do. I've been feeling so guilty about something I did to him, it hid everything else. And I've been dealing with a horrible emotional mess in my life, and it took its toll too.' She tells Laura about Edward.

'Marcia, it sounds an absolute nightmare. No wonder you looked so shattered when we set off. I thought you were just exhausted after the end of the show.'

'I had to sort it out before I left for India, I had to see Edward after that party and tell him I was absolutely wrong to fool him and give him any hope that things could go back as they were.' Marcia stares across the empty museum garden and grounds lit by the low winter afternoon sun. 'Suzanne Baker – my old friend who played the Priestess – hid in the bedroom of my flat when he came to see me, just in case there was more trouble – and I decided I wouldn't tell my solicitor what I was doing, because I had faith Edward and I could sort it out. Suzanne took the portable phone in with her, and we'd arranged she could summon Todd, my neighbour upstairs, to bail us out if the worst came to the worst. Edward was late, and we both got hysterical giggles while we waited. There's nothing like a fit of the giggles for relaxing you – when he arrived I felt able to cope.' Marcia smiles at Laura's round eyes, agog in suspense.

'Then what happened?'

'Not what I expected.'

Edward saw the fading traces of laughter on Marcia's face and in her eyes; he also noticed the bedroom door was firmly shut. The flat was filled with flowers from Marcia's last night, and he held out his bunch of white freesias with a wry shrug.

'You hardly need these, but anyway. Peace offering.'

'They smell so wonderful.' Marcia's hand shook slightly as held the bunch to her nose. 'Thank you, Edward. I hardly recognized you without your beard.'

'I shaved it off as a symbolic gesture.' Marcia stared at the rounded dimpled chin she'd never been aware of, as Edward rubbed his hand over it. 'Everything had to change, so I started with my beard. I got a barber to do it, to make quite sure I didn't change my mind.' He followed Marcia into the sitting-room, where they both sat down stiffly facing each other. The freesias lay on the table between them, lightly underlining the fact that Marcia expected the visit to be brief. Their scent hung in the air. Marcia waited for Edward to speak; he gazed at the flowers as he searched for a way to begin.

'I walked the streets all night after that party. To start with I walked in the wrong direction because I was too drunk to realize it, and as I sobered up I found myself on the Edgware Road and went on walking out of central London until I reached the house where I was born and brought up.' Marcia sat perfectly still as he talked, her eyes on his face; his eyes remained on the flowers. 'I never tell anyone where that is because the area has become such a suburban joke. But what does it matter either way? I was born in Neasden, Dene Street, Neasden, near Dollis Hill Tube station. I called it Mean Street as soon as I was old enough to make judgments, which naturally upset my poor parents. My address afflicted me so much I left home at sixteen. A dire bedsit in the grimmer end of Bloomsbury made me very happy.' Edward looked up. 'I always was a terrible intellectual snob. Still am, I suppose. Ah well, I'm digressing. Back to that night.

'So to try and clear my head and my conscience after that appalling scene on stage, I walked to Neasden. Dene Street looked as it always did – mean-spirited and very proper. Still infested with net curtains – upstairs, downstairs, back, front. I used to think that our neighbours would have worn them on their faces if they could, to signal the fact that they Kept Themselves to Themselves. What a wonderful phrase that is.

'I started to walk down the sleeping street. It's a strange thing, a sleeping street; you know that hundreds of bodies are lying, dreaming or in between dreams, only yards away from you as you pass. I reached my old house, which I hadn't seen since my mother died. It looked different: no net curtains, and dormer windows in the roof where we only had a dusty attic with a gurgling noisy water tank. The front main bedroom, the very room I was born in, had a large smiling paper face stuck to the glass, looking outwards. Mr Happy. I sat on the garden wall opposite and stared at that face. Number 17 Dene Street, Neasden. Because I was tired and still a bit drunk, I wept. I wept for the fact I'd been so ashamed of my parents, of my home. I couldn't disown my parents, but I had certainly disowned my home. What a prig I was! I stared at Mr Happy and I wept.'

Marcia found she couldn't take her eyes off the deep dimple in his chin, plugged with black hair which no razor could reach. She waited for him to go on, puzzled but gripped.

'Somebody put a light on in my old house, probably to go to the lavatory, but I felt my presence had woken them and hurried off, afraid they would look out and see me. Back to the Edgware Road, back through north London. I walked in a daze, and as I walked I saw your face, Marcia, clearer and clearer. I saw your face lying beneath me on that altar as I raised the piece of broken glass, I saw your terrified eyes, and then I thought of another time I'd seen the same expression in your eyes – when they were under mine just before you cut me. A flash of eyes for a nano-second, so brief I'd edited it out, remembering only my excitement, my desire, your softness and seeming compliance, my pain and my frustration at the brutal ending of our love-making. But both times the same terror, though it was only now I realized it.'

Edward shook his head and stood up, walking towards the window. 'What made me see, at four a.m. in the Edgware Road, what I'd hidden so successfully from myself, I don't know. Perhaps the fact I'd seen my old home, let in the past.' He turned and faced Marcia. 'How could I possibly hold you to our relationship if I gave you those feelings? How could I? Say something, Marcia!'

'You did terrify me, both times. The fact is – well, the fact is you like violence, Edward. Too much.'

'Too much. Yes, too much. I would have denied that, you know; I would have said I only enjoyed a little rough stuff if my partner did. I never intended to use that piece of glass, by the way; I found it lying in a corner and decided I'd give you a shock. But when I stood above you as you lay on that altar, I suddenly felt a burst of pleasure like an orgasm at the thought of hurting you. My cock was hard, Marcia – I'd have probably come if I'd cut you. I've never felt anything quite like that excitement. Then wham, Suzanne delivered her bucket of icy water and stopped me. You've got a good friend there. No one else noticed a thing.'

'I know. Even John Alsopp just thought we'd had a row. It was as if Suzanne, you and I were existing in another dimension from the party all around us. Like being in a conscious nightmare.'

'I cut my beard off to remind myself that this time I mustn't cheat. When I shave my face I'll say to myself, "You were going to hurt her and enjoy it." I just hope I never get that feeling again.'

Marcia picked up the freesias and inhaled their scent. 'If I'm honest, a tiny, tiny part of me also got a kick out of hurting you.' She looked at him over the flowers as he stared at her. 'I felt very guilty when I admitted it to myself. Perhaps it's a constant thing in all of us.'

'Perhaps. Not one to encourage.' There was a faint clunk from the bedroom and Edward stiffened and frowned. 'Is there someone in your bedroom?'

'Yes.'

'I knew you had another man in your life!' His voice cracked with sudden jealousy. Marcia got up and fetched Suzanne.

'Moral support, Edward.'

'Hullo, Edward. I can see by the look of you I didn't give you pneumonia, for which I'm grateful as I'm no doubt you are.'

'You tried hard enough.'

'Let's have tea or a drink or something—'

'I must go, Marcia. I think we've said almost everything.'

'Except sorry?'

'I'm sorry about the whole business.'

'So am I.'

'Have a good time in India.'

'I'm sure I will.'

'Who did you say you were going with?'

'I didn't. I'll give you a ring when I get back and tell you how it all went.' She handed the freesias to Suzanne, and hugged him. 'I'm so glad we've had this talk.'

Edward took her by the shoulders and looked into her eyes. His fingers pinched painfully, and as soon as her expression registered this he released her. 'Goodbye, Marcia.'

'Thanks again for the flowers.'

'I hate to accept this is the end.'

'Goodbye, Edward.' She touched his smooth chin. 'You'll surprise everyone without your beard. It suits you.'

'How far is the school, Bitta Singh?' George is not at all sure his driver knows the way. He has stopped his old black and white Ambassador car twice to ask a passerby something in Hindi.

'Just now we are getting there, sahib. No problem.' And indeed after a U-turn, a right turn, and a left turn, Bitta Singh draws up with a flourish and leaps out. George's door has no inside handle so he waits to be ushered forth. 'Chanakyapuri Preparatory School just here, look.' Bitta Singh waves his hand towards a shabby doorway into an unprepossessing building. 'I am waiting for you outside here as long as you want, sahib. No hurry.'

'Thank you.' George wants to postpone the moment of entering but Bitta Singh has already pressed the well-polished brass bell before jumping back into his car. As George waits he reads the painted noticeboard, his eyes unable to move away from the words: 'Founder and Proprietor, Philip Symes' neatly written under the long Hindu name of the headmaster.

A grey-haired Indian woman in a sari leads George through bare wooden corridors echoing with distant school sounds and smelling pervasively of curried food, to a waiting-room lined with school photographs.

'Is Mr Symes expecting you?'

'He told me to come whenever I liked this afternoon.' George hands over his card. 'If you could give him this, I'd be grateful.'

'Certainly. Mr Symes doesn't teach any more, but he has a small flat at the back of the school. Please wait here.' She disappears, and George sits as tensely as any parent hoping for miracles. He can hear the headmaster talking loudly and angrily to a subordinate through a nearby door. A loud bell rings throughout the building and feet pound as the pupils chatter and move to their next lesson. This is the first school George has been inside since leaving Roddick Manor, and he's surprised how familiar the noises sound.

'This way, sir.' The woman leads him to an open door marked Private, and leaves him inside it, shutting the door quietly on him. George stands in a small hall stuffed with wooden filing cabinets, wondering which of two doors to go through.

'In here. I'm in a wheelchair.'

The sitting-room is as full as the hallway, of prints, photographs, Indian hangings, inlaid wooden furniture, brass trays on carved wooden stands, and tottering piles of books everywhere. At first George is not aware of the wheelchair by the window, so surrounded is it by clutter.

Against the light he sees a head of hair, a grizzled version of his own. George's eyes move to the face beneath and he sees his own face distorted by a heart attack, his own big flat ears, his own greenish eyes meeting his, hands held out in greeting, spotted and disfigured by arthritis; he sees his own smile revealing badly fitting dentures. Philip Symes wears tinted reading glasses which he has pushed up on to his forehead.

'Chip off the old block. Come in, come in. At last!'

'Hullo, sir.' George goes forward to shake hands as the blood rises to his face. He can hardly breathe.

'When I saw that school photograph you looked exactly as I did when I was a boy, and now you look like me when I started this school. Uncanny. Look at that.' Philip Symes waves at a photograph on the wall nearby. George sees himself standing in the school group; even the familiar smile of sly triumph is like his own after a successful case.

'It is uncanny. It could certainly be me.'

'Our voices are alike too. Mrs Bannerji told me when she came to announce you that you gave her a real turn when you first spoke. Exactly your voice, Mr Symes, she said, and she's right. Helena doesn't seem to have passed on any of her genes at all! Sit down, George, do sit down. It gives me a neck-crick to stare up at you. How tall are you?'

'Six foot two.'

'I used to be six one. I've been in this bloody wheelchair for six years – had a bit of a turn when I was seventy-seven and fell down the fire-escape to boot. Didn't do me much good, but the old brain is fine, fortunately.' He suddenly shouts something in Hindi, and a little Indian almost as old as his master sticks his head through a hatch and listens, wagging his head from side to side in the characteristic Indian gesture of assent and comprehension.

'*Achcha, sahib.*' He disappears again.

'I'm not surprised to see you, you know.'

George does not know what to reply, but his father is not expecting answers.

'My astrologer told me my son would come soon. Since he didn't know I even had a son, I was rather impressed.'

George clears his throat. 'When did he tell you this?'

'Oh, a few months ago.'

'I only decided to come to India on the spur of the moment, barely a month ago.'

'It makes no difference. It was written in the stars, as they say.' He gives that sly smile, and George returns it. 'So, how is your mother?'

'Lena died in November.'

'Lena – why did she stop calling herself Helena? She always used her full name when I knew her. It was one of her many attractions. How did she die?'

'Her heart.'

Philip makes a glum face and turns to stare out of the window.

His servant brings a large brass tray laden with tea things, and pours out two cups before retiring.

'Thank you, Dilip. Did Helena tell you I came to see her once in that stultifying house in Harrow?'

George laughs and shakes his head. 'I've only recently learned about your visit from a letter she wrote to her sister.'

'She refused, she resolutely refused, to let me come and find you at your school. At the time I was extremely upset – it was one of the biggest frustrations of my life – but now, well I've become completely fatalistic. Inevitable Indian influence. What will be, will be, and there's nothing you can do about it.'

'Did you love my mother?' George is surprised at the complete ease already between them, an ease he never felt with Lena or Geoffrey.

'I adored her and was obsessed by her. Love? In my book that means something different. I loved my wife Madge, who was a typical Raj English woman, daughter of a colonel, a thoroughly good sort but no competition for someone like Helena. When Helena appeared in Jodhpur I was plunged into consuming passion for her at first sight. I couldn't get her out of my head. She nearly ruined my life.' He sips his tea. His hand is steady, however, as he talks about his past; his voice is dry, at odds with what he is saying. 'Your mother was sexy in a way girls in those days just weren't – the sort of thing you see in the West nowadays, but then – well, it was impossible to find in the English women I knew. A bit shocking too. But so exciting. I was obsessed by her, I couldn't see enough of her. Then one day she was gone. No warning, just gone. Nothing to say where.'

'What did you feel?'

'After the first shock, mostly relief! Though of course I missed the sex, relief that I didn't have to live a double life any more with Madge, who knew nothing of my affair. Then I heard Helena had married someone, and eventually I learned his name. Geoffrey Warne. I was also told they had a son.'

'Did you wonder if I was your son?'

'The thought crossed my mind, I admit.' His eyes meet George's, a little shamefaced. 'But she never wrote, never told me. And I was coward enough to be grateful for a quiet life. Madge wanted a big family – the prospect of our children kept me from making further inquiries. Not a very glorious reaction, I know. Then Madge had nothing but miscarriages, so we never achieved our family; finally she died in a riot during Partition – just had the bad luck to be in the wrong place at the wrong time. Poor Madge. That's her.' George gives a quick dutiful look at a fair slab-face woman in a silver frame.

'How did you manage to find Lena in Harrow after all those years of separation?'

'Pure chance, George. I was home on leave and I happened to see a paragraph about Geoffrey Warne in *The Times*. It was easy to discover where he lived. I took a train to Harrow-on-the-Hill, and a taxi delivered me to the door for half-a-crown. I can remember it all as if it was yesterday. Helena nearly passed out when she saw me!' Philip laughs. 'I couldn't help thinking of her as she used to be while we talked over tea-cups. She used to wear a Chinese silk dressing-gown with flowers embroidered all over the back. She didn't wear anything under it when I was visiting.' He laughs again. 'And now here she was all twinsetted and pearled with straight-seamed nylons, and about as sexy as a hot-water bottle. I was feeling very relieved and glad I'd laid – sorry about the choice of verb – that particular ghost when I suddenly noticed the school photograph on the piano. And from the way Helena jumped when I reached for it, and from the horror on her face, I knew I'd see you. And there you were, so patently my son I gave a loud shout – whether more of joy or distress I still couldn't say. But it frightened Helena, and gave her courage too. I couldn't shake her – short of torture, I could see nothing would make her tell me where to find you! So I came back to India, settled in Delhi, and put the rest of my life into founding and running my school. And to be honest, it's been most rewarding. There is nothing like founding a school, opening doors for young brains, giving them a good start. Nothing like it. Better than marriage, certainly better than sex! I'm proud of my school, and I've been happy running it. Don't judge me by my dilapidated appearance now, George.'

'I wouldn't dream of judging you.' He feels his – their – smile grow as he gazes at his father. 'Though it's ironic you should use the word judge.'

'You're not a judge though, are you? From your card I can see you're a QC.'

'Not for much longer.' He desperately wants to call his father something – Philip, Father – but cannot bring himself to use either word. 'I'm about to become a High Court Judge.'

'Congratulations. How gratifying. I shall be able to tell the headmaster that my son is about to become Sir George!' Philip's laugh has a good bite of irony in it. 'It will give me a great deal of credibility in his eyes – he's a terrible snob.'

'Becoming a High Court Judge has certain disadvantages, the title not the least of them.'

'Ah.' Philip takes his glasses off his forehead, and rubs his face. 'Tell me more about your life, George. I've been doing too much talking. Tell me about Geoffrey Warne. I hope he was a good father. Helena made him sound like a saint.'

'He was a good father. And a good provider. Considering that he knew I was someone else's child, what he did for me was beyond the call of duty.' There is a pause which George does not know how to fill. The last person he wants to talk to Philip about is Geoffrey Warne. 'I never got to know him very well – he didn't have much to do with the daily running of the family. And I spent so much time at boarding school I often felt like a visitor in my own home, as boarders often do. Is this school boarding?'

'No, heaven forbid. It started off as a boys-only day school, and when I built the new block rather than turn it into a boarding school I decided to expand and admit girls too. Your school was all boys, I am sure. What was it like?'

'Awful. But I got into Oxford to read history, so it didn't completely fail me. And for me life began at Oxford. I loved it.'

'I never went to university, you know. I have no qualifications whatsoever, but it didn't stop me being a good teacher of basics, and my school now has a very high reputation. You should see the waiting list.'

'Do you play any part now in running the school?'

'None directly. But I bought the property – actually I've made it into a trust to safeguard the future of the school after my death – and I hold a monthly staff meeting in here so that I keep tabs on progress, and everyone knows they can pop in and talk to me at any time. And they do, bless them.' He changes position slightly to ease stiffness. 'So Geoffrey Warne was a bit of a disappointment as a father.'

'I didn't say that.'

'I'm good at construing situations from what people don't say.' Both of them laugh. Dilip comes in at that moment to remove the tea tray, and Philip tells him something in Hindi that makes him stare delightedly at George before he puts his hands together with a little bow.

'*Namaste*.'

'I've just told Dilip you're my son. He said he could see we were related, but is amazed because he thought I had no children.' Dilip's smile splits his face as he says something while wagging his head in his pleasure. 'He's telling you to visit often because he can see how happy you've made me.'

'I'll come as often as I can while I'm in India, but alas it isn't for very long. Tomorrow we go off to Rajasthan for a couple of weeks, and then come back for a final few days here.'

Dilip disappears with the tray as George is speaking; his father asks him who he's travelling with.

'I'm with my cousin Laura and a friend called Marcia Fleckner, and of course we all want to see as much as we can, or I'd be tempted to cut short the stay in Rajasthan so that I could spend more time with you.'

'Don't change your plans on my behalf. You've come here, we've met, and that in itself is enough. Repeating things doesn't always improve them.' He murmurs to himself in Hindi, and there's a pause before he asks George if he's married. As George gives him a brief and edited summary of his marriages, he can see his father is tiring.

'And so my new existence starts at the end of January, when I join the Queen's Bench Division of the High Court.'

'What sort of ceremony do they put you through?'

'I'm sworn in at the House of Lords by the Lord Chancellor, and then I have to go to Buckingham Palace for the knighthood.' George looks at his father and a wild hope fills him. 'Can you still travel?'

'I haven't left Delhi since I was reduced to living in a wheelchair.'

'I'd love you to come to London for the ceremonies. The trip would be my gift. Would you consider it?'

'I couldn't, George. I'm completely dependent on Dilip, I can't do anything for myself. He's my nurse, my bearer, my chauffeur – my salvation.'

'Of course he must come too. I was including him.'

Philip Symes stares out through his window, which looks on to a large tree at the corner of the school playground.

'I'm too old and decrepit, I really am.'

'Are you tempted?'

'Of course I'm tempted. How could I not be? I find my son, and he invites me to see him be sworn on to the Bench and be knighted by the Queen. Of course I'd love to come. But I am very old and I don't want to be a dreadful liability.'

'Please come.'

'Dilip and I will have to discuss it. We never tackle a new idea in a hurry, so it will take several days.'

'I'll come and see you when I return to Delhi, and by then perhaps you'll feel more confident about the journey. Will you forgive me if I hurry off now – I left my friends in the Railway Museum to wait for me, and they must be wondering what on earth has happened to me.'

'Will you write down your birthday for me before you go? Time of day you were born if you know it. My astrologer is bound to ask me if you've come. His son goes to the school, so he gives me his services free as a method of oiling the way for the next child. Since he foretold your arrival so accurately I'm quite happy to accommodate a whole fleet of his sons!'

Philip must have asked her to return at this time, because Mrs Bannerji reappears and offers to show George the way out when he's ready. George takes his father's hand in his.

'I would love it if you could come to London. I – it would make all the difference.'

'I promise you I'll think seriously about it. Dilip will take me on a test drive to the airport, and push me about there, and we'll see how we feel after that.' He calls for Dilip, who comes in and does a *namaste*. George puts his hands together in return.

'*Namaste*, Dilip.' He turns to his father. 'Goodbye. No words can express what this meeting has meant to me. I want to call you Philip or Father – which would you prefer?'

'Call me Philip. I've done nothing for you all your life except kick-start your existence. I don't deserve to be called Father.'

Dilip says something, and Philip gives George the familiar smile. 'Dilip, who understands far more English than he pretends to, says you should call me Bapu, the word used here for father.'

'Bapu.' As George tries this out the bell rings extra loud and long throughout the school, almost drowning his voice. 'Bapu.'

'You must hurry away now, before you are killed in the rush of children going home!'

'Goodbye, Bapu.'

'Goodbye, son.'

Master and servant smile at him as he leaves, and start talking Hindi comfortably together before the door has closed. George follows Mrs Bannerji through the building, now alive in every direction with the din of children getting ready to leave for home. The playground and school gates are crowded with adults – mothers, a few fathers, and servants – waiting to meet the children, some wearing Western clothing but mostly in saries, salwar kameez, turbans and dhotis. Uniformed children emerge carrying their satchels and their tiffin-tins; Georges watches them off-load these on their meeters and immediately run off to gossip. They look confident, happy, full of energy. *There is nothing like founding a school, opening doors for young brains.*

George leaves the playground and sees that Bitta Singh's Ambassador is now surrounded by a blockade of cars and autorickshaws. He raises his shoulders helplessly. 'We must wait, Warne sahib. Nothing to do. All are going home soon with their children.'

'I don't mind in the least. I'm enjoying seeing my father's school in action.'

'This is your *father's* school?'

'Philip Symes is my father, even though my name is Warne.'

'Sahib, you are indeed fortunate. Symes sahib is very good man, all Delhi-wallahs know him.' Bitta Singh is clearly very impressed. 'Symes sahib doing many good things.'

'Tell me about the good things.'

'He funds home for poor girls, sahib. Girls abandoned when they are babies, left to die. This is very bad thing in our country. For them, Symes sahib is tip-top – they have home, they are educated, some even pass into this school. Tip-top. Without him they are in the gutter.'

The blockade of cars has eased and there is a clear space in front of the Ambassador; Bitta Singh accelerates into it with a kangaroo-like motion.

'We go back to Railway Museum to collect memsahibs?'

'Back to the Railway Museum.'

George leans back and shuts his eyes to hide the fact that tears are welling. His father is beyond any of his imaginings. He knows he will never forget Bitta Singh's plump, well-etched lips saying 'tip-top' with such precise gusto.

> *If ever thou gavest hosen and shoon*
>   Every nighte and alle
> *Sit thee down and put them on*
>   And Christe receive thy sawle.
>
> *If ever thou gavest meat and drink,*
>   Every nighte and alle
> *The fire shall never make thee shrink*
>   And Christe receive thy sawle.
>
> *This ane nighte, this ane nighte,*
>   Every nighte and alle
> *Fire and fleet and candlelighte*
>   And Christe receive thy sawle.

'There he is!'

The chipmunks scatter across the empty grounds as Marcia and Laura jump up from the bench and wave at George. The ticket clerk hurries up behind them, scowling more fiercely than ever.

'No tickets available now, sir. Too late.'

'It's all right. I'll come back another time.'

Marcia and Laura stand under the neem tree as George joins them, watched suspiciously by the clerk.

'I'm sorry I've been so long, my dears.'

'We can see from your expression it went well. Oh Jebs!' Laura hugs him. 'What's he like?'

'He's wonderful.' George's voice breaks. He puts his arms round both women and lowers his face; the two women's eyes meet in delighted relief. Then George gives a shaky laugh and takes their hands. 'And I look so like him – he's an older and more decrepit version, that's all. I can't quite believe I've just met him. Even his voice was like mine. It was like looking into a mirror and seeing what I will look like when I'm old.'

'We are closing now, kind sir and ladies—' A second, more friendly, official has come up, with the ticket clerk trailing in his wake. 'It is time to be going now.'

'And we are going.' Marcia smiles at the two men. 'We very much enjoyed your fascinating museum – many thanks.'

George's hand grips hers tightly as they move towards the exit. The official beams, the clerk continues to glower. The chipmunks gather just behind them, re-establishing control over their territory. Hand in hand, George leads Marcia and Laura out of the grounds towards Bitta Singh and the waiting Ambassador as a gust of cool wind blows leaves and dust past their feet. When Marcia looks back she sees the ticket clerk crouching in front of the chipmunks, feeding them nuts from his pocket one by one.

Acknowledgements

Grateful acknowledgements are due to Music Sales Ltd for permission to quote from *I Will Survive* by Gloria Gaynor, and to Penguin for *The Bacchae and other Plays* by Euripedes, translated by Philip Vellacott © 1954.